Goosebumps™

CREEPY CRAWLY COMICS

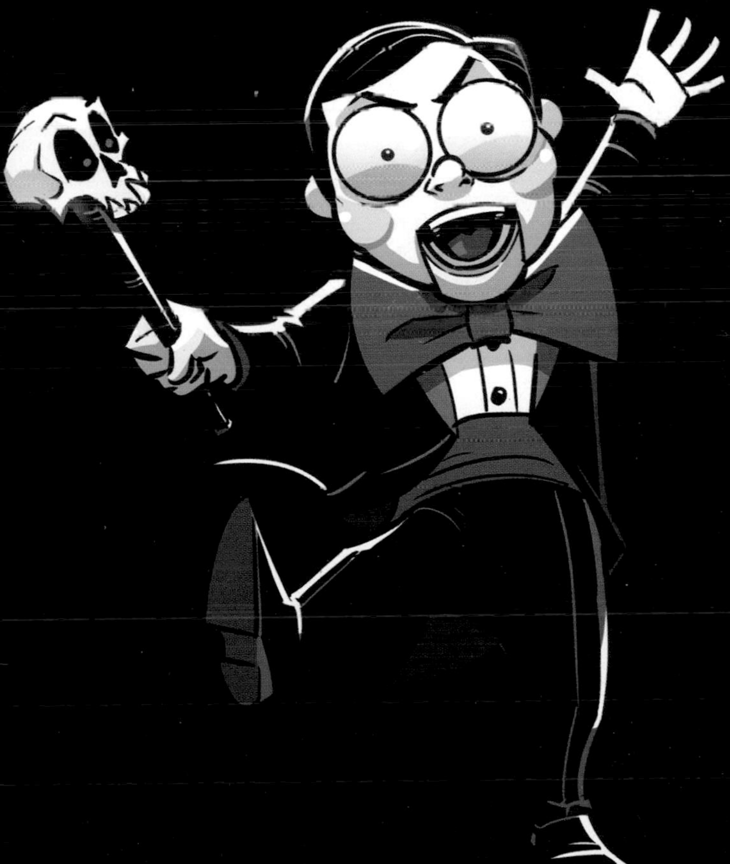

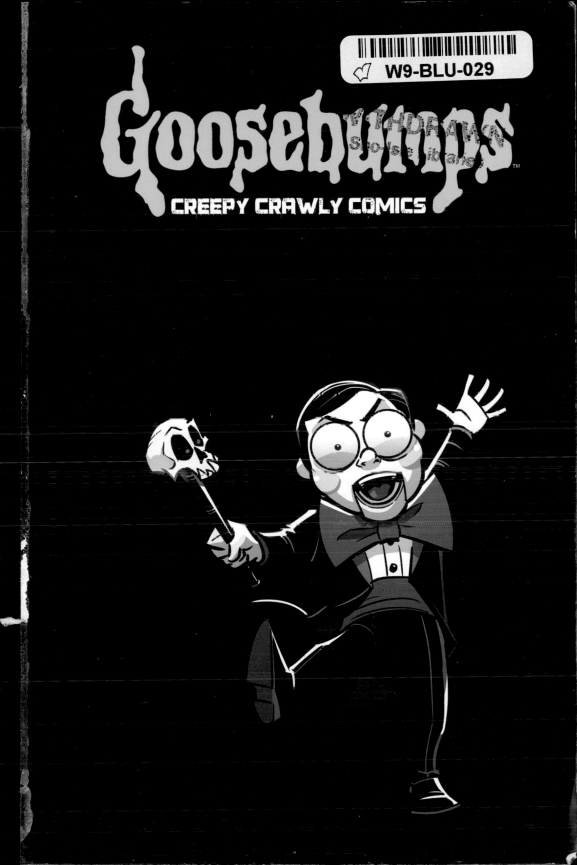

Become our fan on Facebook **facebook.com/idwpublishing**
Follow us on Twitter **@idwpublishing**
Subscribe to us on YouTube **youtube.com/idwpublishing**
See what's new on Tumblr **tumblr.idwpublishing.com**
Check us out on Instagram **instagram.com/idwpublishing**

IDW
www.IDWPUBLISHING.com

Chris Ryall, President & Publisher/CCO
Cara Morrison, Chief Financial Officer
Matthew Ruzicka, Chief Accounting Officer
John Barber, Editor-in-Chief

COVER ARTIST
MEGAN LEVENS

Justin Eisinger, Editorial Director, Graphic Novels and Collections
Jerry Bennington, VP of New Product Development
Lorelei Bunjes, VP of Technology & Information Services

COVER COLORIST
LEONARDO ITO

Jud Meyers, Sales Director
Anna Morrow, Marketing Director
Tara McCrillis, Director of Design & Production

SERIES ASSISTANT EDITORS
ANNI PERHEENTUPA
AND **ELIZABETH BREI**

Mike Ford, Director of Operations
Shauna Monteforte, Manufacturing Operations Director
Rebekah Cahalin, General Manager

SERIES EDITORS
SARAH GAYDOS
AND **CHASE MAROTZ**

Ted Adams and Robbie Robbins, IDW Founders

COLLECTION EDITORS
ALONZO SIMON
AND **ZAC BOONE**

COLLECTION DESIGNER
CLAUDIA CHONG

ISBN: 978-1-68405-765-8   23 22 21 20   1 2 3 4

Originally published as GOOSEBUMPS: MONSTERS AT MIDNIGHT issues #1–3, GOOSEBUMPS: DOWNLOAD AND DIE issues #1–3, and GOOSEBUMPS: HORRORS OF THE WITCH HOUSE issues #1–3.

Special thanks to R.L. Stine.

For international rights, contact licensing@idwpublishing.com

SCHOLASTIC

Goosebumps™

CREEPY CRAWLY COMICS

MONSTERS AT MIDNIGHT

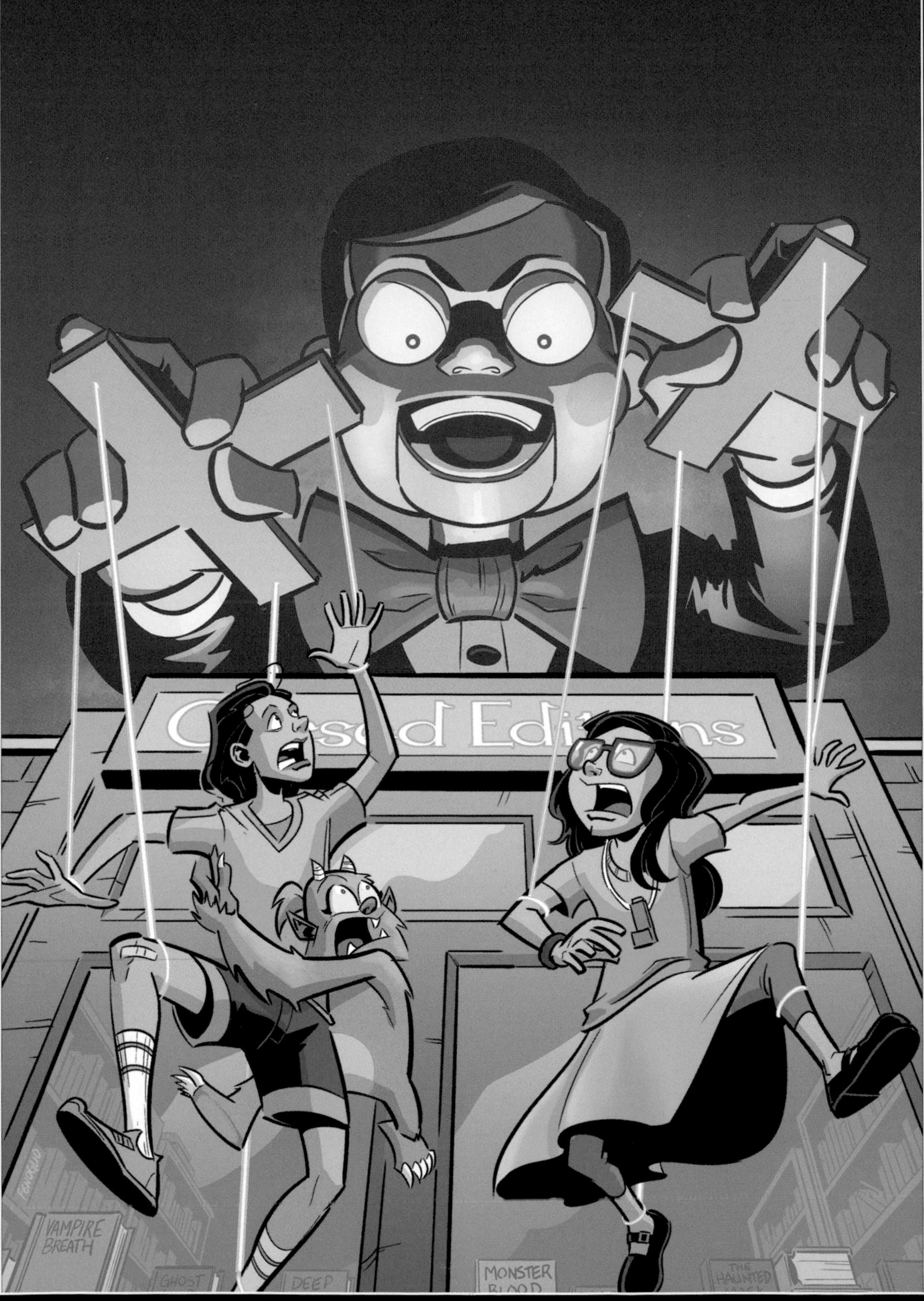
Cursed Editions
VAMPIRE BREATH
GHOST
DEEP
MONSTER BLOOD
THE HAUNTED
FENOGLIO

ART BY
CHRIS FENOGLIO

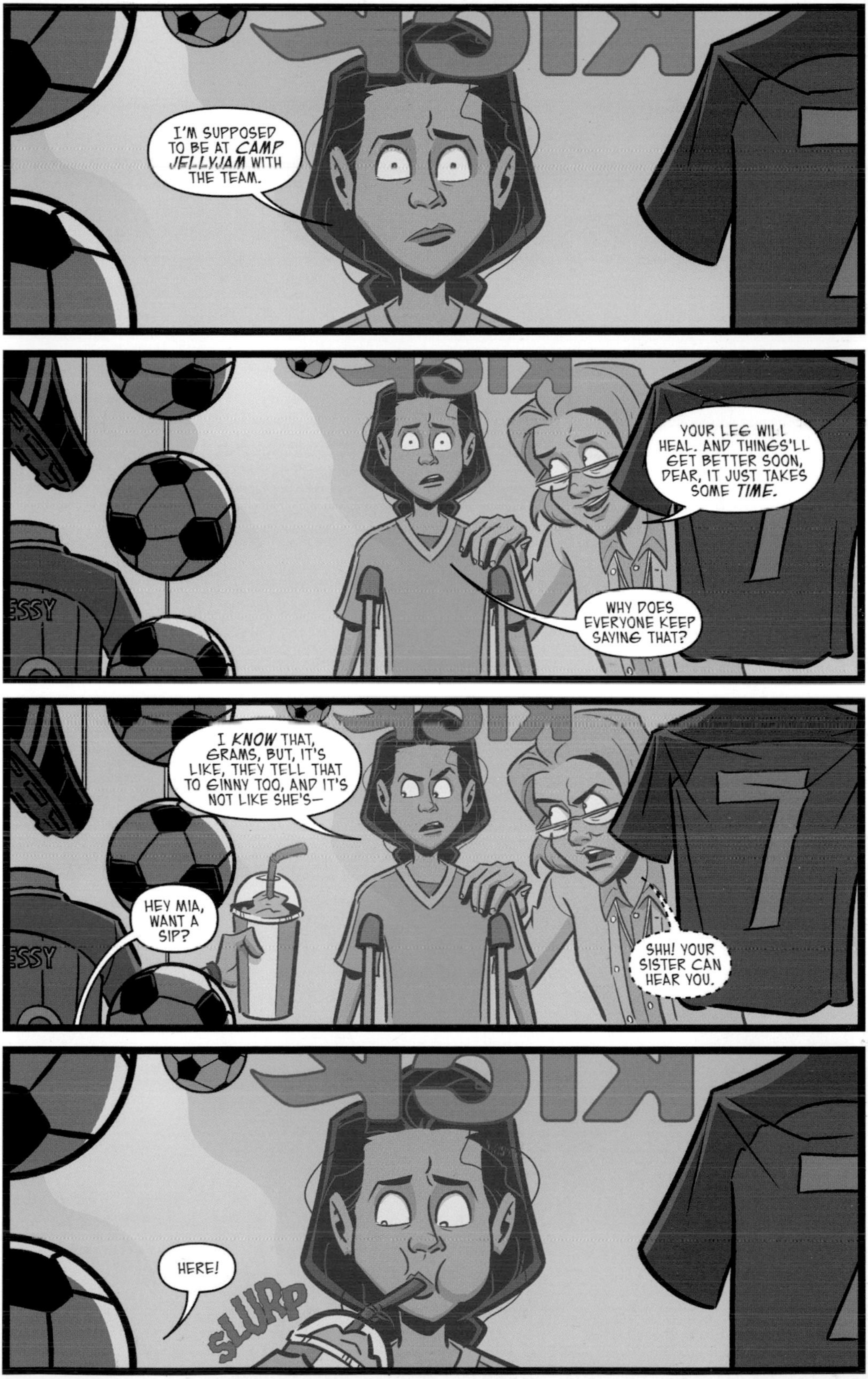
I'M SUPPOSED TO BE AT CAMP JELLYJAM WITH THE TEAM.
YOUR LEG WILL HEAL. AND THINGS'LL GET BETTER SOON, DEAR, IT JUST TAKES SOME TIME.
ESSY
WHY DOES EVERYONE KEEP SAYING THAT?
I KNOW THAT, GRAMS, BUT, IT'S LIKE, THEY TELL THAT TO GINNY TOO, AND IT'S NOT LIKE SHE'S—
HEY MIA, WANT A SIP?
SHH! YOUR SISTER CAN HEAR YOU.
7
HERE!
SLURP

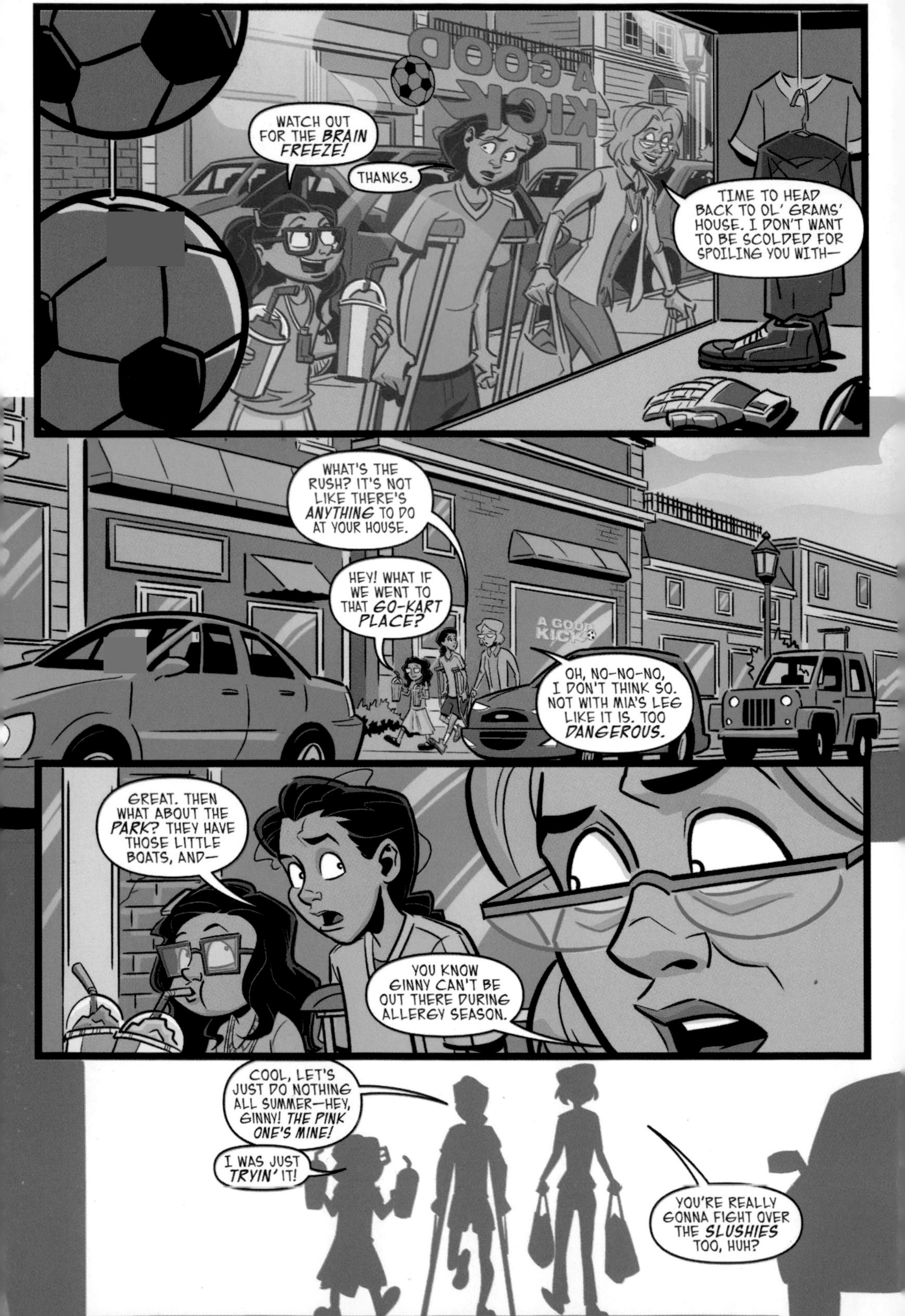
WATCH OUT FOR THE BRAIN FREEZE!
THANKS.
TIME TO HEAD BACK TO OL' GRAMS' HOUSE. I DON'T WANT TO BE SCOLDED FOR SPOILING YOU WITH—
WHAT'S THE RUSH? IT'S NOT LIKE THERE'S ANYTHING TO DO AT YOUR HOUSE.
HEY! WHAT IF WE WENT TO THAT GO-KART PLACE?
A GOOD KICK
OH, NO-NO-NO, I DON'T THINK SO. NOT WITH MIA'S LEG LIKE IT IS. TOO DANGEROUS.
GREAT. THEN WHAT ABOUT THE PARK? THEY HAVE THOSE LITTLE BOATS, AND—
YOU KNOW GINNY CAN'T BE OUT THERE DURING ALLERGY SEASON.
COOL, LET'S JUST DO NOTHING ALL SUMMER—HEY, GINNY! THE PINK ONE'S MINE!
I WAS JUST TRYIN' IT!
YOU'RE REALLY GONNA FIGHT OVER THE SLUSHIES TOO, HUH?

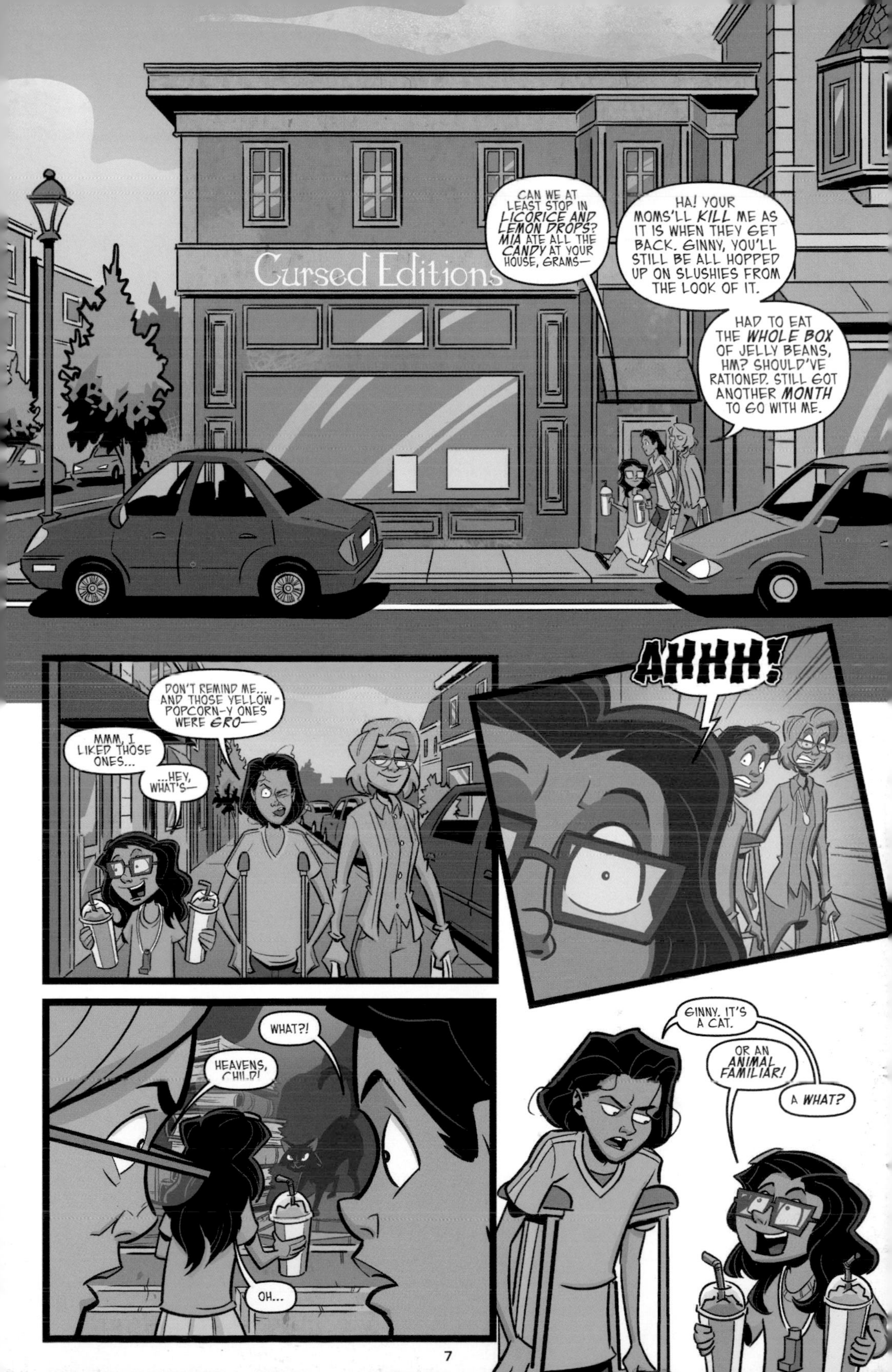
Cursed Editions
CAN WE AT LEAST STOP IN LICORICE AND LEMON DROPS? MIA ATE ALL THE CANDY AT YOUR HOUSE, GRAMS—
HA! YOUR MOMS'LL KILL ME AS IT IS WHEN THEY GET BACK. GINNY, YOU'LL STILL BE ALL HOPPED UP ON SLUSHIES FROM THE LOOK OF IT.
HAD TO EAT THE WHOLE BOX OF JELLY BEANS, HM? SHOULD'VE RATIONED. STILL GOT ANOTHER MONTH TO GO WITH ME.
DON'T REMIND ME... AND THOSE YELLOW-POPCORN-Y ONES WERE GRO—
MMM, I LIKED THOSE ONES...
...HEY, WHAT'S—
AHHH!
WHAT?!
HEAVENS, CHILD!
OH...
GINNY. IT'S A CAT.
OR AN ANIMAL FAMILIAR!
A WHAT?

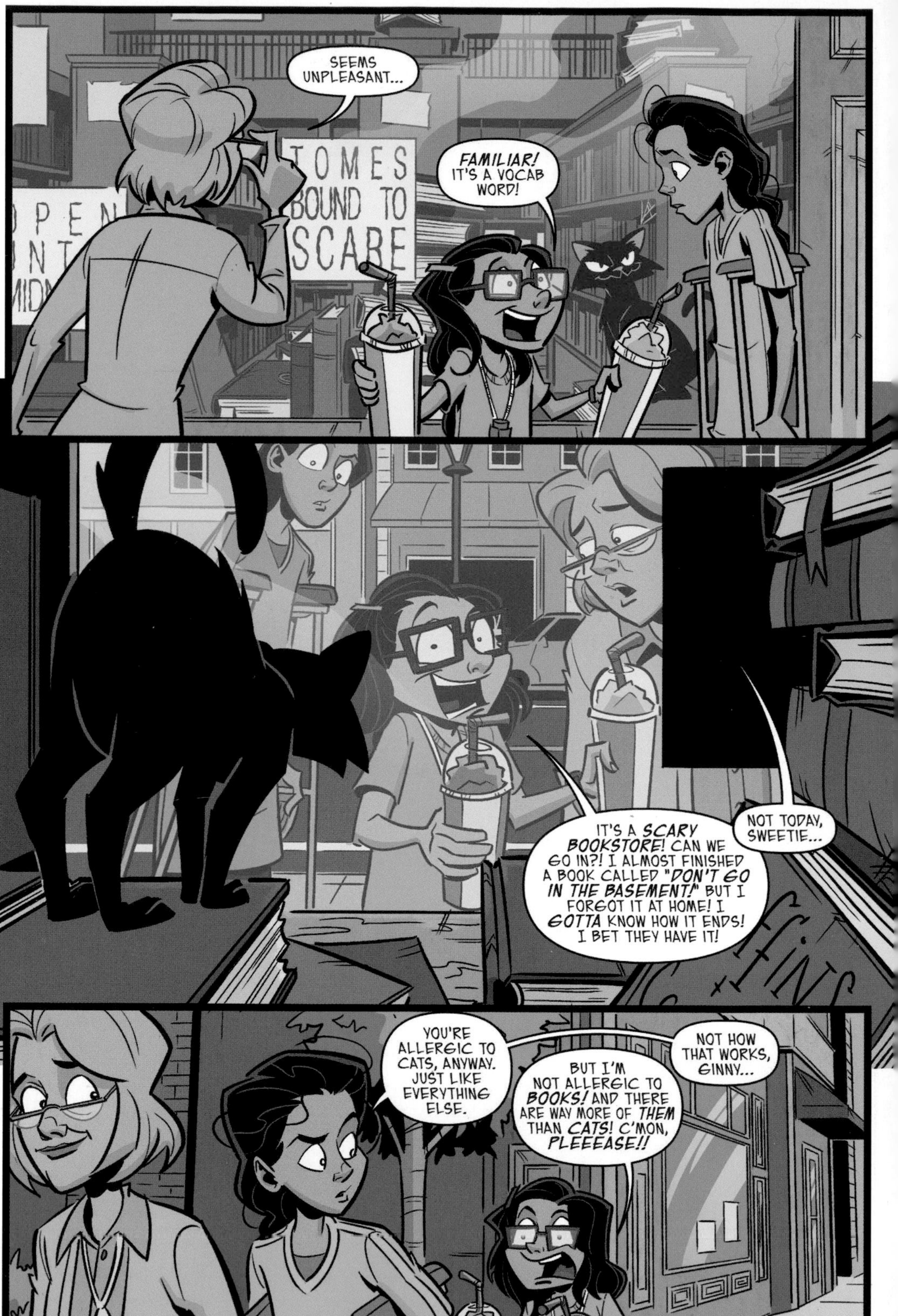
SEEMS UNPLEASANT...
TOMES BOUND TO SCARE
OPEN
FAMILIAR! IT'S A VOCAB WORD!
IT'S A SCARY BOOKSTORE! CAN WE GO IN?! I ALMOST FINISHED A BOOK CALLED "DON'T GO IN THE BASEMENT!" BUT I FORGOT IT AT HOME! I GOTTA KNOW HOW IT ENDS! I BET THEY HAVE IT!
NOT TODAY, SWEETIE...
YOU'RE ALLERGIC TO CATS, ANYWAY. JUST LIKE EVERYTHING ELSE.
BUT I'M NOT ALLERGIC TO BOOKS! AND THERE ARE WAY MORE OF THEM THAN CATS! C'MON, PLEEEASE!!
NOT HOW THAT WORKS, GINNY...

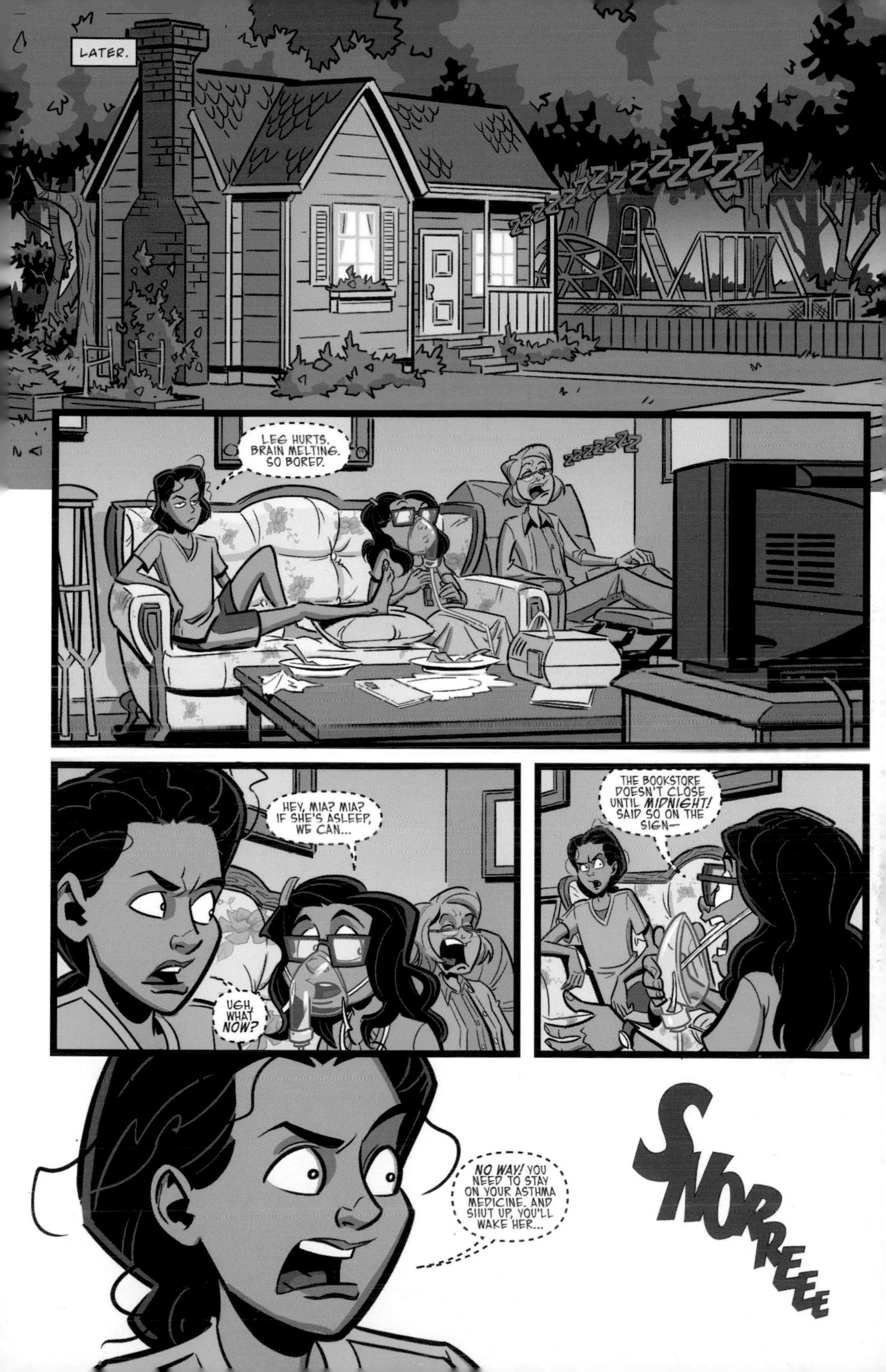
LATER.
ZZZZZZZZZZZZ
LEG HURTS. BRAIN MELTING. SO BORED.
ZZZZZZZ
HEY, MIA? MIA? IF SHE'S ASLEEP, WE CAN...
UGH, WHAT NOW?
THE BOOKSTORE DOESN'T CLOSE UNTIL MIDNIGHT! SAID SO ON THE SIGN—
NO WAY! YOU NEED TO STAY ON YOUR ASTHMA MEDICINE. AND SHUT UP, YOU'LL WAKE HER...
SNORREEEE

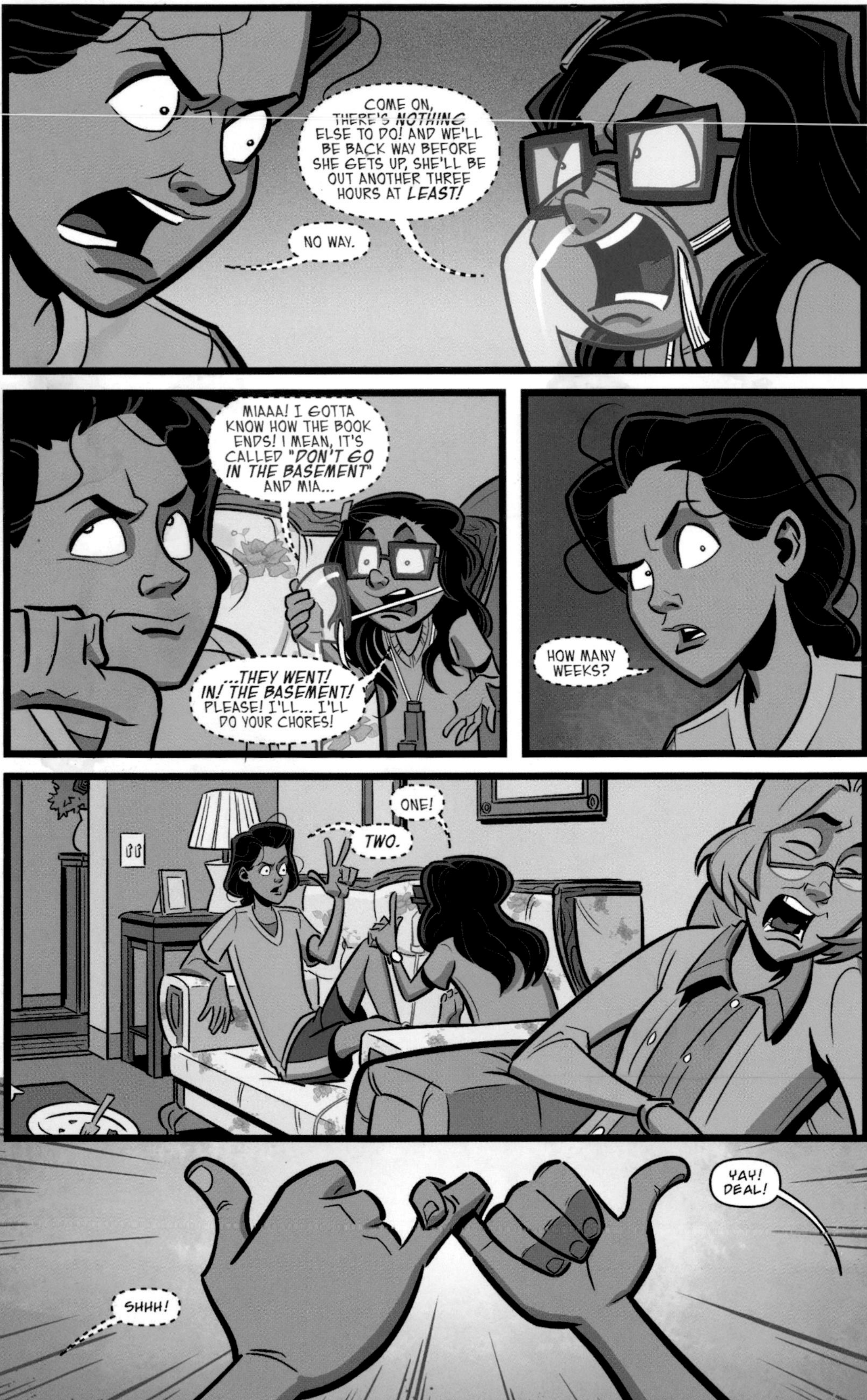
COME ON, THERE'S *NOTHING* ELSE TO DO! AND WE'LL BE BACK WAY BEFORE SHE GETS UP, SHE'LL BE OUT ANOTHER THREE HOURS AT *LEAST!*
NO WAY.
MIAAA! I GOTTA KNOW HOW THE BOOK ENDS! I MEAN, IT'S CALLED *"DON'T GO IN THE BASEMENT"* AND MIA...
...THEY WENT! IN! THE BASEMENT! PLEASE! I'LL... I'LL DO YOUR CHORES!
HOW MANY WEEKS?
ONE!
TWO.
YAY! DEAL!
SHHH!

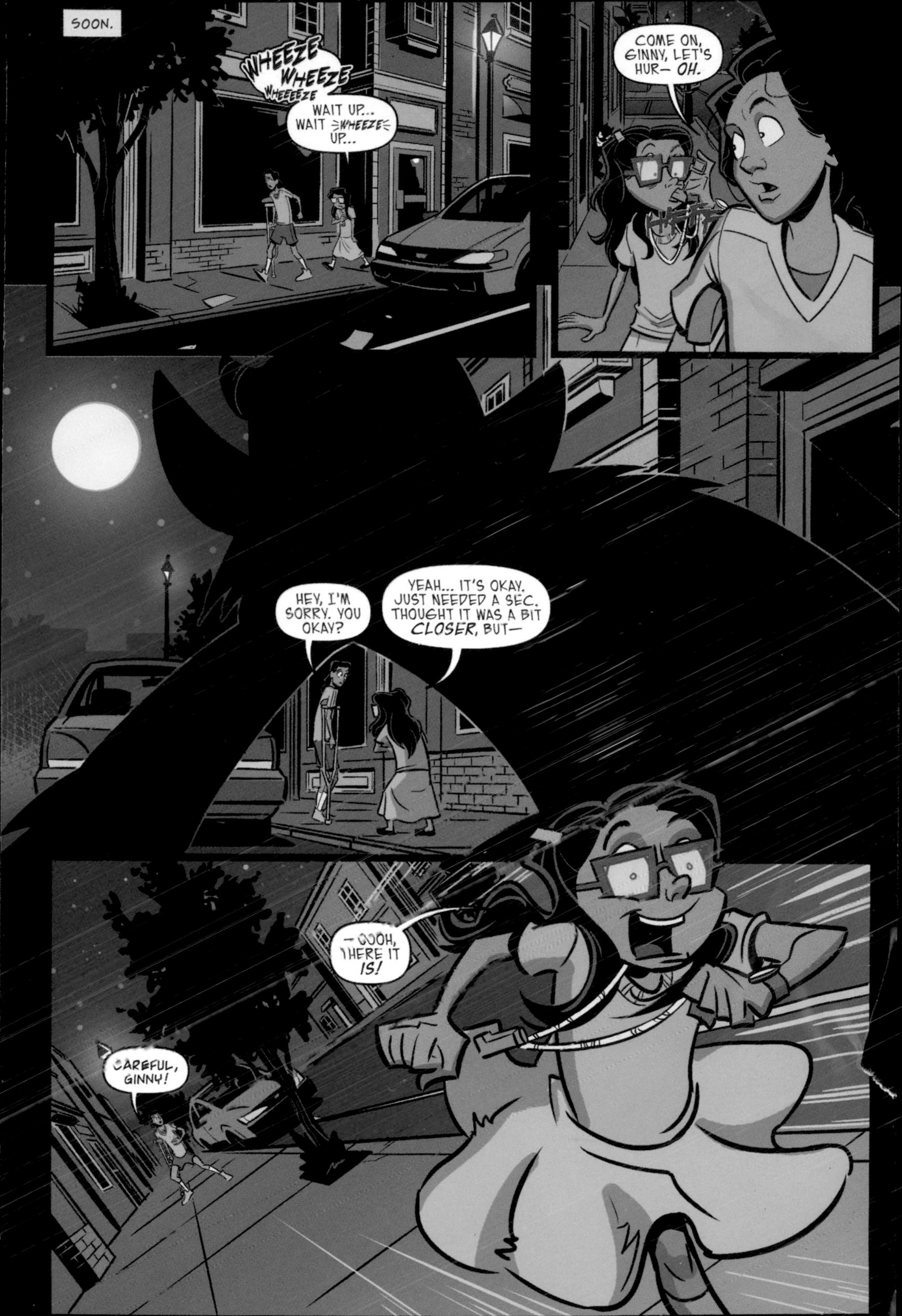
SOON.
WHEEZE WHEEZE WHEEEEZE
WAIT UP... WAIT =WHEEZE= UP...
COME ON, GINNY, LET'S HUR— OH.
HEY, I'M SORRY. YOU OKAY?
YEAH... IT'S OKAY. JUST NEEDED A SEC. THOUGHT IT WAS A BIT CLOSER, BUT—
—OOOH, THERE IT IS!
CAREFUL, GINNY!

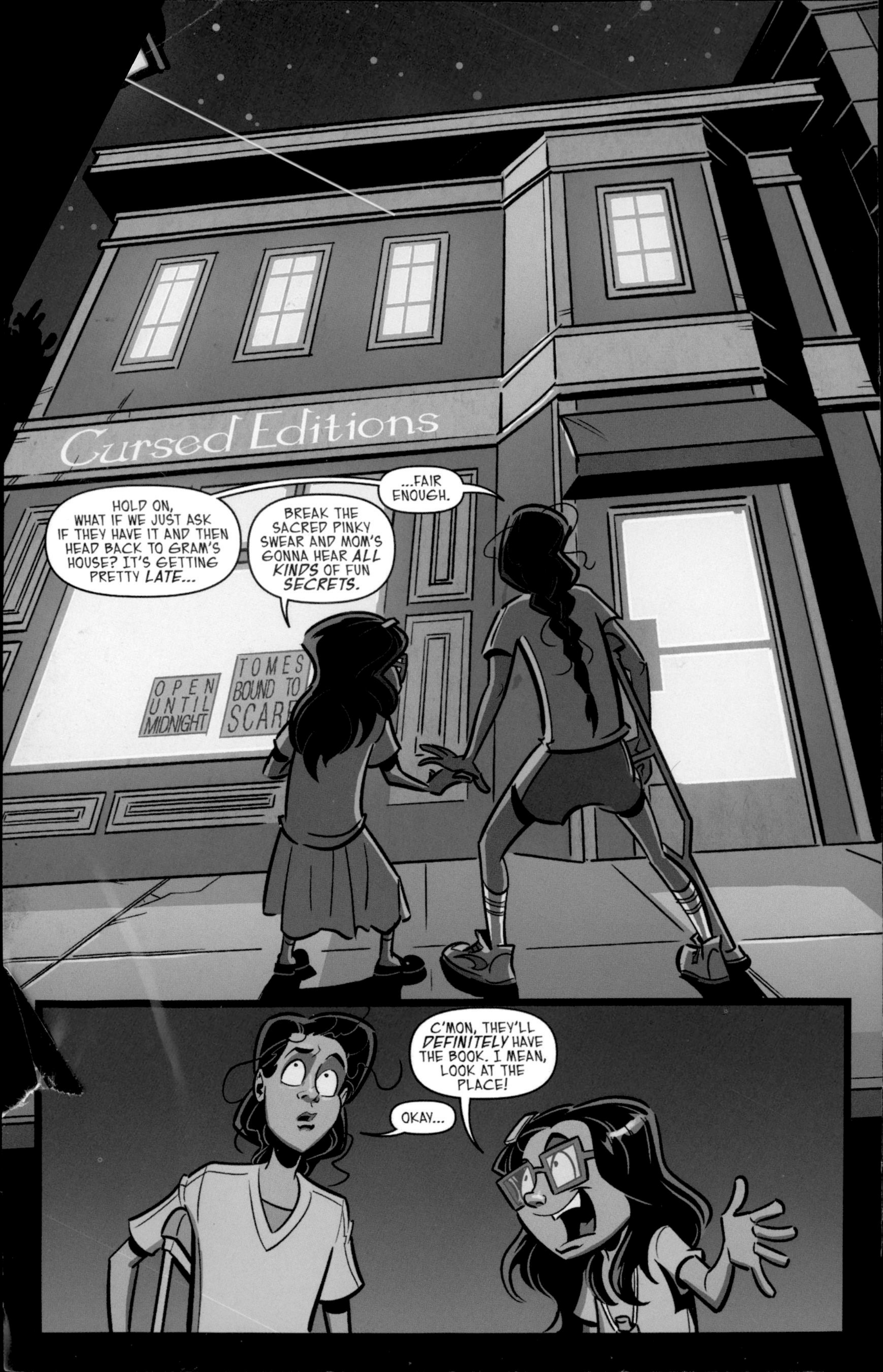
Cursed Editions
HOLD ON, WHAT IF WE JUST ASK IF THEY HAVE IT AND THEN HEAD BACK TO GRAM'S HOUSE? IT'S GETTING PRETTY LATE...
BREAK THE SACRED PINKY SWEAR AND MOM'S GONNA HEAR ALL KINDS OF FUN SECRETS.
...FAIR ENOUGH.
OPEN UNTIL MIDNIGHT
TOMES BOUND TO SCARE
C'MON, THEY'LL DEFINITELY HAVE THE BOOK. I MEAN, LOOK AT THE PLACE!
OKAY...

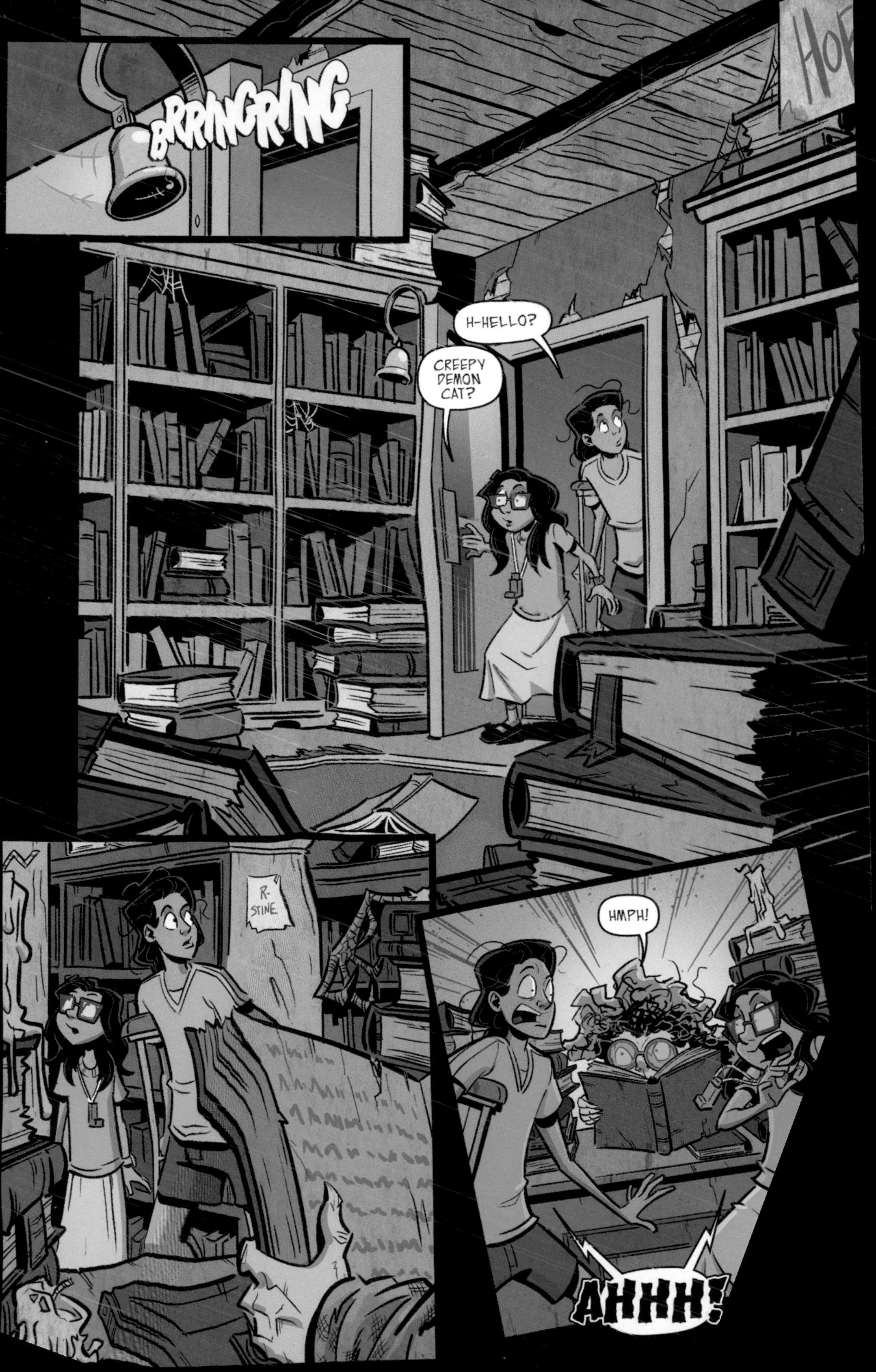
BRRINGRING
H-HELLO?
CREEPY DEMON CAT?
R-STINE
HMPH!
AHHH!

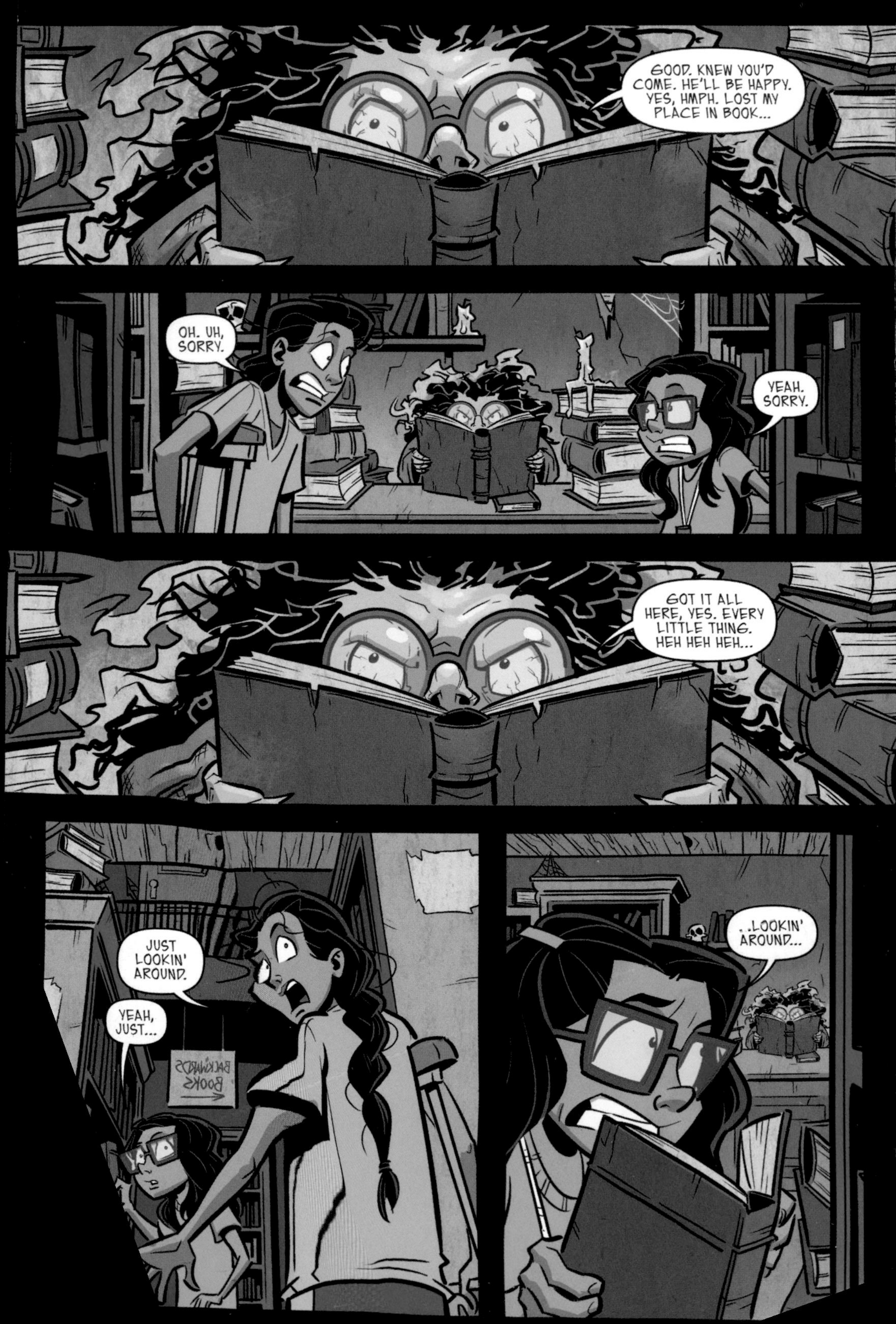
GOOD. KNEW YOU'D COME. HE'LL BE HAPPY. YES, HMPH. LOST MY PLACE IN BOOK...
OH. UH, SORRY.
YEAH. SORRY.
GOT IT ALL HERE, YES. EVERY LITTLE THING. HEH HEH HEH...
JUST LOOKIN' AROUND.
YEAH, JUST...
BACKWARDS BOOKS
...LOOKIN' AROUND...

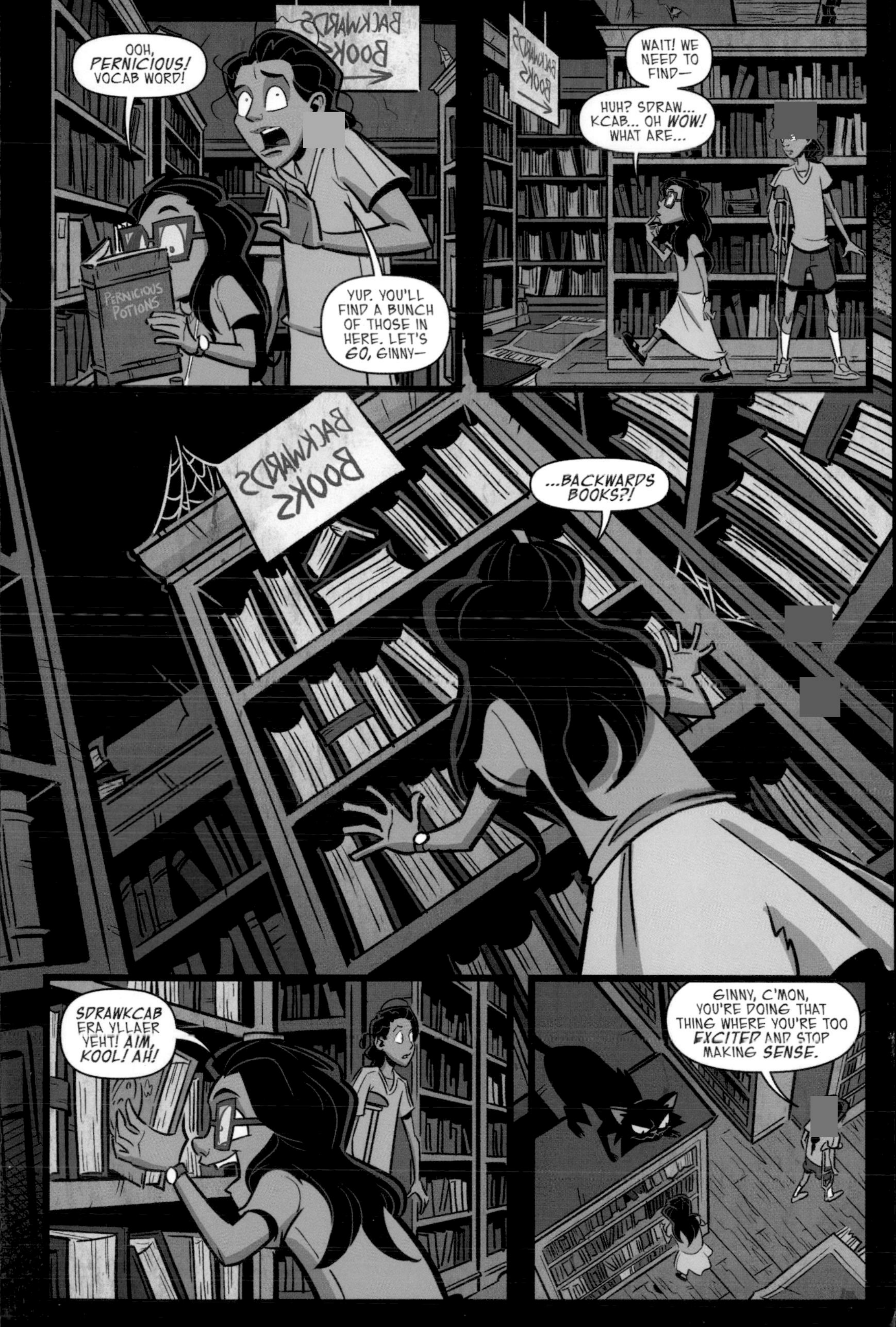
BACKWARDS BOOKS
OOH, PERNICIOUS! VOCAB WORD!
PERNICIOUS POTIONS
YUP. YOU'LL FIND A BUNCH OF THOSE IN HERE. LET'S GO, GINNY—
WAIT! WE NEED TO FIND—
HUH? SDRAW... KCAB... OH WOW! WHAT ARE...
...BACKWARDS BOOKS?!
SDRAWKCAB ERA YLLAER YEHT! AIM, KOOL! AH!
GINNY, C'MON, YOU'RE DOING THAT THING WHERE YOU'RE TOO EXCITED AND STOP MAKING SENSE.

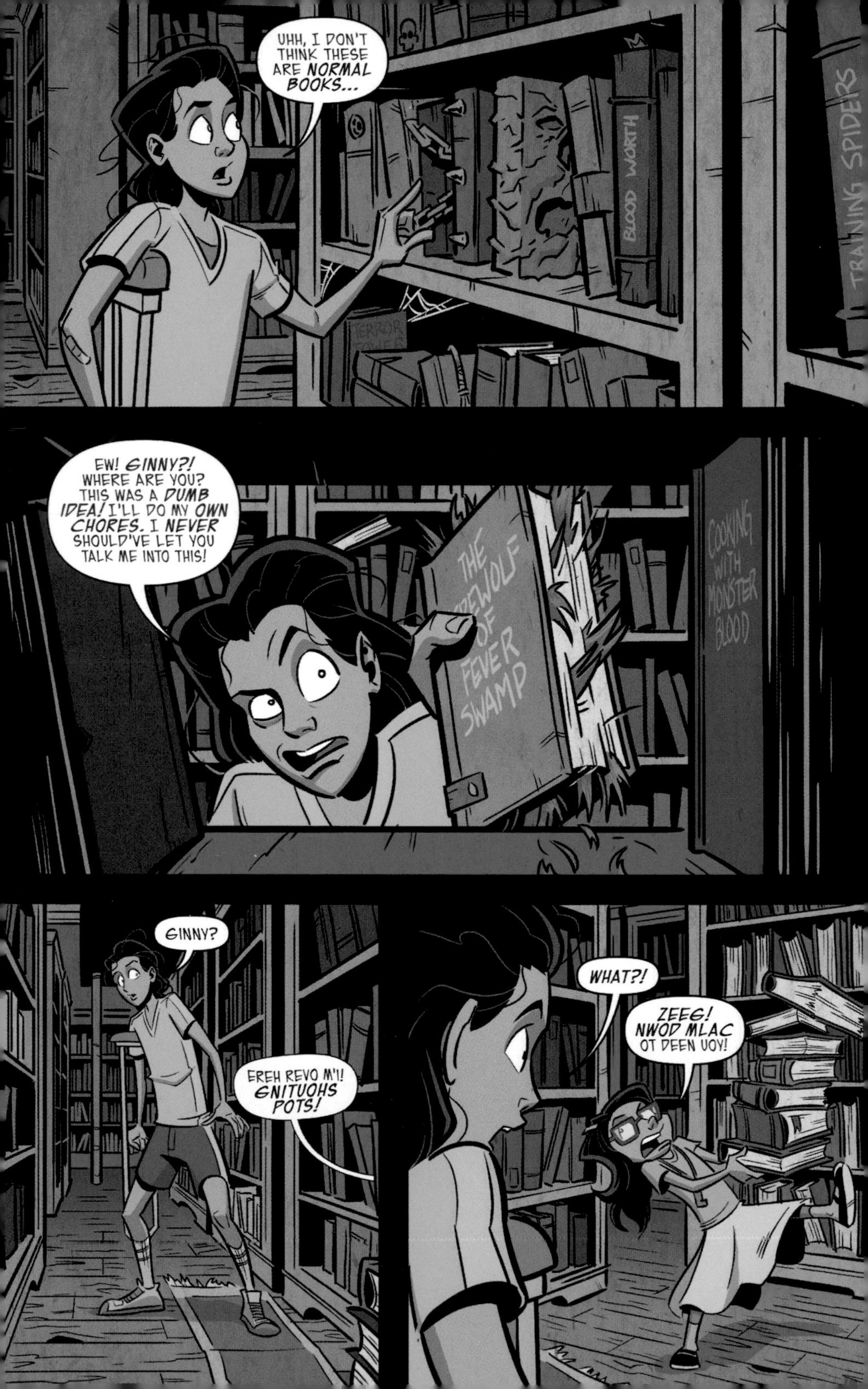
UHH, I DON'T THINK THESE ARE NORMAL BOOKS...
BLOOD WORTH
TRAINING SPIDERS
EW! GINNY?! WHERE ARE YOU? THIS WAS A DUMB IDEA! I'LL DO MY OWN CHORES. I NEVER SHOULD'VE LET YOU TALK ME INTO THIS!
FEVER SWAMP
COOKING WITH MONSTER BLOOD
GINNY?
EREH REVO M'I! GNITUOHS POTS!
WHAT?!
ZEEG! NWOD MLAC OT DEEN UOY!

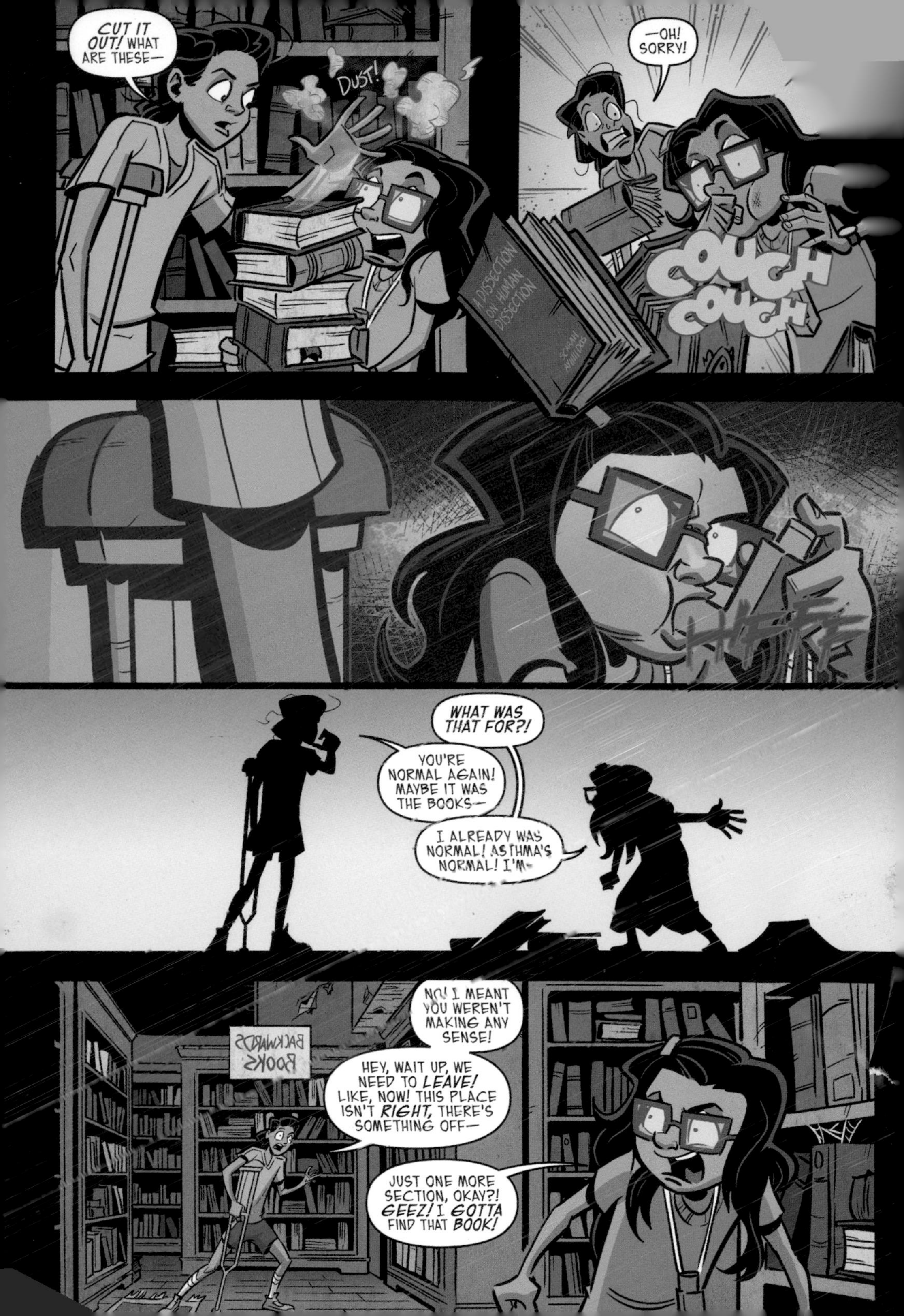
CUT IT OUT! WHAT ARE THESE—
DUST!
A DISSECTION ON HUMAN DISSECTION
—OH! SORRY!
COUGH COUGH
WHAT WAS THAT FOR?!
YOU'RE NORMAL AGAIN! MAYBE IT WAS THE BOOKS—
I ALREADY WAS NORMAL! ASTHMA'S NORMAL! I'M—
NO! I MEANT YOU WEREN'T MAKING ANY SENSE!
HEY, WAIT UP, WE NEED TO LEAVE! LIKE, NOW! THIS PLACE ISN'T RIGHT, THERE'S SOMETHING OFF—
JUST ONE MORE SECTION, OKAY?! GEEZ! I GOTTA FIND THAT BOOK!

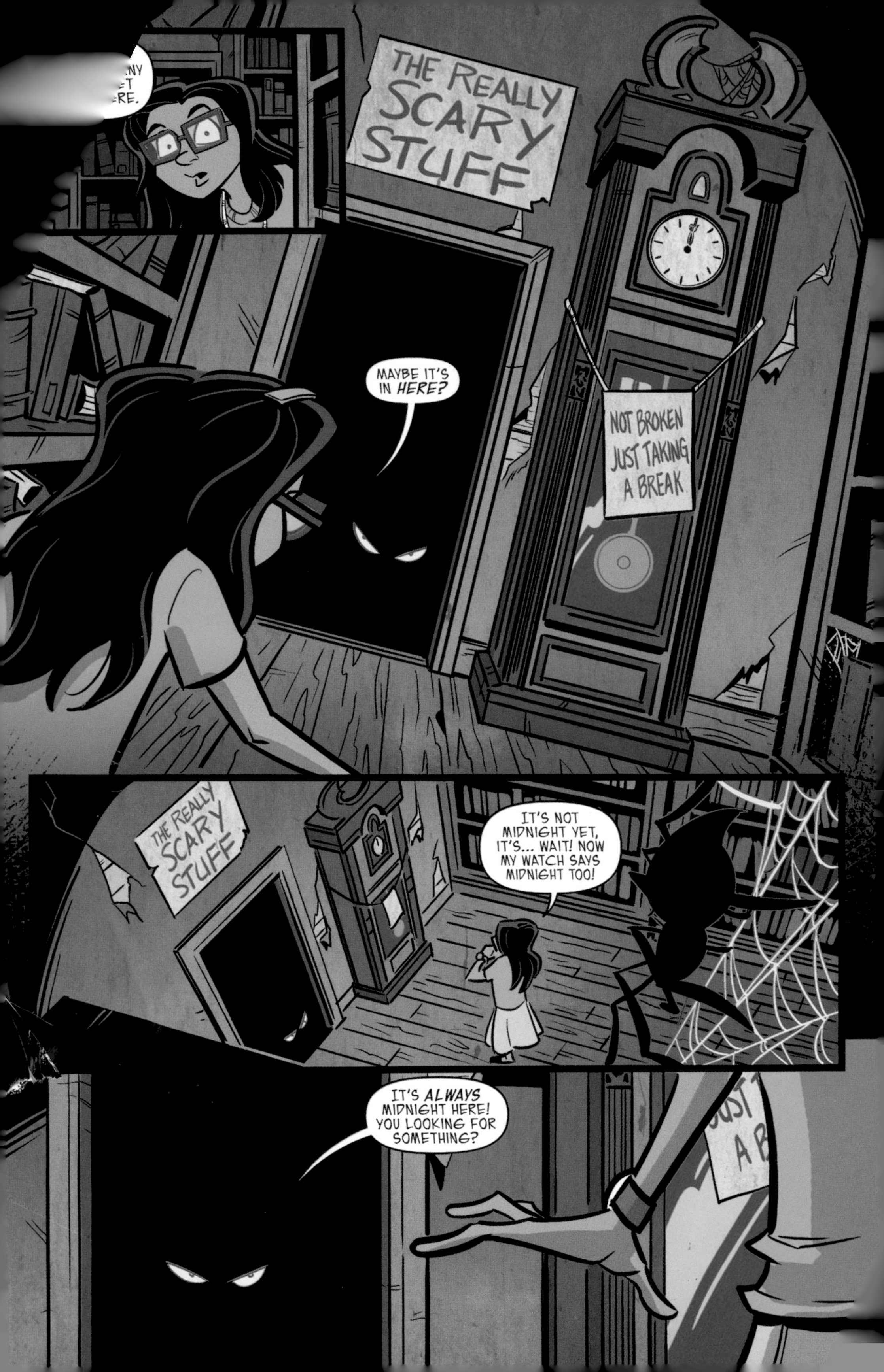
THE REALLY SCARY STUFF
NOT BROKEN JUST TAKING A BREAK
MAYBE IT'S IN HERE?
THE REALLY SCARY STUFF
IT'S NOT MIDNIGHT YET, IT'S... WAIT! NOW MY WATCH SAYS MIDNIGHT TOO!
IT'S ALWAYS MIDNIGHT HERE! YOU LOOKING FOR SOMETHING?

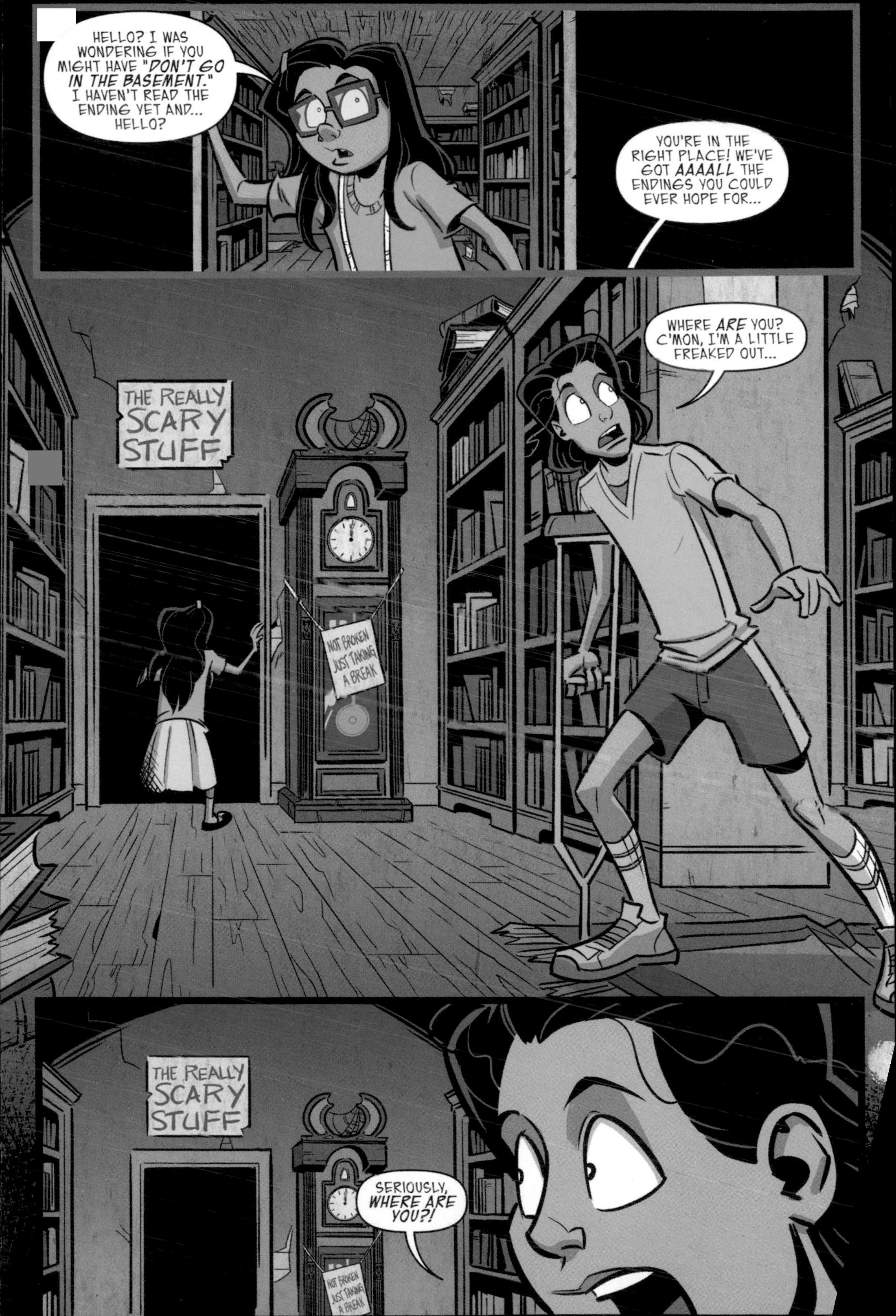

HELLO? I WAS WONDERING IF YOU MIGHT HAVE "DON'T GO IN THE BASEMENT." I HAVEN'T READ THE ENDING YET AND... HELLO?
YOU'RE IN THE RIGHT PLACE! WE'VE GOT AAAALL THE ENDINGS YOU COULD EVER HOPE FOR...
WHERE ARE YOU? C'MON, I'M A LITTLE FREAKED OUT...
THE REALLY SCARY STUFF
NOT BROKEN JUST TAKING A BREAK
THE REALLY SCARY STUFF
SERIOUSLY, WHERE ARE YOU?!
NOT BROKEN JUST TAKING A BREAK

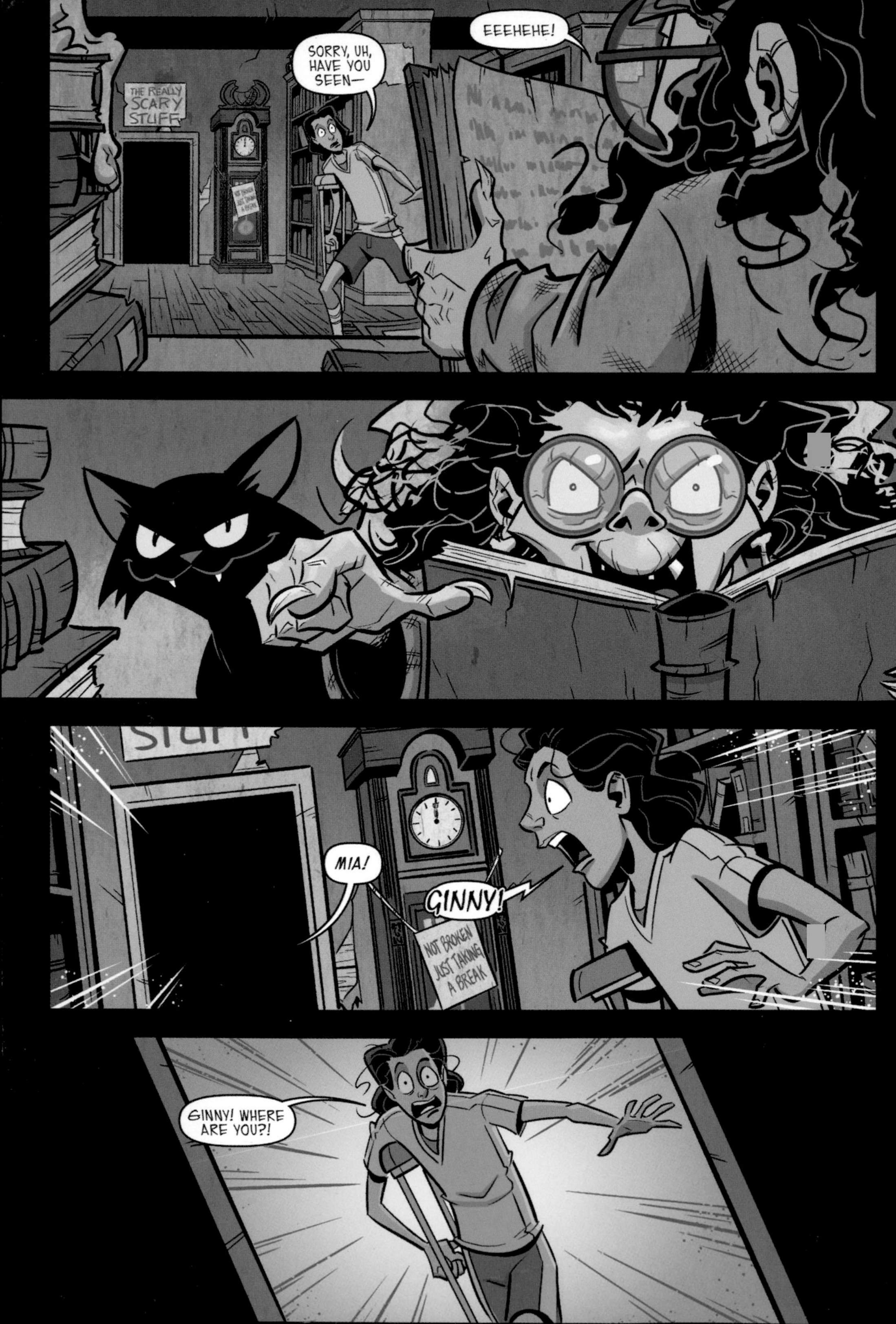
THE REALLY SCARY STUFF
SORRY, UH, HAVE YOU SEEN—
EEEHEHE!
MIA!
GINNY!
NOT BROKEN JUST TAKING A BREAK
GINNY! WHERE ARE YOU?!

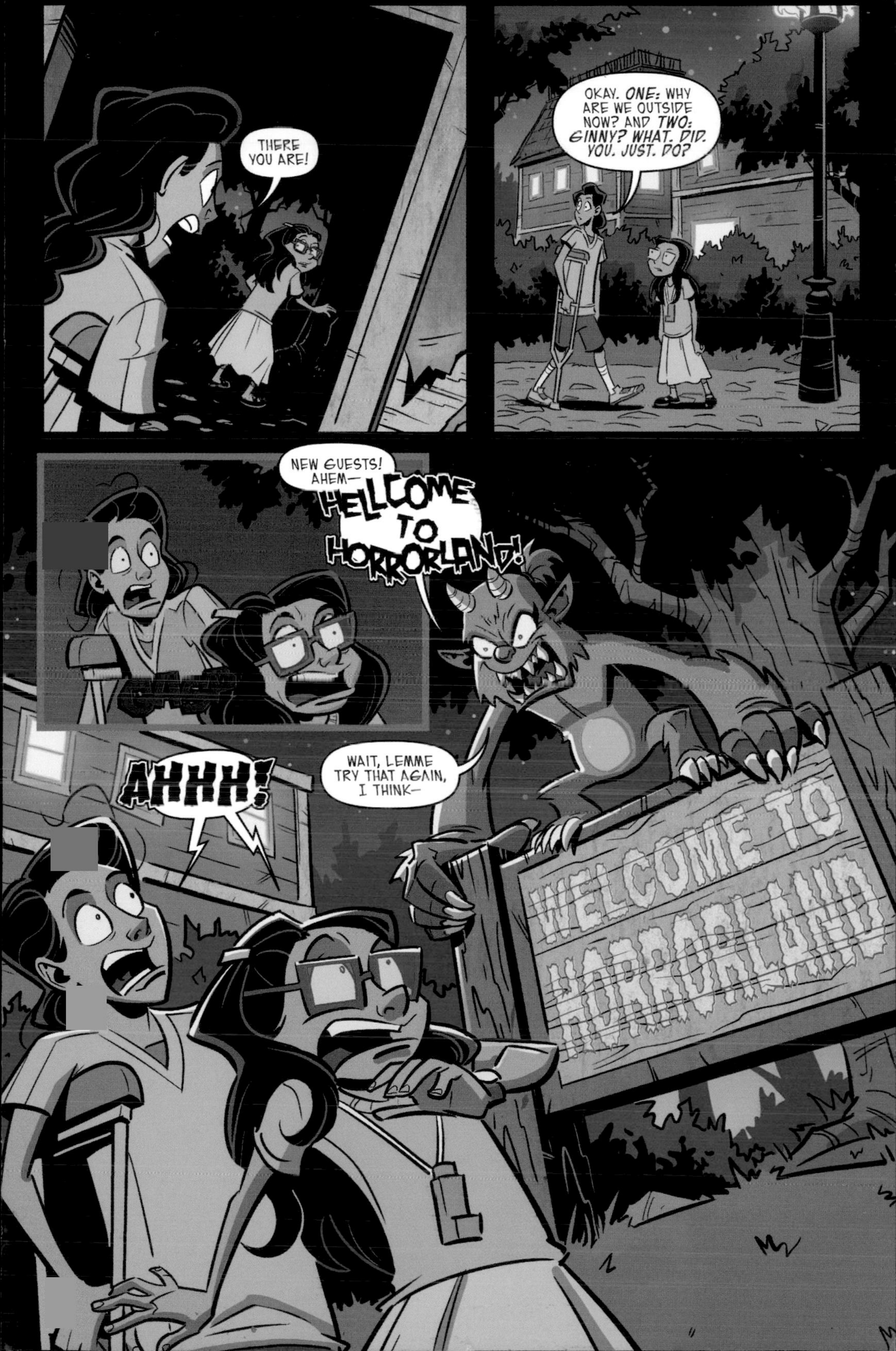
THERE YOU ARE!
OKAY. ONE: WHY ARE WE OUTSIDE NOW? AND TWO: GINNY? WHAT. DID. YOU. JUST. DO?
NEW GUESTS! AHEM—
HELLCOME TO HORRORLAND!
AHHH!
WAIT, LEMME TRY THAT AGAIN, I THINK—
WELCOME TO HORRORLAND

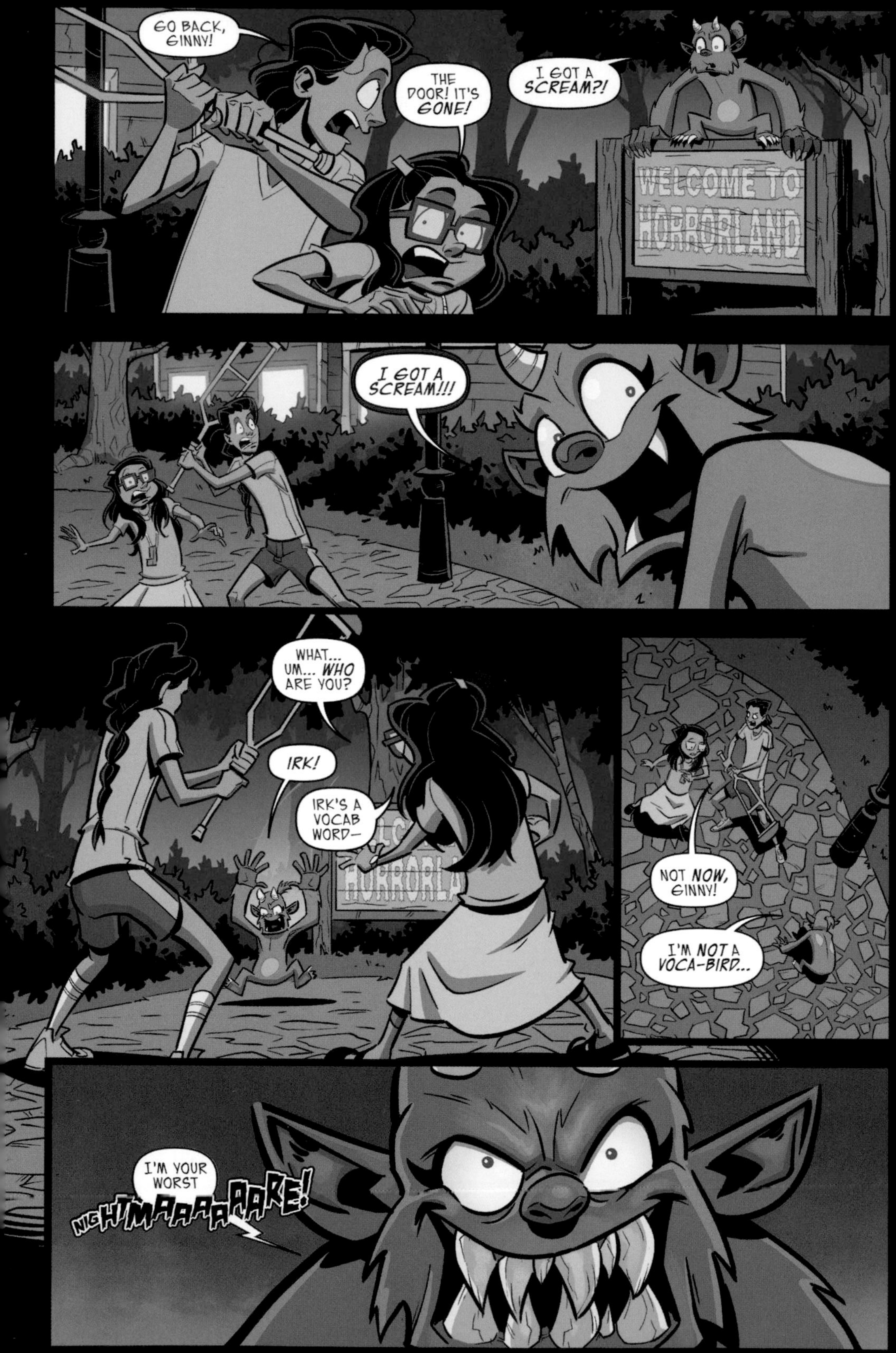
GO BACK, GINNY!
THE DOOR! IT'S GONE!
I GOT A SCREAM?!
WELCOME TO HORRORLAND
I GOT A SCREAM!!!
WHAT... UM... WHO ARE YOU?
IRK!
IRK'S A VOCAB WORD—
NOT NOW, GINNY!
I'M NOT A VOCA-BIRD...
I'M YOUR WORST
NIGHTMAAAAAARE!

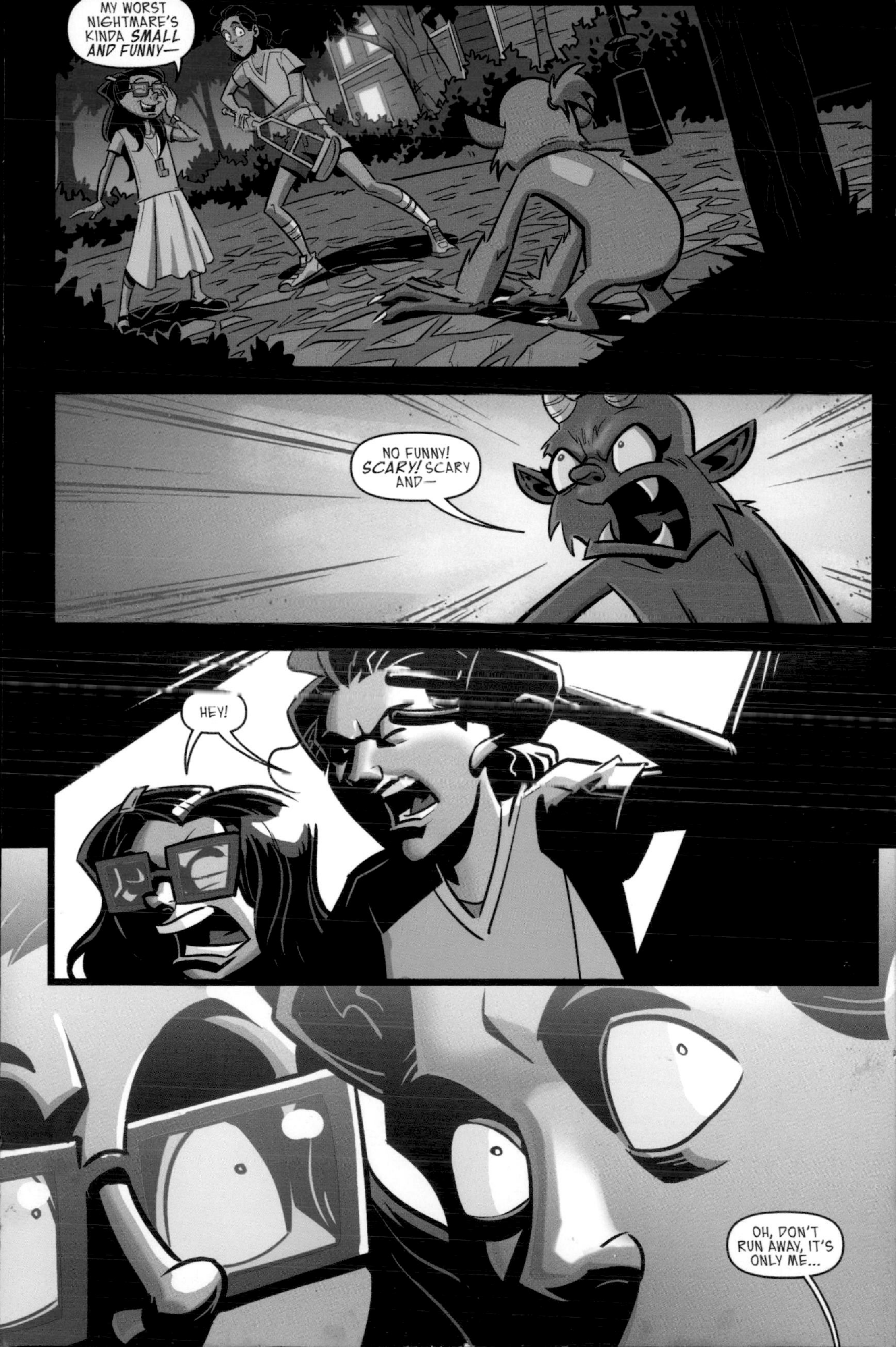
MY WORST NIGHTMARE'S KINDA SMALL AND FUNNY—
NO FUNNY! SCARY! SCARY AND—
HEY!
OH, DON'T RUN AWAY, IT'S ONLY ME...

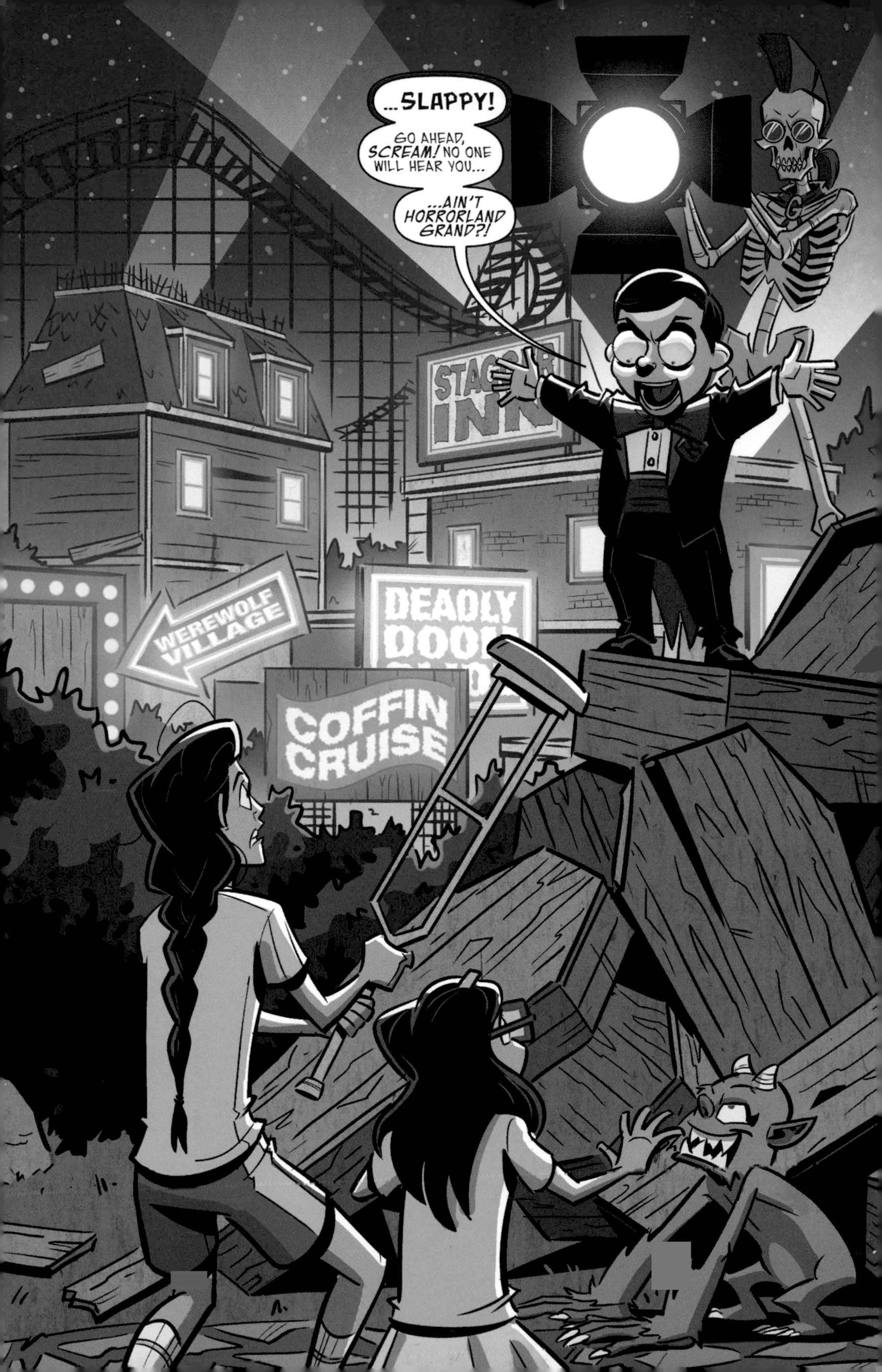
...SLAPPY!
GO AHEAD, SCREAM! NO ONE WILL HEAR YOU...
...AIN'T HORRORLAND GRAND?!
WEREWOLF VILLAGE
DEADLY
COFFIN CRUISE

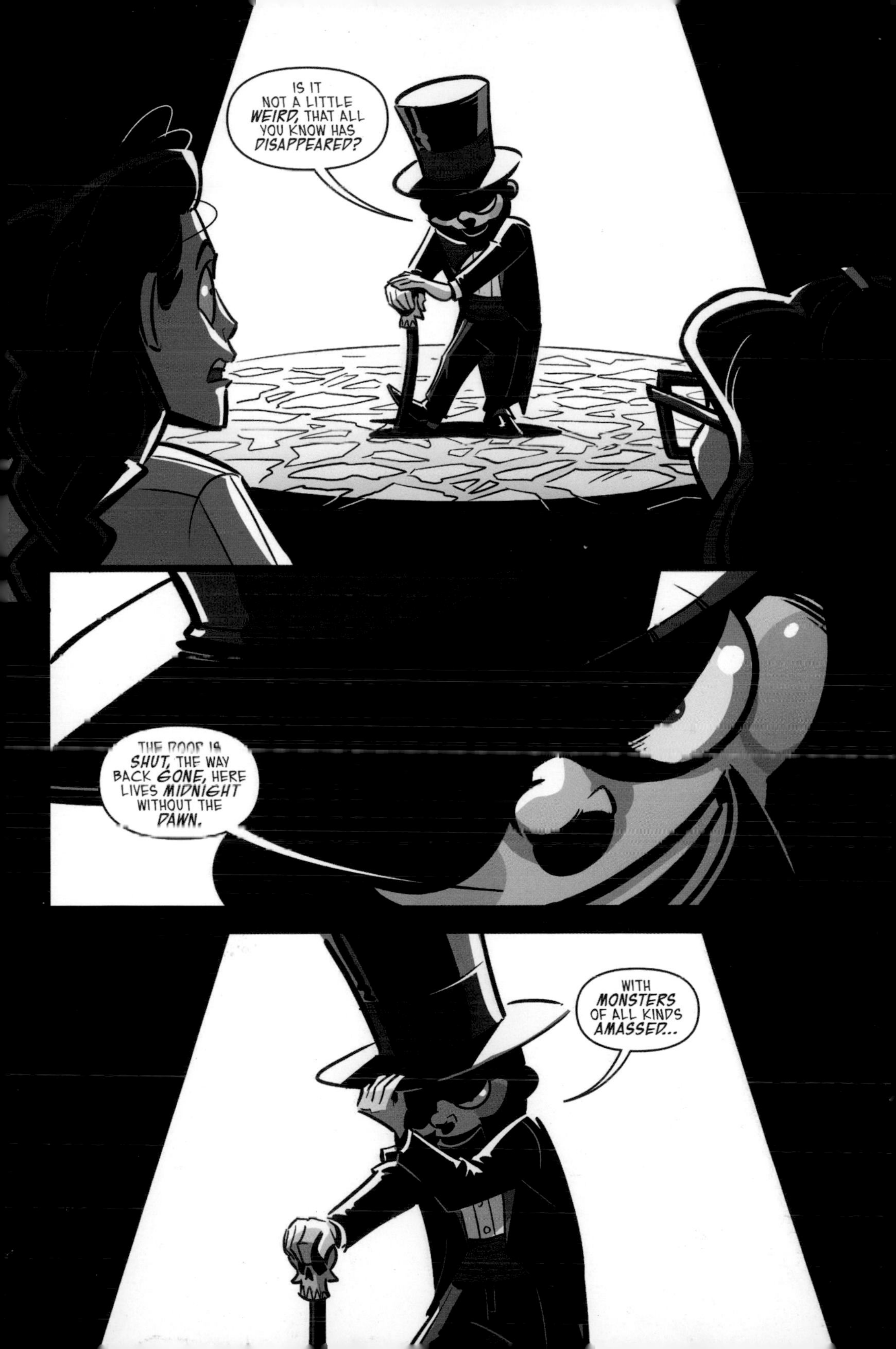
IS IT NOT A LITTLE WEIRD, THAT ALL YOU KNOW HAS DISAPPEARED?
THE DOOR IS SHUT, THE WAY BACK GONE, HERE LIVES MIDNIGHT WITHOUT THE DAWN.
WITH MONSTERS OF ALL KINDS AMASSED...

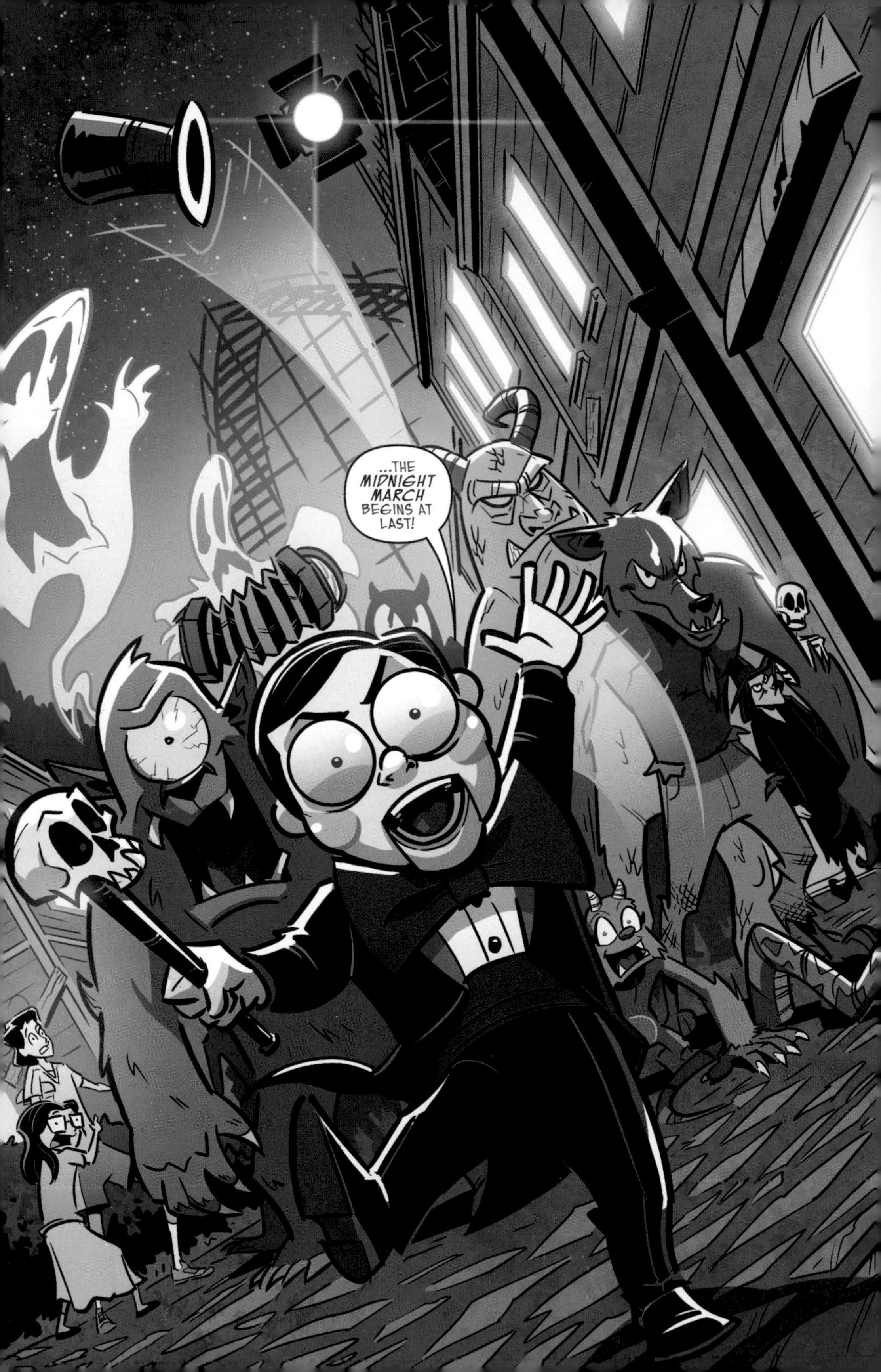
...THE MIDNIGHT MARCH BEGINS AT LAST!

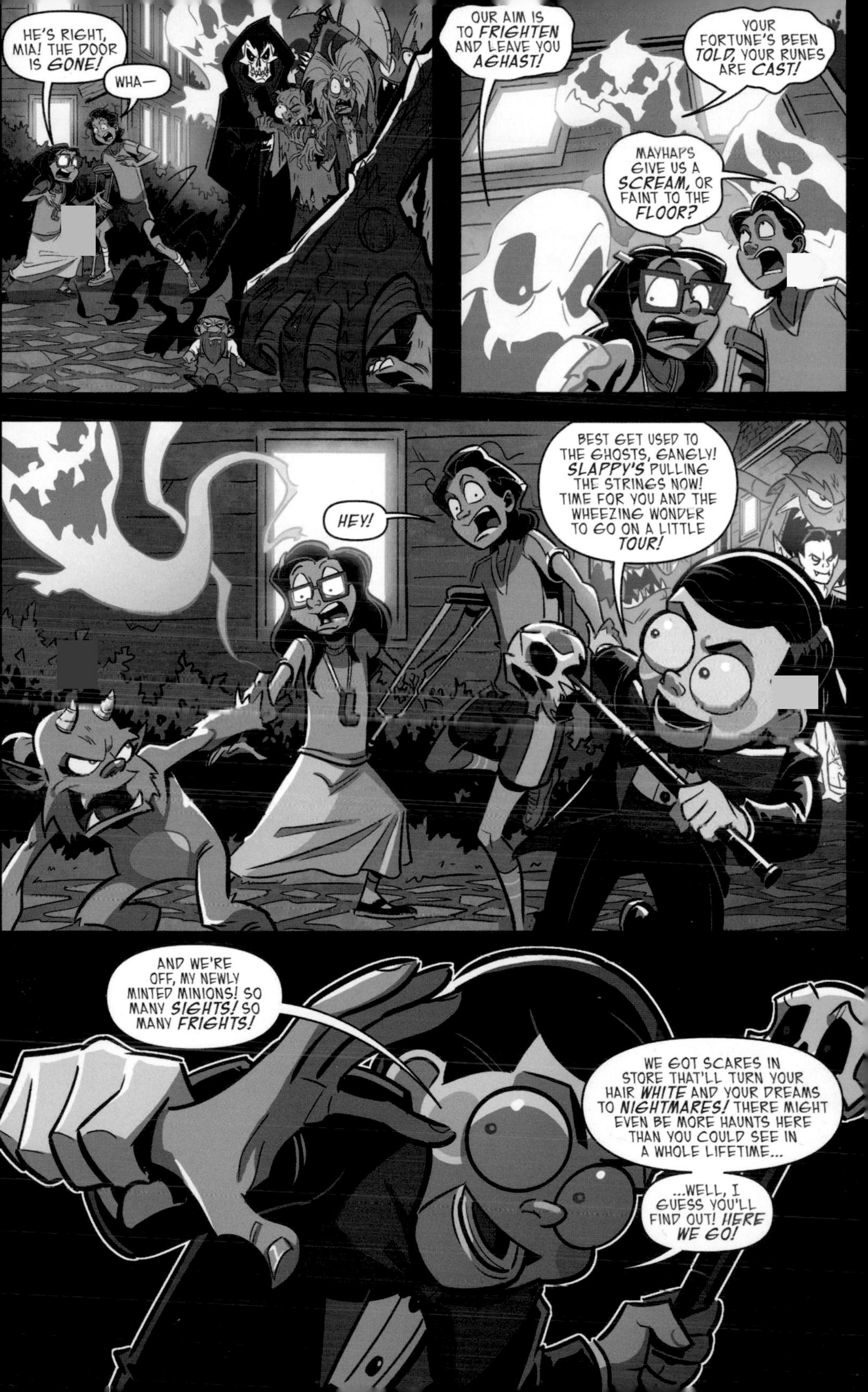
HE'S RIGHT, MIA! THE DOOR IS GONE!
WHA—
OUR AIM IS TO FRIGHTEN AND LEAVE YOU AGHAST!
YOUR FORTUNE'S BEEN TOLD, YOUR RUNES ARE CAST!
MAYHAPS GIVE US A SCREAM, OR FAINT TO THE FLOOR?
HEY!
BEST GET USED TO THE GHOSTS, GANGLY! SLAPPY'S PULLING THE STRINGS NOW! TIME FOR YOU AND THE WHEEZING WONDER TO GO ON A LITTLE TOUR!
AND WE'RE OFF, MY NEWLY MINTED MINIONS! SO MANY SIGHTS! SO MANY FRIGHTS!
WE GOT SCARES IN STORE THAT'LL TURN YOUR HAIR WHITE AND YOUR DREAMS TO NIGHTMARES! THERE MIGHT EVEN BE MORE HAUNTS HERE THAN YOU COULD SEE IN A WHOLE LIFETIME...
...WELL, I GUESS YOU'LL FIND OUT! HERE WE GO!

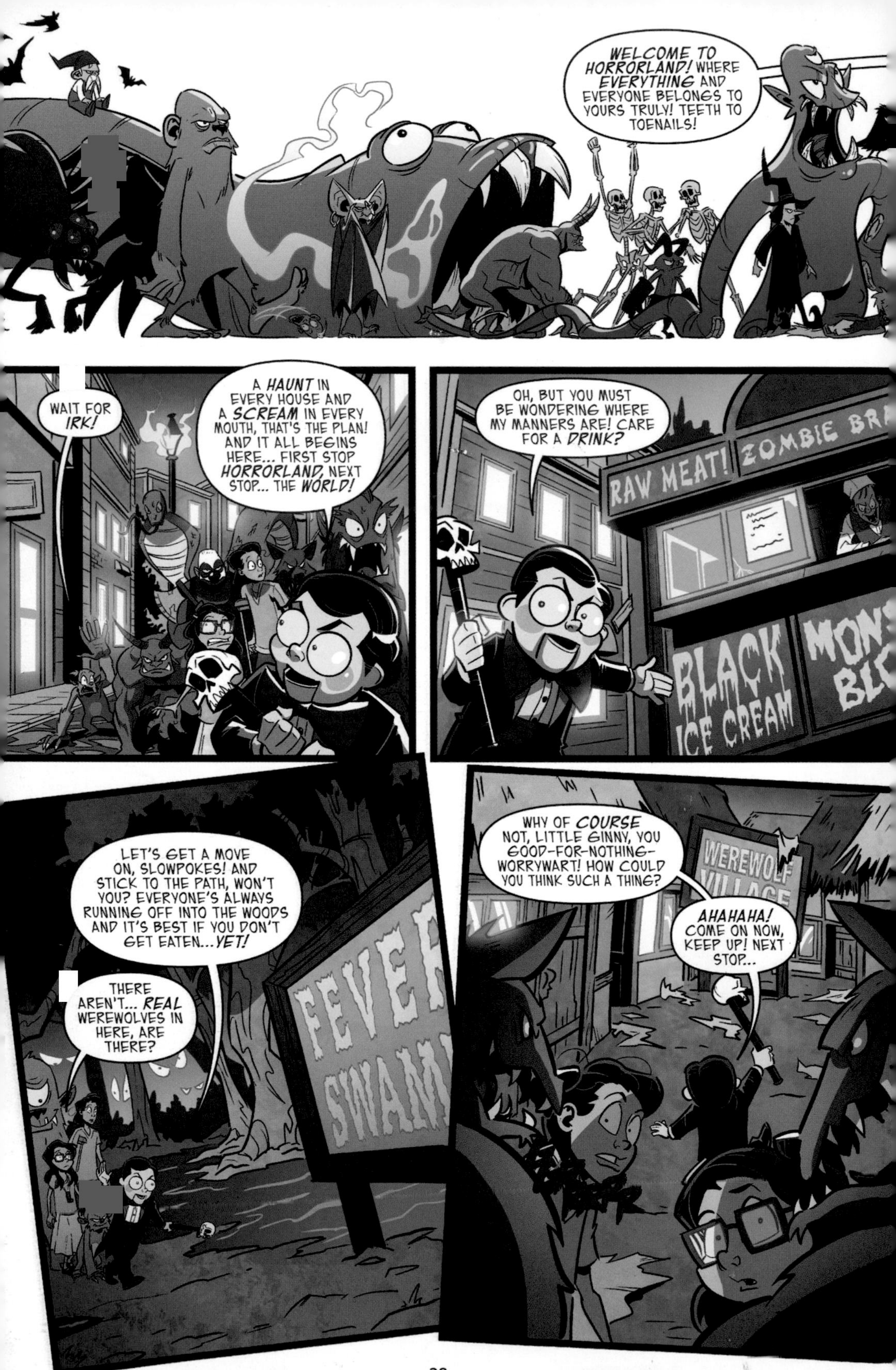
WELCOME TO HORRORLAND! WHERE EVERYTHING AND EVERYONE BELONGS TO YOURS TRULY! TEETH TO TOENAILS!
WAIT FOR IRK!
A HAUNT IN EVERY HOUSE AND A SCREAM IN EVERY MOUTH, THAT'S THE PLAN! AND IT ALL BEGINS HERE... FIRST STOP HORRORLAND, NEXT STOP... THE WORLD!
OH, BUT YOU MUST BE WONDERING WHERE MY MANNERS ARE! CARE FOR A DRINK?
RAW MEAT!
ZOMBIE BRA
BLACK ICE CREAM
LET'S GET A MOVE ON, SLOWPOKES! AND STICK TO THE PATH, WON'T YOU? EVERYONE'S ALWAYS RUNNING OFF INTO THE WOODS AND IT'S BEST IF YOU DON'T GET EATEN...YET!
THERE AREN'T... REAL WEREWOLVES IN HERE, ARE THERE?
FEVER SWAM
WHY OF COURSE NOT, LITTLE GINNY, YOU GOOD-FOR-NOTHING-WORRYWART! HOW COULD YOU THINK SUCH A THING?
WEREWOLF VILLAGE
AHAHAHA! COME ON NOW, KEEP UP! NEXT STOP...

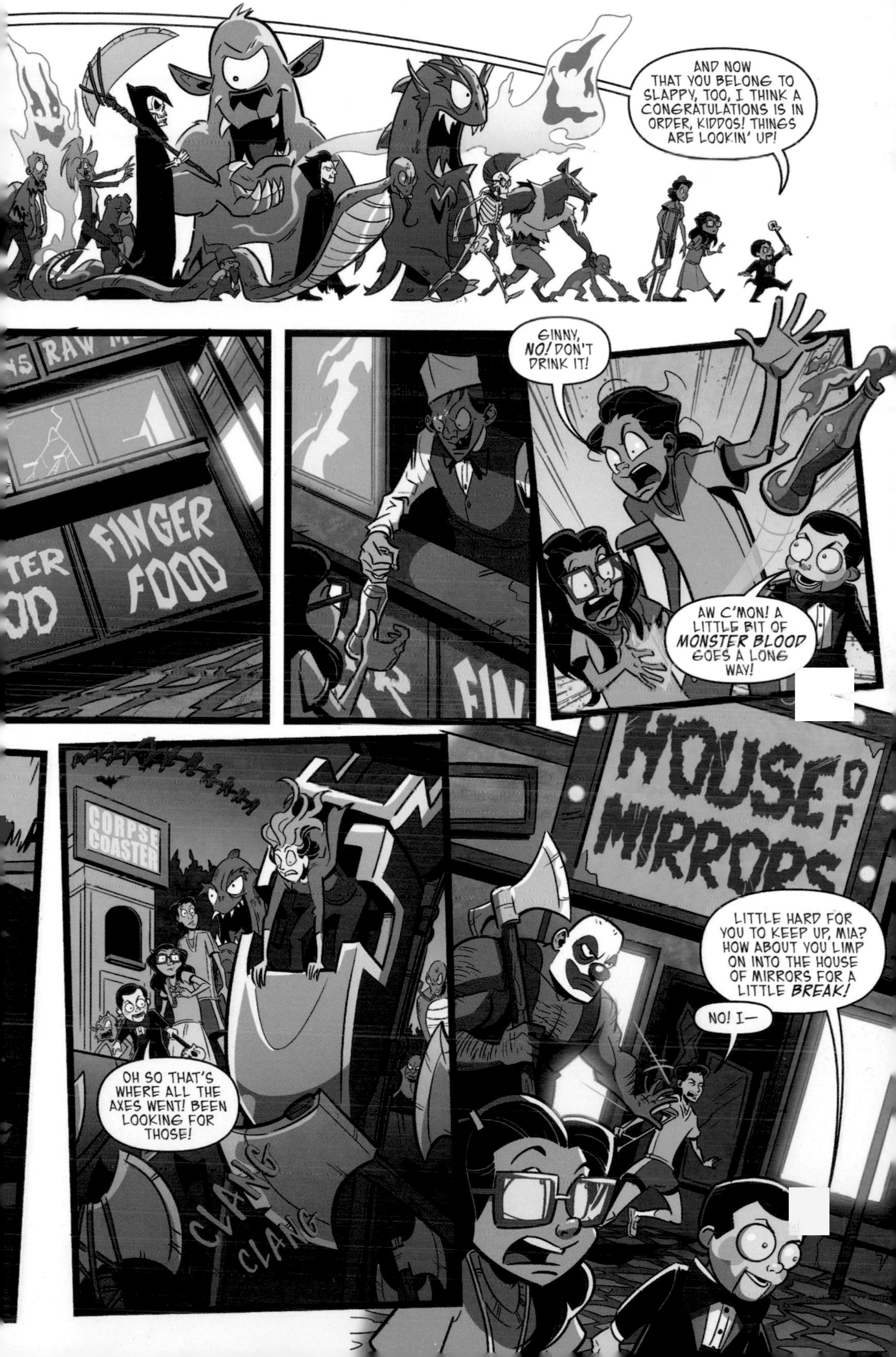
AND NOW THAT YOU BELONG TO SLAPPY, TOO, I THINK A CONGRATULATIONS IS IN ORDER, KIDDOS! THINGS ARE LOOKIN' UP!
RAW
FINGER FOOD
GINNY, NO! DON'T DRINK IT!
AW C'MON! A LITTLE BIT OF MONSTER BLOOD GOES A LONG WAY!
CORPSE COASTER
OH SO THAT'S WHERE ALL THE AXES WENT! BEEN LOOKING FOR THOSE!
CLANG
CLANG
HOUSE OF MIRRORS
LITTLE HARD FOR YOU TO KEEP UP, MIA? HOW ABOUT YOU LIMP ON INTO THE HOUSE OF MIRRORS FOR A LITTLE BREAK!
NO! I—

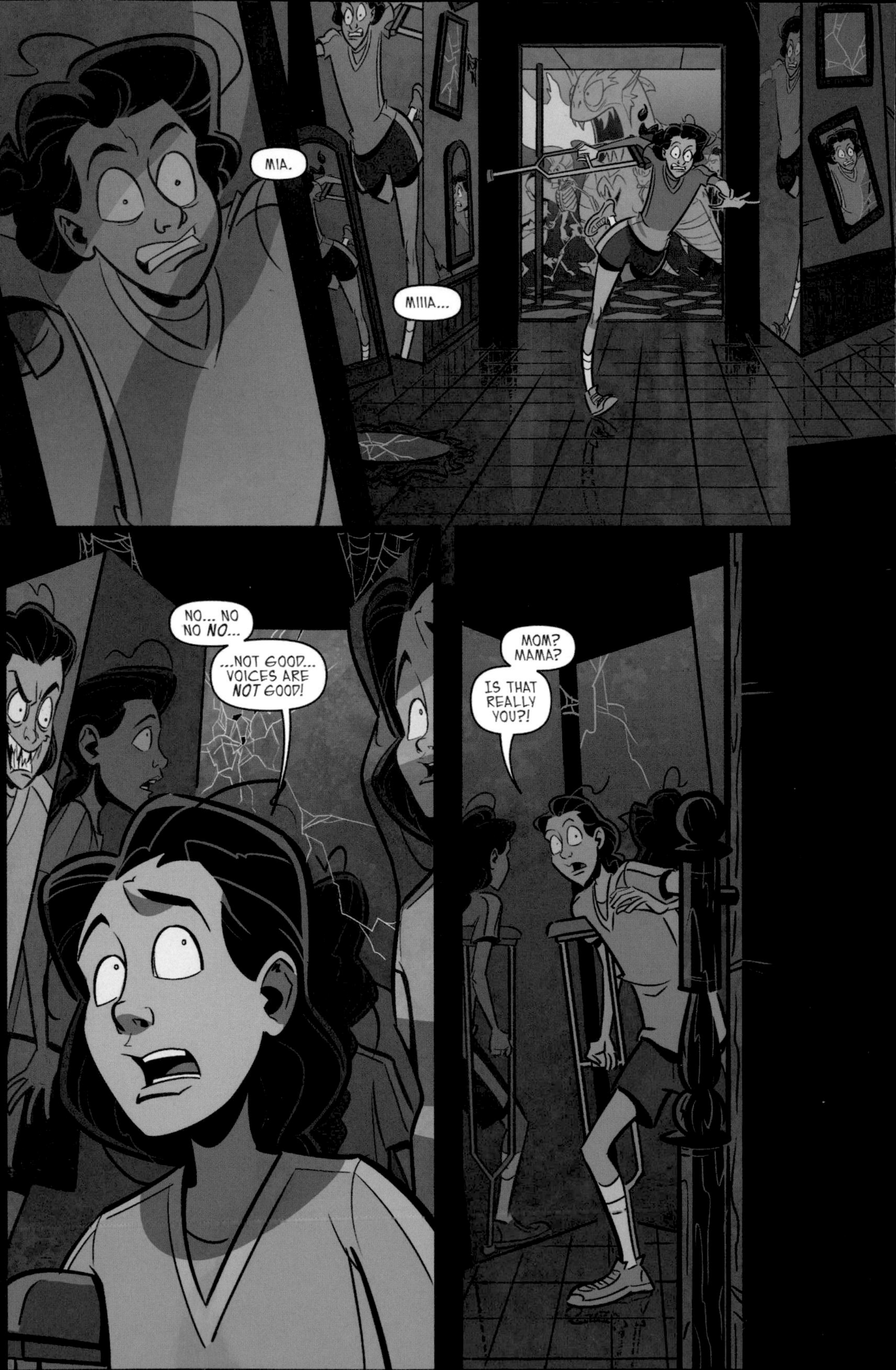
MIA.
MIIIA...
NO... NO NO NO...
...NOT GOOD... VOICES ARE NOT GOOD!
MOM? MAMA?
IS THAT REALLY YOU?!

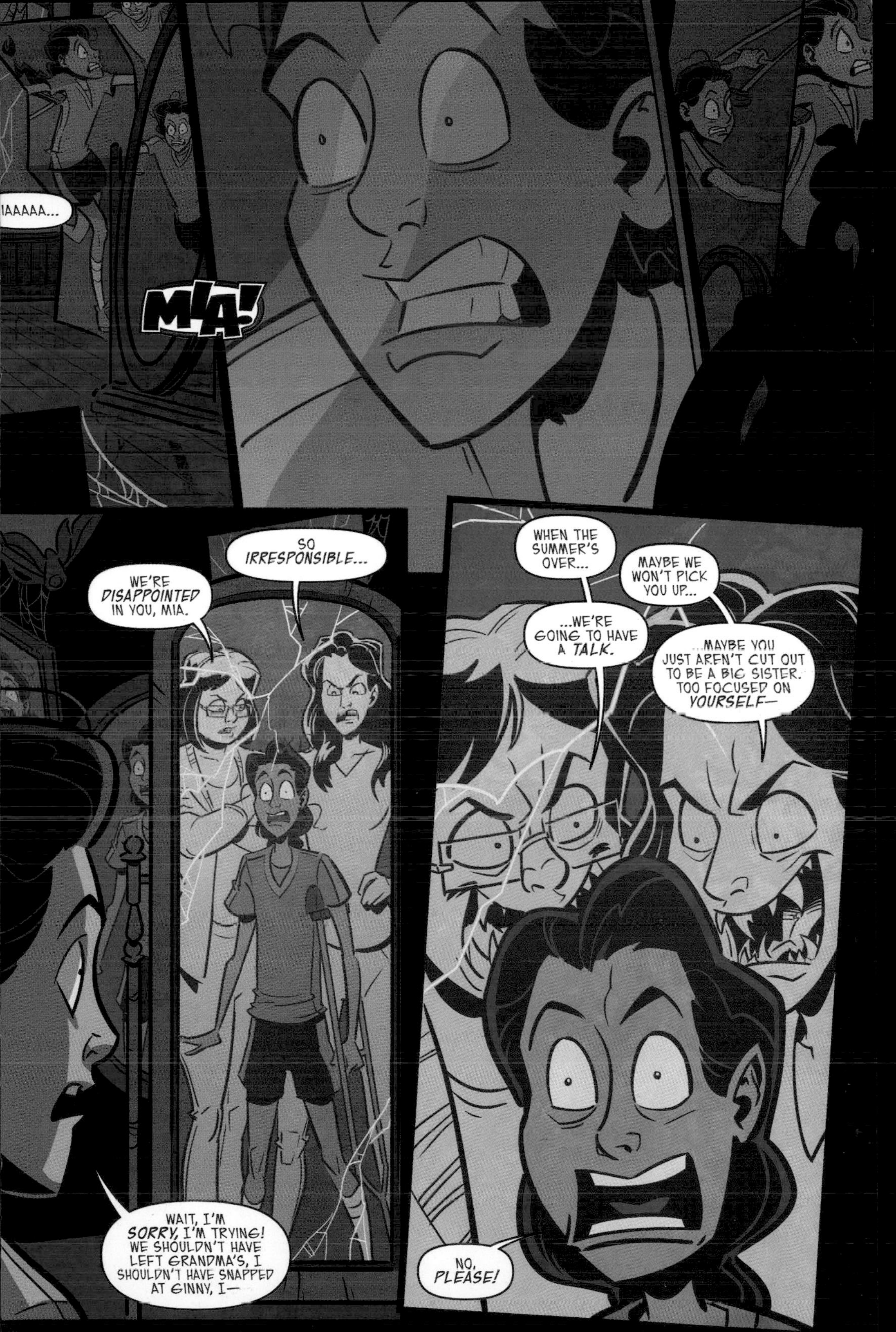

IAAAAA...
MIA!
WE'RE DISAPPOINTED IN YOU, MIA.
SO IRRESPONSIBLE...
WAIT, I'M SORRY, I'M TRYING! WE SHOULDN'T HAVE LEFT GRANDMA'S, I SHOULDN'T HAVE SNAPPED AT GINNY, I—
WHEN THE SUMMER'S OVER...
...WE'RE GOING TO HAVE A TALK.
MAYBE WE WON'T PICK YOU UP...
...MAYBE YOU JUST AREN'T CUT OUT TO BE A BIG SISTER. TOO FOCUSED ON YOURSELF—
NO, PLEASE!

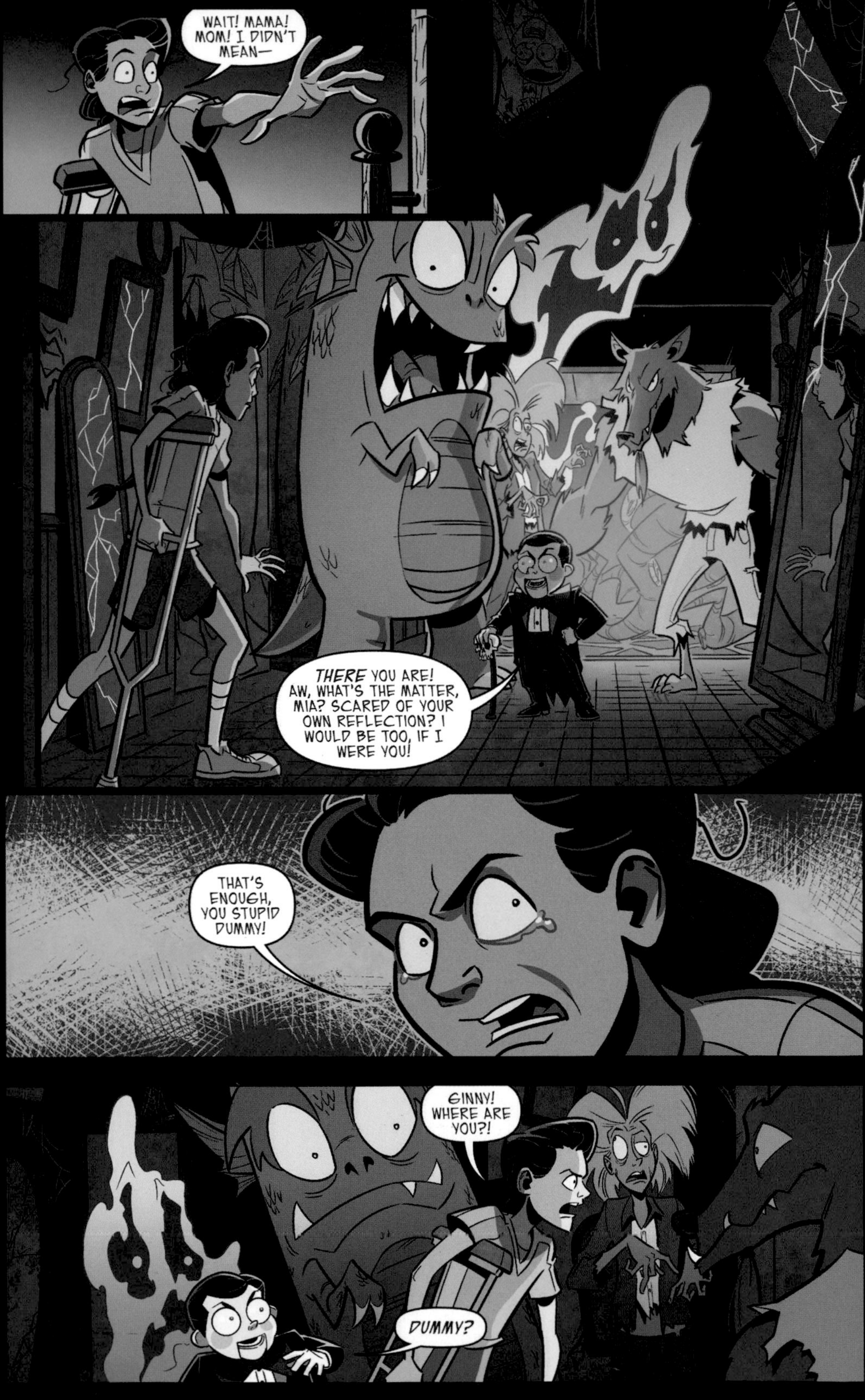
WAIT! MAMA! MOM! I DIDN'T MEAN—
THERE YOU ARE! AW, WHAT'S THE MATTER, MIA? SCARED OF YOUR OWN REFLECTION? I WOULD BE TOO, IF I WERE YOU!
THAT'S ENOUGH, YOU STUPID DUMMY!
GINNY! WHERE ARE YOU?!
DUMMY?

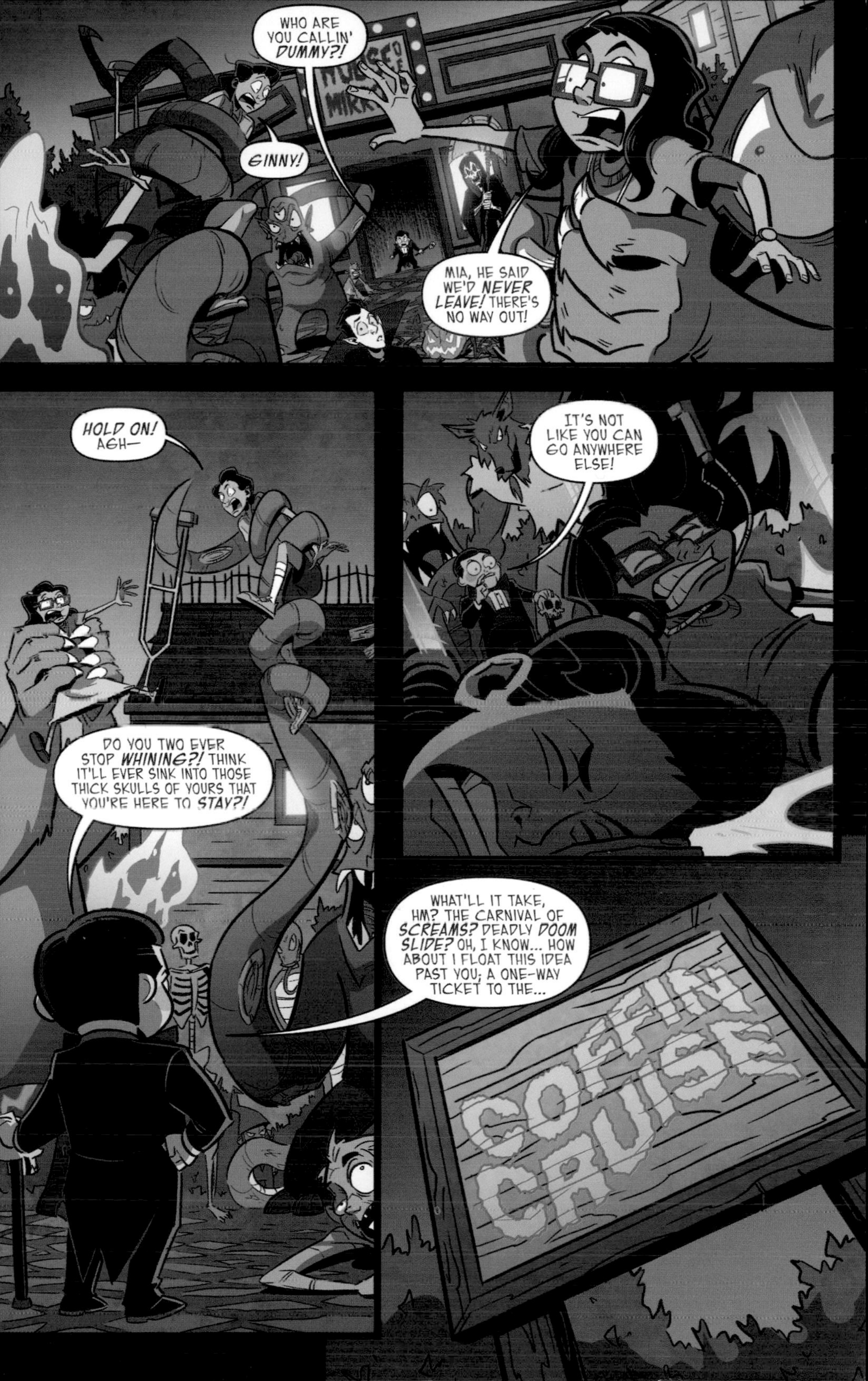

WHO ARE YOU CALLIN' DUMMY?!
GINNY!
MIA, HE SAID WE'D NEVER LEAVE! THERE'S NO WAY OUT!
HOLD ON! AGH—
IT'S NOT LIKE YOU CAN GO ANYWHERE ELSE!
DO YOU TWO EVER STOP WHINING?! THINK IT'LL EVER SINK INTO THOSE THICK SKULLS OF YOURS THAT YOU'RE HERE TO STAY?!
WHAT'LL IT TAKE, HM? THE CARNIVAL OF SCREAMS? DEADLY DOOM SLIDE? OH, I KNOW... HOW ABOUT I FLOAT THIS IDEA PAST YOU; A ONE-WAY TICKET TO THE...
COFFIN CRUISE

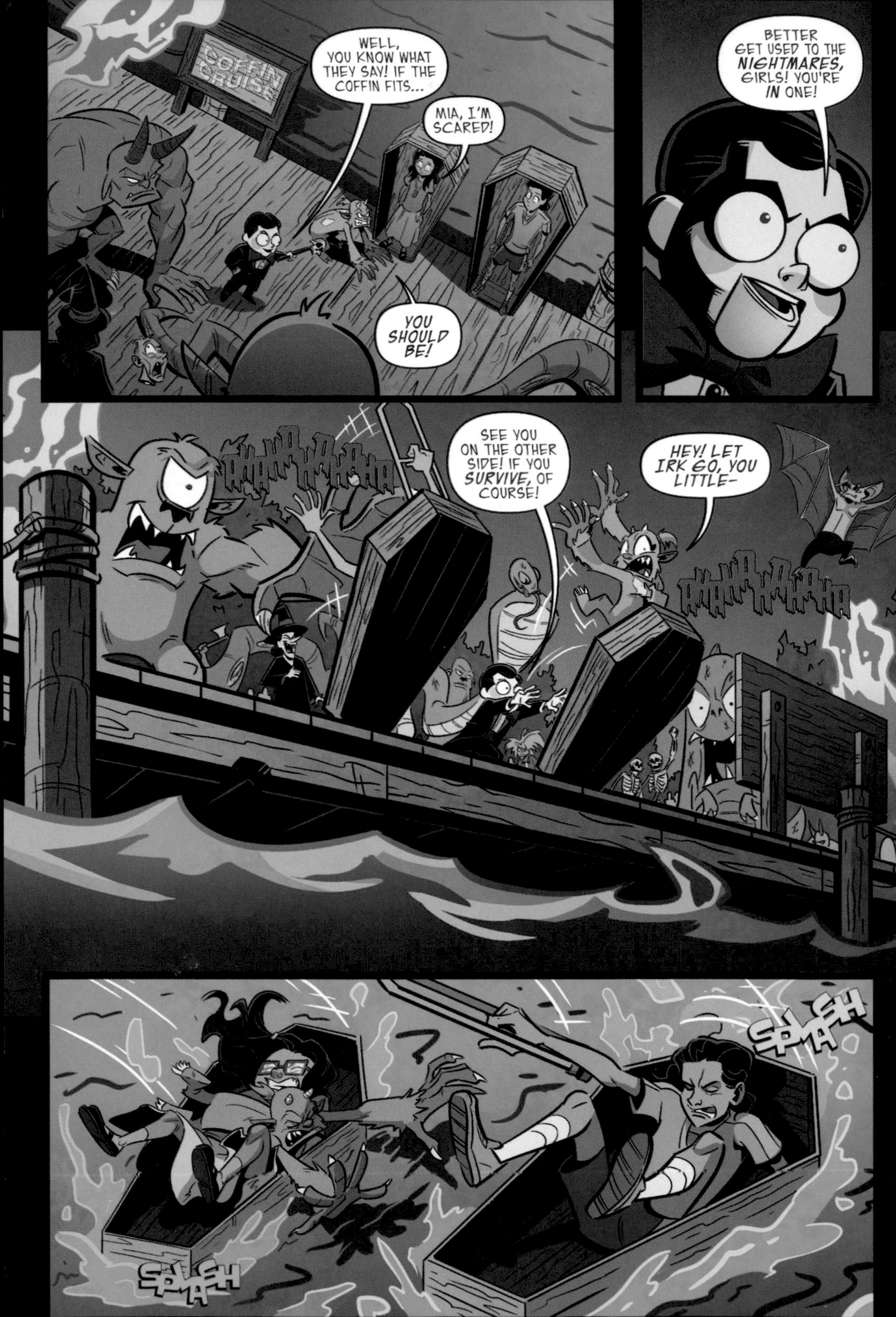
COFFIN CRUISE
WELL, YOU KNOW WHAT THEY SAY! IF THE COFFIN FITS...
MIA, I'M SCARED!
YOU SHOULD BE!
BETTER GET USED TO THE NIGHTMARES, GIRLS! YOU'RE IN ONE!
AHAHAHAHAHA
SEE YOU ON THE OTHER SIDE! IF YOU SURVIVE, OF COURSE!
HEY! LET IRK GO, YOU LITTLE-
AHAHAHAHAHA
SPLASH
SPLASH

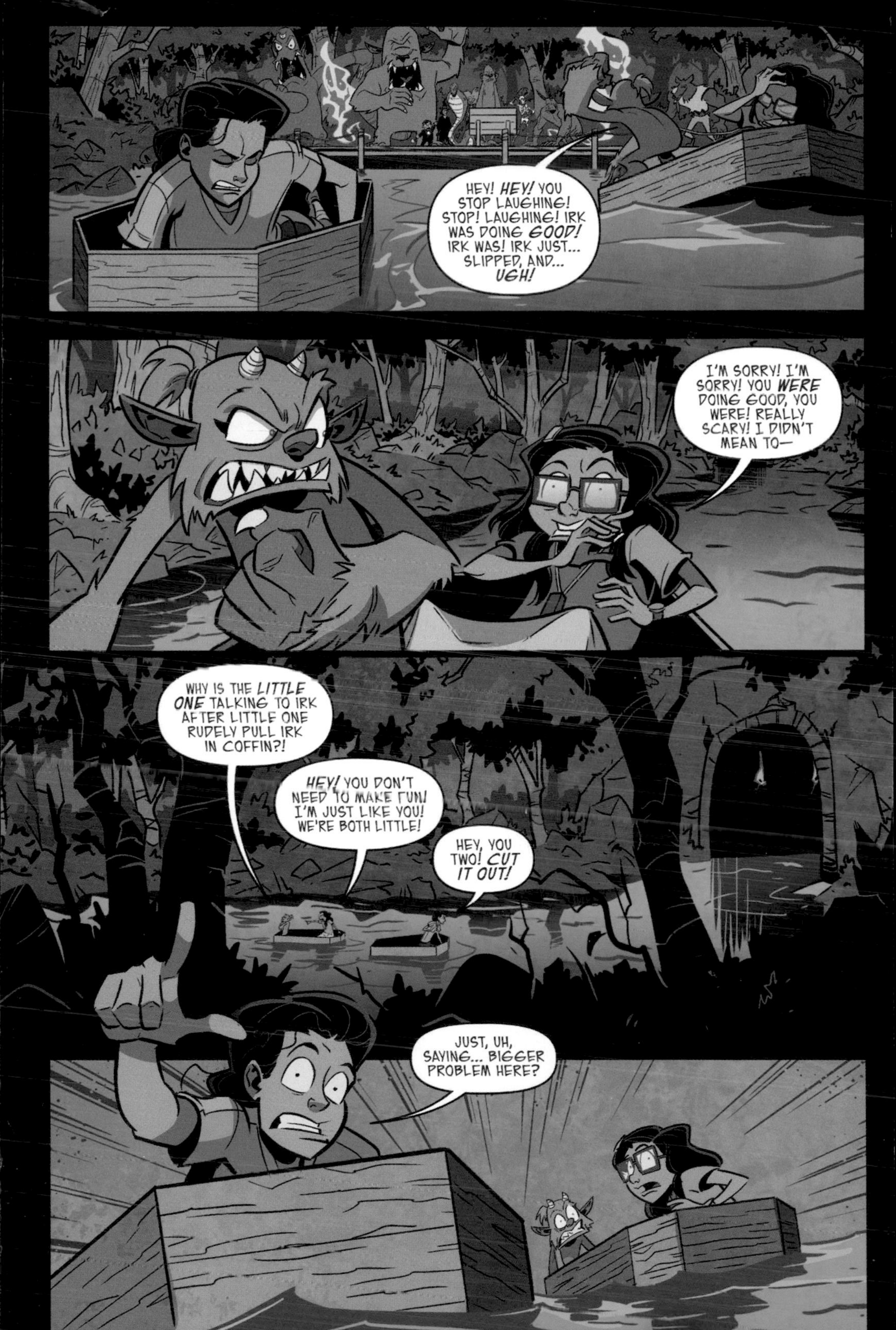
HEY! HEY! YOU STOP LAUGHING! STOP! LAUGHING! IRK WAS DOING GOOD! IRK WAS! IRK JUST... SLIPPED, AND... UGH!
I'M SORRY! I'M SORRY! YOU WERE DOING GOOD, YOU WERE! REALLY SCARY! I DIDN'T MEAN TO—
WHY IS THE LITTLE ONE TALKING TO IRK AFTER LITTLE ONE RUDELY PULL IRK IN COFFIN?!
HEY! YOU DON'T NEED TO MAKE FUN! I'M JUST LIKE YOU! WE'RE BOTH LITTLE!
HEY, YOU TWO! CUT IT OUT!
JUST, UH, SAYING... BIGGER PROBLEM HERE?

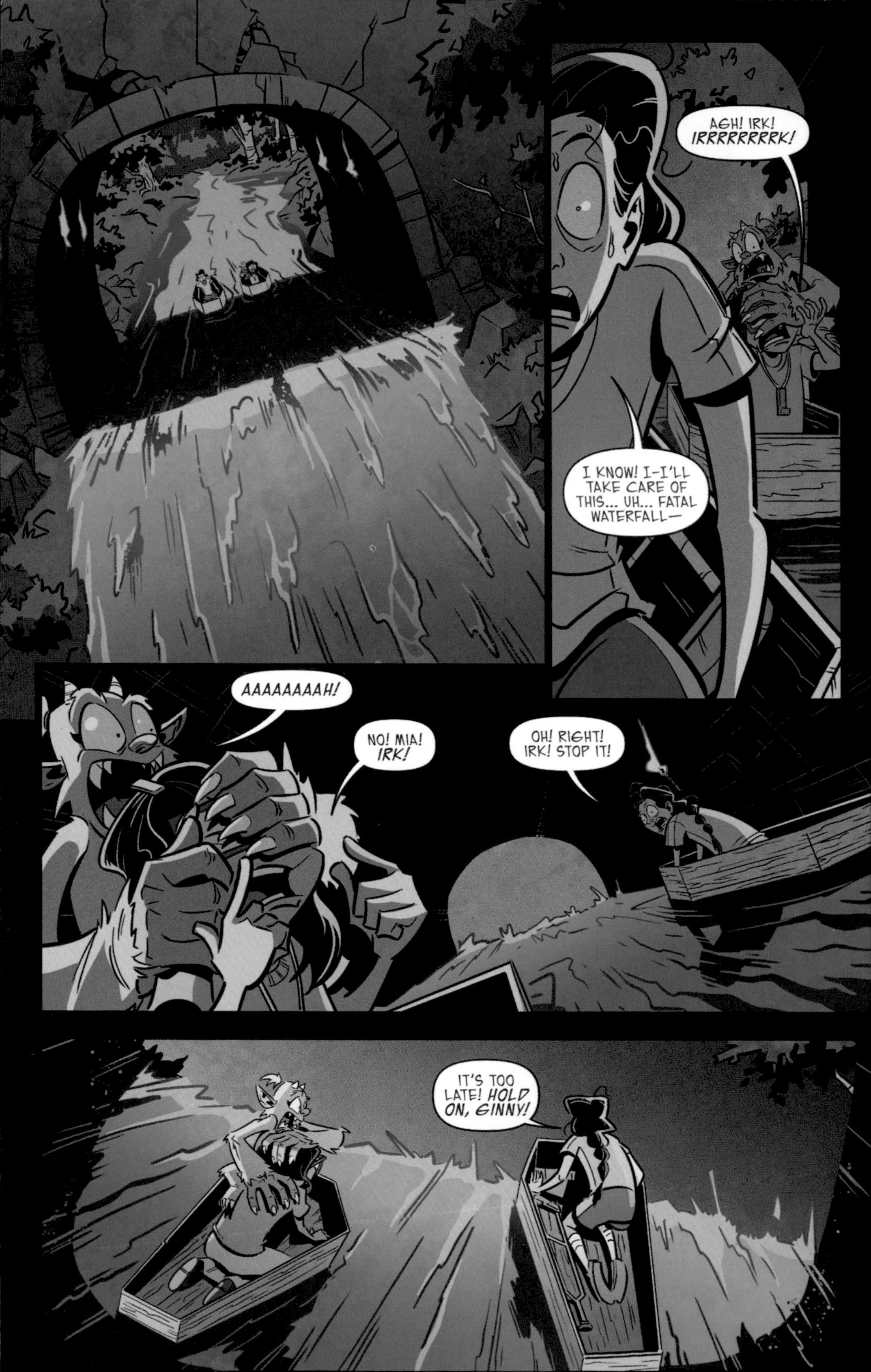
AGH! IRK! IRRRRRRRRK!
I KNOW! I-I'LL TAKE CARE OF THIS... UH... FATAL WATERFALL—
AAAAAAAAH!
NO! MIA! IRK!
OH! RIGHT! IRK! STOP IT!
IT'S TOO LATE! HOLD ON, GINNY!

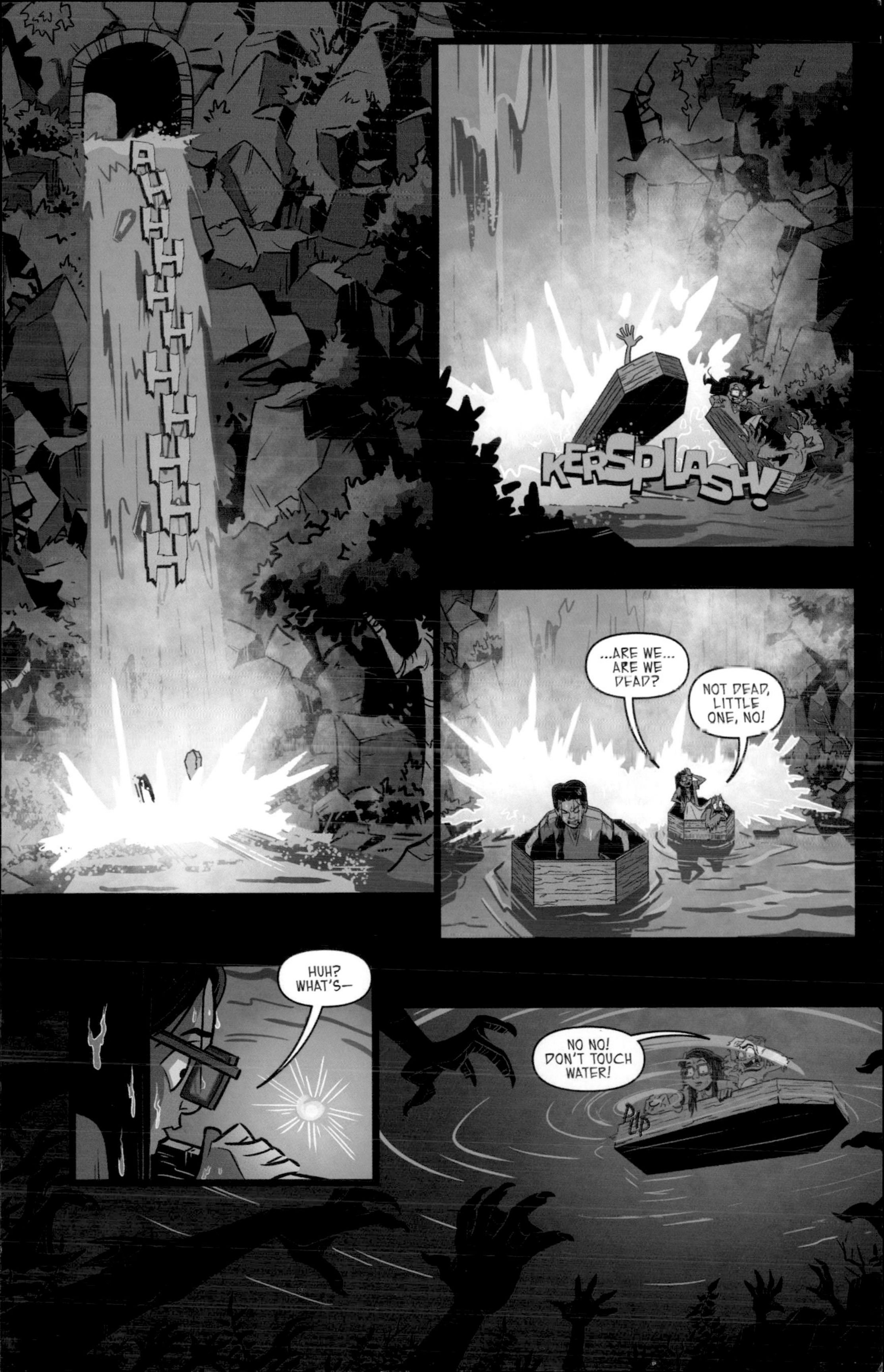
AHHHHHHHHHHHHH
KERSPLASH!
...ARE WE... ARE WE DEAD?
NOT DEAD, LITTLE ONE, NO!
HUH? WHAT'S—
NO NO! DON'T TOUCH WATER!
PLIP

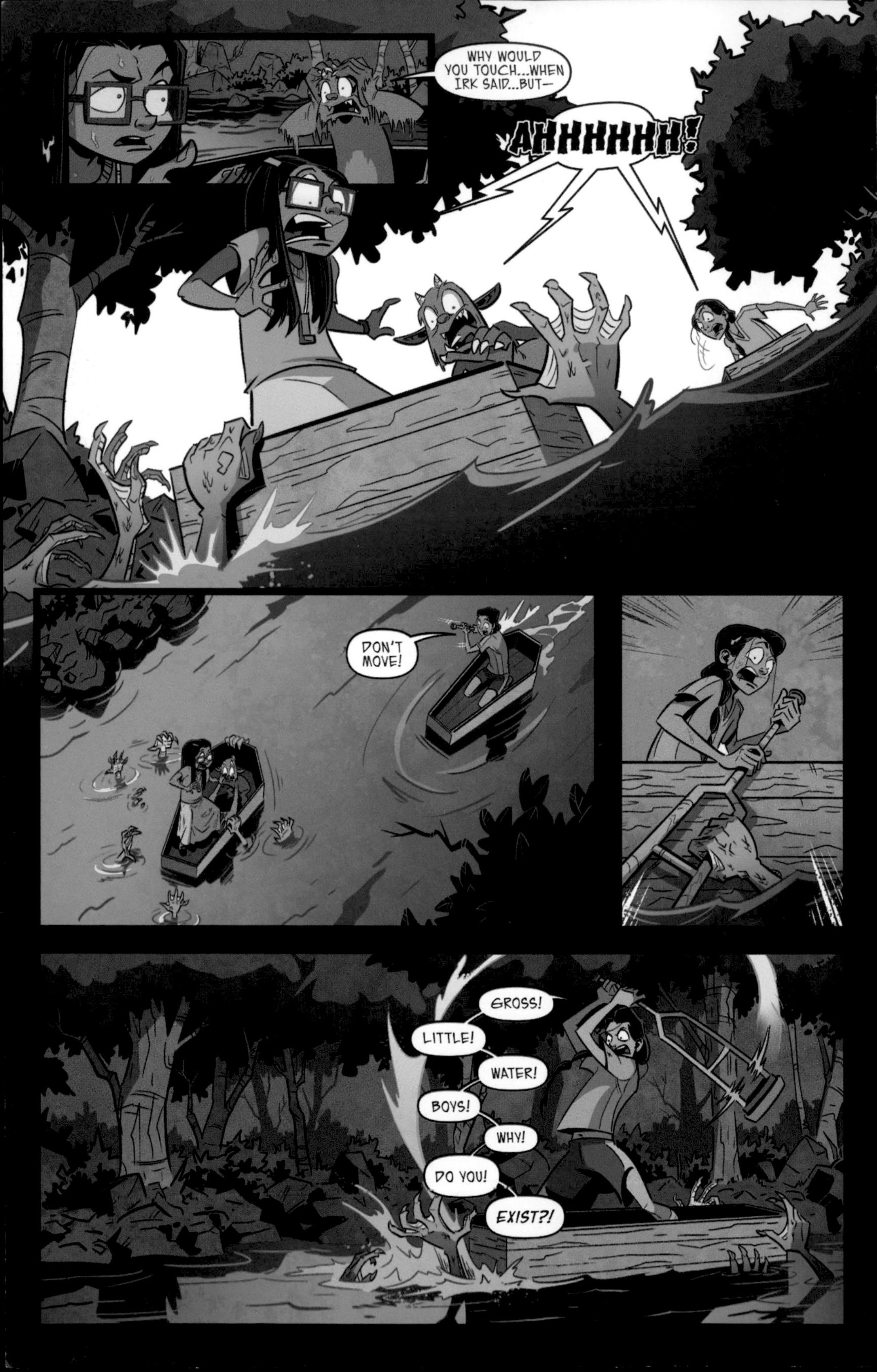
WHY WOULD YOU TOUCH...WHEN IRK SAID...BUT—
AHHHHHH!
DON'T MOVE!
GROSS!
LITTLE!
WATER!
BOYS!
WHY!
DO YOU!
EXIST?!

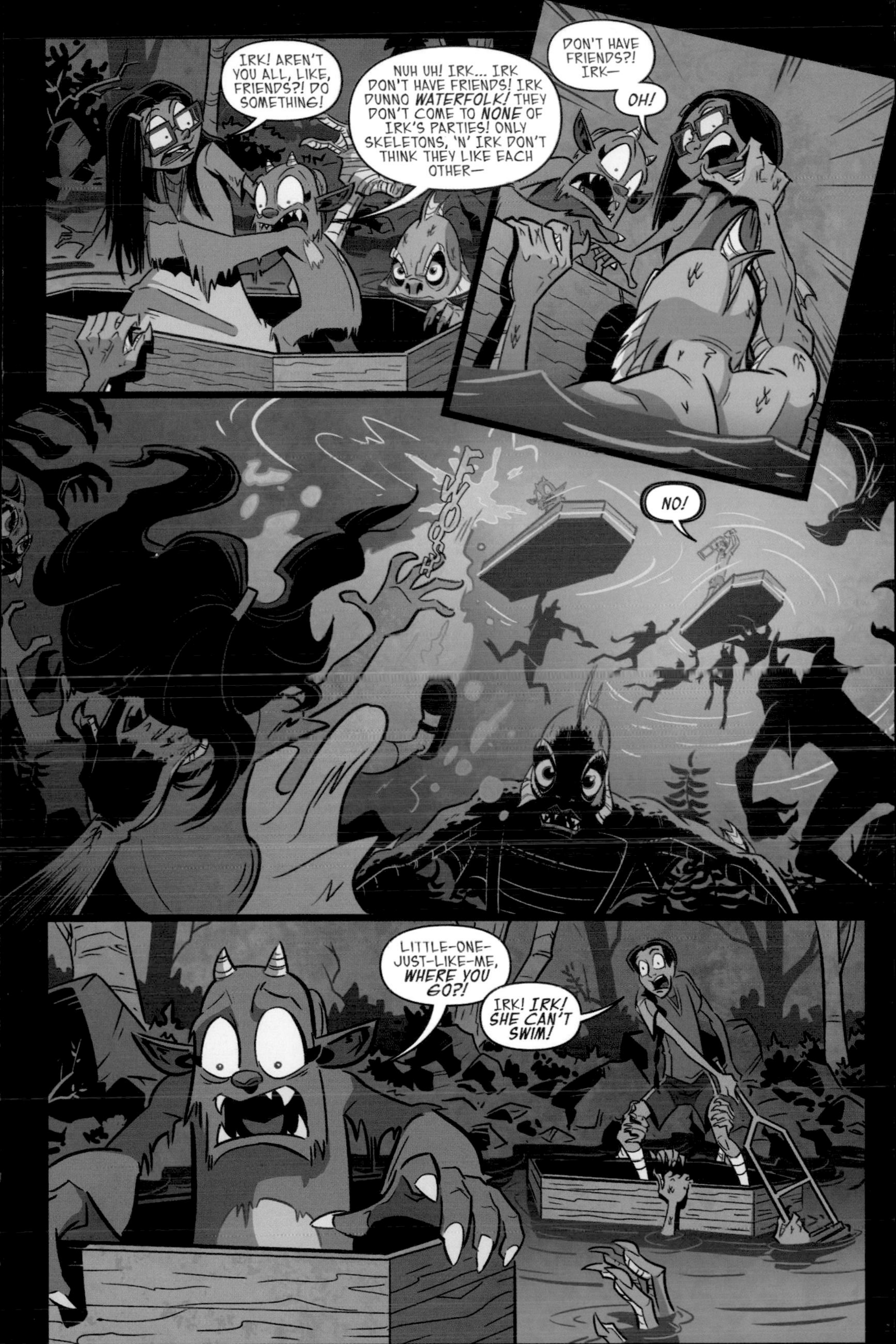
IRK! AREN'T YOU ALL, LIKE, FRIENDS?! DO SOMETHING!
NUH UH! IRK... IRK DON'T HAVE FRIENDS! IRK DUNNO WATERFOLK! THEY DON'T COME TO NONE OF IRK'S PARTIES! ONLY SKELETONS, 'N' IRK DON'T THINK THEY LIKE EACH OTHER—
DON'T HAVE FRIENDS?! IRK—
OH!
FWOOSH
NO!
LITTLE-ONE-JUST-LIKE-ME, WHERE YOU GO?!
IRK! IRK! SHE CAN'T SWIM!

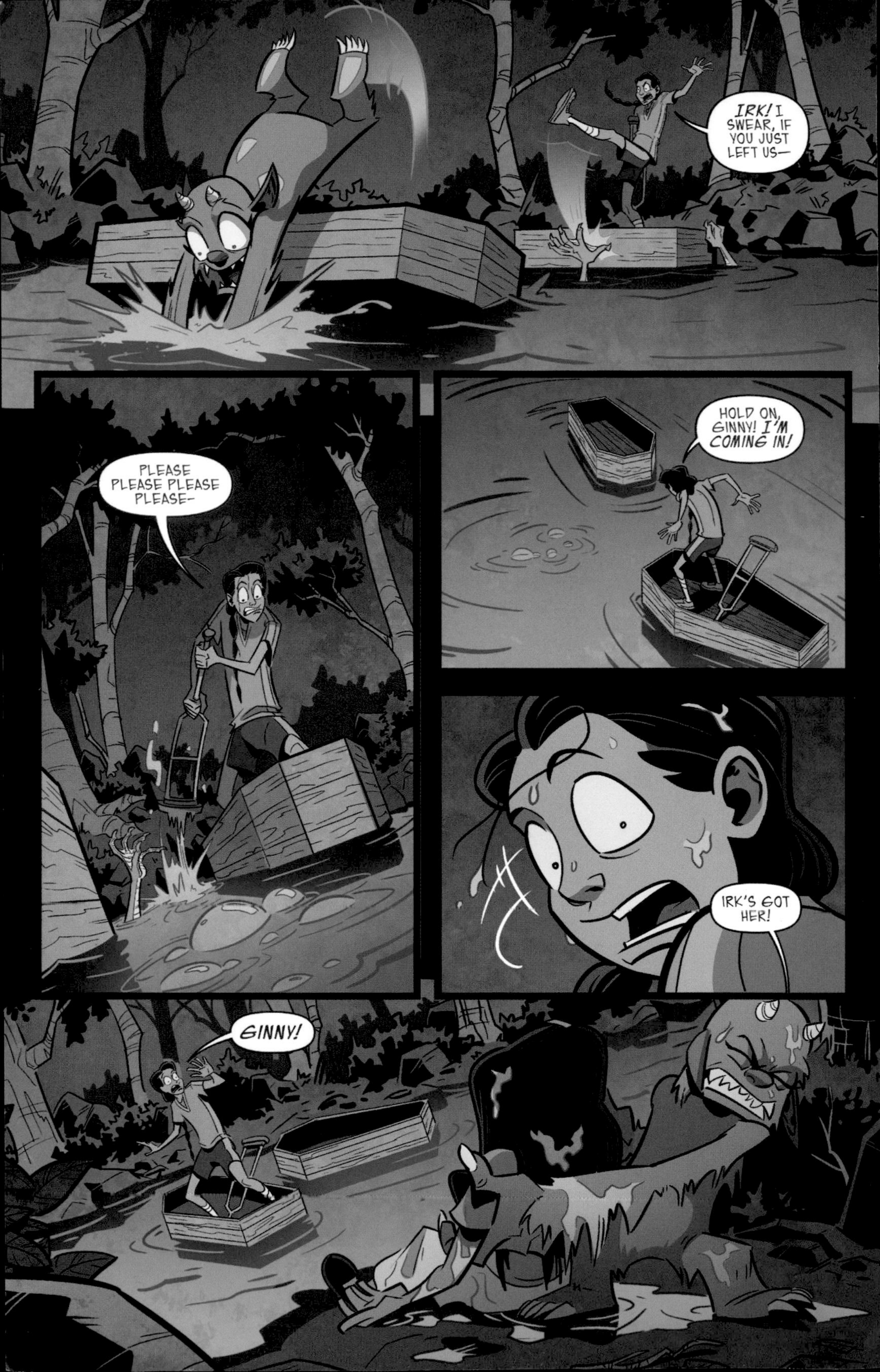
IRK! I SWEAR, IF YOU JUST LEFT US—
PLEASE PLEASE PLEASE PLEASE-
HOLD ON, GINNY! I'M COMING IN!
IRK'S GOT HER!
GINNY!

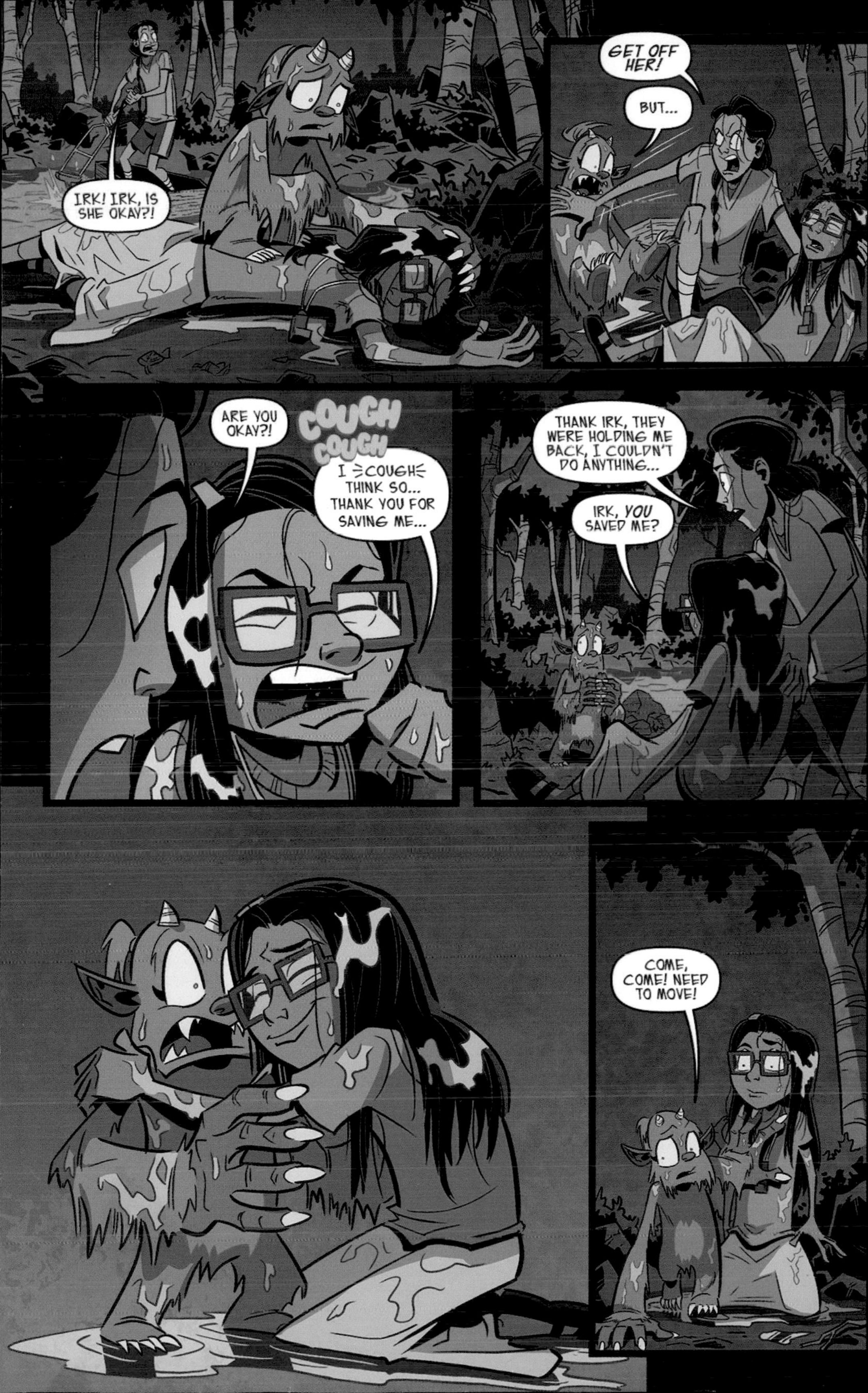
IRK! IRK, IS SHE OKAY?!
GET OFF HER!
BUT...
ARE YOU OKAY?!
COUGH COUGH
I COUGH THINK SO... THANK YOU FOR SAVING ME...
THANK IRK, THEY WERE HOLDING ME BACK, I COULDN'T DO ANYTHING...
IRK, YOU SAVED ME?
COME, COME! NEED TO MOVE!

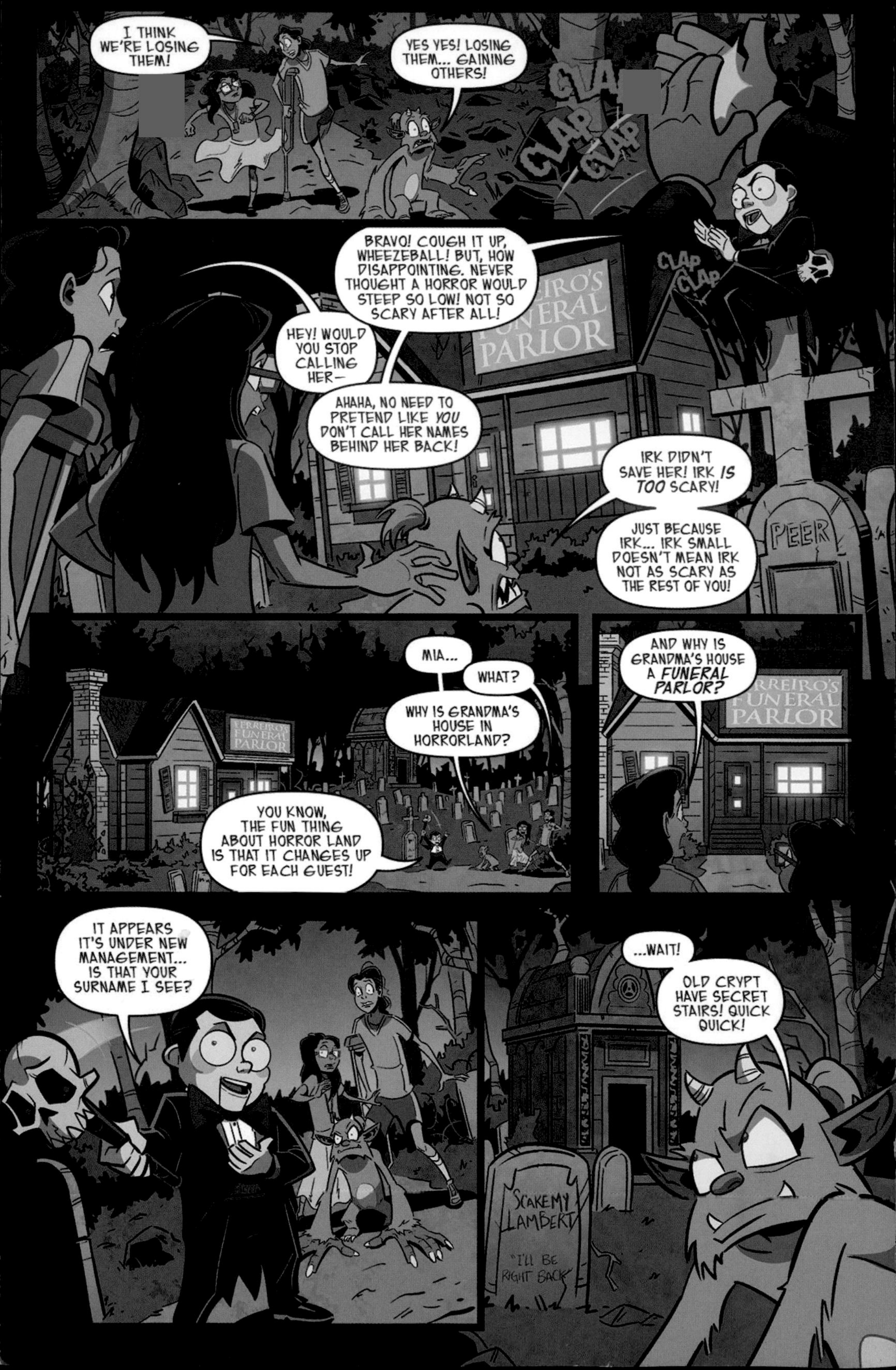
I THINK WE'RE LOSING THEM!
YES YES! LOSING THEM... GAINING OTHERS!
CLAP CLAP CLAP
CLAP CLAP
BRAVO! COUGH IT UP, WHEEZEBALL! BUT, HOW DISAPPOINTING. NEVER THOUGHT A HORROR WOULD STEEP SO LOW! NOT SO SCARY AFTER ALL!
FERREIRO'S FUNERAL PARLOR
HEY! WOULD YOU STOP CALLING HER—
AHAHA, NO NEED TO PRETEND LIKE *YOU* DON'T CALL HER NAMES BEHIND HER BACK!
IRK DIDN'T SAVE HER! IRK *IS TOO* SCARY!
JUST BECAUSE IRK... IRK SMALL DOESN'T MEAN IRK NOT AS SCARY AS THE REST OF YOU!
PEER
MIA...
WHAT?
WHY IS GRANDMA'S HOUSE IN HORRORLAND?
YOU KNOW, THE FUN THING ABOUT HORROR LAND IS THAT IT CHANGES UP FOR EACH GUEST!
AND WHY IS GRANDMA'S HOUSE A *FUNERAL PARLOR?*
IT APPEARS IT'S UNDER NEW MANAGEMENT... IS THAT YOUR SURNAME I SEE?
...WAIT!
OLD CRYPT HAVE SECRET STAIRS! QUICK QUICK!
SCAKEMY LAMBERT
"I'LL BE RIGHT BACK"

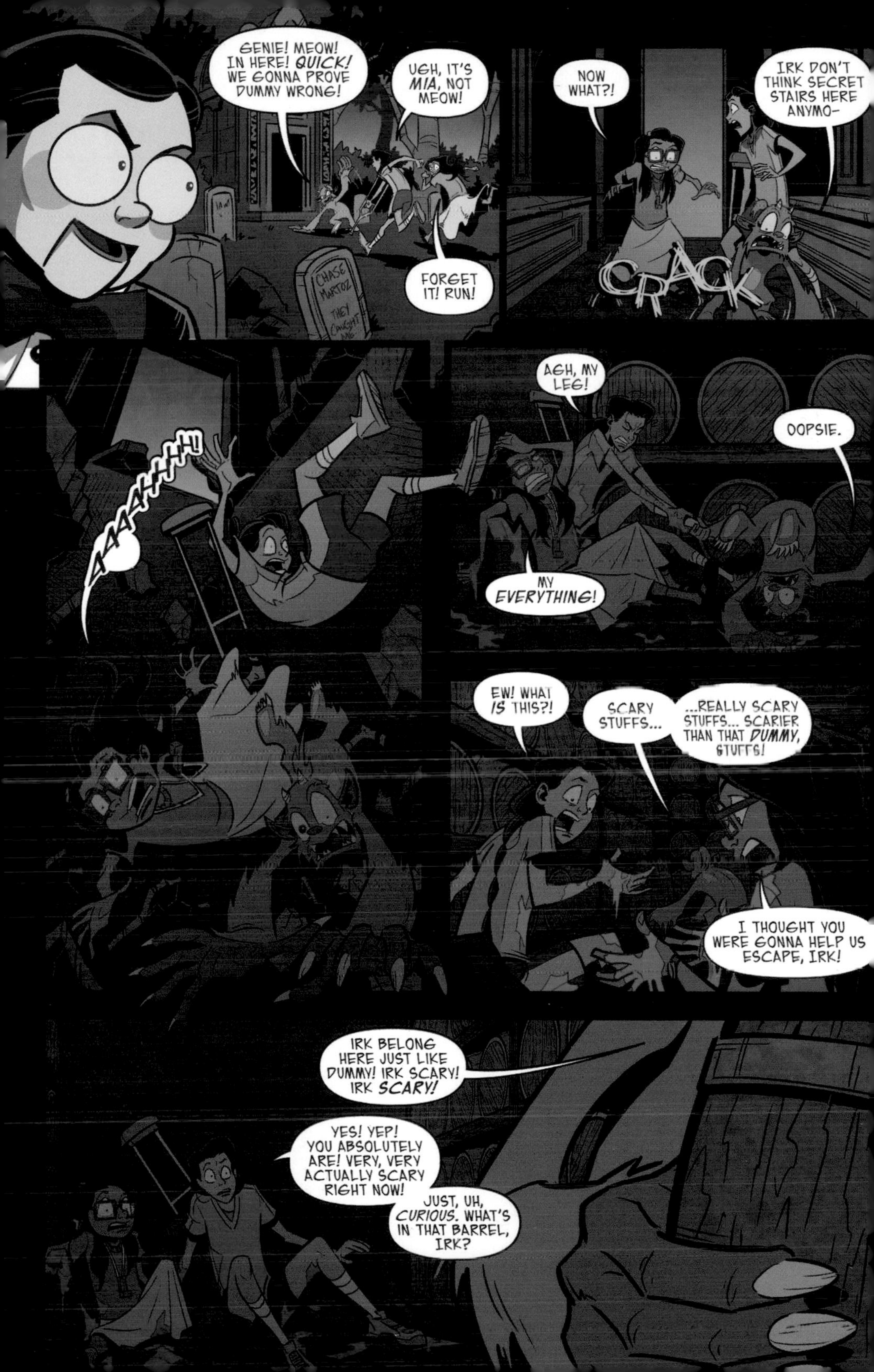
GENIE! MEOW! IN HERE! QUICK! WE GONNA PROVE DUMMY WRONG!
UGH, IT'S MIA, NOT MEOW!
FORGET IT! RUN!
CHASE MARTOZ THEY CAUGHT ME
NOW WHAT?!
IRK DON'T THINK SECRET STAIRS HERE ANYMO–
CRACK
AAAAHHHHH!
AGH, MY LEG!
OOPSIE.
MY EVERYTHING!
EW! WHAT IS THIS?!
SCARY STUFFS...
...REALLY SCARY STUFFS... SCARIER THAN THAT DUMMY, STUFFS!
I THOUGHT YOU WERE GONNA HELP US ESCAPE, IRK!
IRK BELONG HERE JUST LIKE DUMMY! IRK SCARY! IRK SCARY!
YES! YEP! YOU ABSOLUTELY ARE! VERY, VERY ACTUALLY SCARY RIGHT NOW!
JUST, UH, CURIOUS. WHAT'S IN THAT BARREL, IRK?

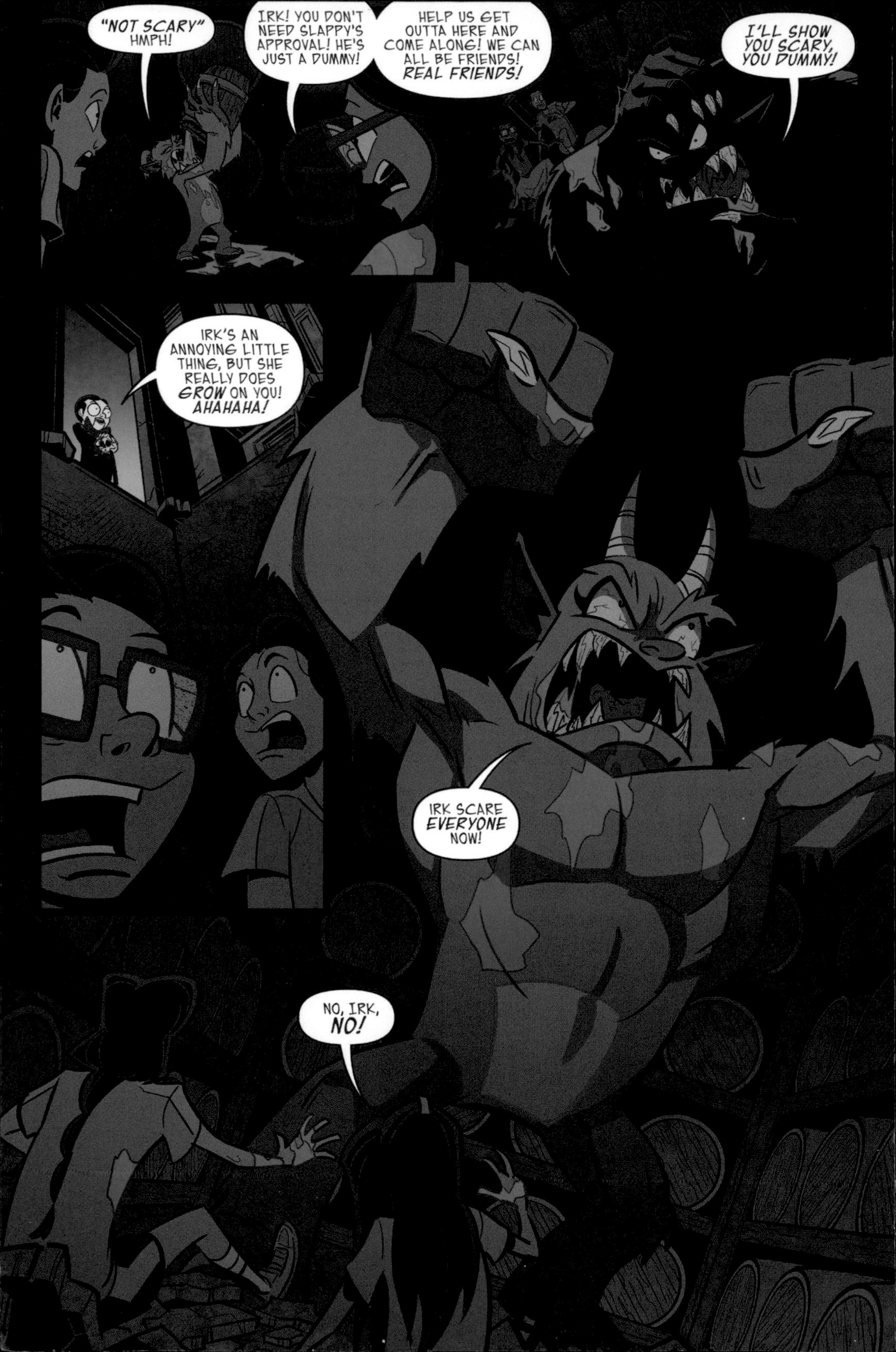
"NOT SCARY" HMPH!
IRK! YOU DON'T NEED SLAPPY'S APPROVAL! HE'S JUST A DUMMY!
HELP US GET OUTTA HERE AND COME ALONG! WE CAN ALL BE FRIENDS! REAL FRIENDS!
I'LL SHOW YOU SCARY, YOU DUMMY!
IRK'S AN ANNOYING LITTLE THING, BUT SHE REALLY DOES GROW ON YOU! AHAHAHA!
IRK SCARE EVERYONE NOW!
NO, IRK, NO!

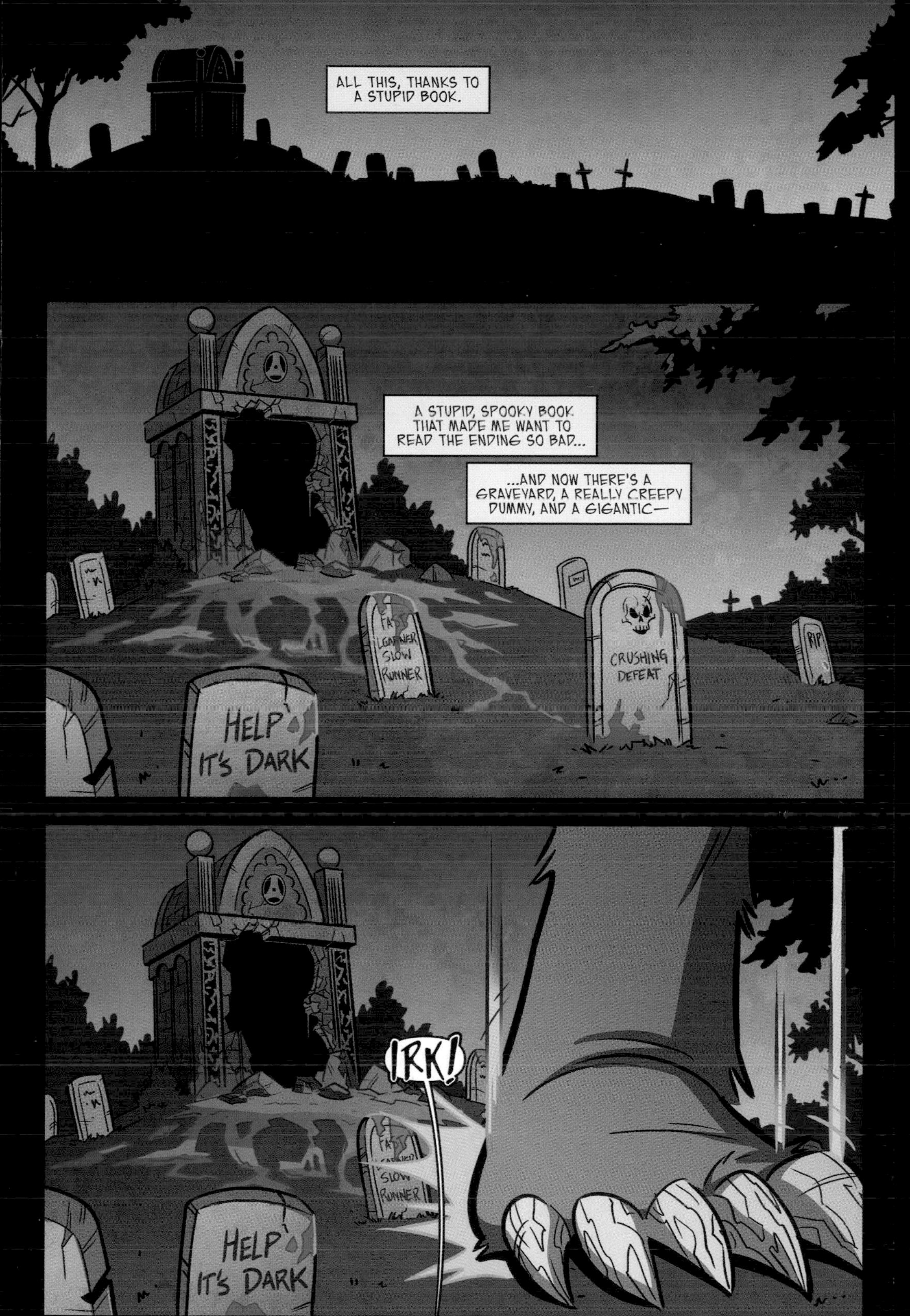

ALL THIS, THANKS TO A STUPID BOOK.
A STUPID, SPOOKY BOOK THAT MADE ME WANT TO READ THE ENDING SO BAD...
...AND NOW THERE'S A GRAVEYARD, A REALLY CREEPY DUMMY, AND A GIGANTIC—
SLOW RUNNER
CRUSHING DEFEAT
RIP
HELP IT'S DARK
IRK!
SLOW RUNNER
HELP IT'S DARK

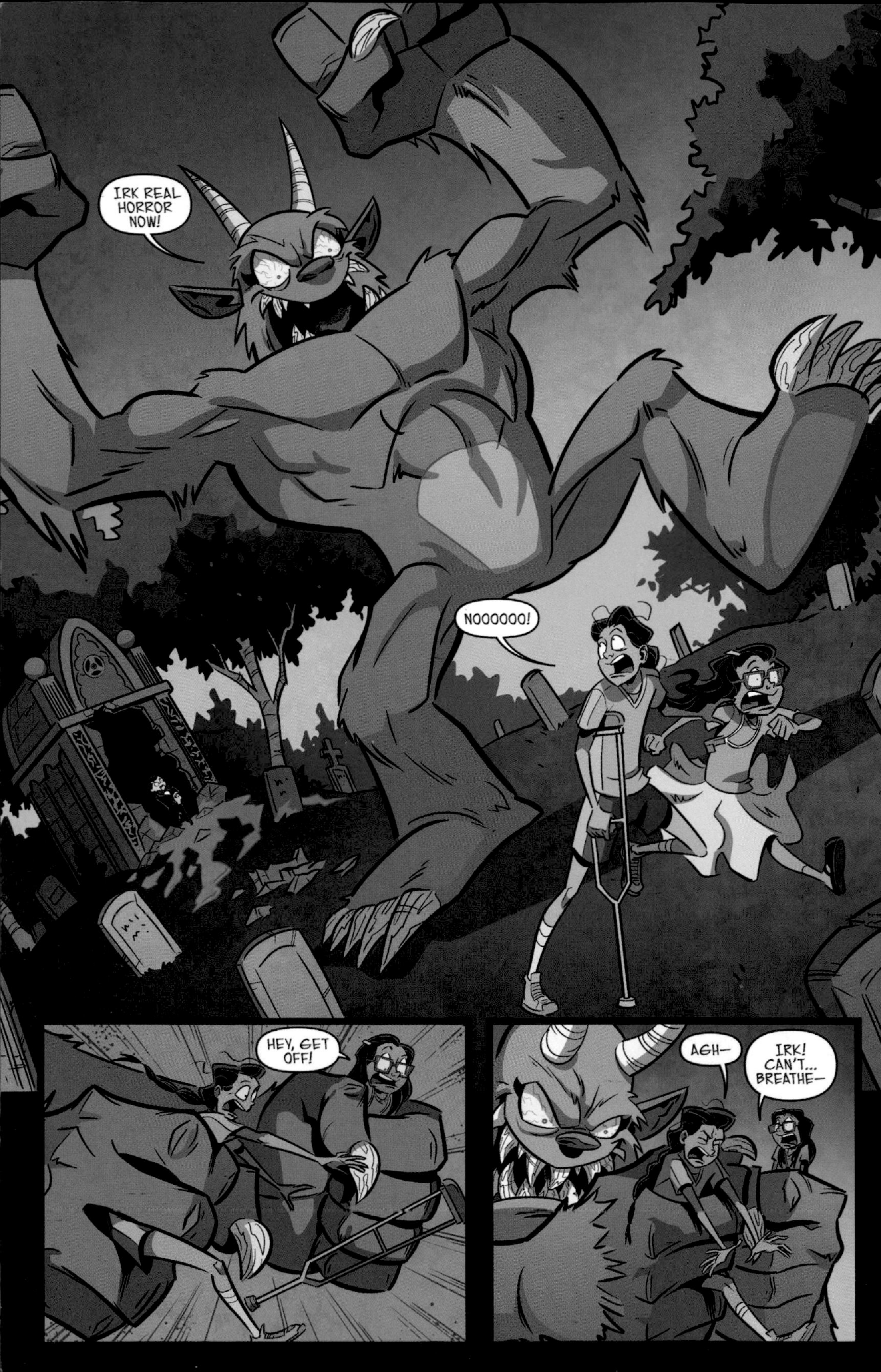
IRK REAL HORROR NOW!
NOOOOOO!
HEY, GET OFF!
AGH—
IRK! CAN'T... BREATHE—

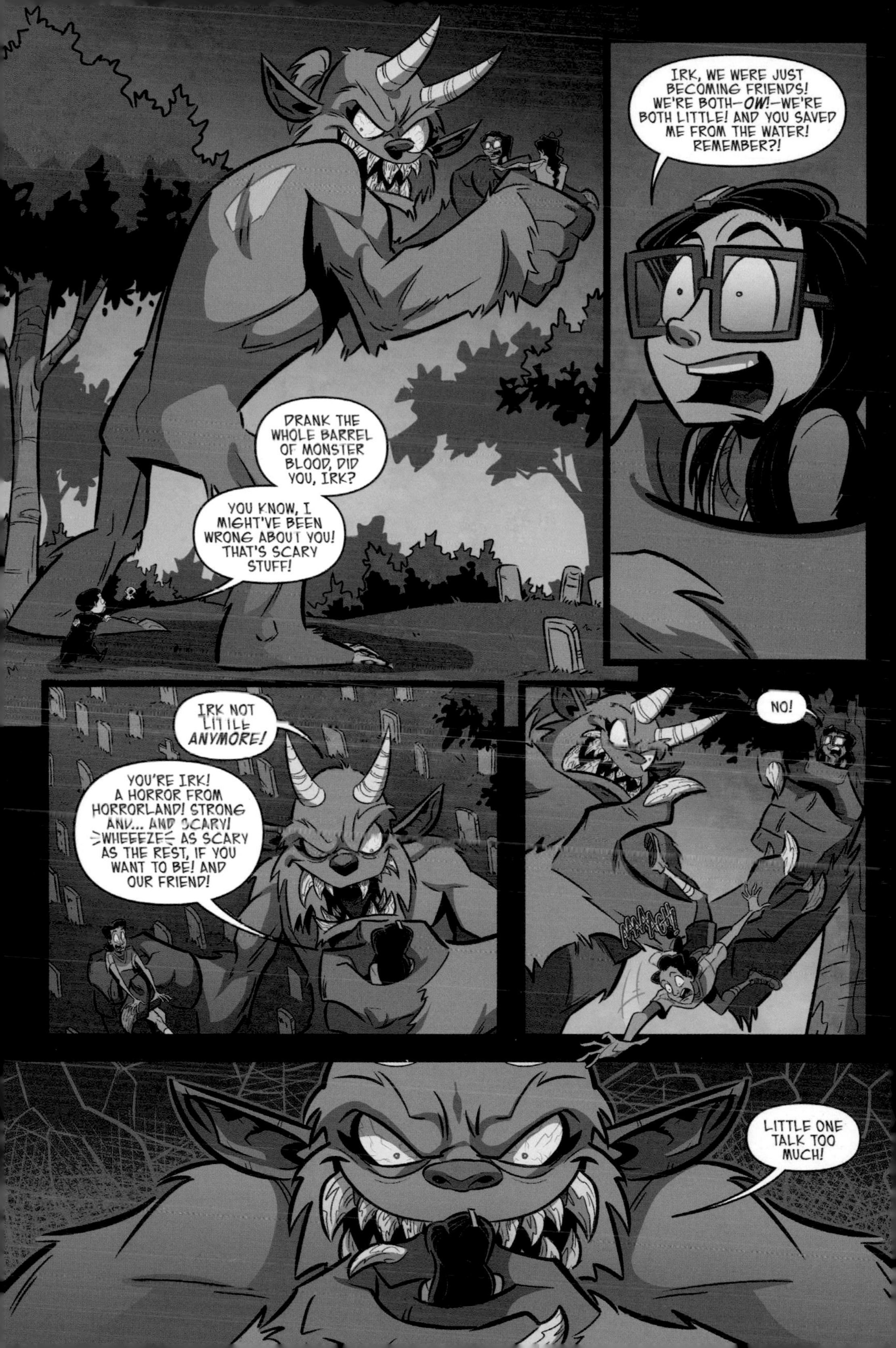
IRK, WE WERE JUST BECOMING FRIENDS! WE'RE BOTH—*OW!*—WE'RE BOTH LITTLE! AND YOU SAVED ME FROM THE WATER! REMEMBER?!
DRANK THE WHOLE BARREL OF MONSTER BLOOD, DID YOU, IRK?
YOU KNOW, I MIGHT'VE BEEN WRONG ABOUT YOU! THAT'S SCARY STUFF!
IRK NOT LITTLE ***ANYMORE!***
YOU'RE IRK! A HORROR FROM HORRORLAND! STRONG AND... AND SCARY! *WHEEEZE* AS SCARY AS THE REST, IF YOU WANT TO BE! AND OUR FRIEND!
NO!
LITTLE ONE TALK TOO MUCH!

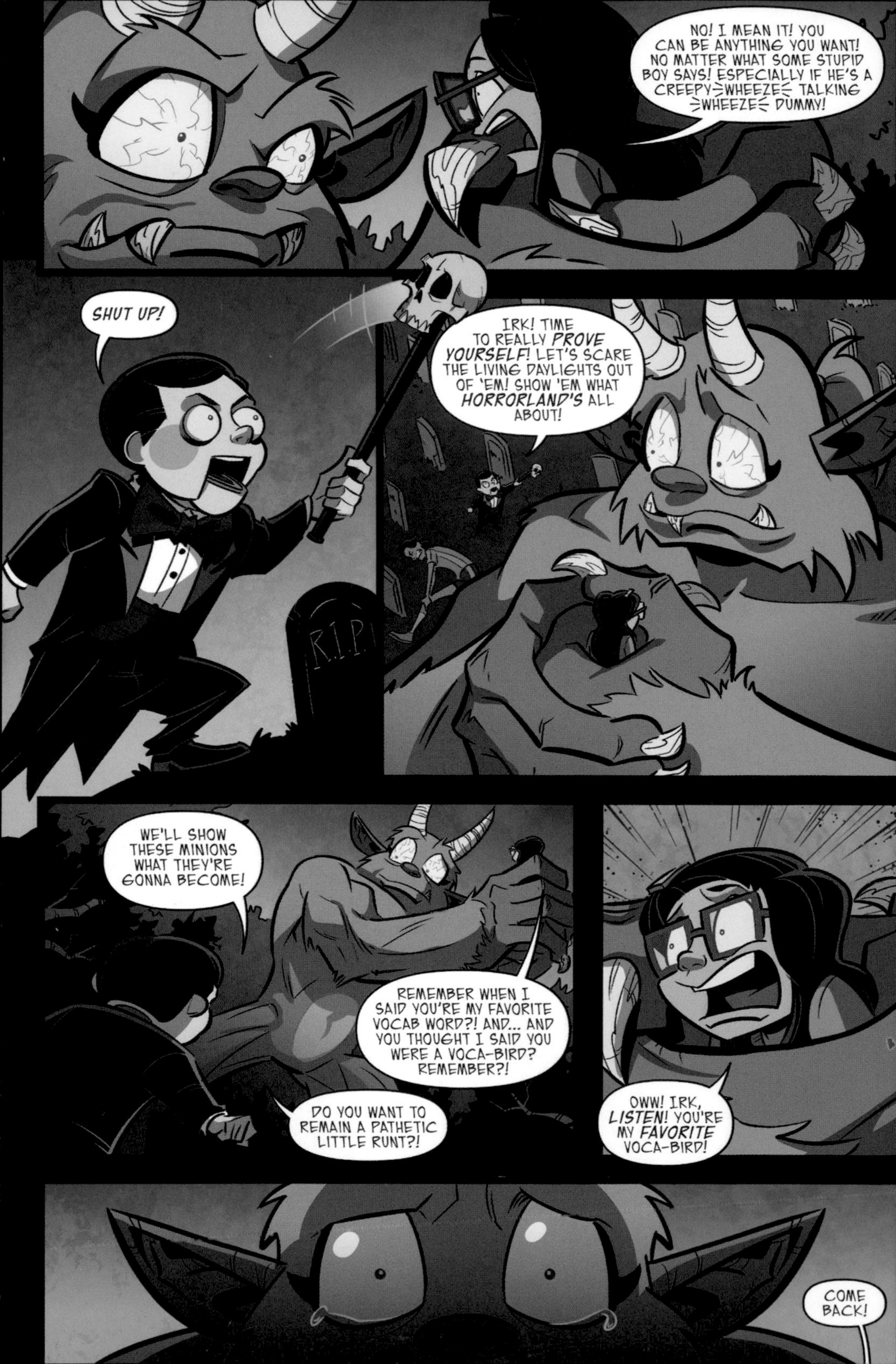
NO! I MEAN IT! YOU CAN BE ANYTHING YOU WANT! NO MATTER WHAT SOME STUPID BOY SAYS! ESPECIALLY IF HE'S A CREEPY *WHEEZE* TALKING *WHEEZE* DUMMY!
SHUT UP!
IRK! TIME TO REALLY PROVE YOURSELF! LET'S SCARE THE LIVING DAYLIGHTS OUT OF 'EM! SHOW 'EM WHAT HORRORLAND'S ALL ABOUT!
R.I.P.
WE'LL SHOW THESE MINIONS WHAT THEY'RE GONNA BECOME!
REMEMBER WHEN I SAID YOU'RE MY FAVORITE VOCAB WORD?! AND... AND YOU THOUGHT I SAID YOU WERE A VOCA-BIRD? REMEMBER?!
DO YOU WANT TO REMAIN A PATHETIC LITTLE RUNT?!
OWW! IRK, LISTEN! YOU'RE MY FAVORITE VOCA-BIRD!
COME BACK!

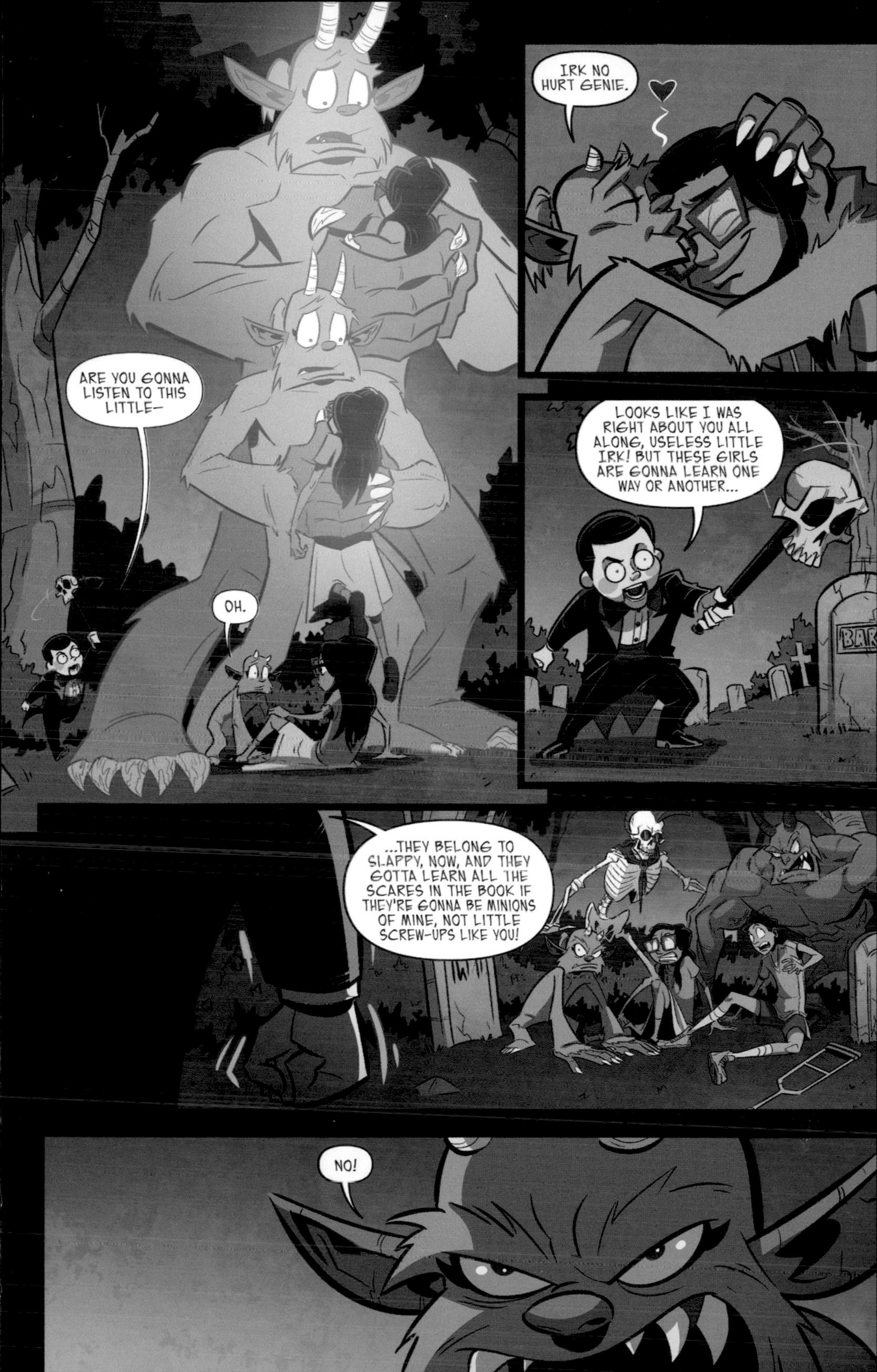
ARE YOU GONNA LISTEN TO THIS LITTLE-
OH.
IRK NO HURT GENIE.
LOOKS LIKE I WAS RIGHT ABOUT YOU ALL ALONG, USELESS LITTLE IRK! BUT THESE GIRLS ARE GONNA LEARN ONE WAY OR ANOTHER...
BAR
...THEY BELONG TO SLAPPY, NOW, AND THEY GOTTA LEARN ALL THE SCARES IN THE BOOK IF THEY'RE GONNA BE MINIONS OF MINE, NOT LITTLE SCREW-UPS LIKE YOU!
NO!

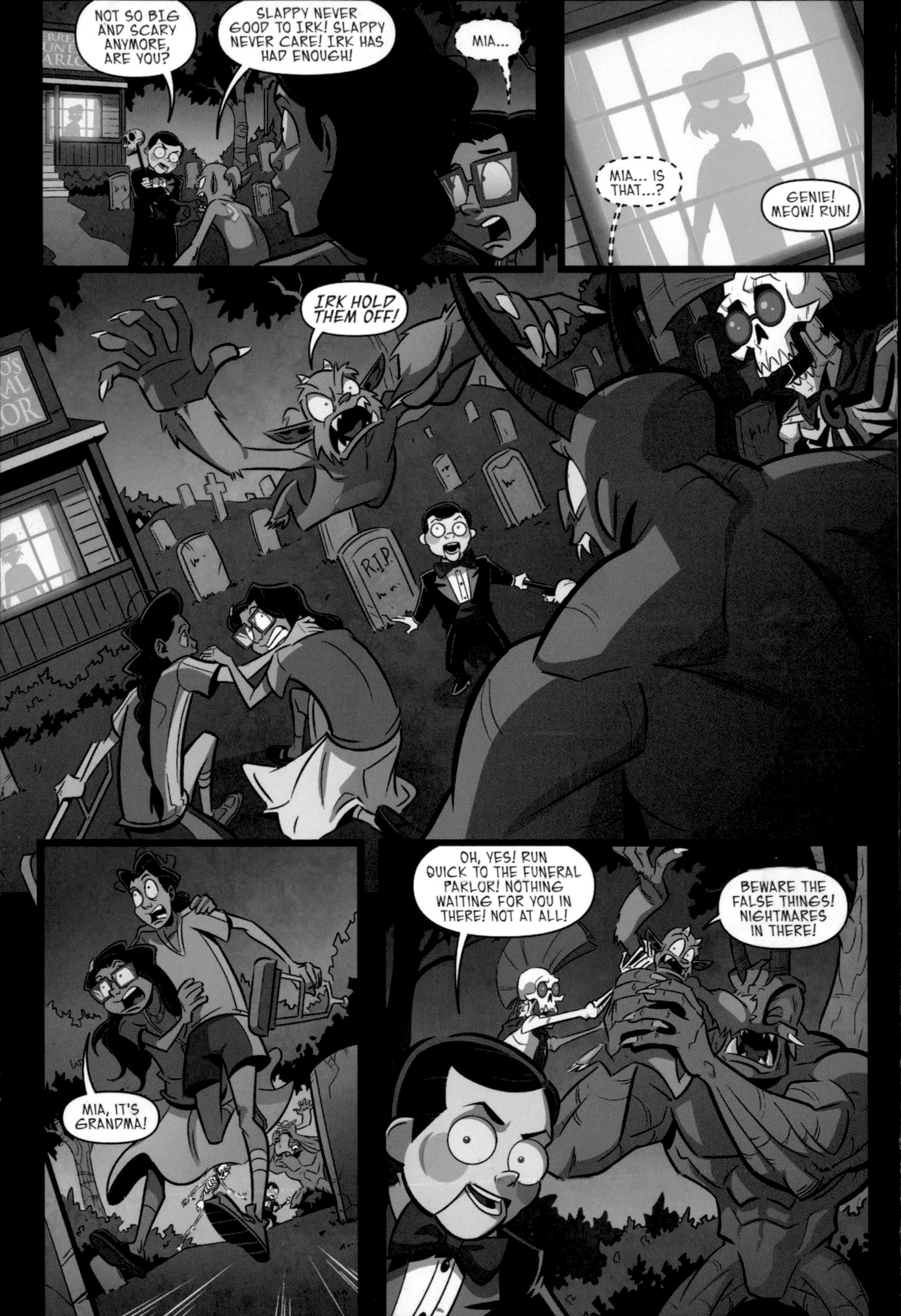

NOT SO BIG AND SCARY ANYMORE, ARE YOU?
SLAPPY NEVER GOOD TO IRK! SLAPPY NEVER CARE! IRK HAS HAD ENOUGH!
MIA...
MIA... IS THAT...?
GENIE! MEOW! RUN!
IRK HOLD THEM OFF!
R.I.P.
MIA, IT'S GRANDMA!
OH, YES! RUN QUICK TO THE FUNERAL PARLOR! NOTHING WAITING FOR YOU IN THERE! NOT AT ALL!
BEWARE THE FALSE THINGS! NIGHTMARES IN THERE!

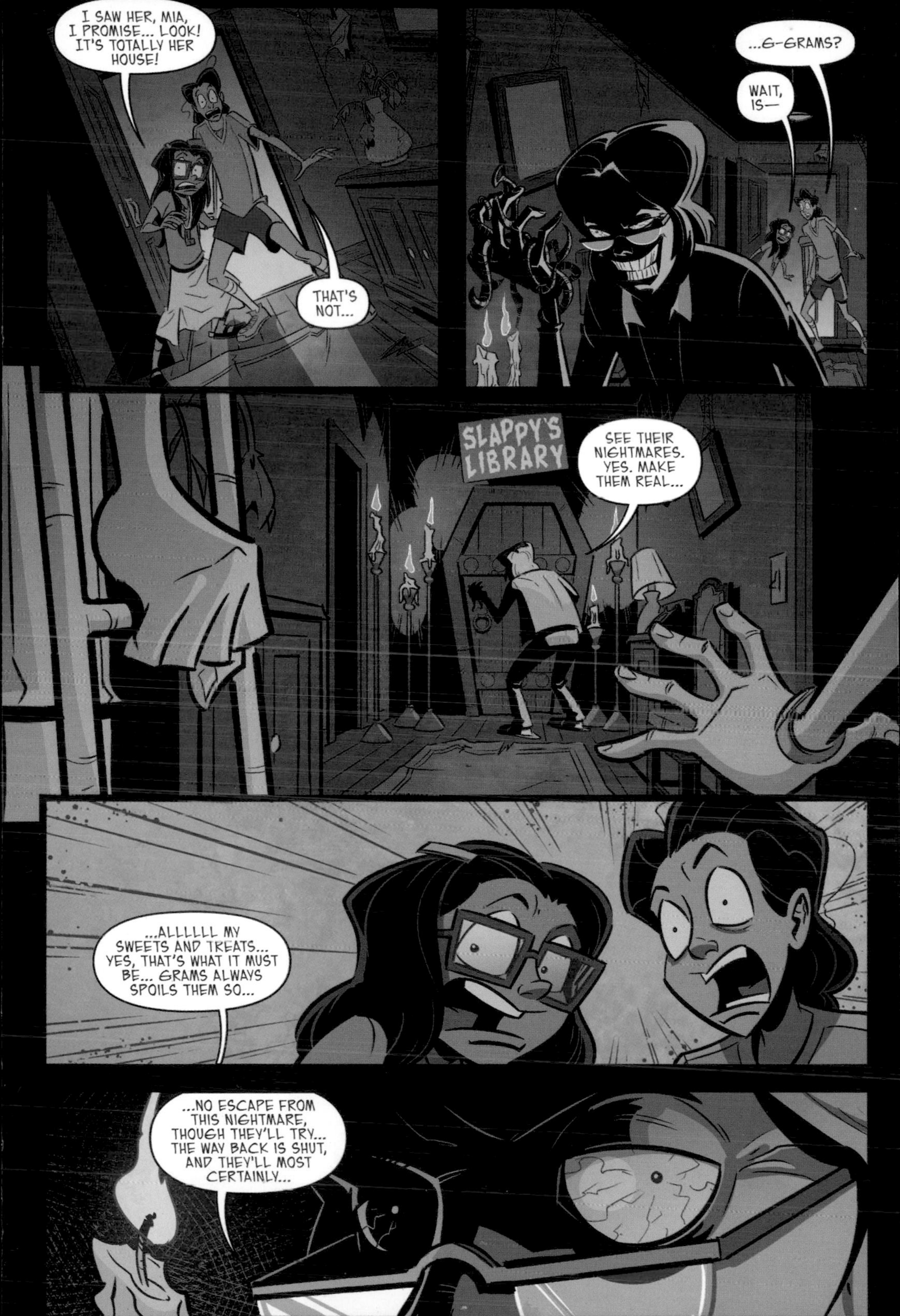
I SAW HER, MIA, I PROMISE... LOOK! IT'S TOTALLY HER HOUSE!
THAT'S NOT...
...G-GRAMS?
WAIT, IS—
SLAPPY'S LIBRARY
SEE THEIR NIGHTMARES. YES. MAKE THEM REAL...
...ALLLLLL MY SWEETS AND TREATS... YES, THAT'S WHAT IT MUST BE... GRAMS ALWAYS SPOILS THEM SO...
...NO ESCAPE FROM THIS NIGHTMARE, THOUGH THEY'LL TRY... THE WAY BACK IS SHUT, AND THEY'LL MOST CERTAINLY...

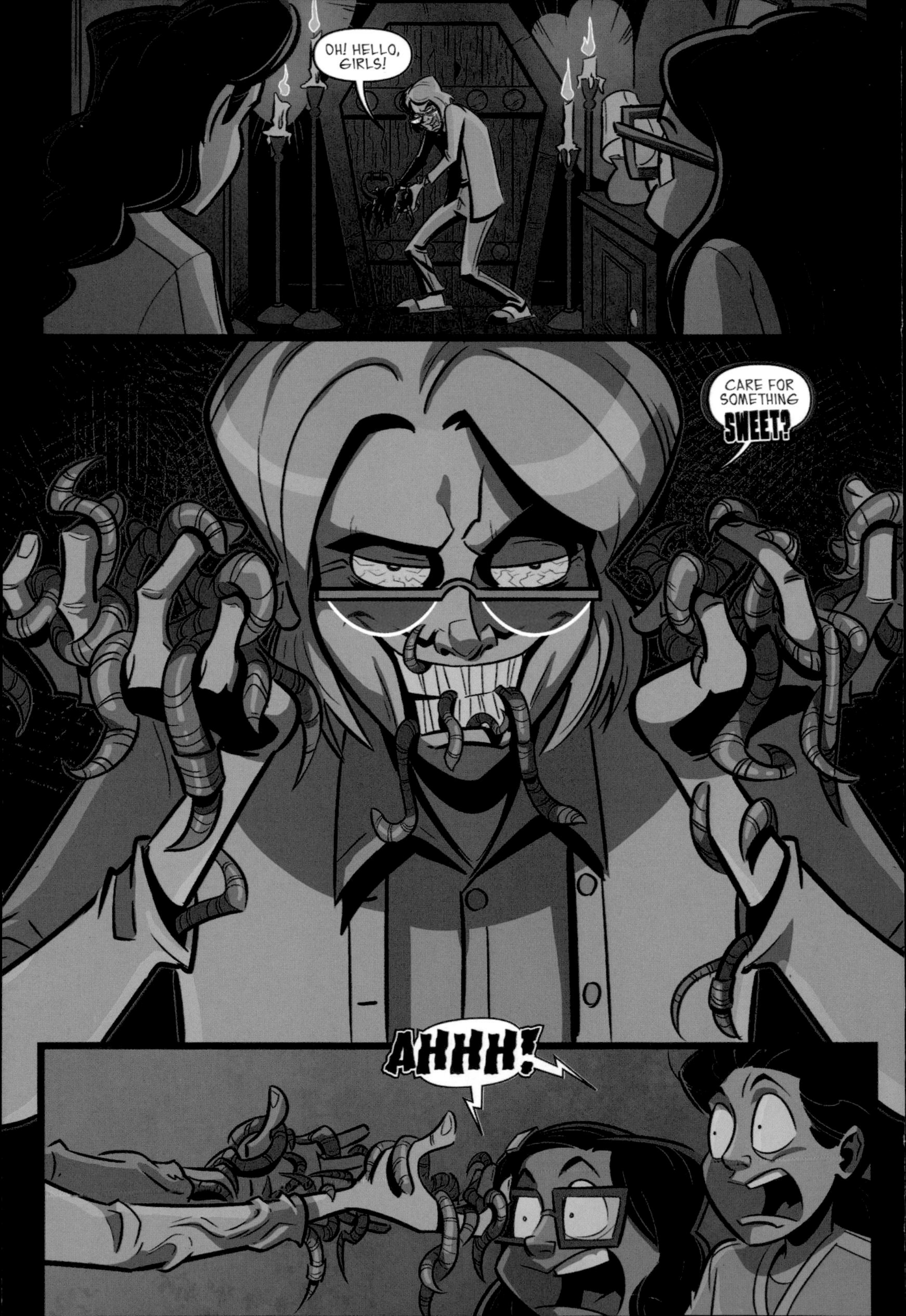
OH! HELLO, GIRLS!
CARE FOR SOMETHING SWEET?
AHHH!

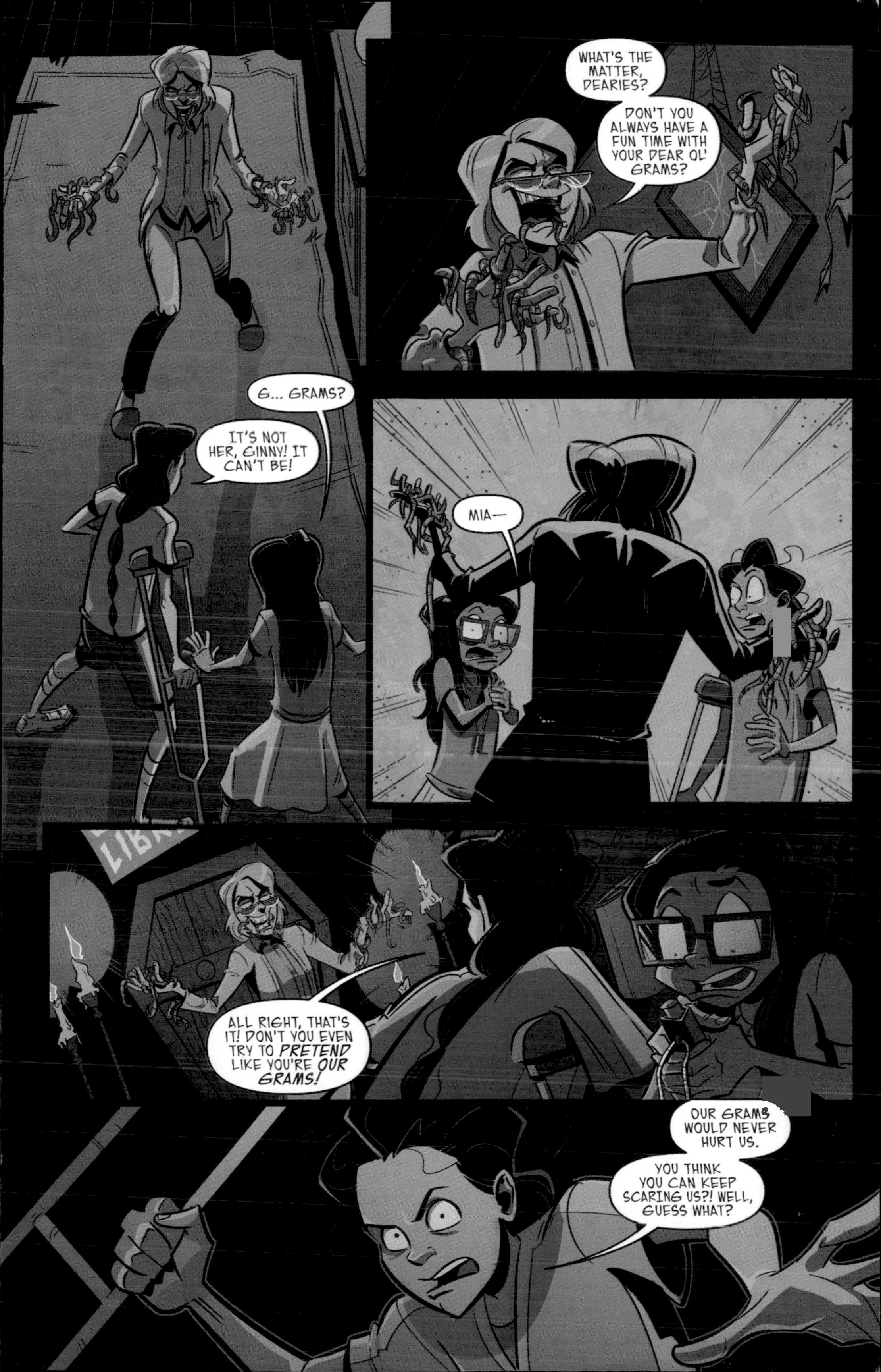
WHAT'S THE MATTER, DEARIES?
DON'T YOU ALWAYS HAVE A FUN TIME WITH YOUR DEAR OL' GRAMS?
G... GRAMS?
IT'S NOT HER, GINNY! IT CAN'T BE!
MIA—
ALL RIGHT, THAT'S IT! DON'T YOU EVEN TRY TO *PRETEND* LIKE YOU'RE *OUR GRAMS!*
OUR GRAMS WOULD NEVER HURT US.
YOU THINK YOU CAN KEEP SCARING US?! WELL, GUESS WHAT?

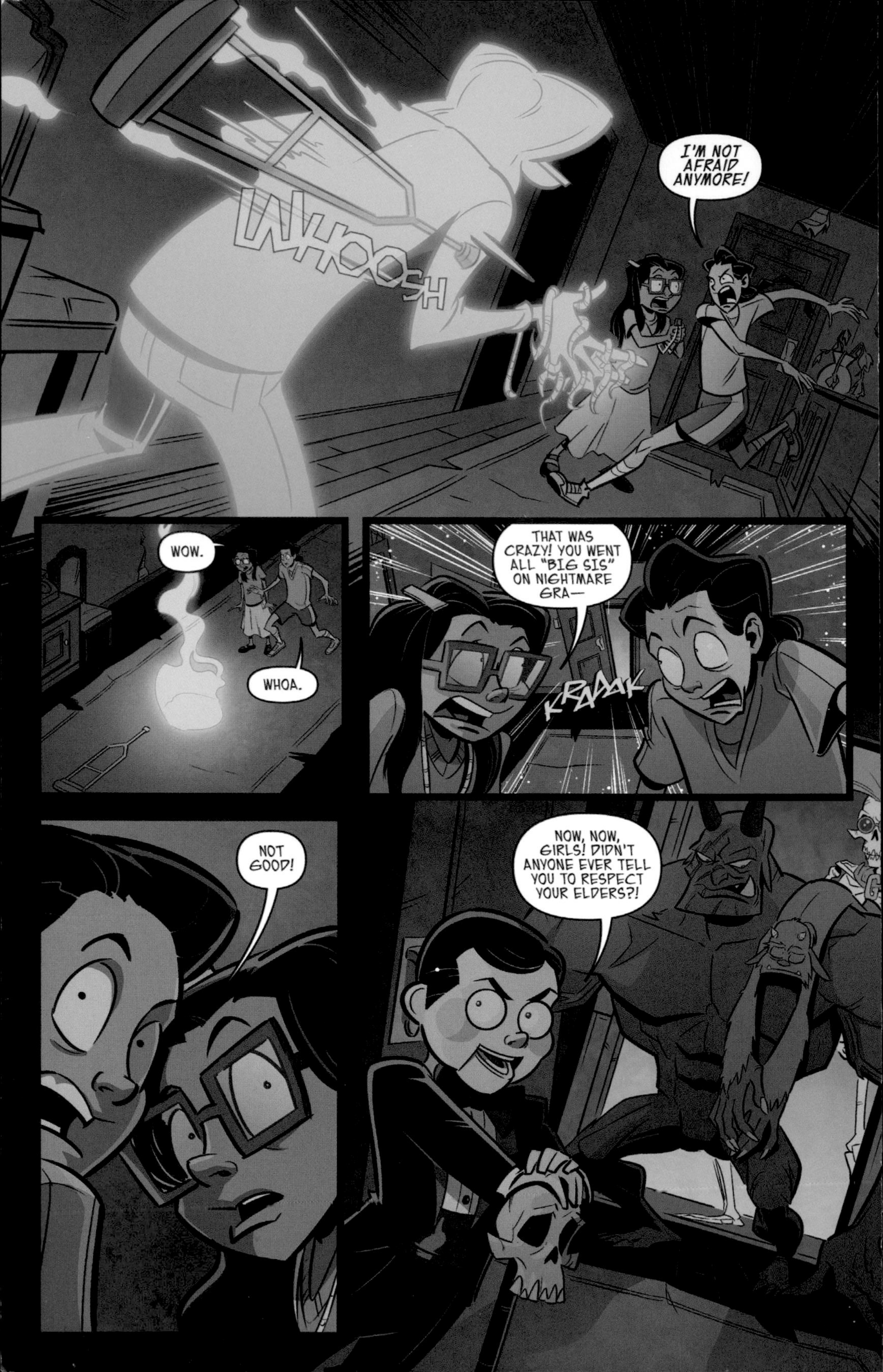
I'M NOT AFRAID ANYMORE!
WHOOSH
WOW.
WHOA.
THAT WAS CRAZY! YOU WENT ALL "BIG SIS" ON NIGHTMARE GRA—
KRAAAK
NOT GOOD!
NOW, NOW, GIRLS! DIDN'T ANYONE EVER TELL YOU TO RESPECT YOUR ELDERS?!

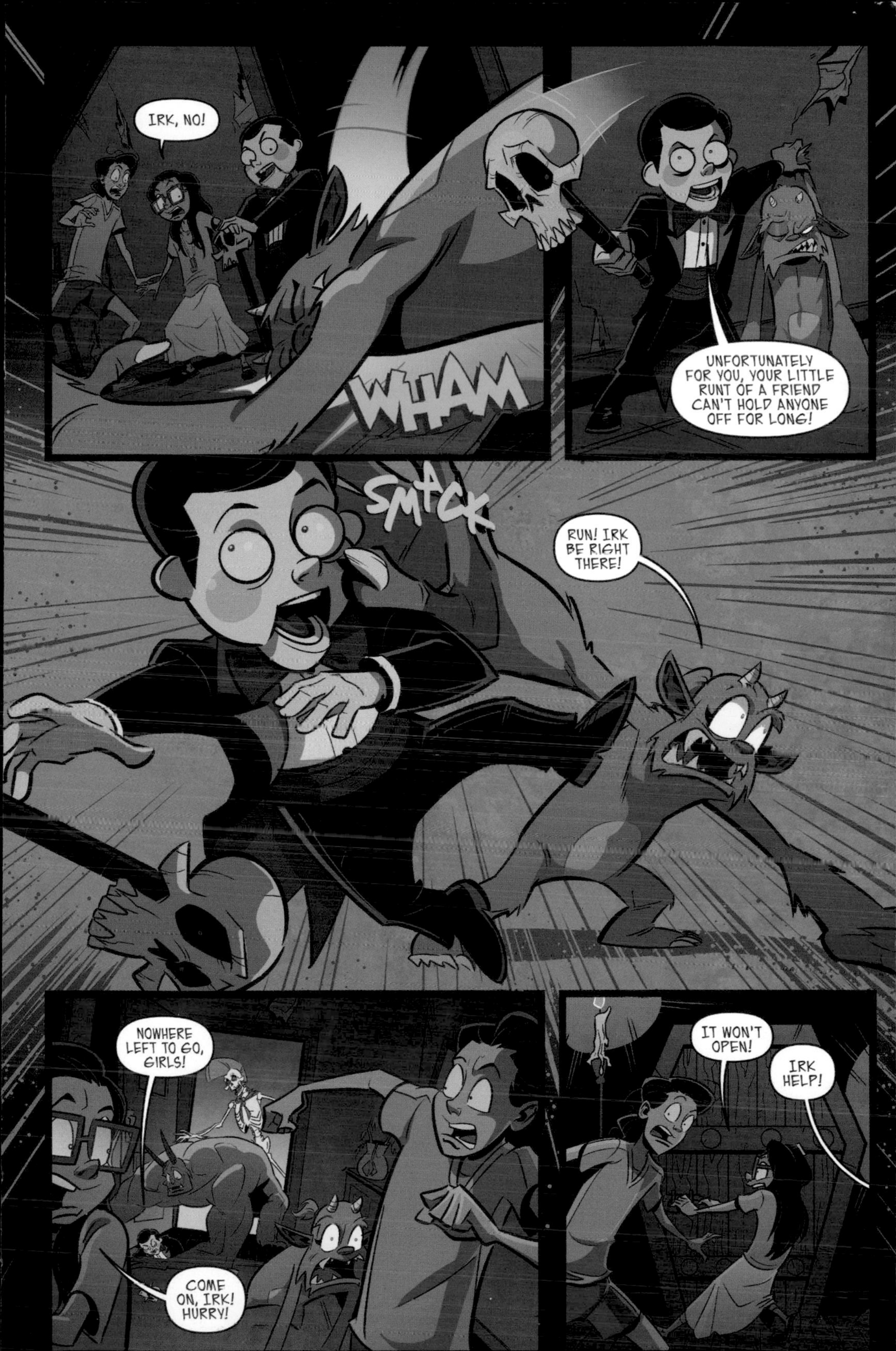
IRK, NO!
WHAM
UNFORTUNATELY FOR YOU, YOUR LITTLE RUNT OF A FRIEND CAN'T HOLD ANYONE OFF FOR LONG!
SMACK
RUN! IRK BE RIGHT THERE!
NOWHERE LEFT TO GO, GIRLS!
COME ON, IRK! HURRY!
IT WON'T OPEN!
IRK HELP!

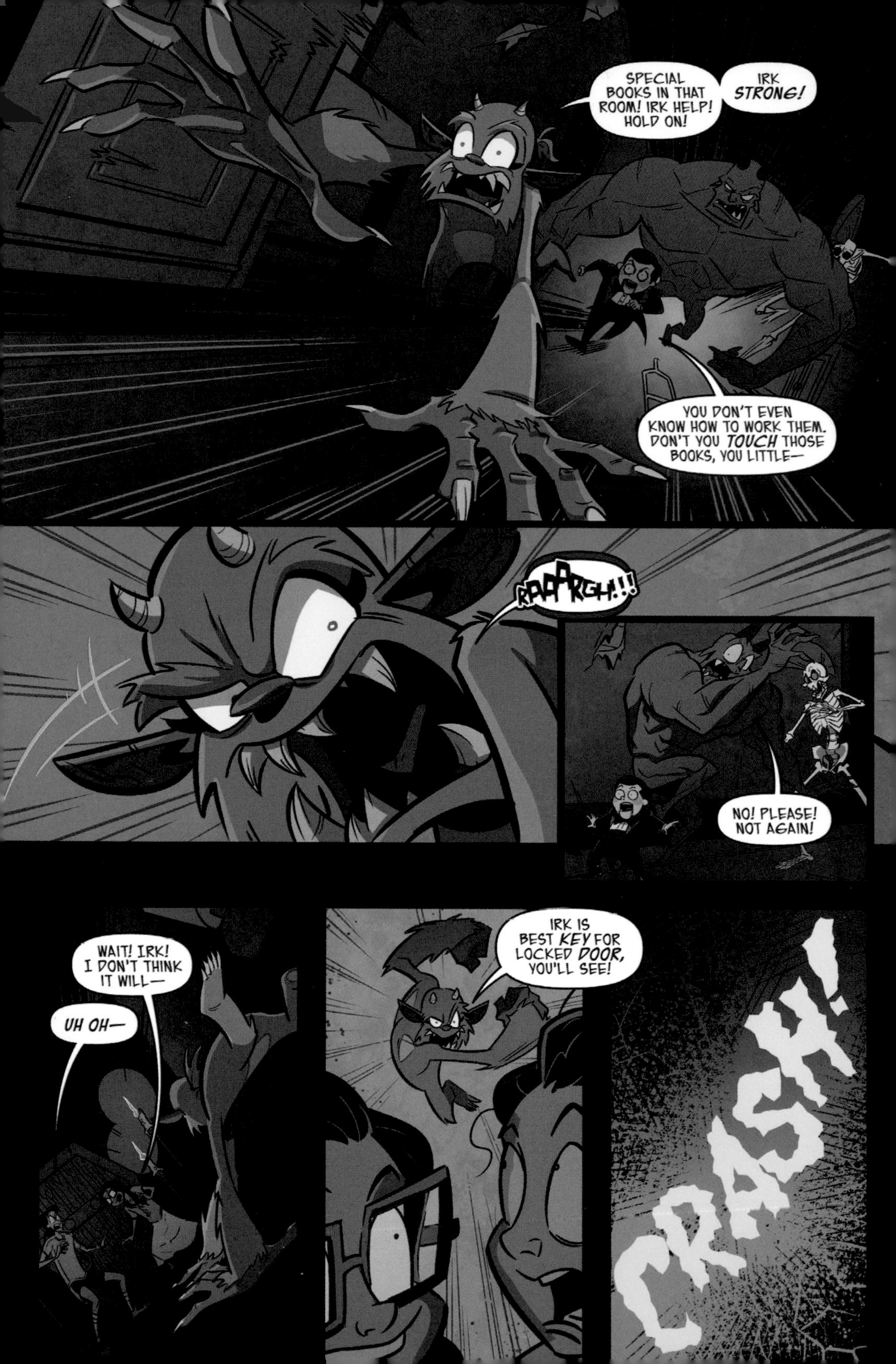
SPECIAL BOOKS IN THAT ROOM! IRK HELP! HOLD ON!
IRK STRONG!
YOU DON'T EVEN KNOW HOW TO WORK THEM. DON'T YOU TOUCH THOSE BOOKS, YOU LITTLE—
RAAARGH!!!
NO! PLEASE! NOT AGAIN!
WAIT! IRK! I DON'T THINK IT WILL—
UH OH—
IRK IS BEST KEY FOR LOCKED DOOR, YOU'LL SEE!
CRASH!

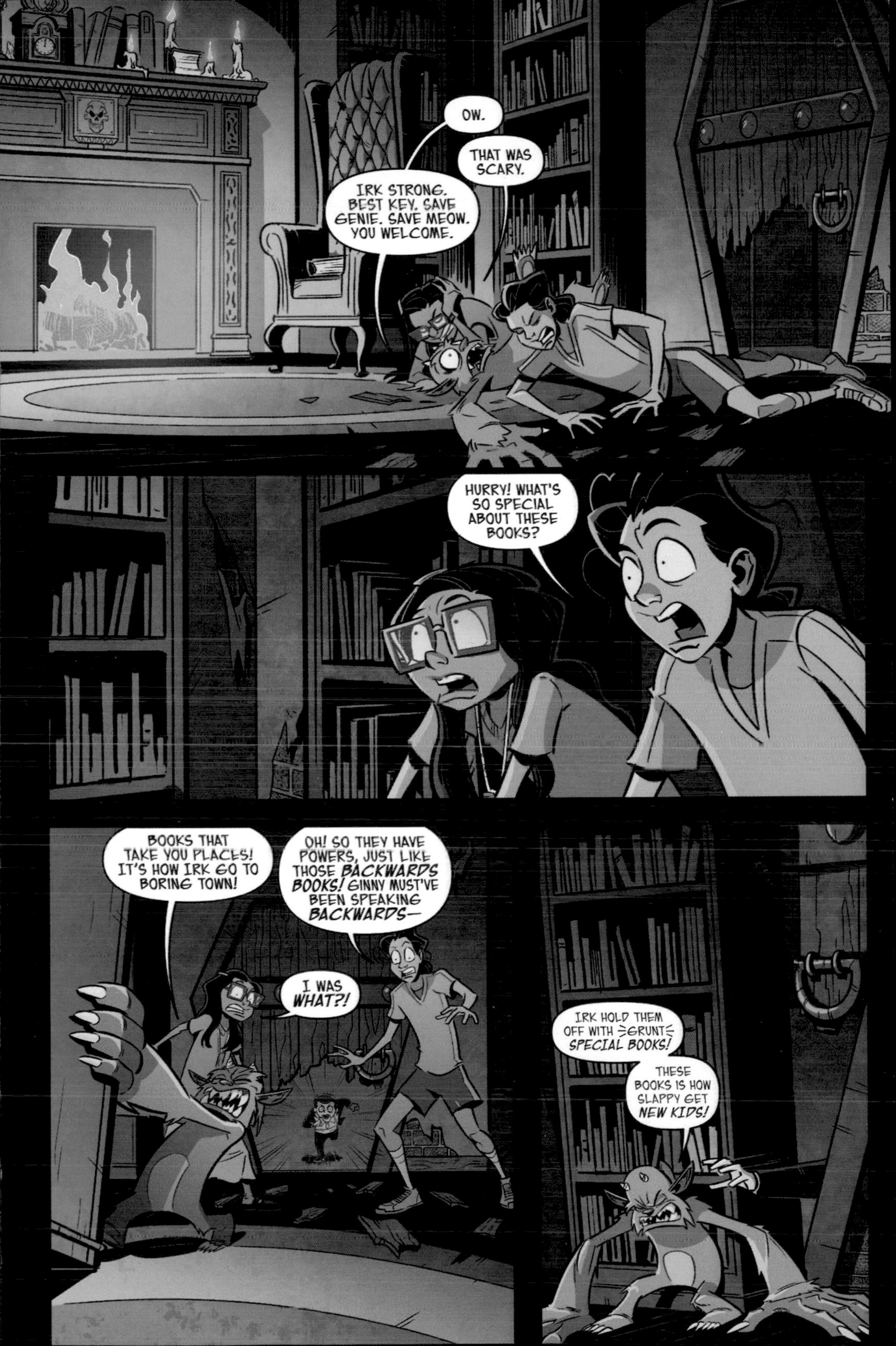
OW.
THAT WAS SCARY.
IRK STRONG. BEST KEY. SAVE GENIE. SAVE MEOW. YOU WELCOME.
HURRY! WHAT'S SO SPECIAL ABOUT THESE BOOKS?
BOOKS THAT TAKE YOU PLACES! IT'S HOW IRK GO TO BORING TOWN!
OH! SO THEY HAVE POWERS, JUST LIKE THOSE *BACKWARDS BOOKS!* GINNY MUST'VE BEEN SPEAKING *BACKWARDS*—
I WAS *WHAT?!*
IRK HOLD THEM OFF WITH ≶GRUNT≶ *SPECIAL BOOKS!*
THESE BOOKS IS HOW SLAPPY GET *NEW KIDS!*

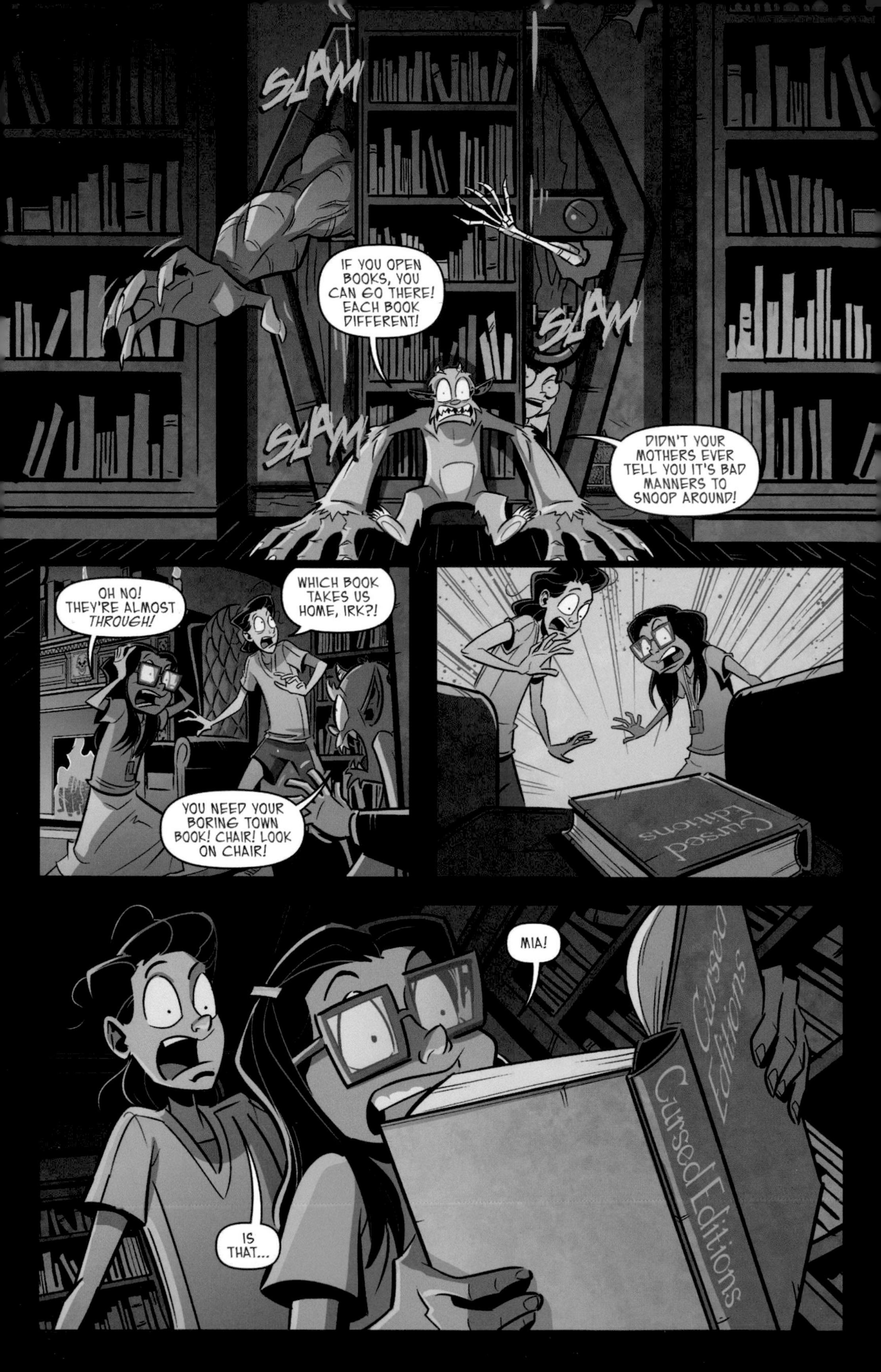
SLAM
IF YOU OPEN BOOKS, YOU CAN GO THERE! EACH BOOK DIFFERENT!
SLAM
SLAM
DIDN'T YOUR MOTHERS EVER TELL YOU IT'S BAD MANNERS TO SNOOP AROUND!
OH NO! THEY'RE ALMOST *THROUGH!*
WHICH BOOK TAKES US HOME, IRK?!
YOU NEED YOUR BORING TOWN BOOK! CHAIR! LOOK ON CHAIR!
Cursed Editions
MIA!
Cursed Editions
Cursed Editions
IS THAT...

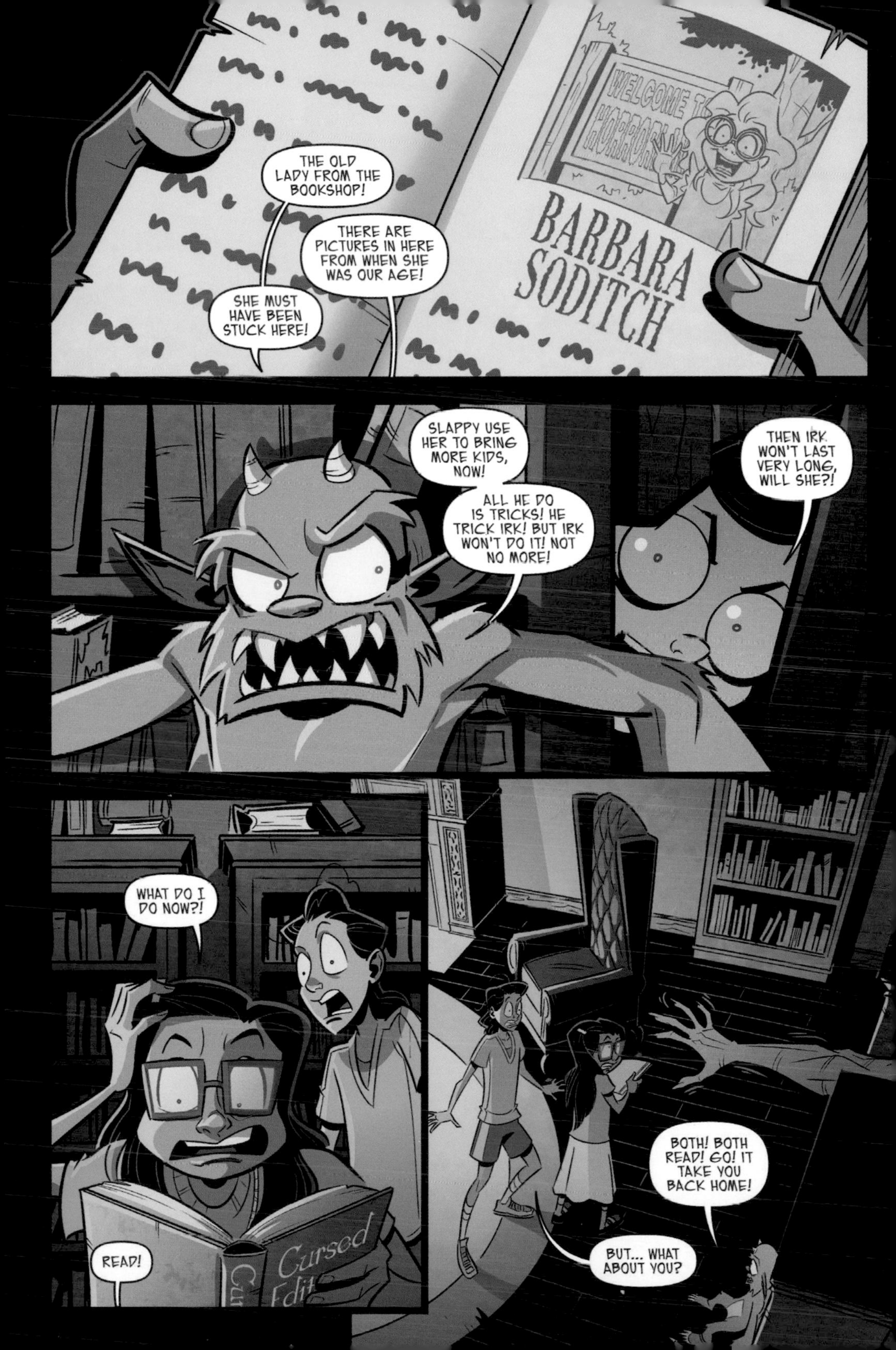
WELCOME TO HORRORLAND
BARBARA SODITCH
THE OLD LADY FROM THE BOOKSHOP!
SHE MUST HAVE BEEN STUCK HERE!
THERE ARE PICTURES IN HERE FROM WHEN SHE WAS OUR AGE!
SLAPPY USE HER TO BRING MORE KIDS, NOW!
ALL HE DO IS TRICKS! HE TRICK IRK! BUT IRK WON'T DO IT! NOT NO MORE!
THEN IRK WON'T LAST VERY LONG, WILL SHE?!
WHAT DO I DO NOW?!
READ!
Cursed Edit
BOTH! BOTH READ! GO! IT TAKE YOU BACK HOME!
BUT... WHAT ABOUT YOU?

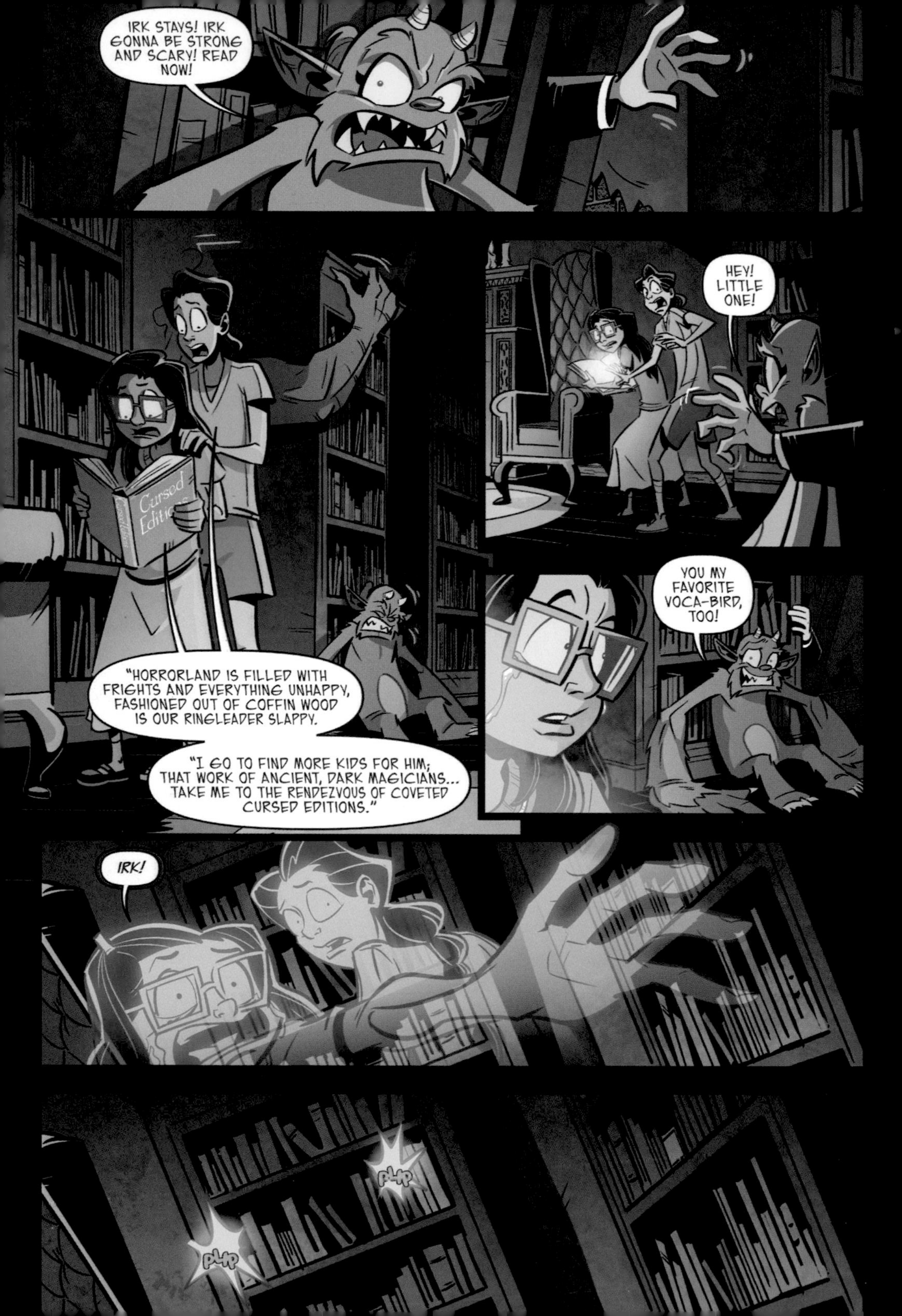

IRK STAYS! IRK GONNA BE STRONG AND SCARY! READ NOW!
Cursed Editions
HEY! LITTLE ONE!
YOU MY FAVORITE VOCA-BIRD, TOO!
"HORRORLAND IS FILLED WITH FRIGHTS AND EVERYTHING UNHAPPY, FASHIONED OUT OF COFFIN WOOD IS OUR RINGLEADER SLAPPY.
"I GO TO FIND MORE KIDS FOR HIM; THAT WORK OF ANCIENT, DARK MAGICIANS... TAKE ME TO THE RENDEZVOUS OF COVETED CURSED EDITIONS."
IRK!
PLIP
PLIP

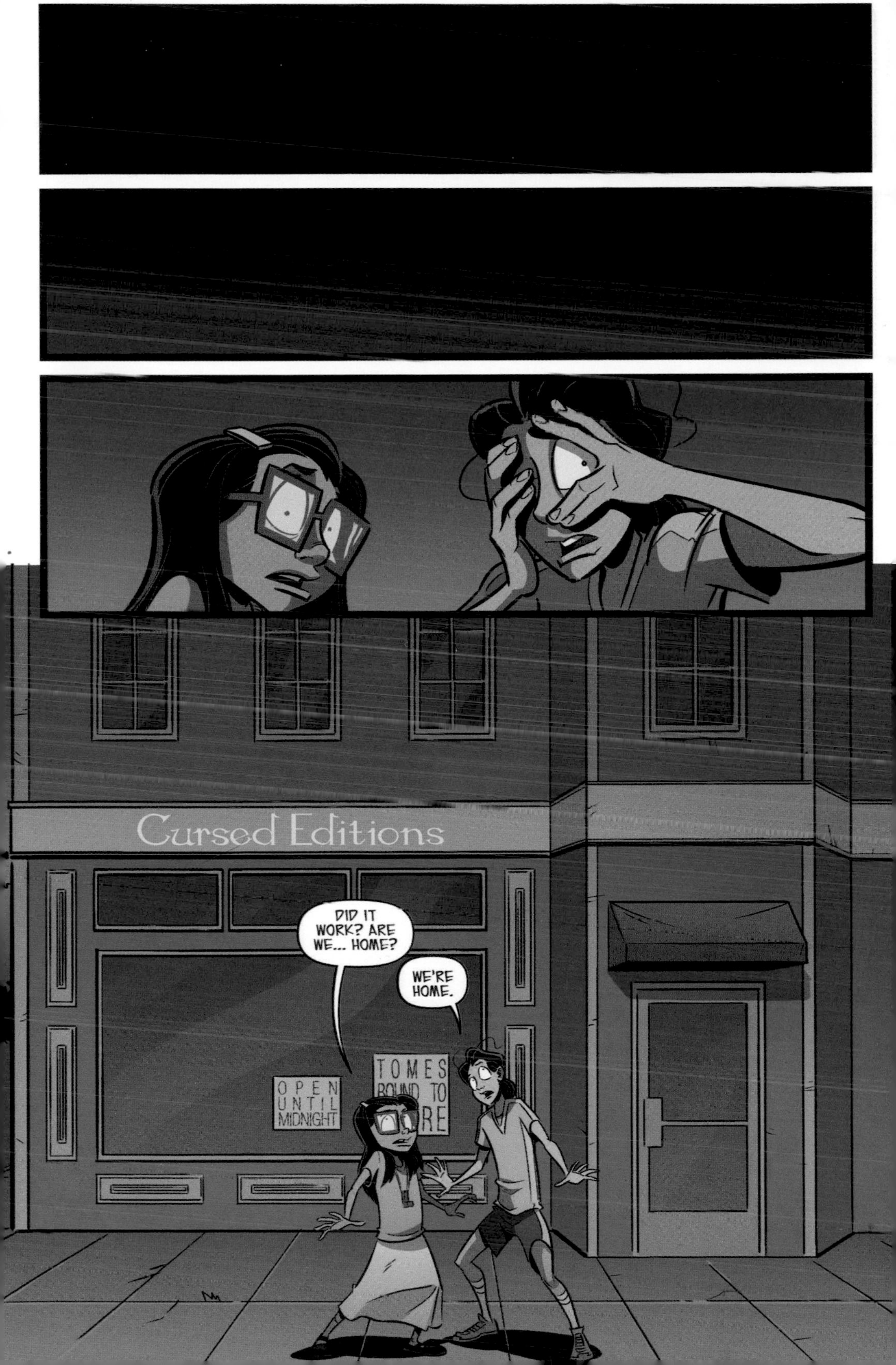
Cursed Editions
DID IT WORK? ARE WE... HOME?
WE'RE HOME.
OPEN UNTIL MIDNIGHT
TOMES BOUND TO

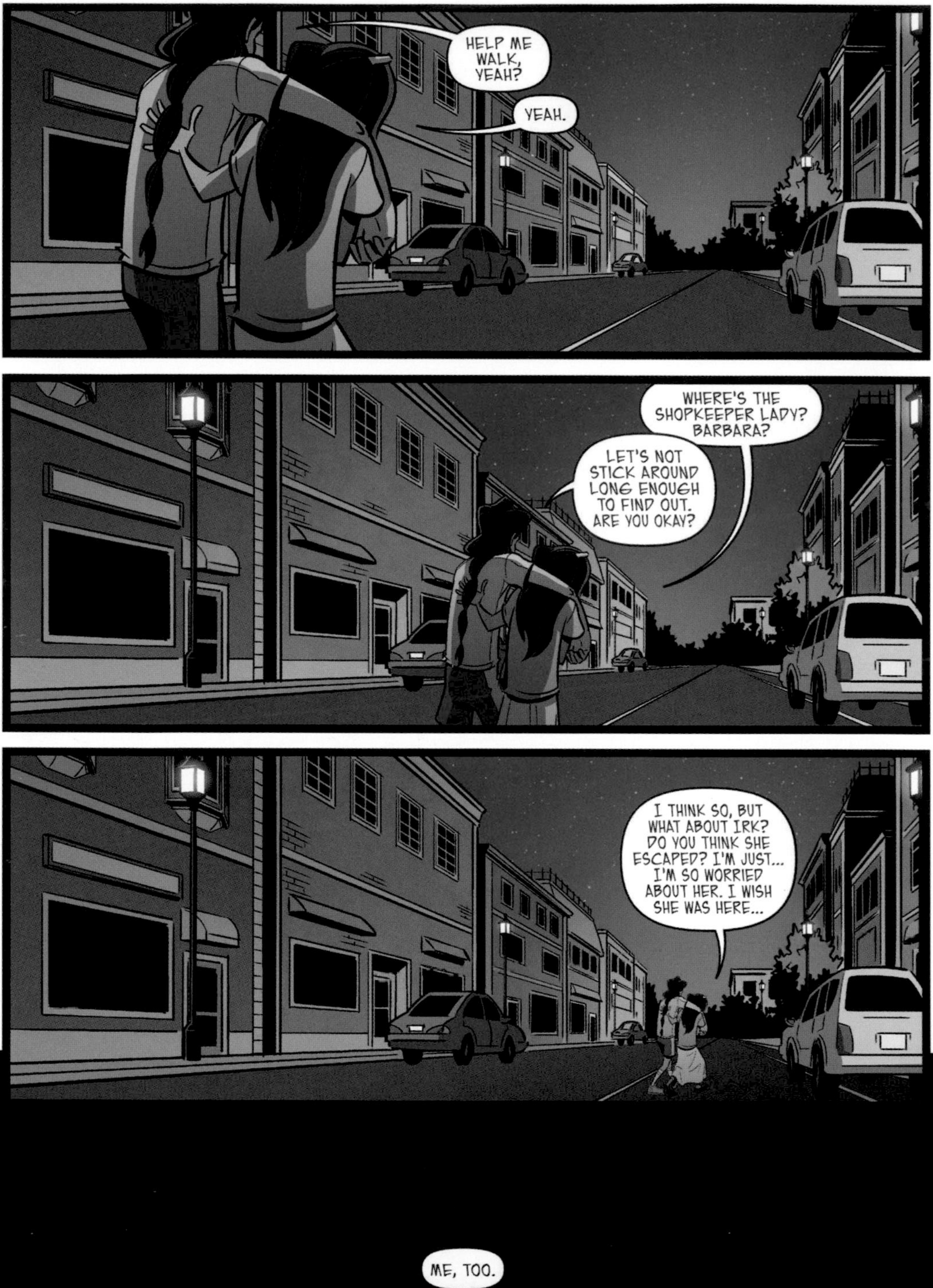
HELP ME WALK, YEAH?
YEAH.
WHERE'S THE SHOPKEEPER LADY? BARBARA?
LET'S NOT STICK AROUND LONG ENOUGH TO FIND OUT. ARE YOU OKAY?
I THINK SO, BUT WHAT ABOUT IRK? DO YOU THINK SHE ESCAPED? I'M JUST... I'M SO WORRIED ABOUT HER. I WISH SHE WAS HERE...
ME, TOO.

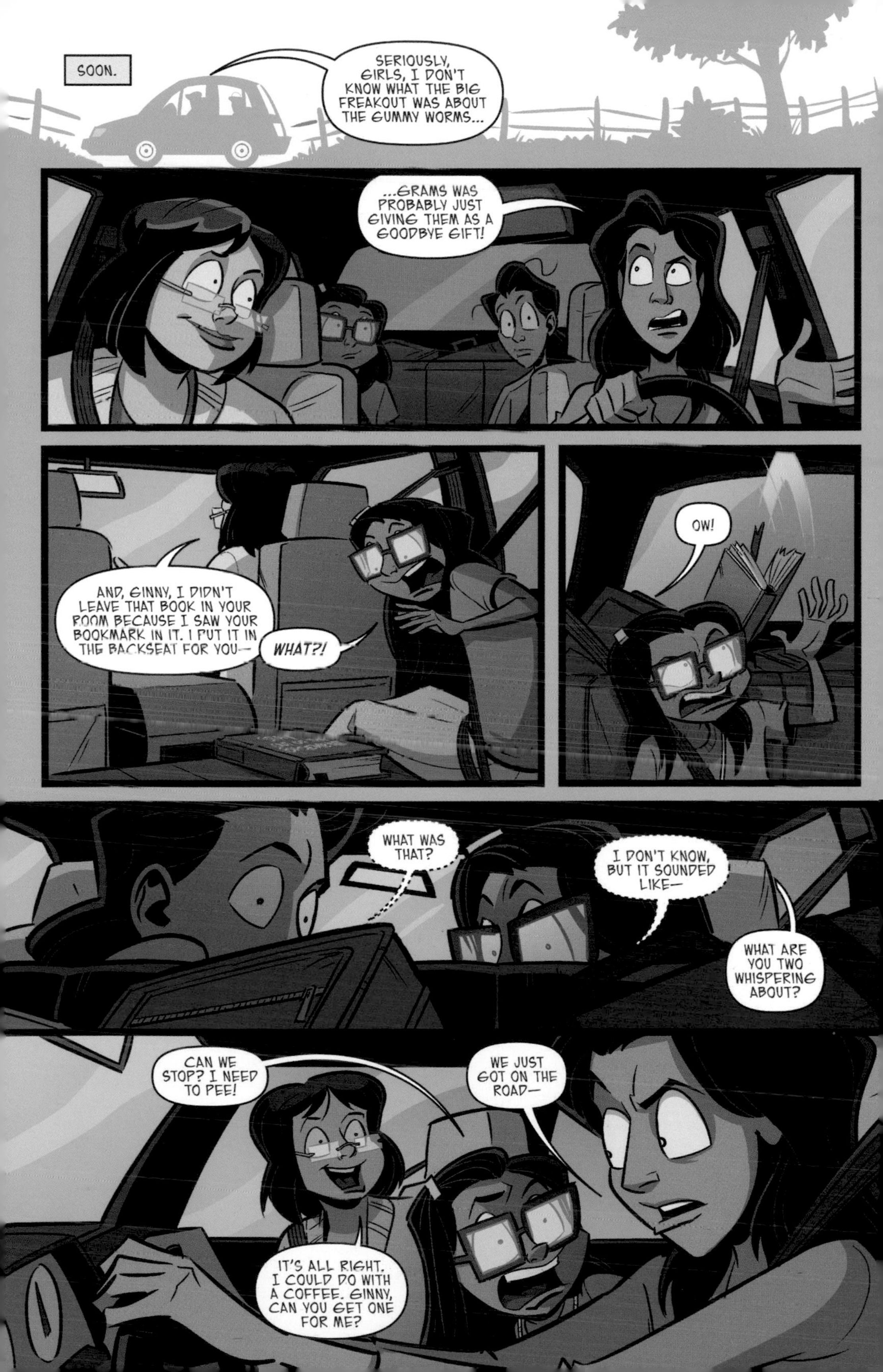
SOON.
SERIOUSLY, GIRLS, I DON'T KNOW WHAT THE BIG FREAKOUT WAS ABOUT THE GUMMY WORMS...
...GRAMS WAS PROBABLY JUST GIVING THEM AS A GOODBYE GIFT!
AND, GINNY, I DIDN'T LEAVE THAT BOOK IN YOUR ROOM BECAUSE I SAW YOUR BOOKMARK IN IT. I PUT IT IN THE BACKSEAT FOR YOU—
WHAT?!
OW!
WHAT WAS THAT?
I DON'T KNOW, BUT IT SOUNDED LIKE—
WHAT ARE YOU TWO WHISPERING ABOUT?
CAN WE STOP? I NEED TO PEE!
WE JUST GOT ON THE ROAD—
IT'S ALL RIGHT. I COULD DO WITH A COFFEE. GINNY, CAN YOU GET ONE FOR ME?

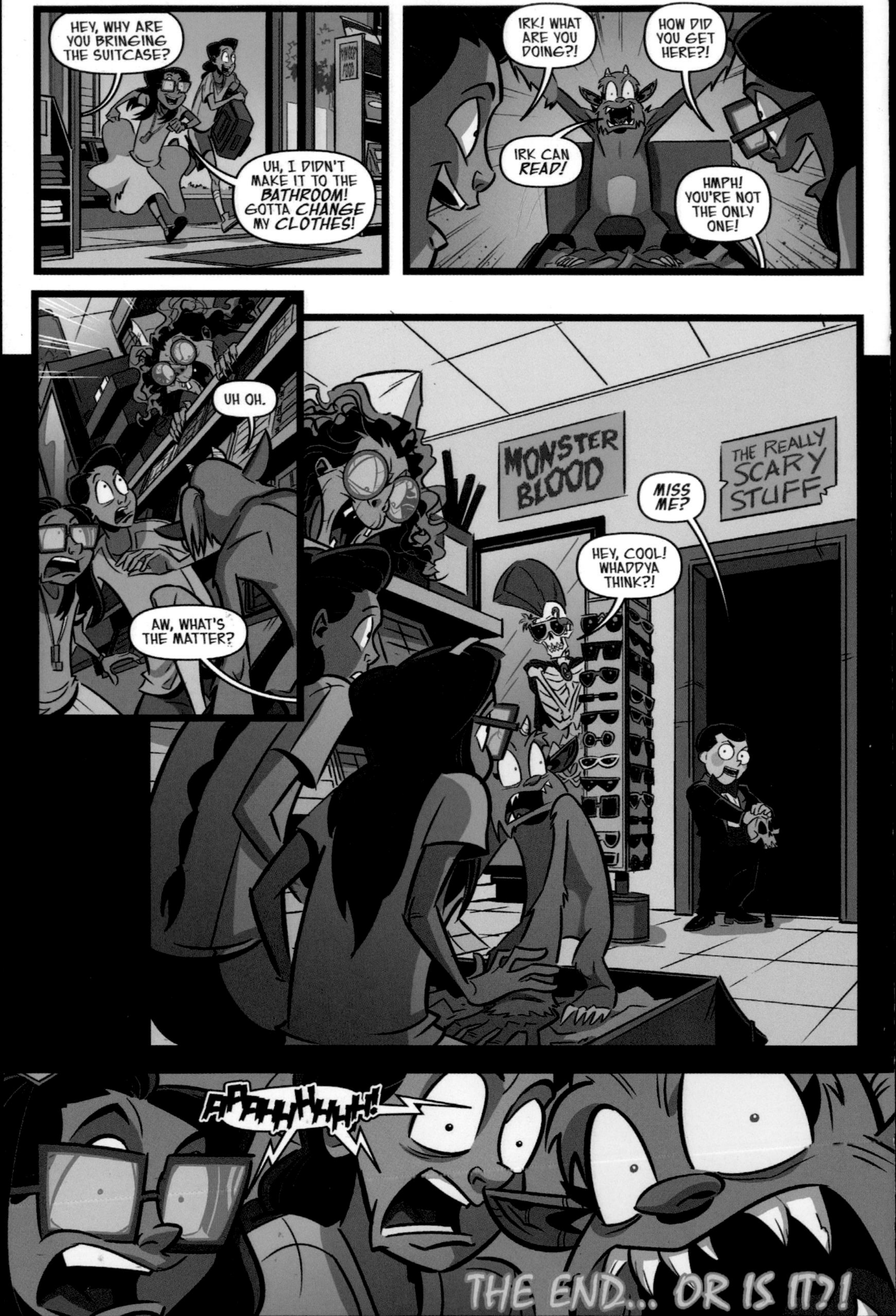
HEY, WHY ARE YOU BRINGING THE SUITCASE?
UH, I DIDN'T MAKE IT TO THE BATHROOM! GOTTA CHANGE MY CLOTHES!
IRK! WHAT ARE YOU DOING?!
HOW DID YOU GET HERE?!
IRK CAN READ!
HMPH! YOU'RE NOT THE ONLY ONE!
UH OH.
AW, WHAT'S THE MATTER?
MONSTER BLOOD
THE REALLY SCARY STUFF
MISS ME?
HEY, COOL! WHADDYA THINK?!
AAAHHHHHH!
THE END... OR IS IT?!

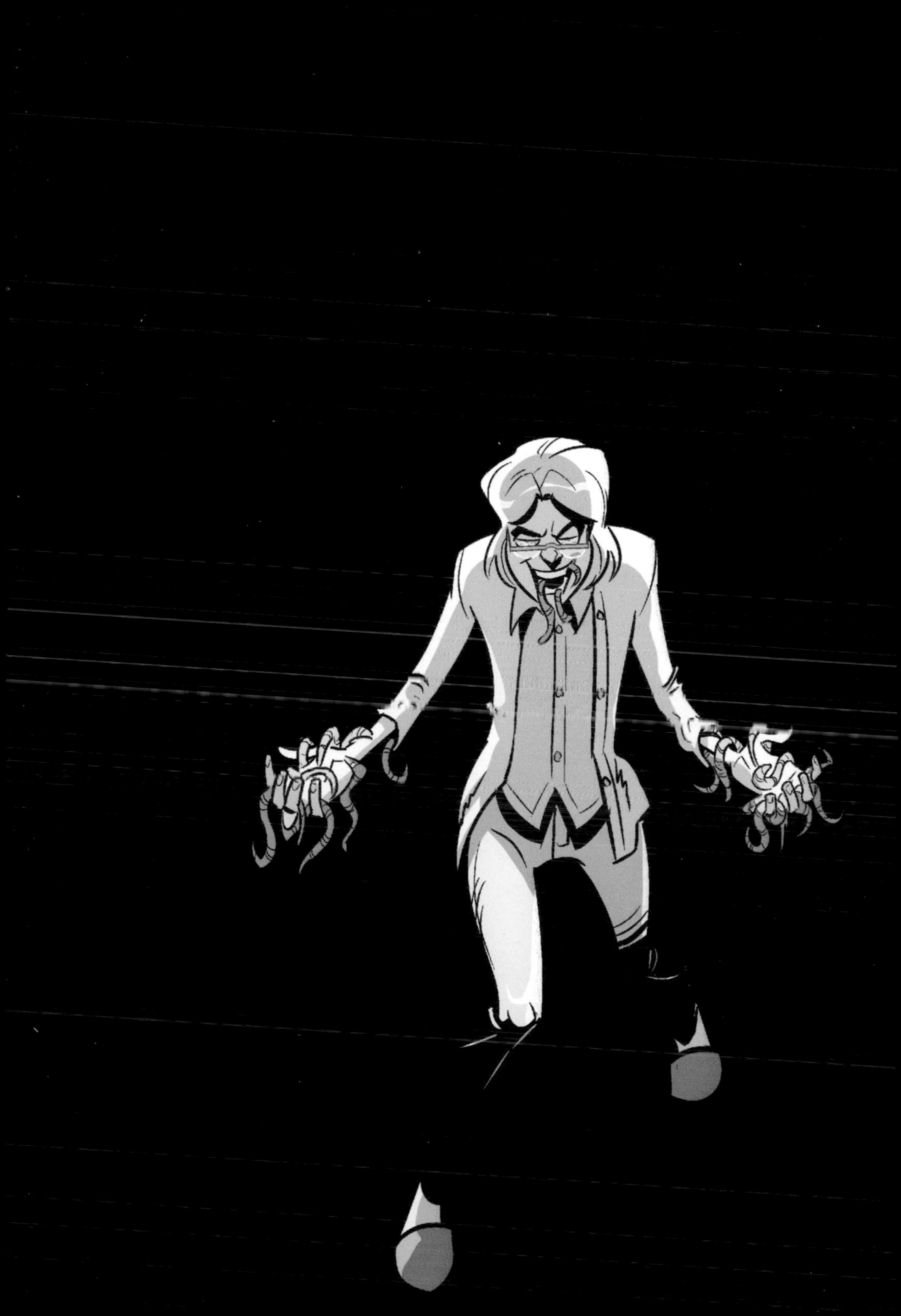

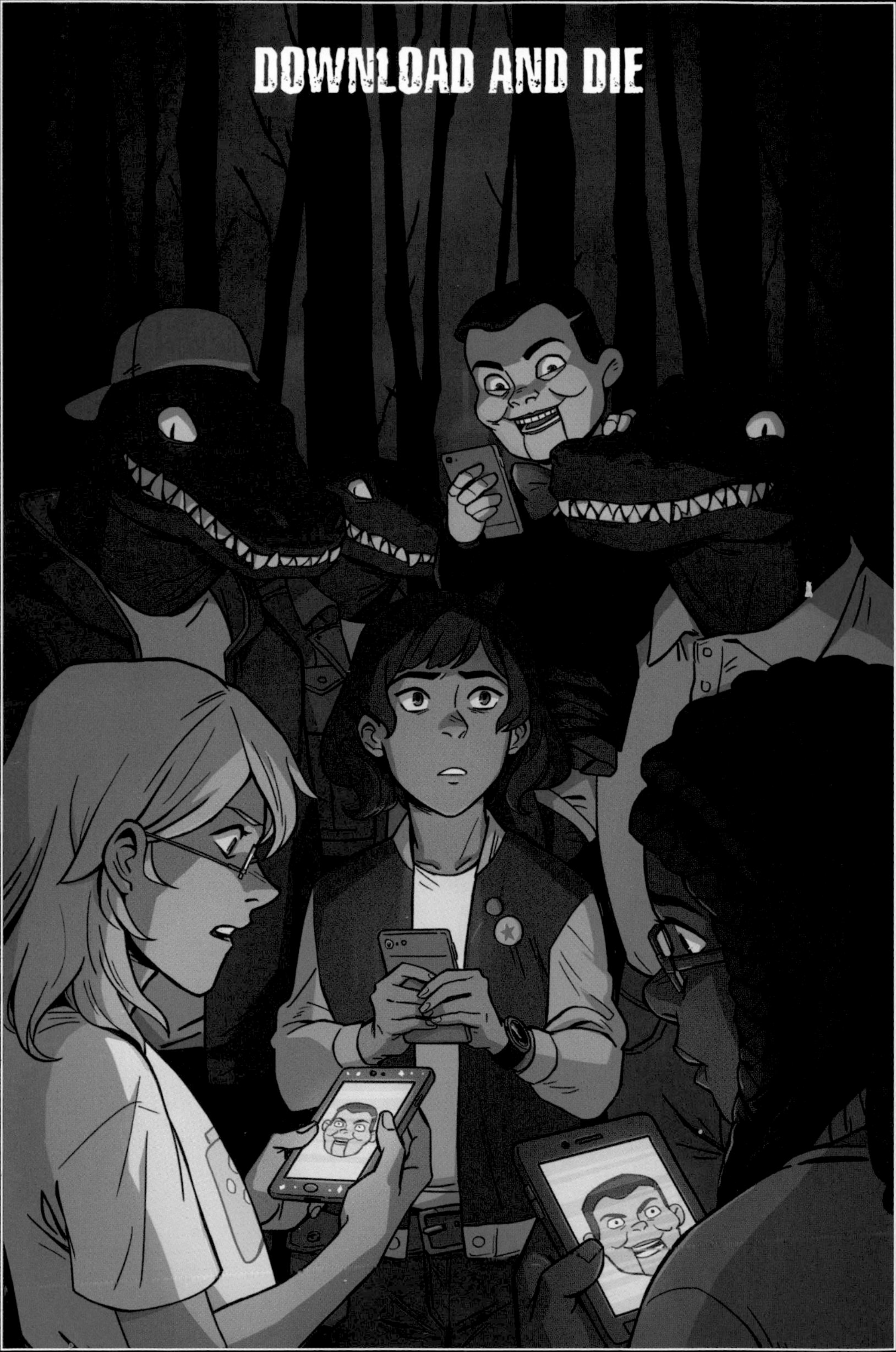
DOWNLOAD AND DIE

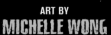

ART BY
MICHELLE WONG

FIRST DAY OF A NEW SCHOOL YEAR.

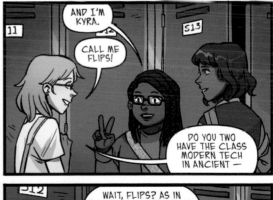

LOCK...ER ....BUDS. LOCKER BUDS!

HEY, UHM, ARE THESE THE "S" LOCKERS?

"ESSS" THEY ARE!

DON'T BE A CREEP, MITRA!

AND I'M KYRA.

CALL ME FLIPS!

DO YOU TWO HAVE THE CLASS MODERN TECH IN ANCIENT —

WAIT, FLIPS? AS IN "FLIPS1101101"? AREN'T YOU ON THE *TRAVELERS OF THE FROST* LEADERBOARD?

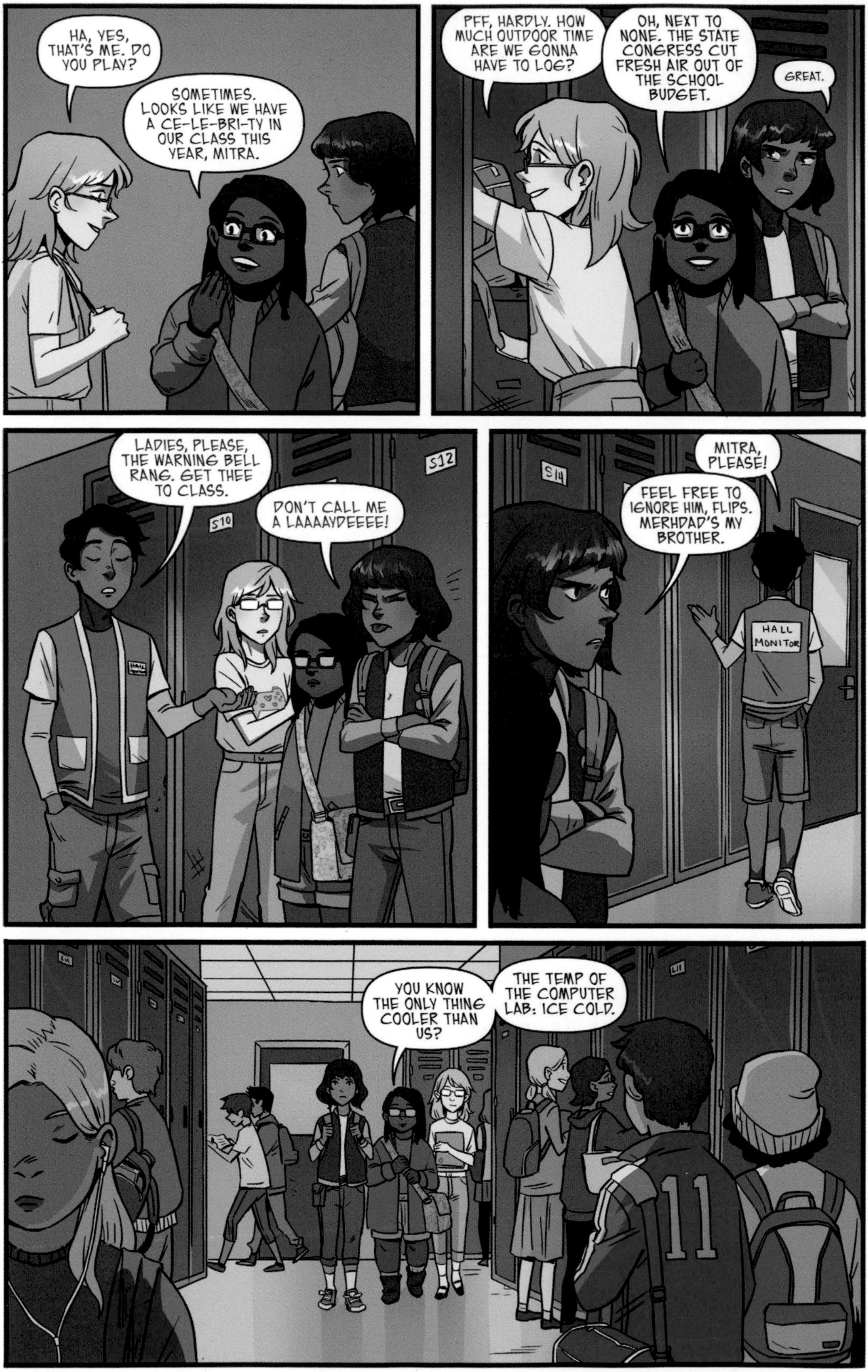
HA, YES, THAT'S ME. DO YOU PLAY?
SOMETIMES. LOOKS LIKE WE HAVE A CE-LE-BRI-TY IN OUR CLASS THIS YEAR, MITRA.
PFF, HARDLY. HOW MUCH OUTDOOR TIME ARE WE GONNA HAVE TO LOG?
OH, NEXT TO NONE. THE STATE CONGRESS CUT FRESH AIR OUT OF THE SCHOOL BUDGET.
GREAT.
LADIES, PLEASE, THE WARNING BELL RANG. GET THEE TO CLASS.
DON'T CALL ME A LAAAAYDEEEE!
S12
S10
HALL
MITRA, PLEASE!
FEEL FREE TO IGNORE HIM, FLIPS. MERHDAD'S MY BROTHER.
S14
HALL MONITOR
YOU KNOW THE ONLY THING COOLER THAN US?
THE TEMP OF THE COMPUTER LAB: ICE COLD.
11

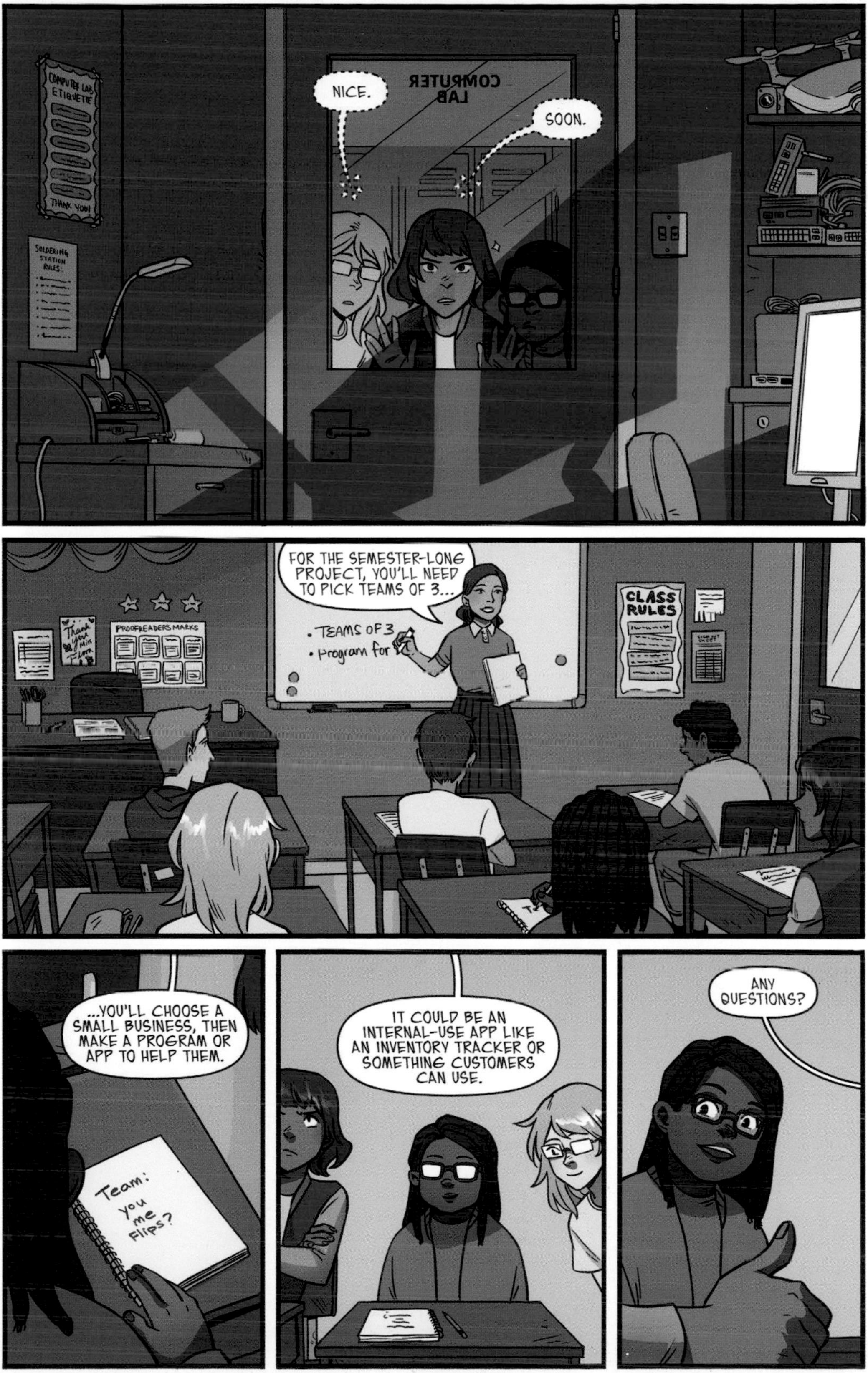
COMPUTER LAB
NICE.
SOON.
FOR THE SEMESTER-LONG PROJECT, YOU'LL NEED TO PICK TEAMS OF 3...
CLASS RULES
PROOFREADERS MARKS
• TEAMS OF 3
• Program for
...YOU'LL CHOOSE A SMALL BUSINESS, THEN MAKE A PROGRAM OR APP TO HELP THEM.
Team: you me Flips?
IT COULD BE AN INTERNAL-USE APP LIKE AN INVENTORY TRACKER OR SOMETHING CUSTOMERS CAN USE.
ANY QUESTIONS?

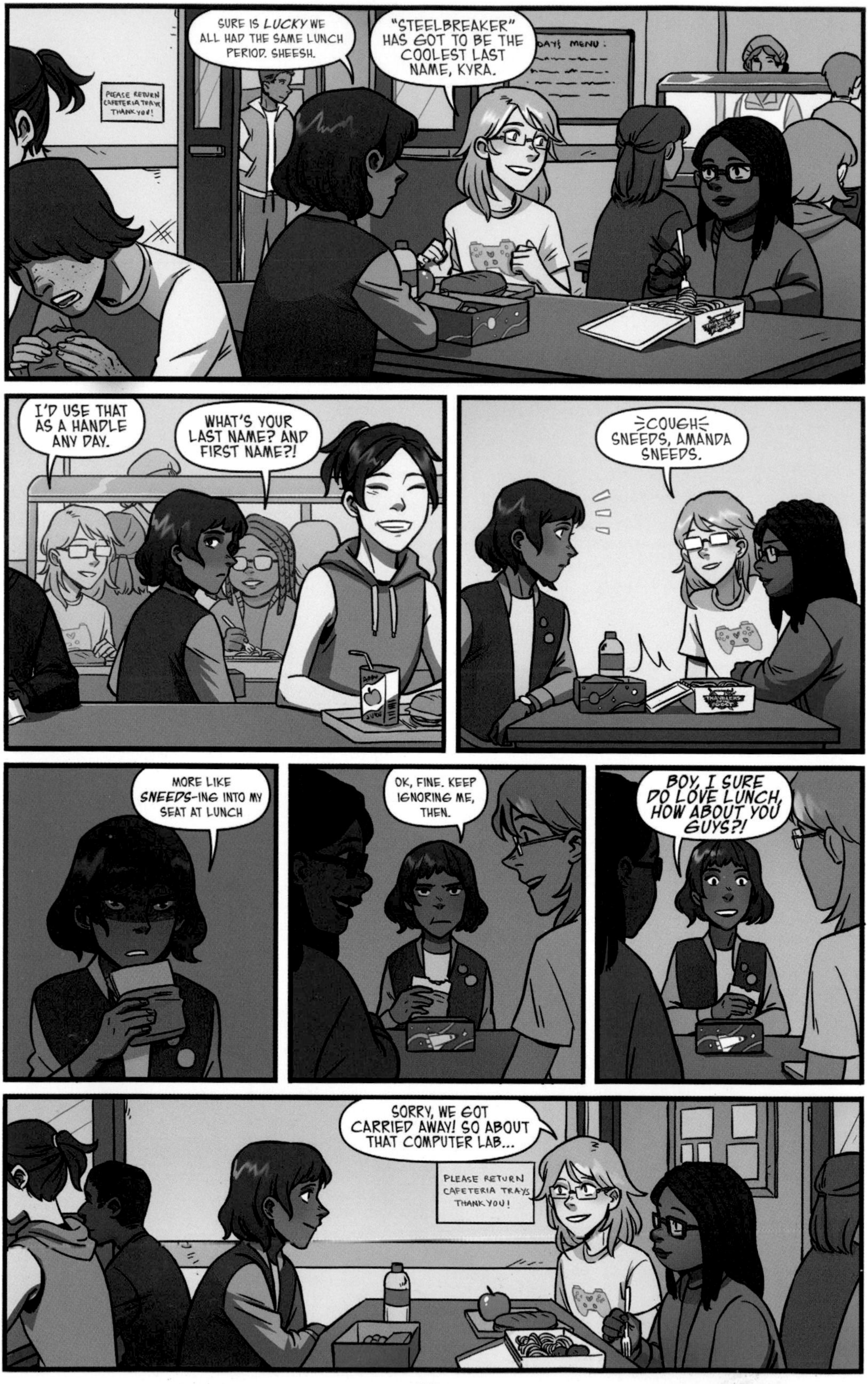
PLEASE RETURN CAFETERIA TRAYS THANK YOU!
SURE IS LUCKY WE ALL HAD THE SAME LUNCH PERIOD. SHEESH.
"STEELBREAKER" HAS GOT TO BE THE COOLEST LAST NAME, KYRA.
I'D USE THAT AS A HANDLE ANY DAY.
WHAT'S YOUR LAST NAME? AND FIRST NAME?!
COUGH SNEEDS, AMANDA SNEEDS.
MORE LIKE SNEEDS-ING INTO MY SEAT AT LUNCH
OK, FINE. KEEP IGNORING ME, THEN.
BOY, I SURE DO LOVE LUNCH, HOW ABOUT YOU GUYS?!
SORRY, WE GOT CARRIED AWAY! SO ABOUT THAT COMPUTER LAB...
PLEASE RETURN CAFETERIA TRAYS THANK YOU!

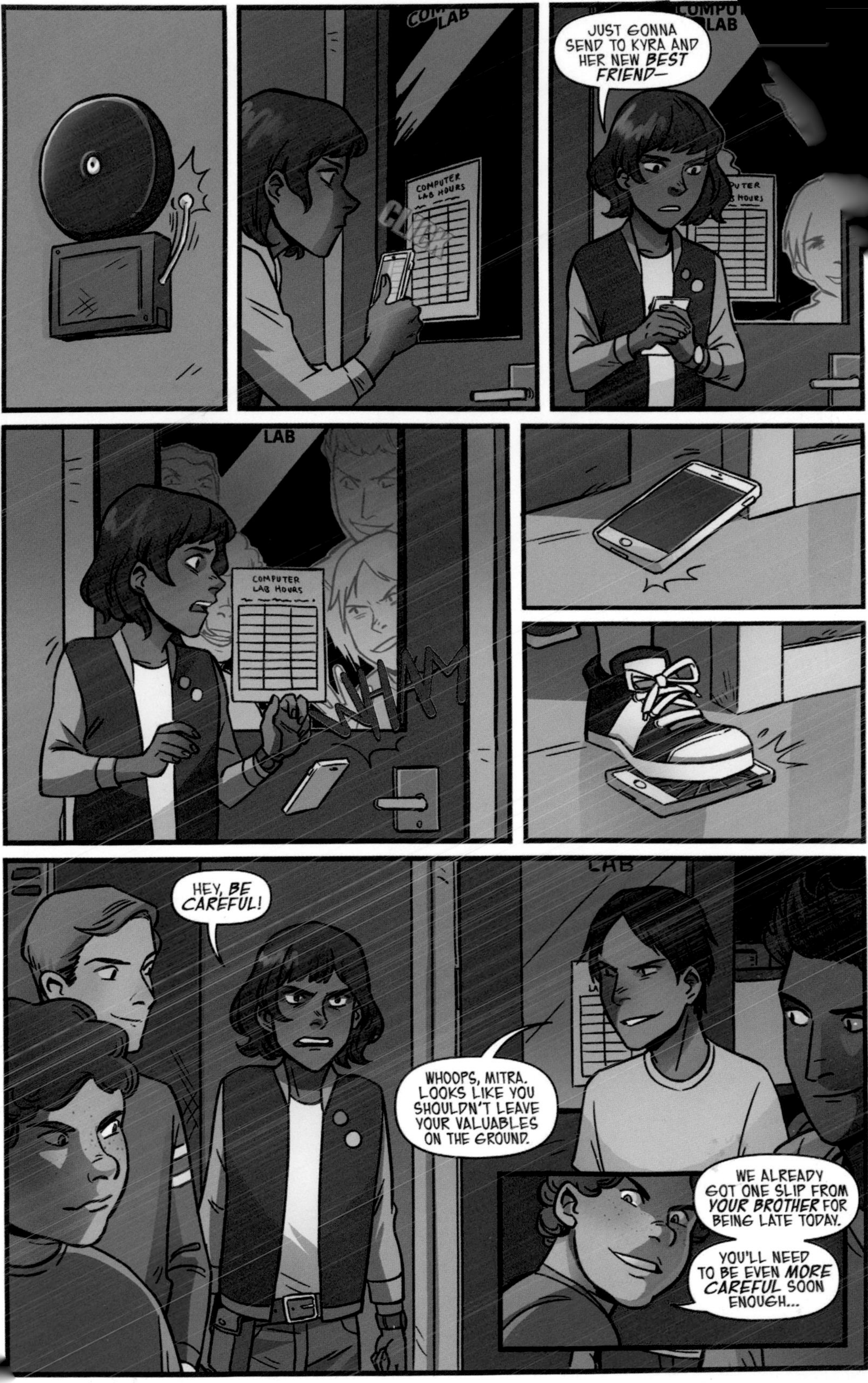
COMPUTER LAB
COMPUTER LAB HOURS
CLICK
JUST GONNA SEND TO KYRA AND HER NEW BEST FRIEND—
LAB
COMPUTER LAB HOURS
WHAM
HEY, BE CAREFUL!
LAB
WHOOPS, MITRA. LOOKS LIKE YOU SHOULDN'T LEAVE YOUR VALUABLES ON THE GROUND.
WE ALREADY GOT ONE SLIP FROM YOUR BROTHER FOR BEING LATE TODAY.
YOU'LL NEED TO BE EVEN MORE CAREFUL SOON ENOUGH...

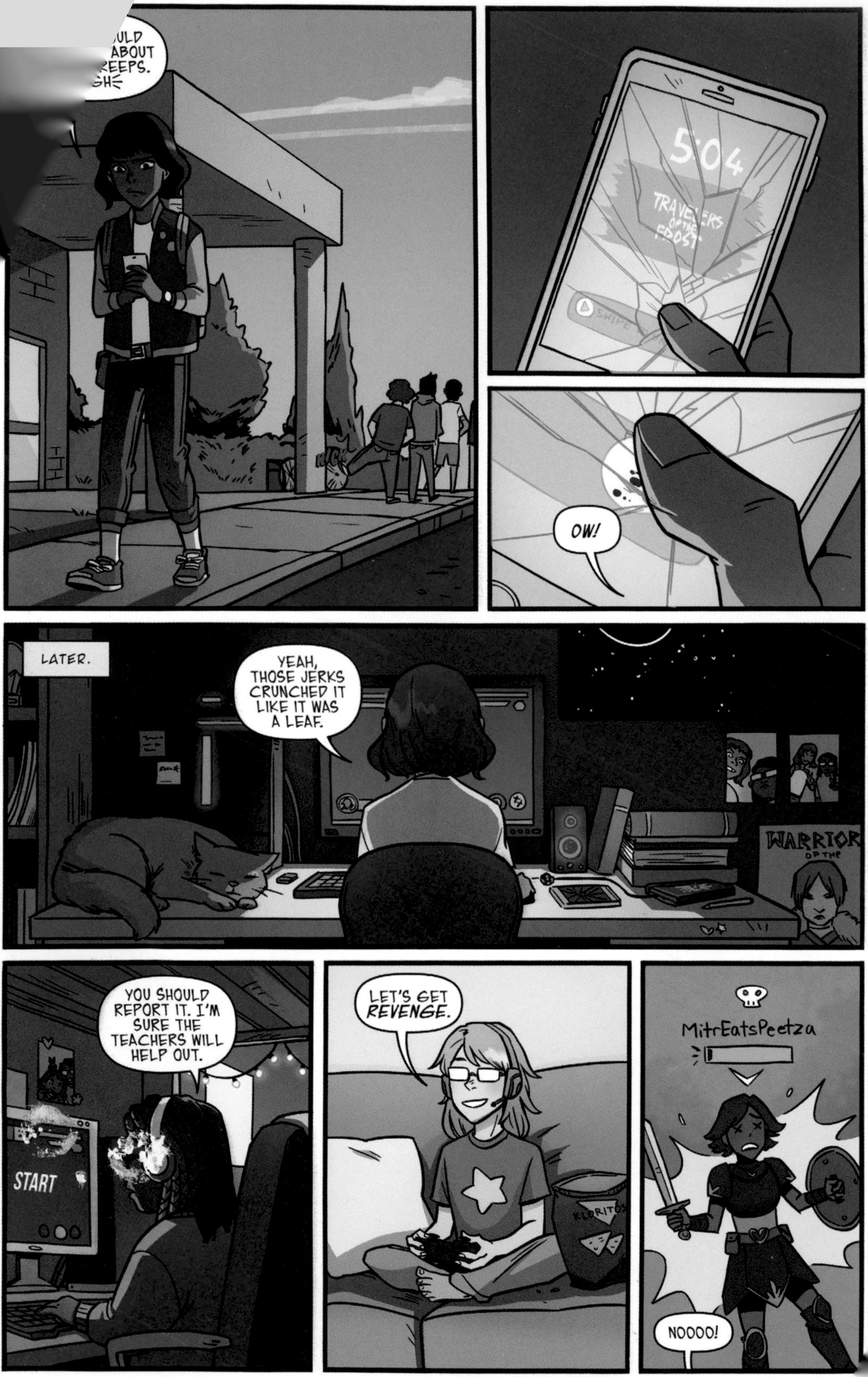
5:04
TRAVELERS OF THE FROST
SWIPE
OW!
LATER.
YEAH, THOSE JERKS CRUNCHED IT LIKE IT WAS A LEAF.
WARRIOR OF THE
YOU SHOULD REPORT IT. I'M SURE THE TEACHERS WILL HELP OUT.
START
LET'S GET *REVENGE.*
MitrEatsPeetza
NOOOO!

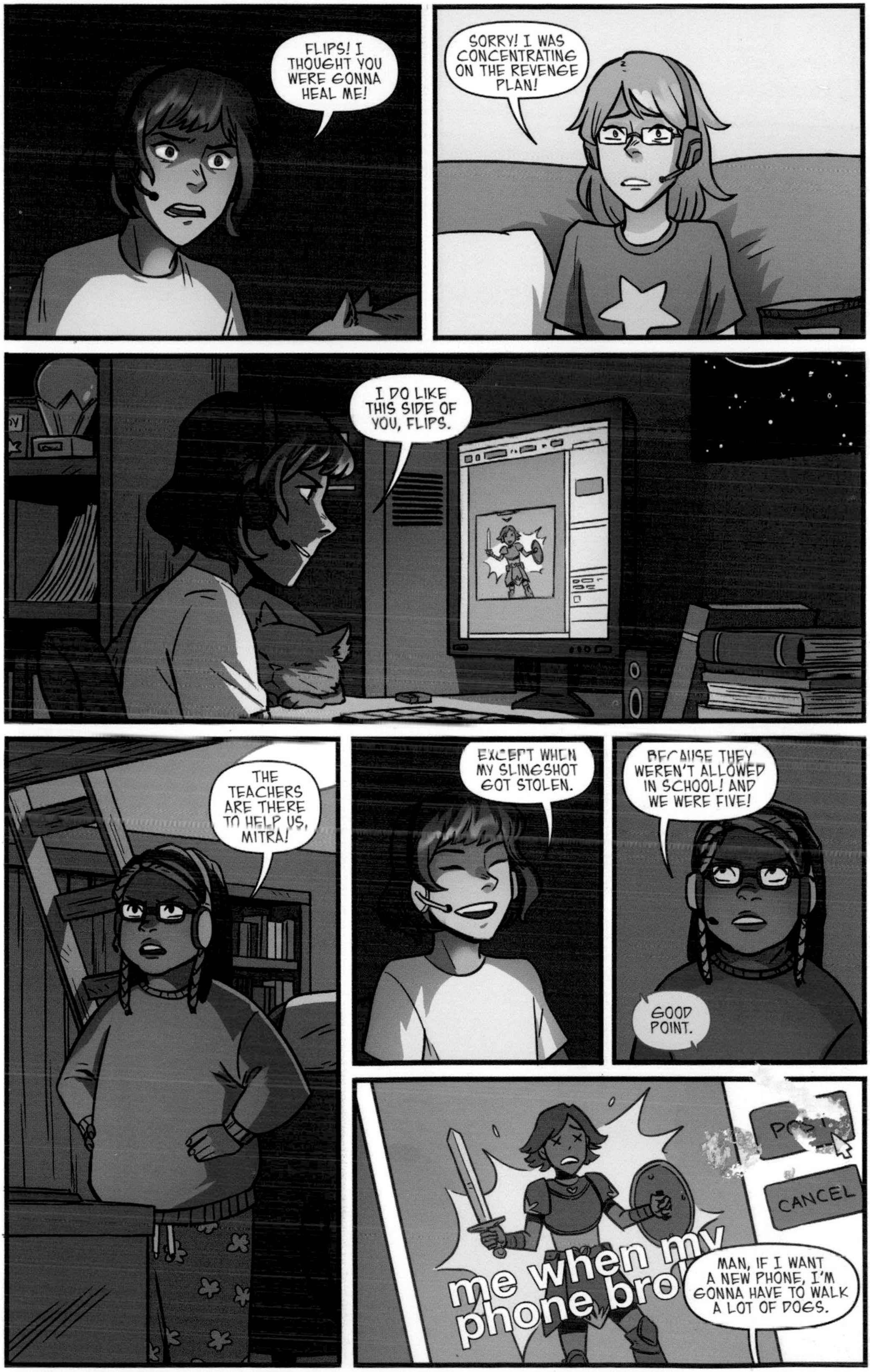
FLIPS! I THOUGHT YOU WERE GONNA HEAL ME!
SORRY! I WAS CONCENTRATING ON THE REVENGE PLAN!
I DO LIKE THIS SIDE OF YOU, FLIPS.
THE TEACHERS ARE THERE TO HELP US, MITRA!
EXCEPT WHEN MY SLINGSHOT GOT STOLEN.
BECAUSE THEY WEREN'T ALLOWED IN SCHOOL! AND WE WERE FIVE!
GOOD POINT.
CANCEL
me when my phone bro
MAN, IF I WANT A NEW PHONE, I'M GONNA HAVE TO WALK A LOT OF DOGS.

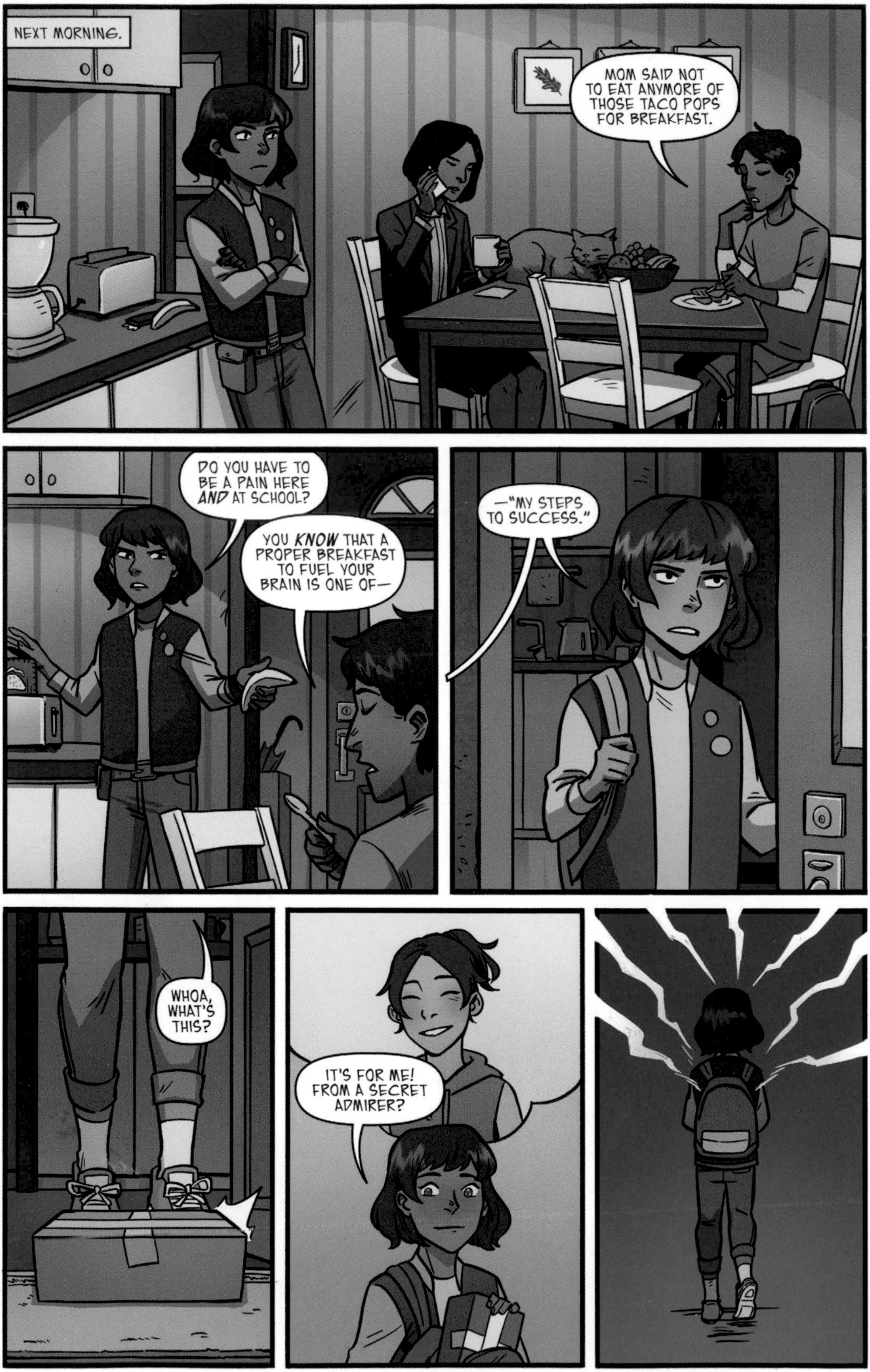
NEXT MORNING.
MOM SAID NOT TO EAT ANYMORE OF THOSE TACO POPS FOR BREAKFAST.
DO YOU HAVE TO BE A PAIN HERE *AND* AT SCHOOL?
YOU *KNOW* THAT A PROPER BREAKFAST TO FUEL YOUR BRAIN IS ONE OF—
—"MY STEPS TO SUCCESS."
WHOA, WHAT'S THIS?
IT'S FOR ME! FROM A SECRET ADMIRER?

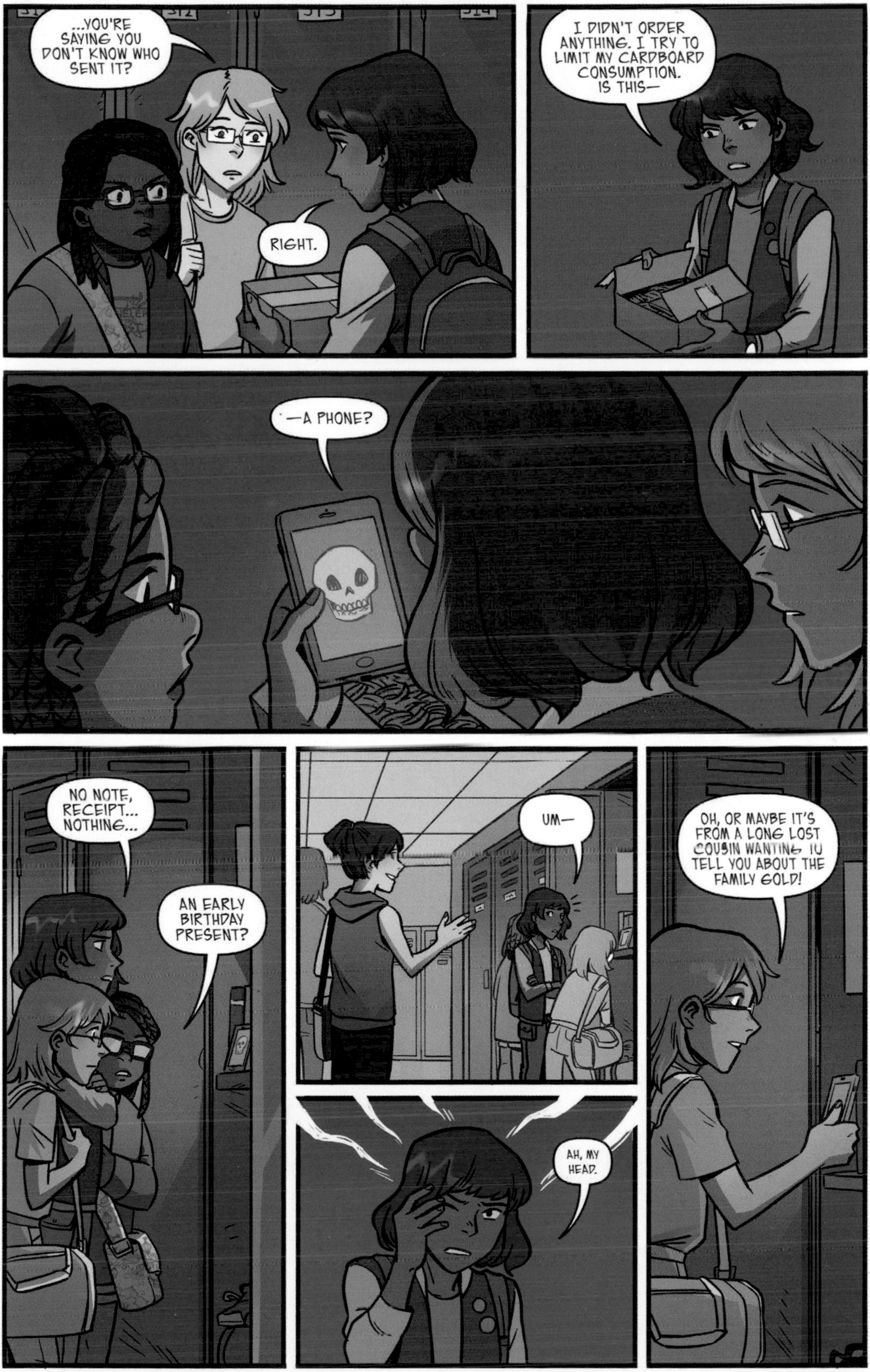
...YOU'RE SAYING YOU DON'T KNOW WHO SENT IT?
RIGHT.
I DIDN'T ORDER ANYTHING. I TRY TO LIMIT MY CARDBOARD CONSUMPTION. IS THIS—
—A PHONE?
NO NOTE, RECEIPT... NOTHING...
AN EARLY BIRTHDAY PRESENT?
UM—
AH, MY HEAD.
OH, OR MAYBE IT'S FROM A LONG LOST COUSIN WANTING TO TELL YOU ABOUT THE FAMILY GOLD!

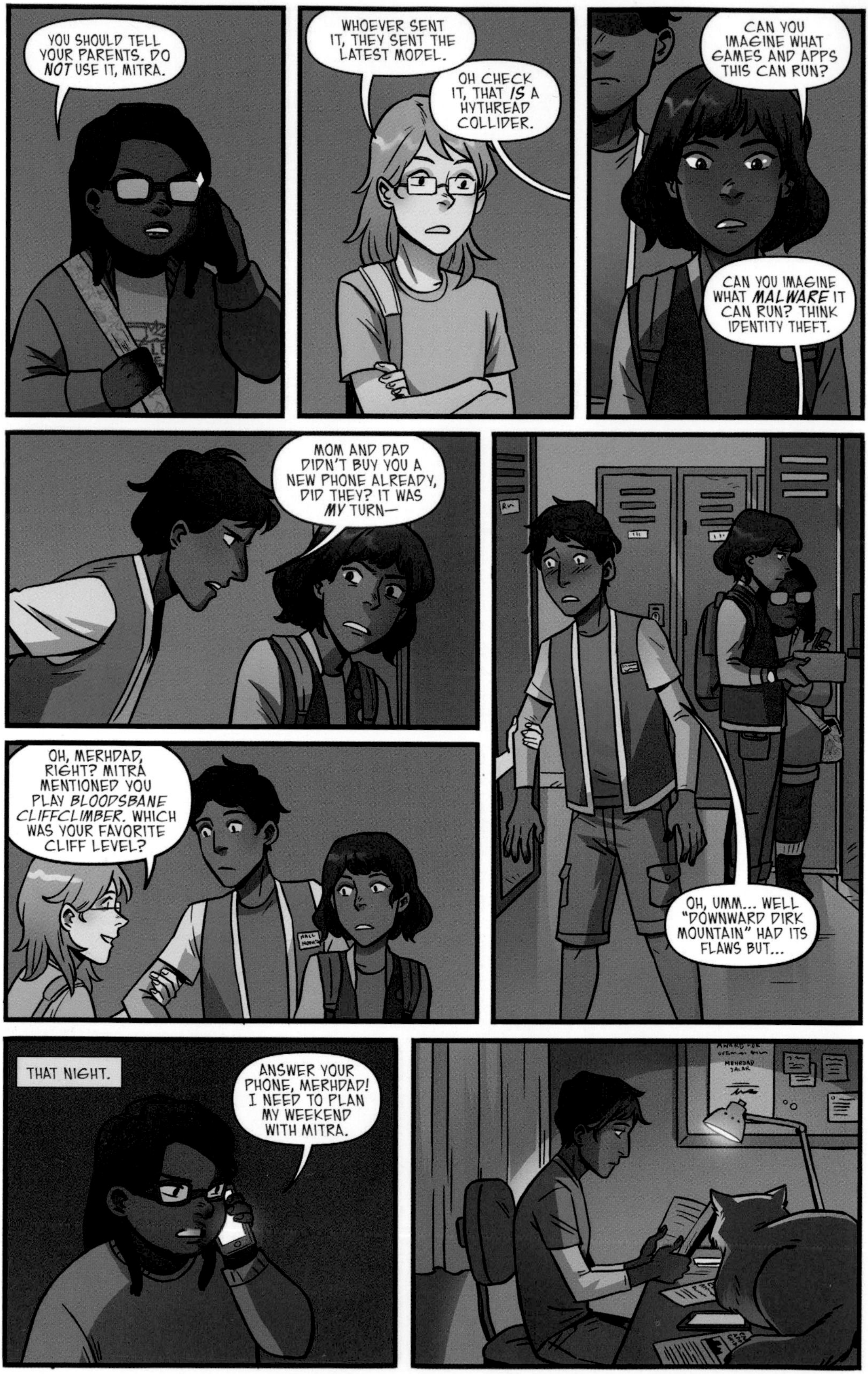
YOU SHOULD TELL YOUR PARENTS. DO NOT USE IT, MITRA.
WHOEVER SENT IT, THEY SENT THE LATEST MODEL.
OH CHECK IT, THAT IS A HYTHREAD COLLIDER.
CAN YOU IMAGINE WHAT GAMES AND APPS THIS CAN RUN?
CAN YOU IMAGINE WHAT MALWARE IT CAN RUN? THINK IDENTITY THEFT.
MOM AND DAD DIDN'T BUY YOU A NEW PHONE ALREADY, DID THEY? IT WAS MY TURN—
OH, MERHDAD, RIGHT? MITRA MENTIONED YOU PLAY BLOODSBANE CLIFFCLIMBER. WHICH WAS YOUR FAVORITE CLIFF LEVEL?
OH, UMM... WELL "DOWNWARD DIRK MOUNTAIN" HAD ITS FLAWS BUT...
THAT NIGHT.
ANSWER YOUR PHONE, MERHDAD! I NEED TO PLAN MY WEEKEND WITH MITRA.

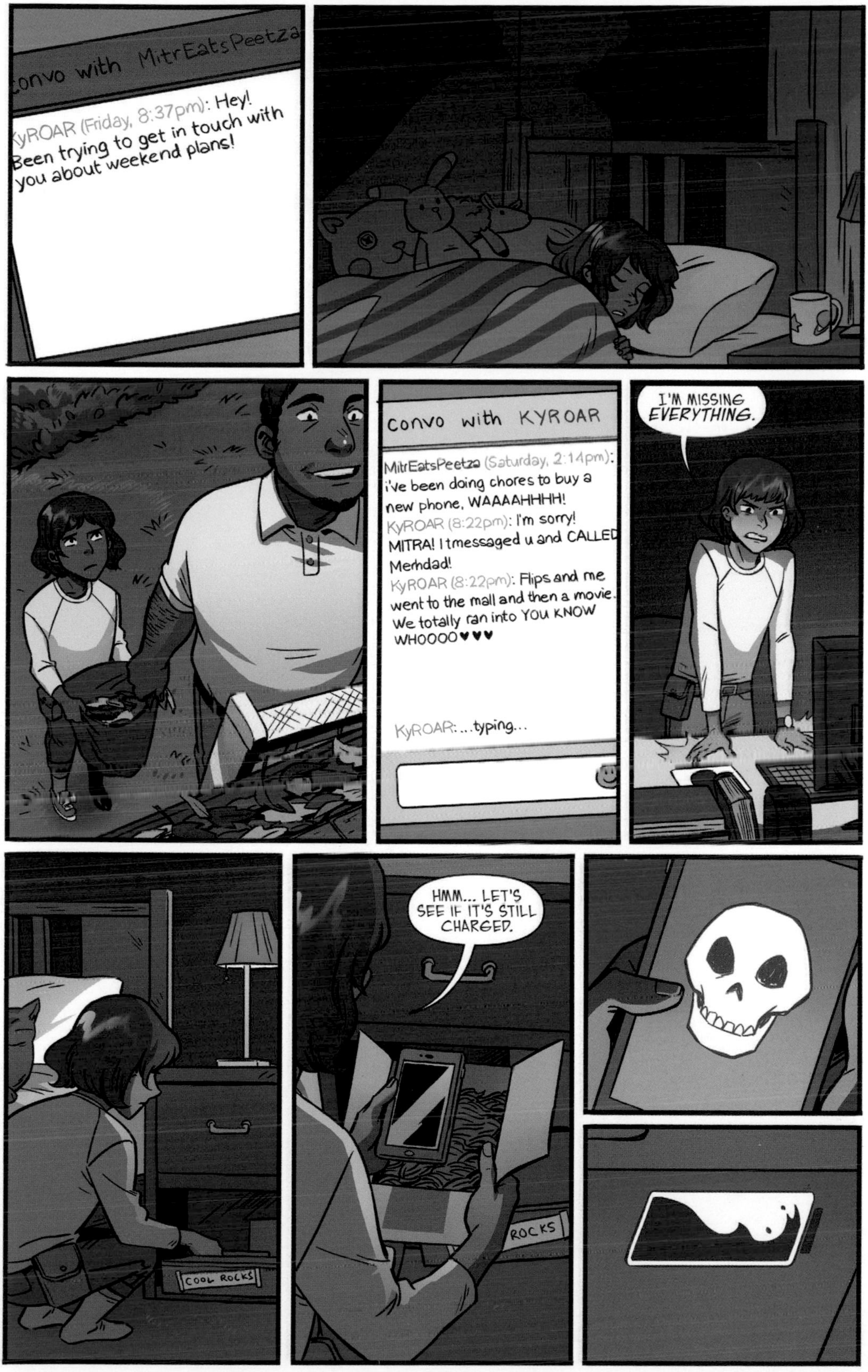
convo with MitrEatsPeetza
KyROAR (Friday, 8:37pm): Hey! Been trying to get in touch with you about weekend plans!
convo with KYROAR
MitrEatsPeetza (Saturday, 2:14pm): i've been doing chores to buy a new phone, WAAAAHHHH!
KyROAR (8:22pm): I'm sorry! MITRA! I tmessaged u and CALLED Mehdad!
KyROAR (8:22pm): Flips and me went to the mall and then a movie. We totally ran into YOU KNOW WHOOOO♥♥♥
KyROAR: ...typing...
I'M MISSING EVERYTHING.
COOL ROCKS
HMM... LET'S SEE IF IT'S STILL CHARGED.
ROCKS

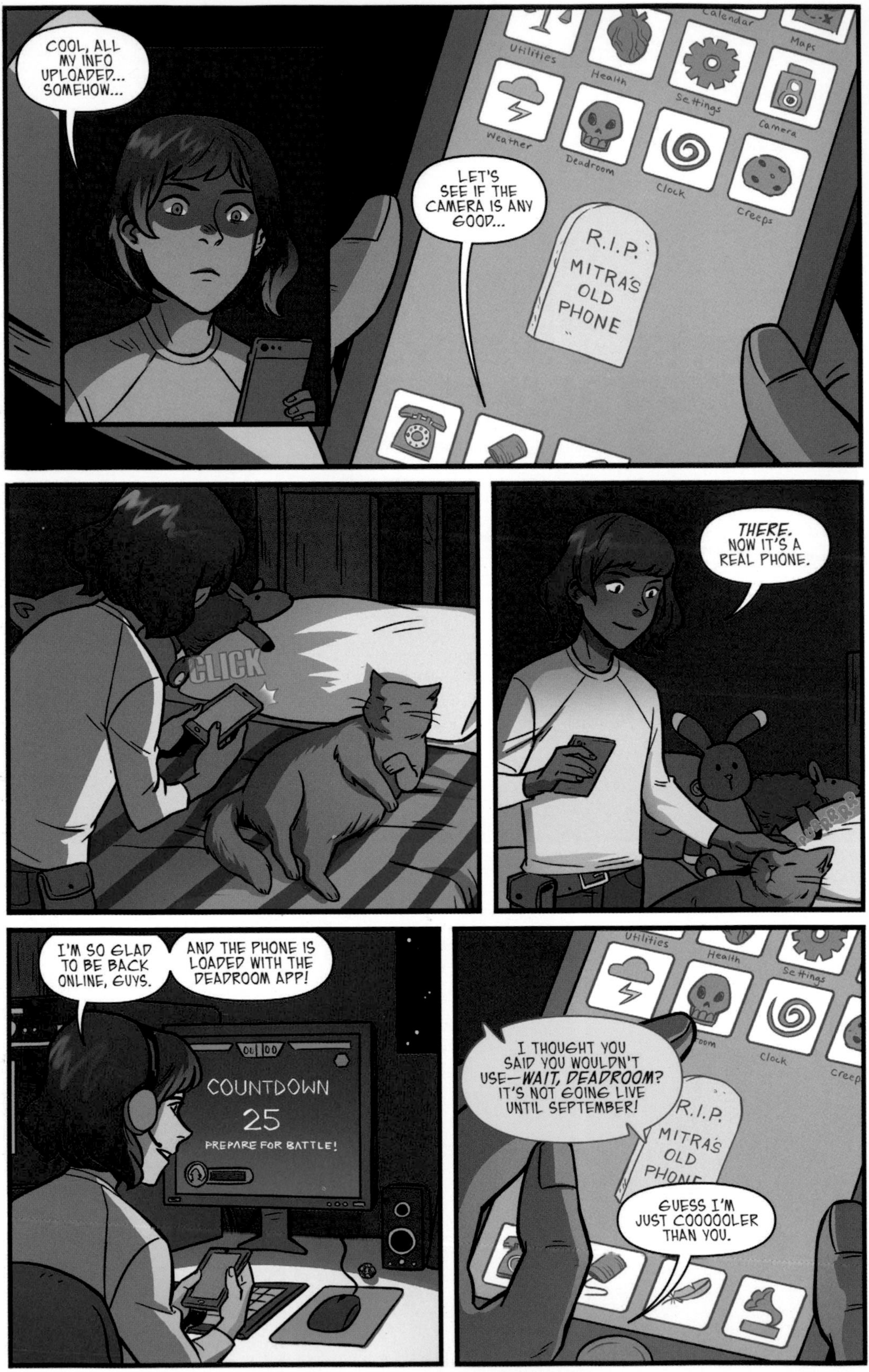
COOL, ALL MY INFO UPLOADED... SOMEHOW...
Calendar
Maps
Utilities
Health
Settings
Camera
Weather
Deadroom
Clock
Creeps
LET'S SEE IF THE CAMERA IS ANY GOOD...
R.I.P. MITRA'S OLD PHONE
CLICK
THERE. NOW IT'S A REAL PHONE.
I'M SO GLAD TO BE BACK ONLINE, GUYS.
AND THE PHONE IS LOADED WITH THE DEADROOM APP!
COUNTDOWN
25
PREPARE FOR BATTLE!
I THOUGHT YOU SAID YOU WOULDN'T USE—WAIT, DEADROOM? IT'S NOT GOING LIVE UNTIL SEPTEMBER!
GUESS I'M JUST COOOOOLER THAN YOU.

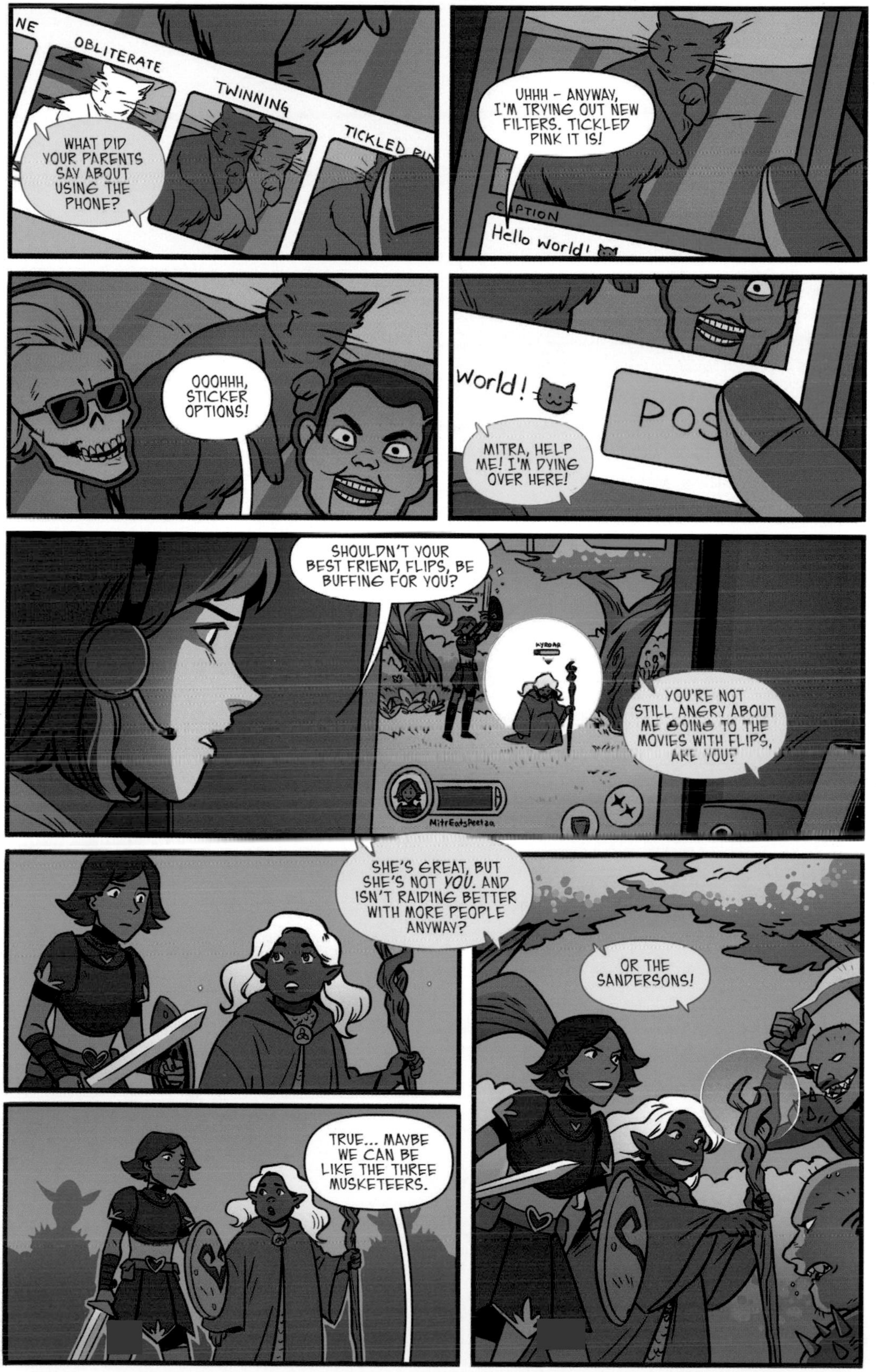
NE
OBLITERATE
TWINNING
TICKLED PI
WHAT DID YOUR PARENTS SAY ABOUT USING THE PHONE?
UHHH – ANYWAY, I'M TRYING OUT NEW FILTERS. TICKLED PINK IT IS!
CAPTION
Hello world!
OOOHHH, STICKER OPTIONS!
World!
POS
MITRA, HELP ME! I'M DYING OVER HERE!
SHOULDN'T YOUR BEST FRIEND, FLIPS, BE BUFFING FOR YOU?
YOU'RE NOT STILL ANGRY ABOUT ME GOING TO THE MOVIES WITH FLIPS, ARE YOU?
MitrEatsPeetza
SHE'S GREAT, BUT SHE'S NOT *YOU*. AND ISN'T RAIDING BETTER WITH MORE PEOPLE ANYWAY?
OR THE SANDERSONS!
TRUE... MAYBE WE CAN BE LIKE THE THREE MUSKETEERS.

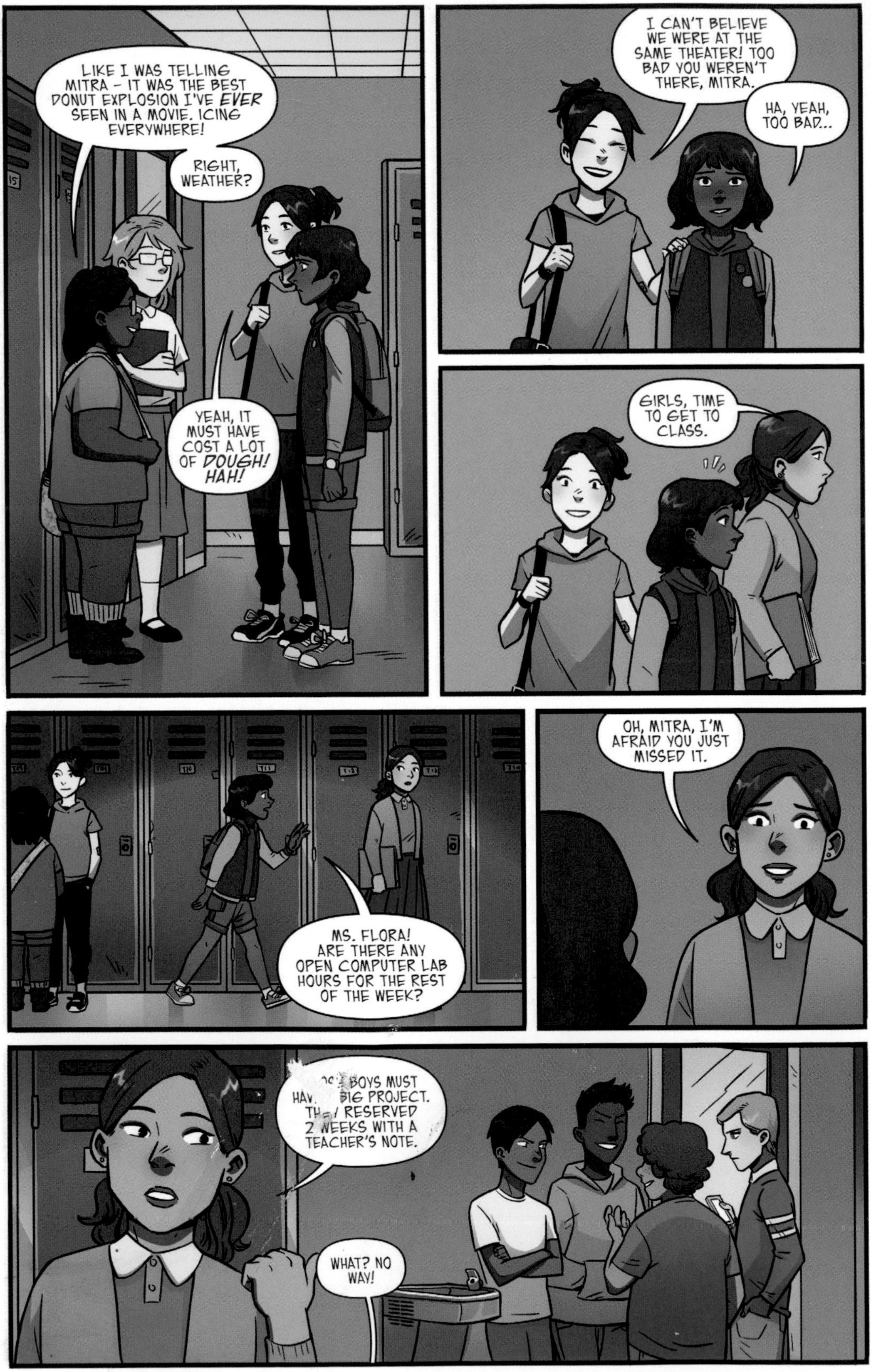
LIKE I WAS TELLING MITRA – IT WAS THE BEST DONUT EXPLOSION I'VE *EVER* SEEN IN A MOVIE. ICING EVERYWHERE!
RIGHT, WEATHER?
YEAH, IT MUST HAVE COST A LOT OF *DOUGH! HAH!*
I CAN'T BELIEVE WE WERE AT THE SAME THEATER! TOO BAD YOU WEREN'T THERE, MITRA.
HA, YEAH, TOO BAD...
GIRLS, TIME TO GET TO CLASS.
MS. FLORA! ARE THERE ANY OPEN COMPUTER LAB HOURS FOR THE REST OF THE WEEK?
OH, MITRA, I'M AFRAID YOU JUST MISSED IT.
BOYS MUST BIG PROJECT. RESERVED 2 WEEKS WITH A TEACHER'S NOTE.
WHAT? NO WAY!

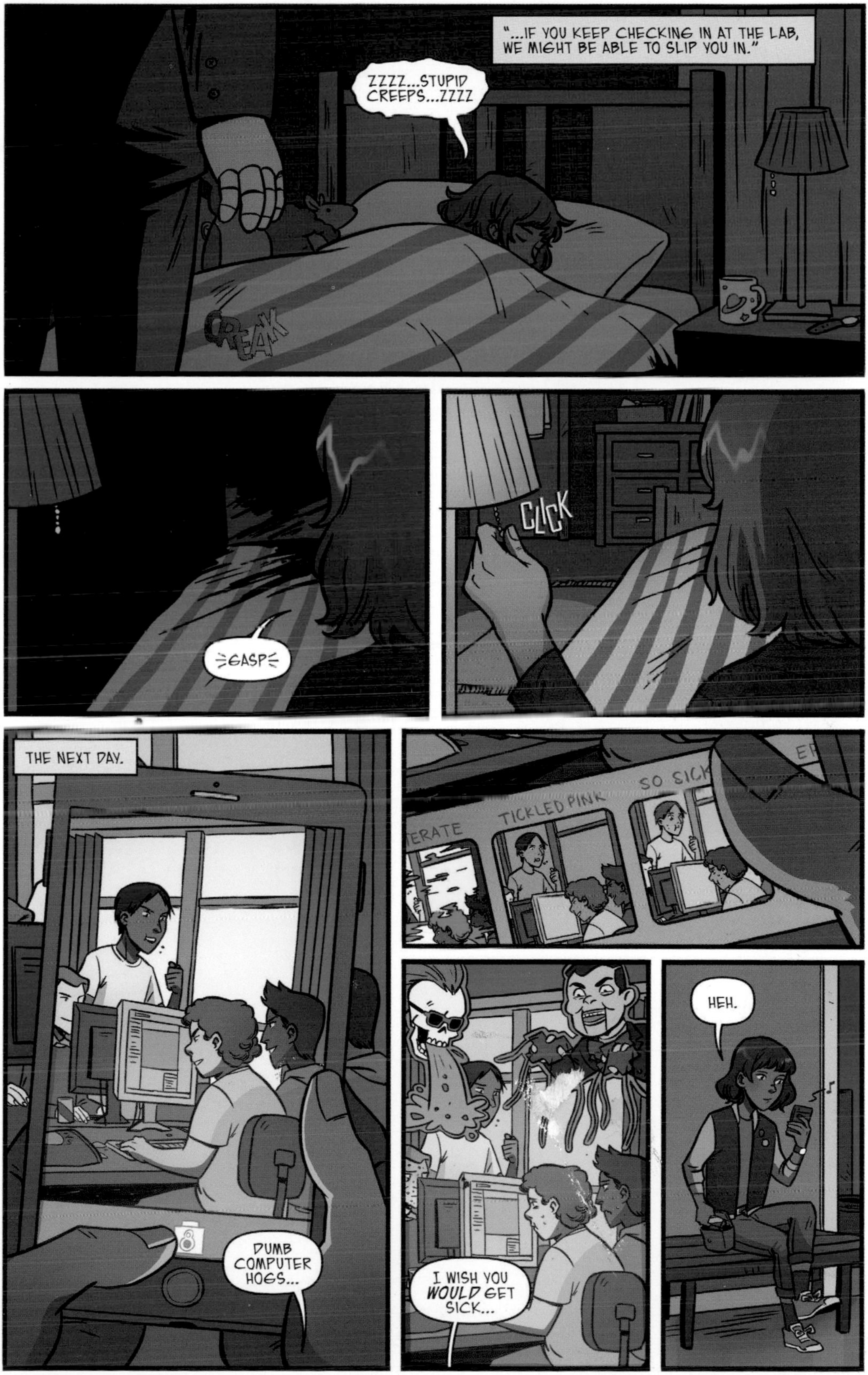
"...IF YOU KEEP CHECKING IN AT THE LAB, WE MIGHT BE ABLE TO SLIP YOU IN."
ZZZZ...STUPID CREEPS...ZZZZ
CREAK
GASP
CLICK
THE NEXT DAY.
SO SICK
TICKLED PINK
DUMB COMPUTER HOGS...
I WISH YOU *WOULD* GET SICK...
HEH.

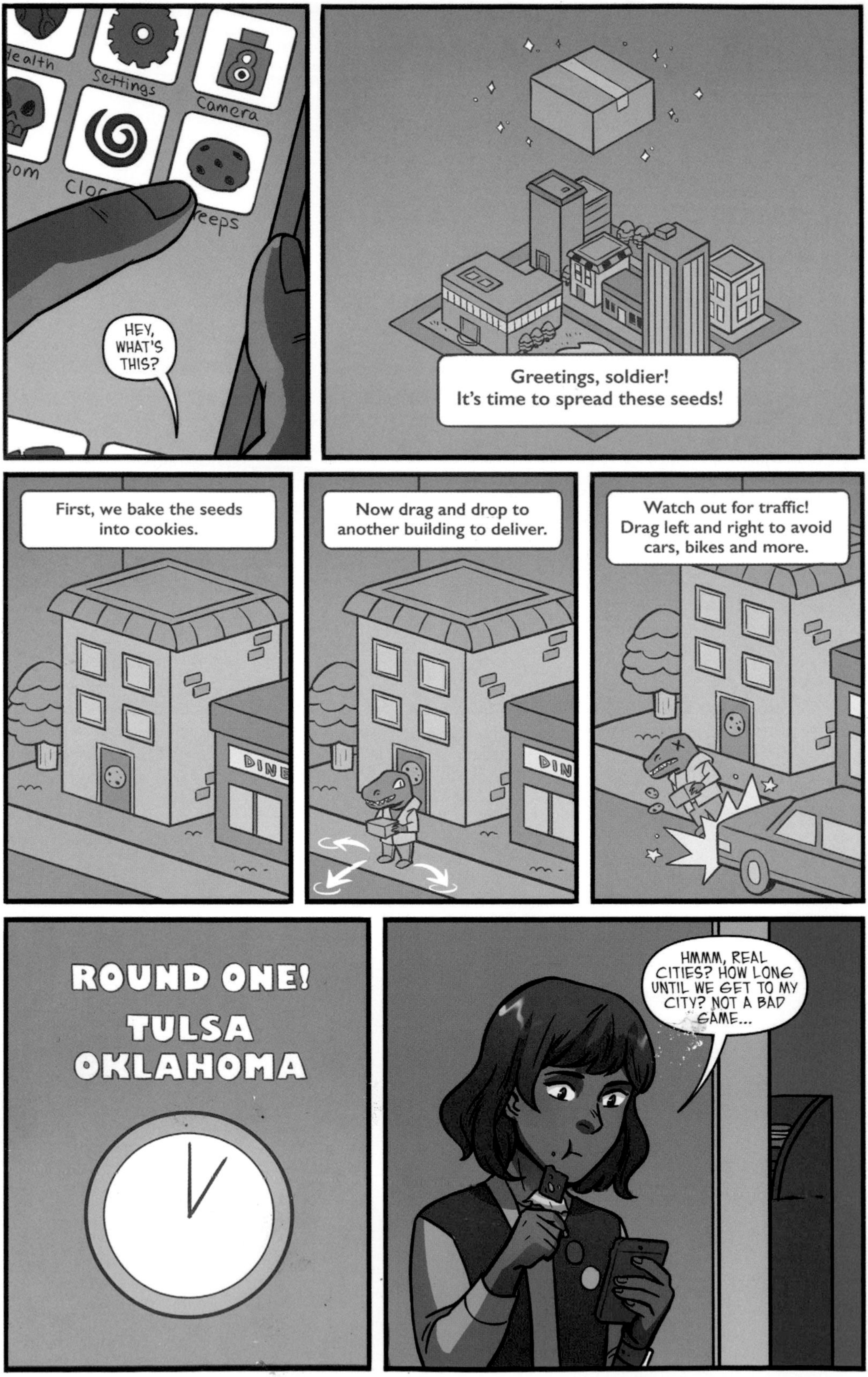

Health
Settings
Camera
Clo
eeps
HEY, WHAT'S THIS?
Greetings, soldier!
It's time to spread these seeds!
First, we bake the seeds into cookies.
DINE
Now drag and drop to another building to deliver.
DIN
Watch out for traffic! Drag left and right to avoid cars, bikes and more.
ROUND ONE!
TULSA
OKLAHOMA
HMMM, REAL CITIES? HOW LONG UNTIL WE GET TO MY CITY? NOT A BAD GAME...

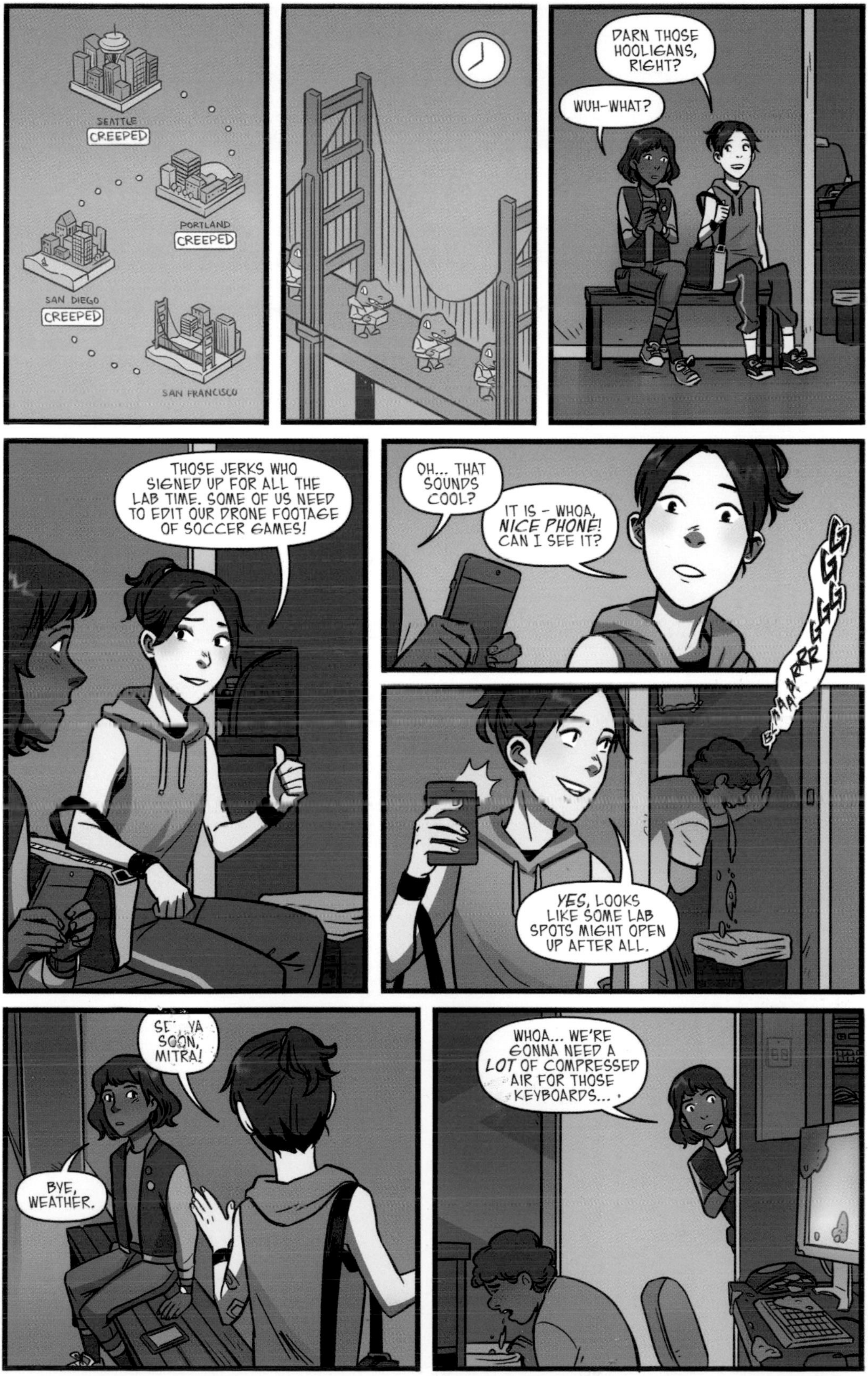
SEATTLE
CREEPED
PORTLAND
CREEPED
SAN DIEGO
CREEPED
SAN FRANCISCO
DARN THOSE HOOLIGANS, RIGHT?
WUH-WHAT?
THOSE JERKS WHO SIGNED UP FOR ALL THE LAB TIME. SOME OF US NEED TO EDIT OUR DRONE FOOTAGE OF SOCCER GAMES!
OH... THAT SOUNDS COOL?
IT IS - WHOA, NICE PHONE! CAN I SEE IT?
B-MAAARRRGGGGG
YES, LOOKS LIKE SOME LAB SPOTS MIGHT OPEN UP AFTER ALL.
SEE YA SOON, MITRA!
BYE, WEATHER.
WHOA... WE'RE GONNA NEED A LOT OF COMPRESSED AIR FOR THOSE KEYBOARDS...

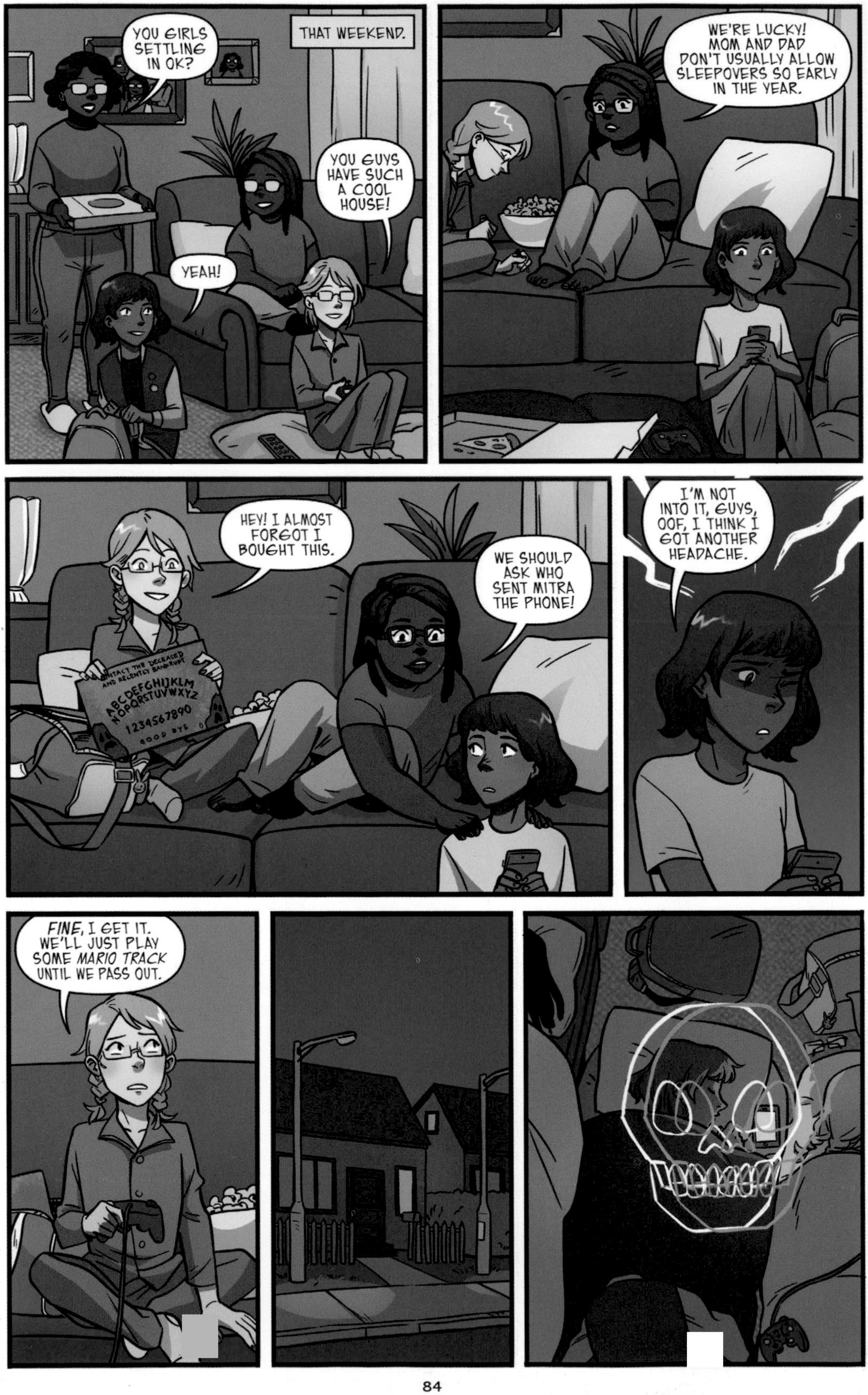

YOU GIRLS SETTLING IN OK?
THAT WEEKEND.
YOU GUYS HAVE SUCH A COOL HOUSE!
YEAH!
WE'RE LUCKY! MOM AND DAD DON'T USUALLY ALLOW SLEEPOVERS SO EARLY IN THE YEAR.
HEY! I ALMOST FORGOT I BOUGHT THIS.
CONTACT THE DECEASED AND RECENTLY BANKRUPT
ABCDEFGHIJKLM
NOPQRSTUVWXYZ
1234567890
GOOD BYE
WE SHOULD ASK WHO SENT MITRA THE PHONE!
I'M NOT INTO IT, GUYS, OOF, I THINK I GOT ANOTHER HEADACHE.
FINE, I GET IT. WE'LL JUST PLAY SOME MARIO TRACK UNTIL WE PASS OUT.

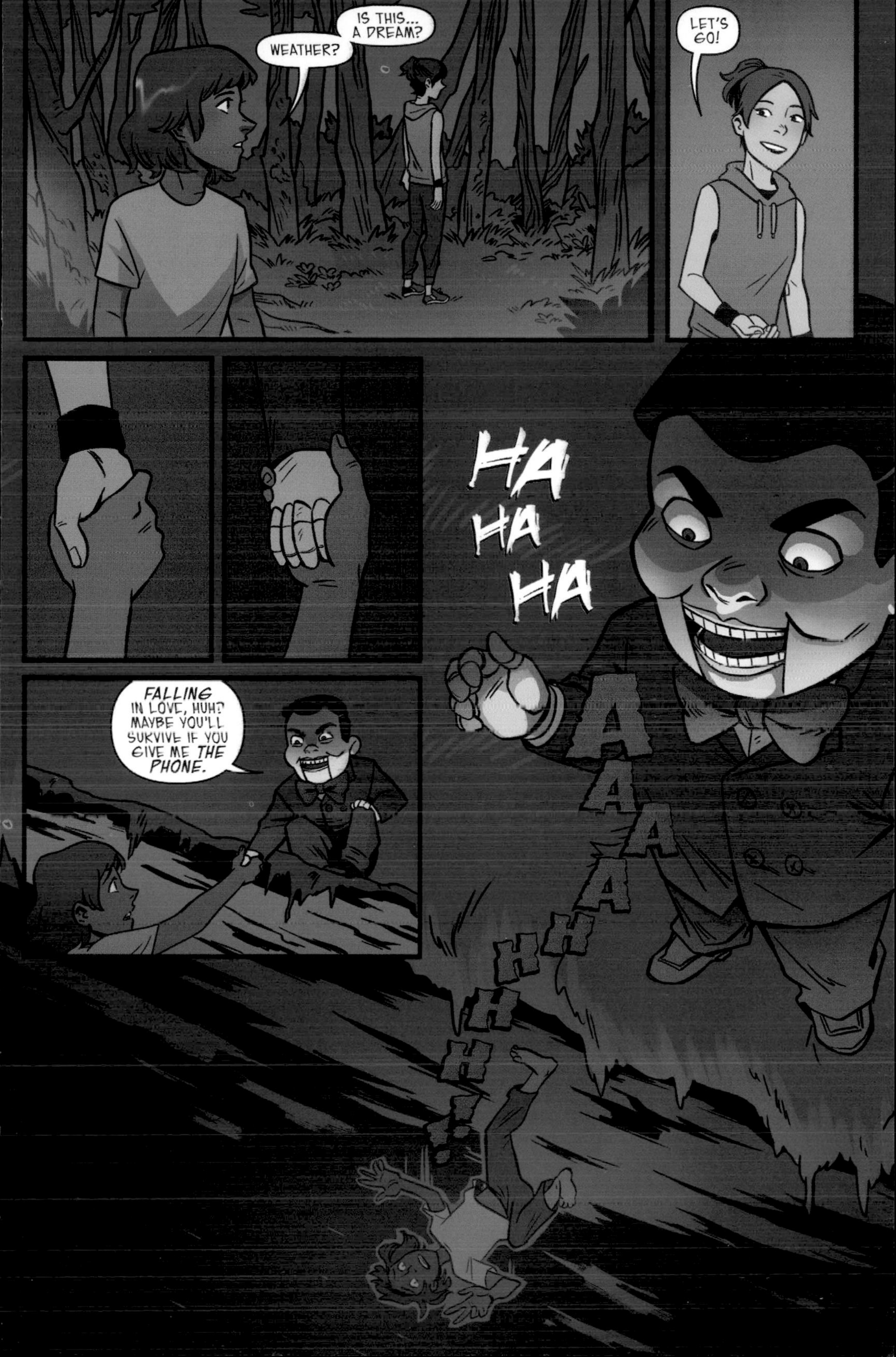
WEATHER?
IS THIS... A DREAM?
LET'S GO!
FALLING IN LOVE, HUH? MAYBE YOU'LL SURVIVE IF YOU GIVE ME THE PHONE.
HA HA HA
AAAAAHHHHH!

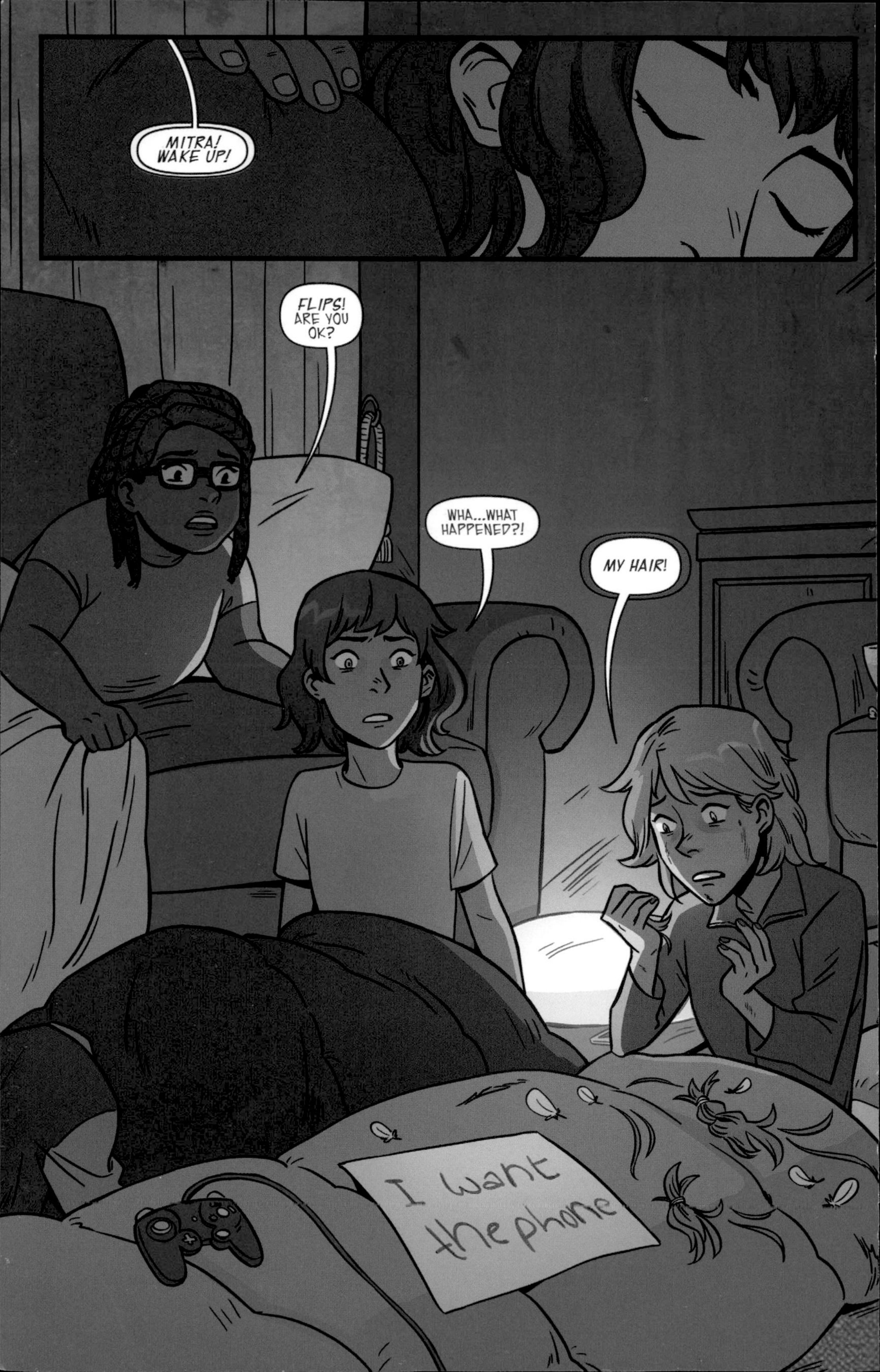
MITRA! WAKE UP!
FLIPS! ARE YOU OK?
WHA...WHAT HAPPENED?!
MY HAIR!
I want the phone

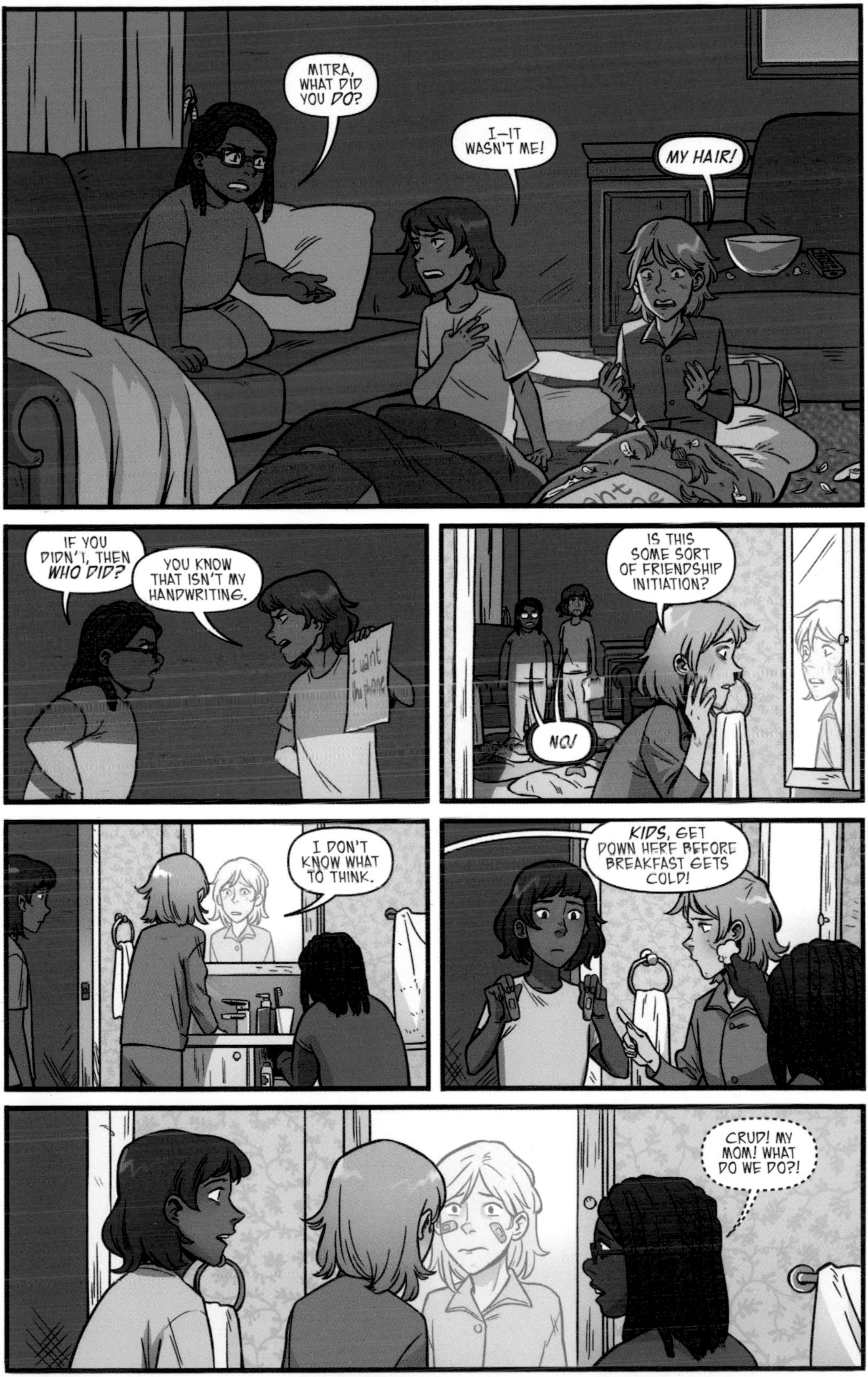
MITRA, WHAT DID YOU DO?
I—IT WASN'T ME!
MY HAIR!
IF YOU DIDN'T, THEN WHO DID?
YOU KNOW THAT ISN'T MY HANDWRITING.
I want the phone
IS THIS SOME SORT OF FRIENDSHIP INITIATION?
NO!
I DON'T KNOW WHAT TO THINK.
KIDS, GET DOWN HERE BEFORE BREAKFAST GETS COLD!
CRUD! MY MOM! WHAT DO WE DO?!

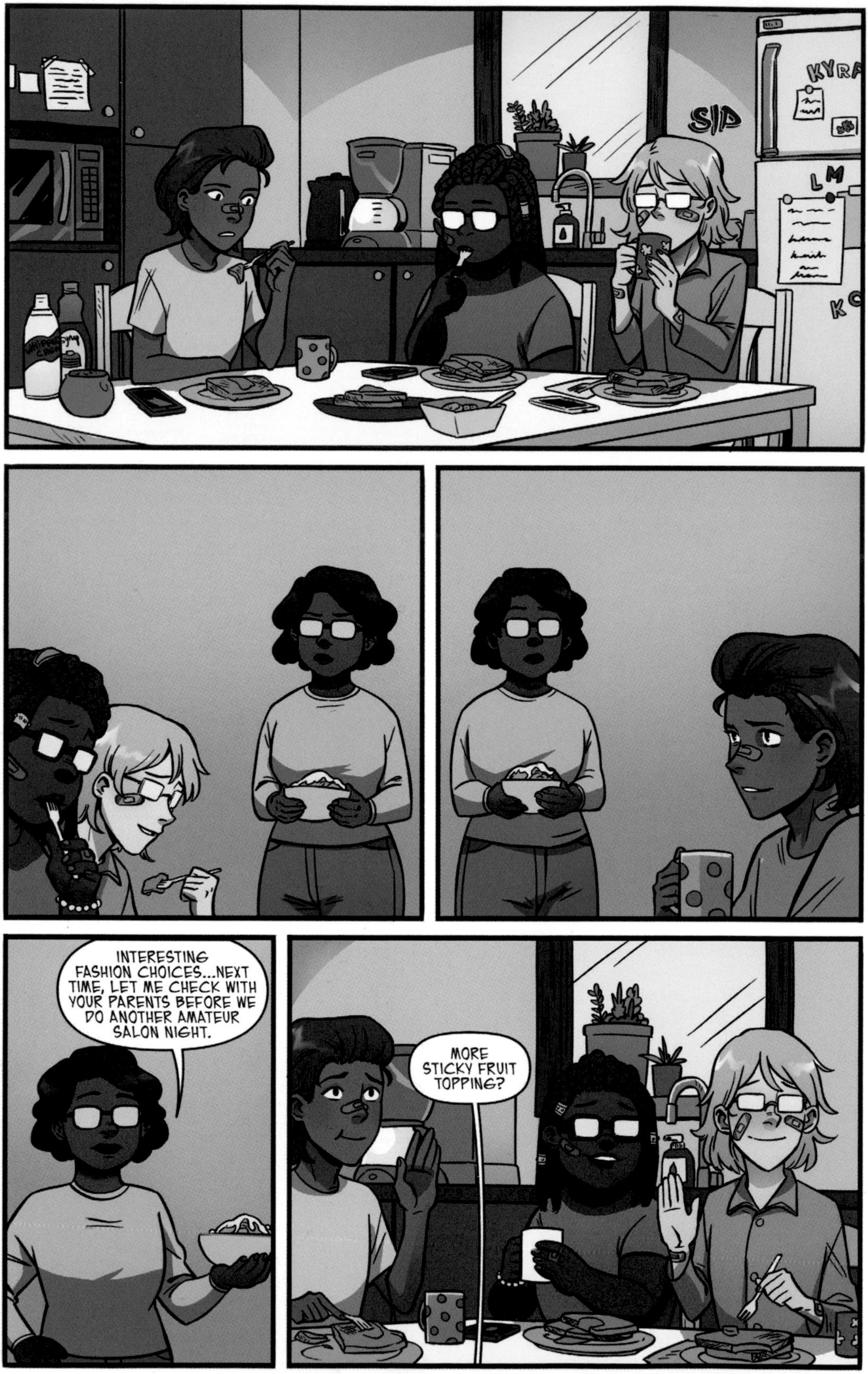
KYRA
SIP
LM
INTERESTING FASHION CHOICES...NEXT TIME, LET ME CHECK WITH YOUR PARENTS BEFORE WE DO ANOTHER AMATEUR SALON NIGHT.
MORE STICKY FRUIT TOPPING?

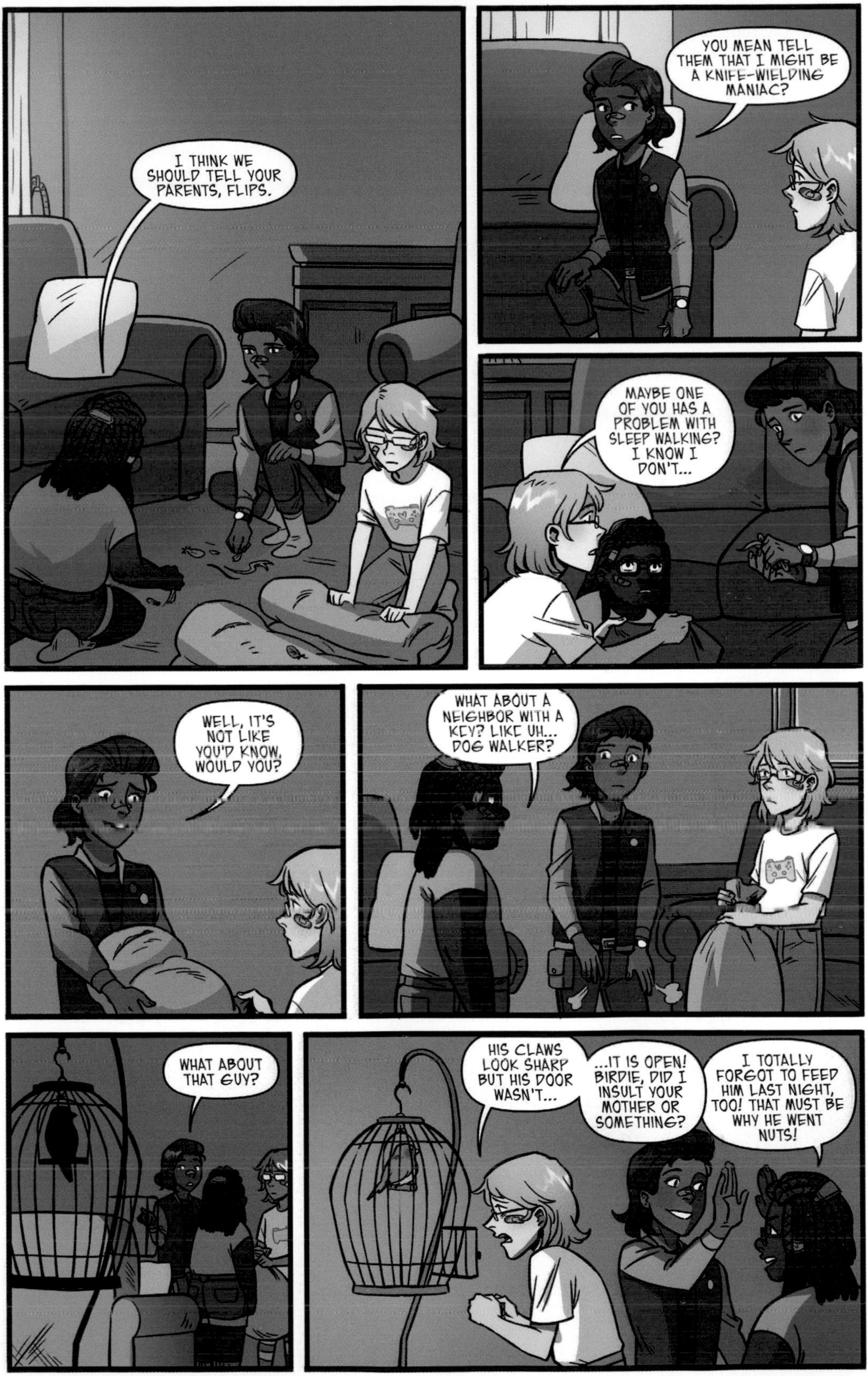
I THINK WE SHOULD TELL YOUR PARENTS, FLIPS.
YOU MEAN TELL THEM THAT I MIGHT BE A KNIFE-WIELDING MANIAC?
MAYBE ONE OF YOU HAS A PROBLEM WITH SLEEP WALKING? I KNOW I DON'T...
WELL, IT'S NOT LIKE YOU'D KNOW, WOULD YOU?
WHAT ABOUT A NEIGHBOR WITH A KEY? LIKE UH... DOG WALKER?
WHAT ABOUT THAT GUY?
HIS CLAWS LOOK SHARP BUT HIS DOOR WASN'T...
...IT IS OPEN! BIRDIE, DID I INSULT YOUR MOTHER OR SOMETHING?
I TOTALLY FORGOT TO FEED HIM LAST NIGHT, TOO! THAT MUST BE WHY HE WENT NUTS!

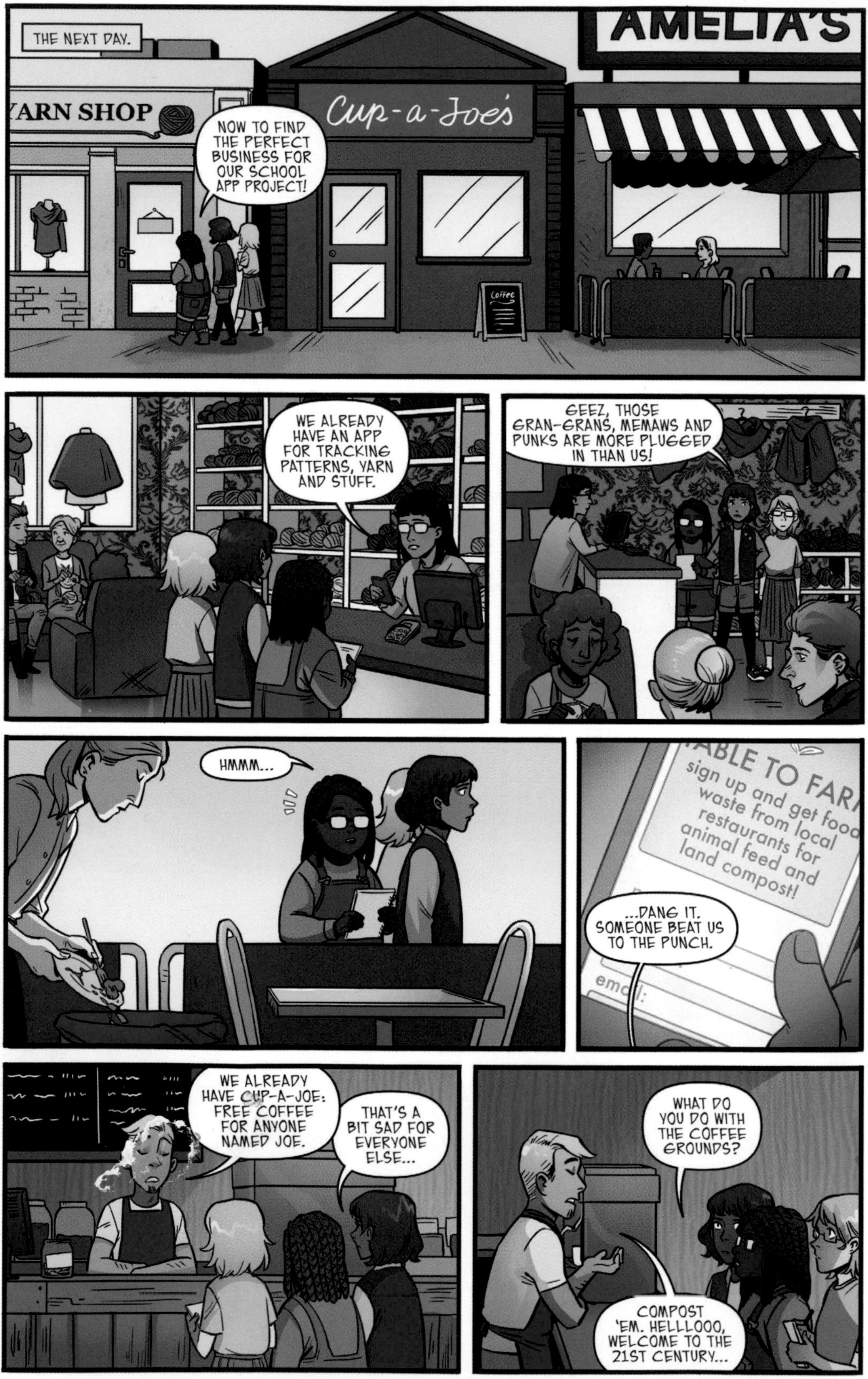
THE NEXT DAY.
AMELIA'S
YARN SHOP
Cup-a-Joe's
NOW TO FIND THE PERFECT BUSINESS FOR OUR SCHOOL APP PROJECT!
Coffee
WE ALREADY HAVE AN APP FOR TRACKING PATTERNS, YARN AND STUFF.
GEEZ, THOSE GRAN-GRANS, MEMAWS AND PUNKS ARE MORE PLUGGED IN THAN US!
HMMM...
ABLE TO FAR
sign up and get food waste from local restaurants for animal feed and land compost!
email:
...DANG IT. SOMEONE BEAT US TO THE PUNCH.
WE ALREADY HAVE CUP-A-JOE: FREE COFFEE FOR ANYONE NAMED JOE.
THAT'S A BIT SAD FOR EVERYONE ELSE...
WHAT DO YOU DO WITH THE COFFEE GROUNDS?
COMPOST 'EM. HELLLOOO, WELCOME TO THE 21ST CENTURY...

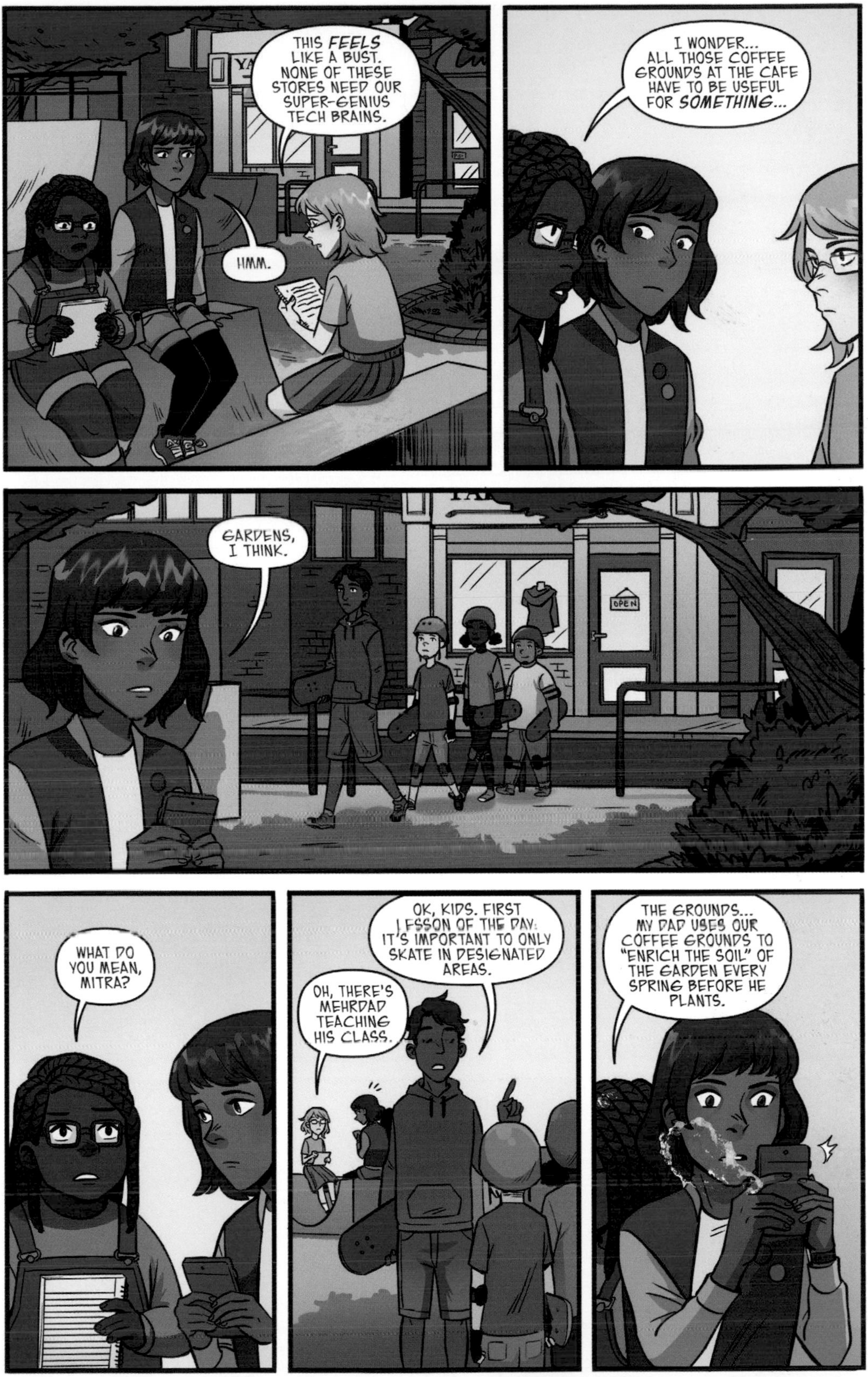
THIS FEELS LIKE A BUST. NONE OF THESE STORES NEED OUR SUPER-GENIUS TECH BRAINS.
HMM.
I WONDER... ALL THOSE COFFEE GROUNDS AT THE CAFE HAVE TO BE USEFUL FOR SOMETHING...
GARDENS, I THINK.
OPEN
WHAT DO YOU MEAN, MITRA?
OK, KIDS. FIRST LESSON OF THE DAY: IT'S IMPORTANT TO ONLY SKATE IN DESIGNATED AREAS.
OH, THERE'S MEHRDAD TEACHING HIS CLASS.
THE GROUNDS... MY DAD USES OUR COFFEE GROUNDS TO "ENRICH THE SOIL" OF THE GARDEN EVERY SPRING BEFORE HE PLANTS.

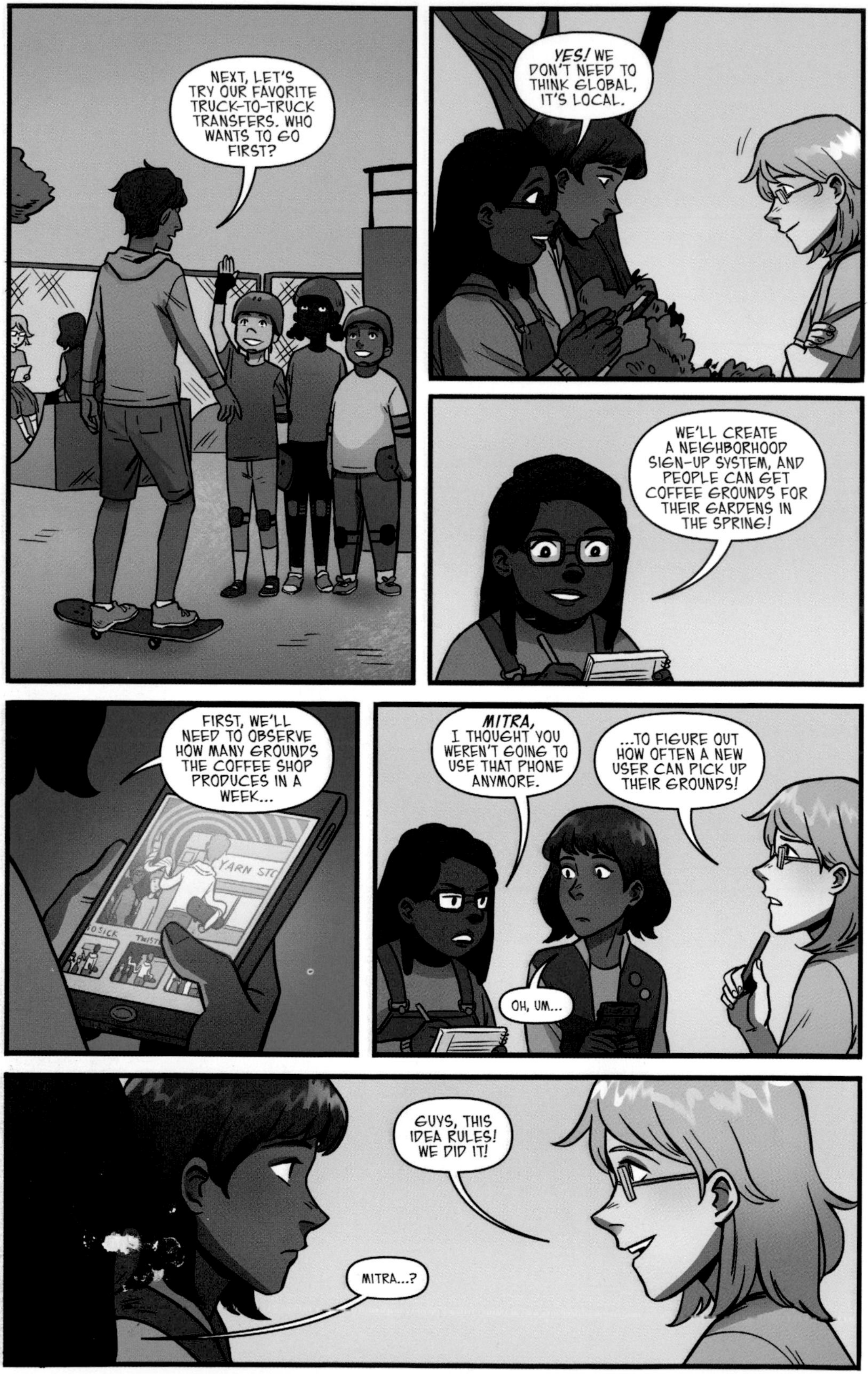
NEXT, LET'S TRY OUR FAVORITE TRUCK-TO-TRUCK TRANSFERS. WHO WANTS TO GO FIRST?
YES! WE DON'T NEED TO THINK GLOBAL, IT'S LOCAL.
WE'LL CREATE A NEIGHBORHOOD SIGN-UP SYSTEM, AND PEOPLE CAN GET COFFEE GROUNDS FOR THEIR GARDENS IN THE SPRING!
FIRST, WE'LL NEED TO OBSERVE HOW MANY GROUNDS THE COFFEE SHOP PRODUCES IN A WEEK...
YARN STO
MITRA, I THOUGHT YOU WEREN'T GOING TO USE THAT PHONE ANYMORE.
...TO FIGURE OUT HOW OFTEN A NEW USER CAN PICK UP THEIR GROUNDS!
OH, UM...
GUYS, THIS IDEA RULES! WE DID IT!
MITRA...?

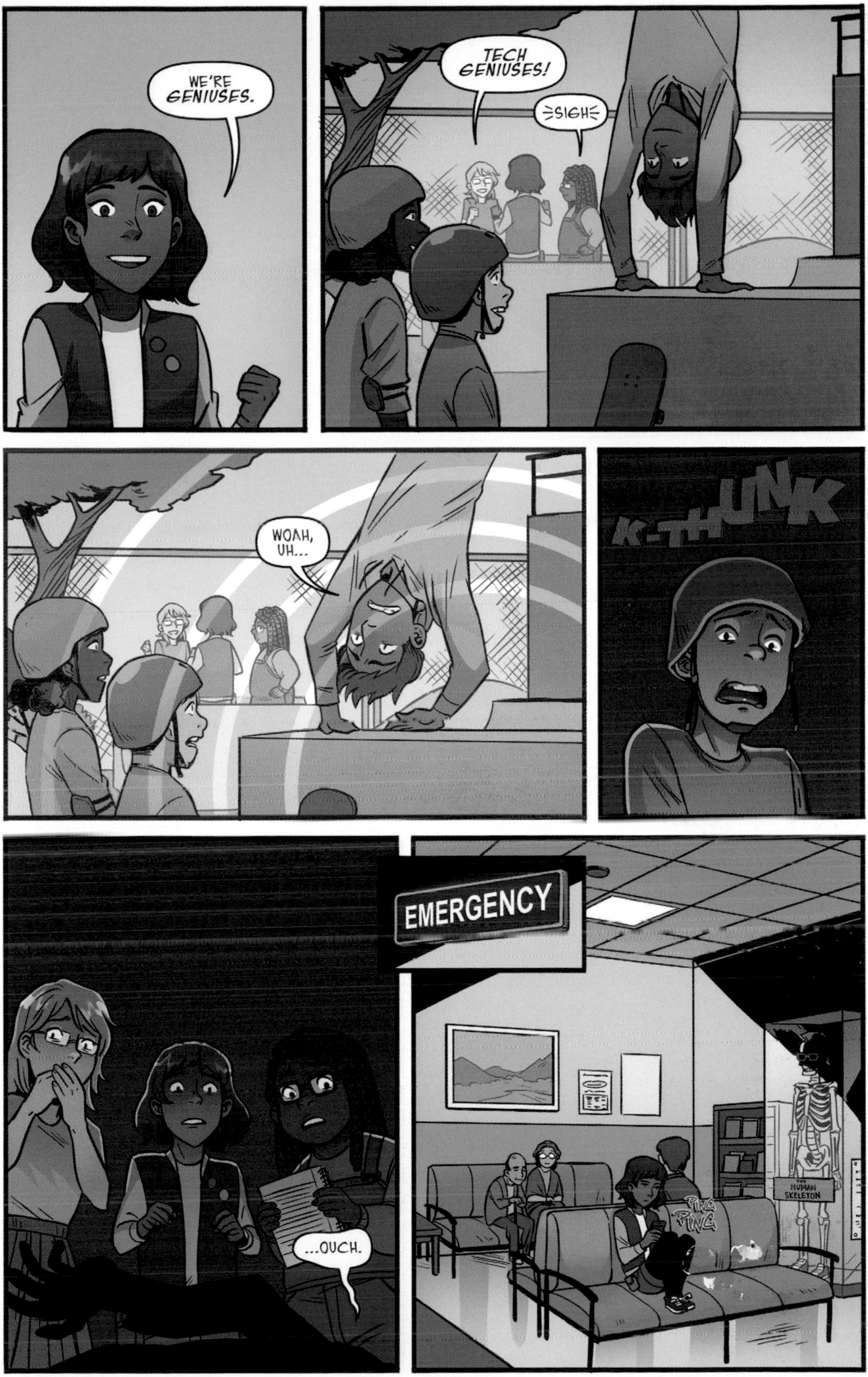
WE'RE GENIUSES.
TECH GENIUSES!
SIGH
WOAH, UH...
K-THUNK
...OUCH.
EMERGENCY
PING PING
HUMAN SKELETON

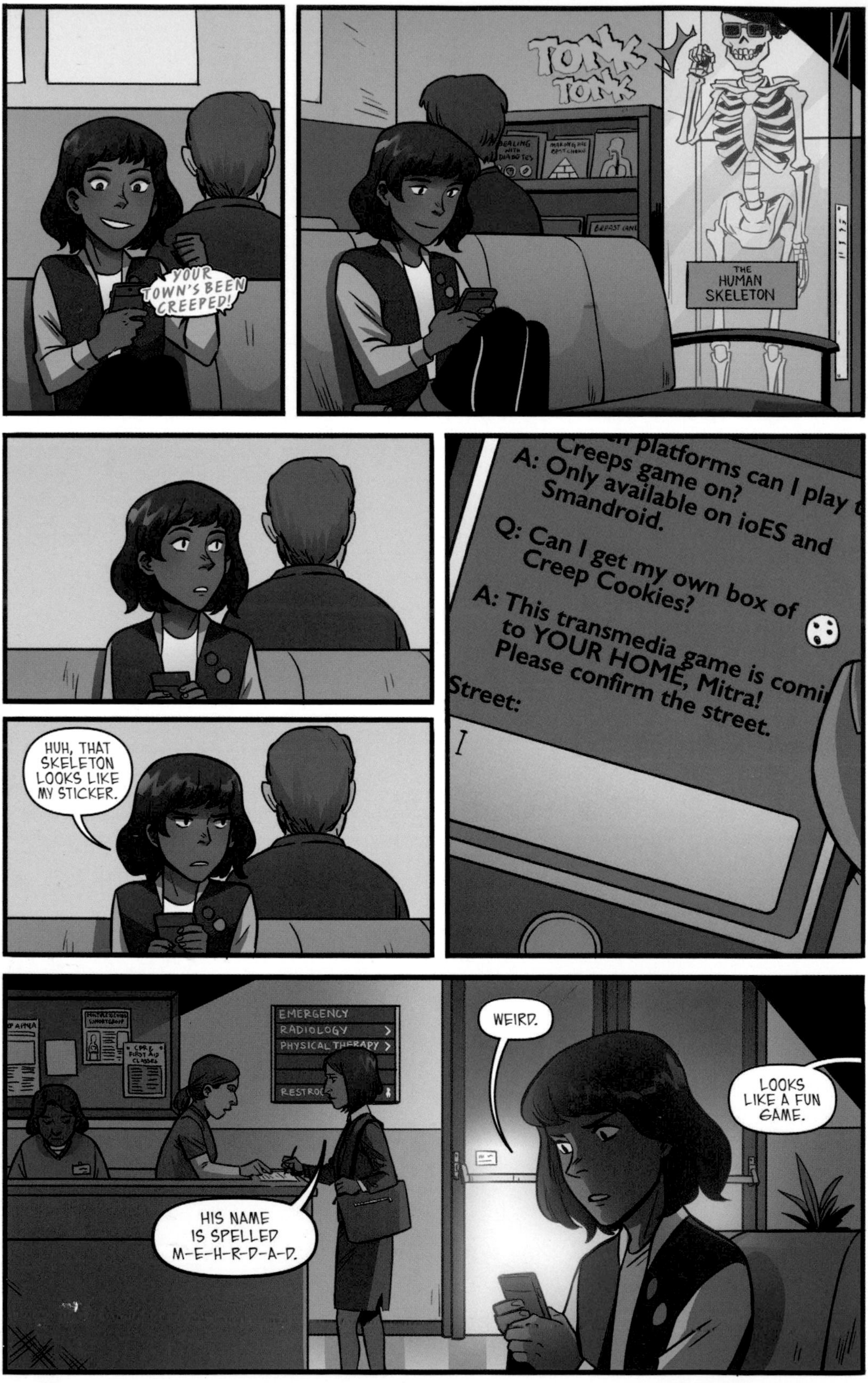
YOUR TOWN'S BEEN CREEPED!
TONK TONK
DEALING WITH DIABETES
THE HUMAN SKELETON
platforms can I play
Creeps game on?
A: Only available on ioES and Smandroid.
Q: Can I get my own box of Creep Cookies?
A: This transmedia game is comi
to YOUR HOME, Mitra!
Please confirm the street.
Street:
HUH, THAT SKELETON LOOKS LIKE MY STICKER.
EMERGENCY
RADIOLOGY
PHYSICAL THERAPY
HIS NAME IS SPELLED M-E-H-R-D-A-D.
WEIRD.
LOOKS LIKE A FUN GAME.

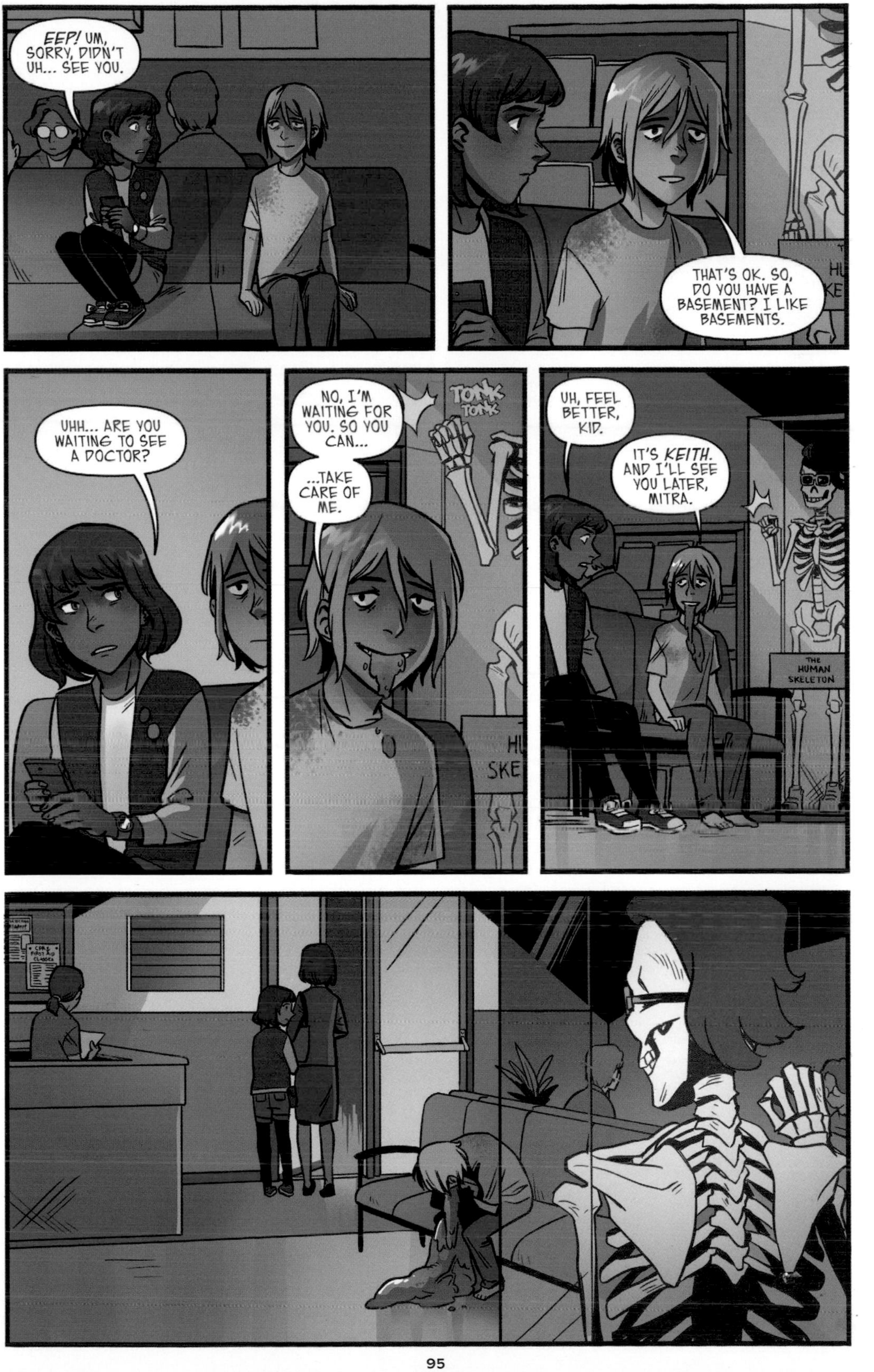
EEP! UM, SORRY, DIDN'T UH... SEE YOU.
THAT'S OK. SO, DO YOU HAVE A BASEMENT? I LIKE BASEMENTS.
THE HUMAN SKELETON
UHH... ARE YOU WAITING TO SEE A DOCTOR?
NO, I'M WAITING FOR YOU. SO YOU CAN...
...TAKE CARE OF ME.
TONK TONK
UH, FEEL BETTER, KID.
IT'S KEITH. AND I'LL SEE YOU LATER, MITRA.
THE HUMAN SKELETON

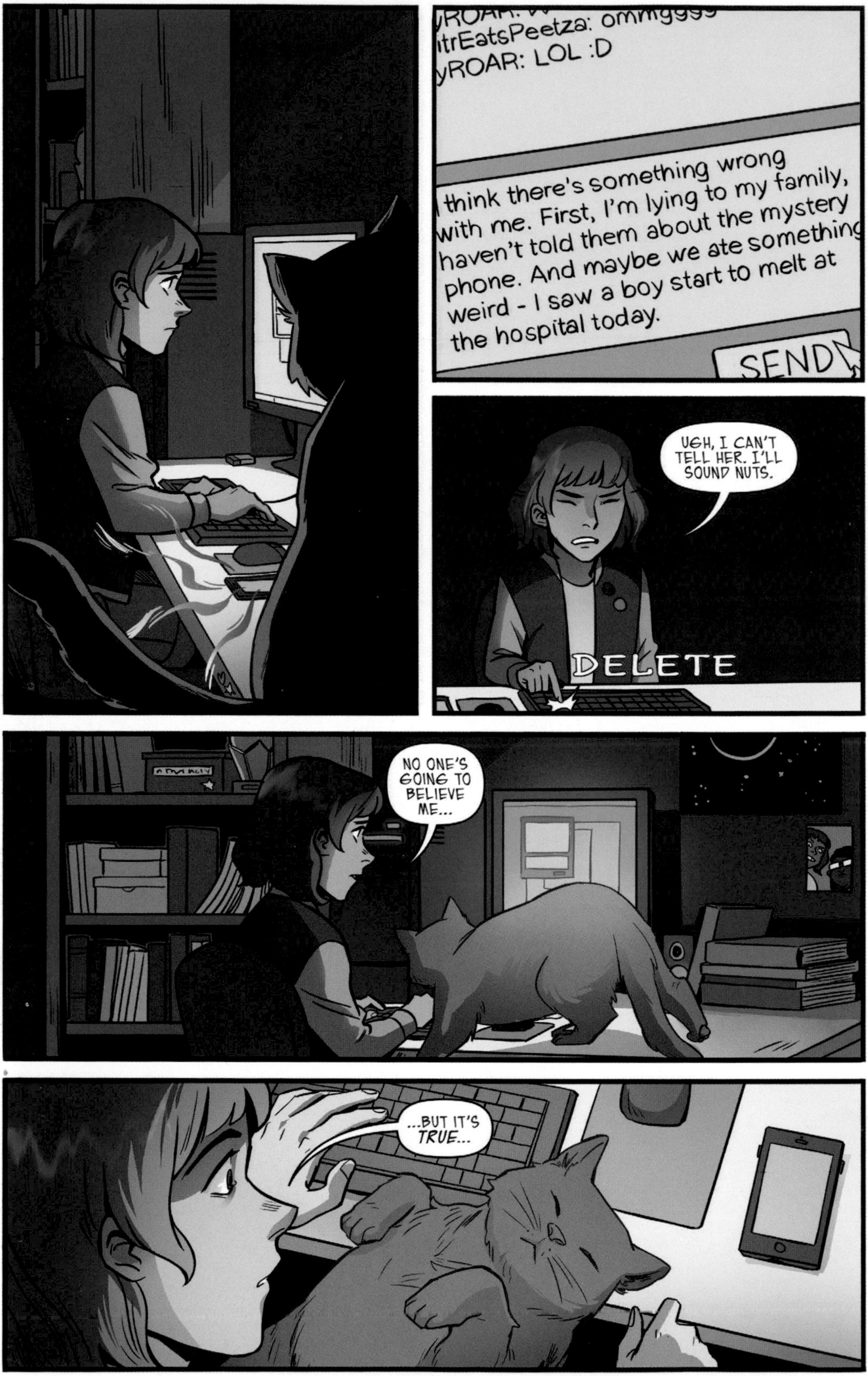
yROAR: W...
itrEatsPeetza: ommggg
yROAR: LOL :D
I think there's something wrong with me. First, I'm lying to my family, haven't told them about the mystery phone. And maybe we ate something weird - I saw a boy start to melt at the hospital today.
SEND
UGH, I CAN'T TELL HER. I'LL SOUND NUTS.
DELETE
NO ONE'S GOING TO BELIEVE ME...
...BUT IT'S *TRUE*...

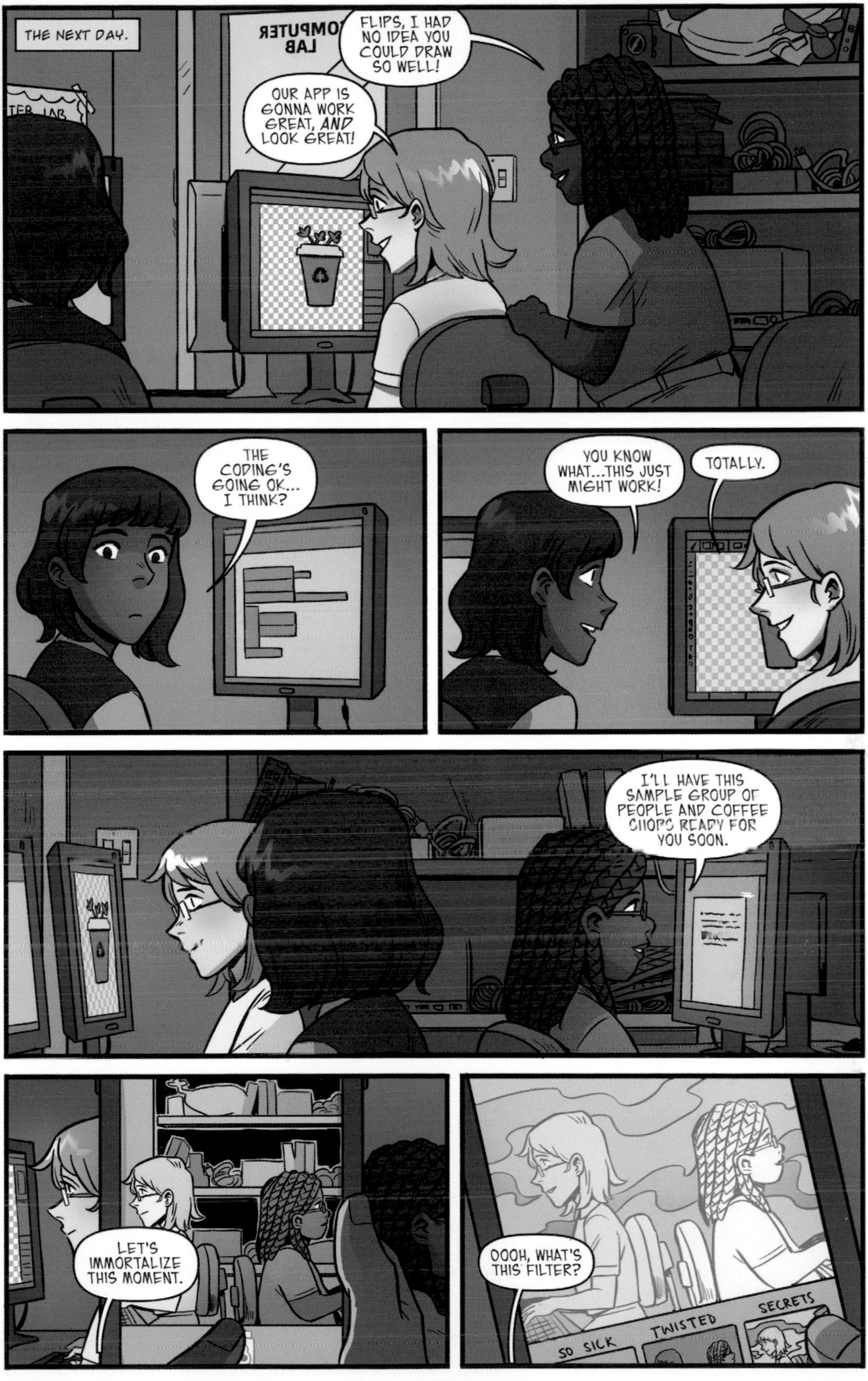
THE NEXT DAY.
FLIPS, I HAD NO IDEA YOU COULD DRAW SO WELL!
OUR APP IS GONNA WORK GREAT, AND LOOK GREAT!
THE CODING'S GOING OK... I THINK?
YOU KNOW WHAT...THIS JUST MIGHT WORK!
TOTALLY.
I'LL HAVE THIS SAMPLE GROUP OF PEOPLE AND COFFEE SHOPS READY FOR YOU SOON.
LET'S IMMORTALIZE THIS MOMENT.
OOOH, WHAT'S THIS FILTER?
SO SICK
TWISTED
SECRETS

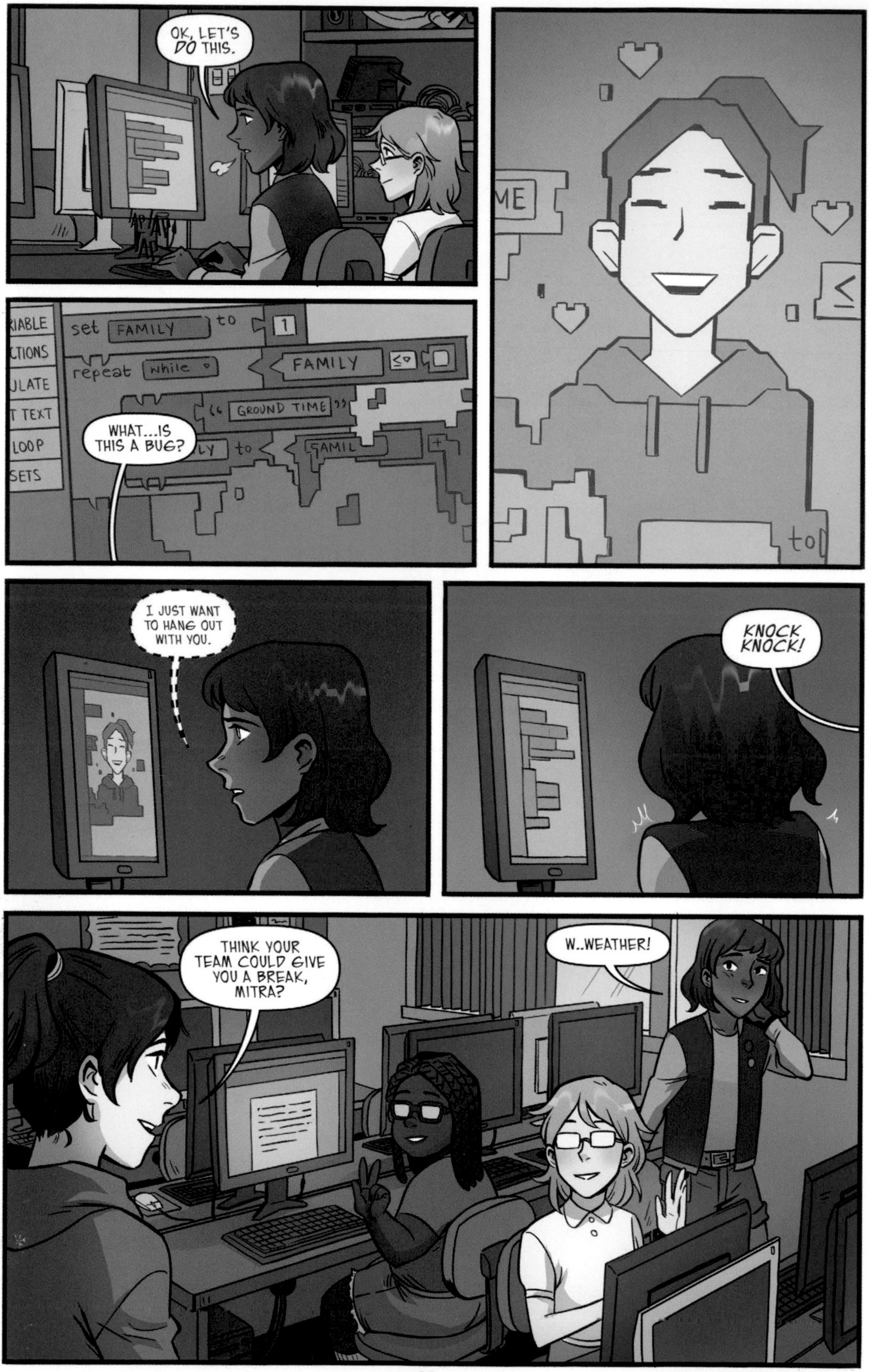
OK, LET'S DO THIS.
set FAMILY to 1
repeat while FAMILY ≤
"GROUND TIME"
WHAT...IS THIS A BUG?
ME
to
I JUST WANT TO HANG OUT WITH YOU.
KNOCK KNOCK!
THINK YOUR TEAM COULD GIVE YOU A BREAK, MITRA?
W..WEATHER!

COMPUTER LAB

COMPUTER LAB ETIQUETTE

WE WERE IN A GROOVE, BUT MAYBE—

TAKE A BREAK, BUT GET OUTTA HERE...I NEED *COMPLETE* SILENCE.

JOHN

SO.... HOW IS YOUR SPORTS VIDEO PROJECT GOING?

GREAT, *MORE* THAN GREAT.

YOU KNOW HOW PEOPLE REACT WHEN THE BALL IS COMING TOWARDS THEM, BUT THERE'S ALSO THIS RUSH OF PLAYERS...?

UH-HUH.

I GOT THAT ON FILM, THE SMALL TICKS AND WAYS THEIR FACES CHANGE.

YEAH...KINDA LIKE HOW YOUR FACE LOOKS RIGHT NOW.

I JUST WANT TO HANG OUT WITH YOU.

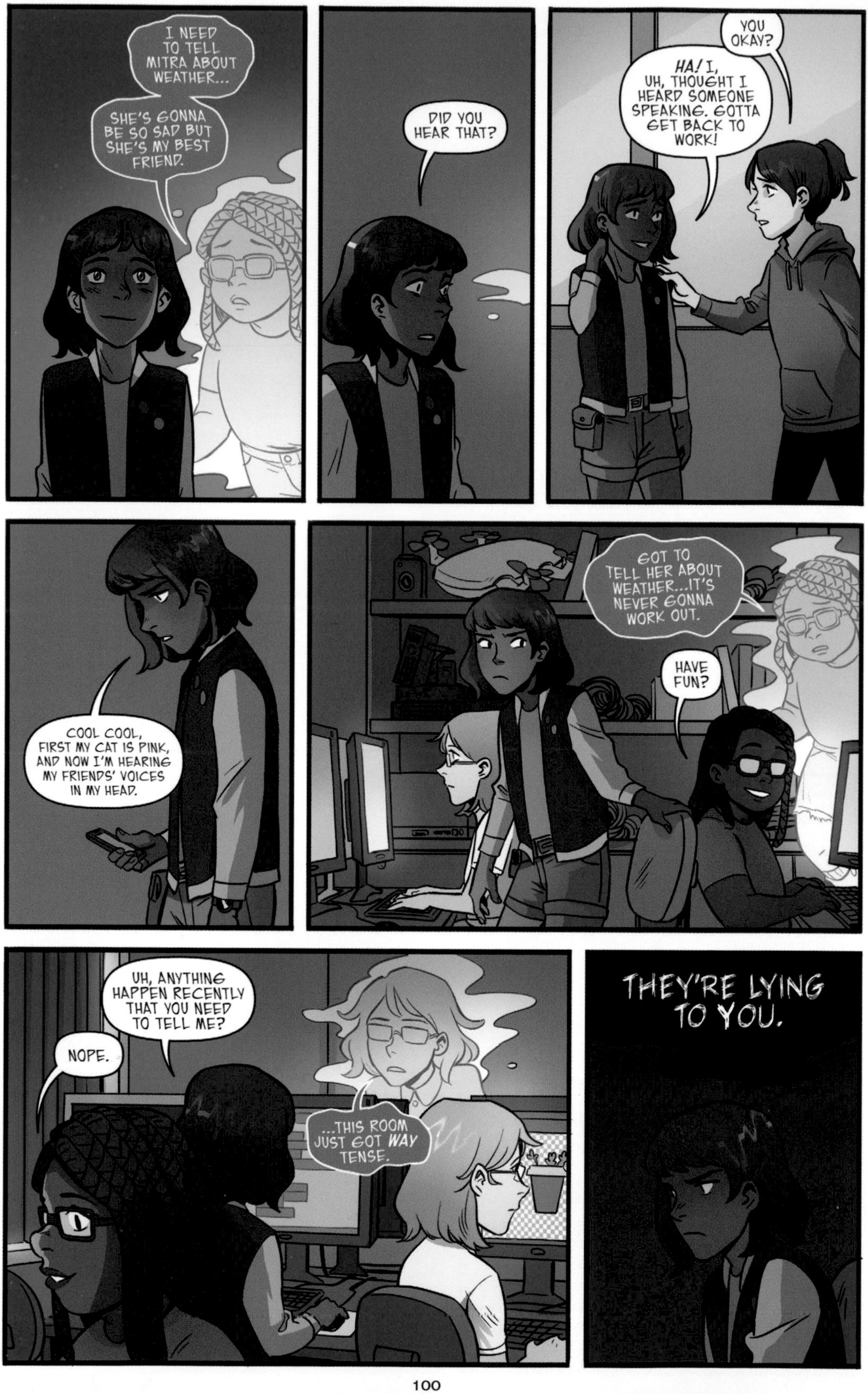
I NEED TO TELL MITRA ABOUT WEATHER...
SHE'S GONNA BE SO SAD BUT SHE'S MY BEST FRIEND.
DID YOU HEAR THAT?
YOU OKAY?
HA! I, UH, THOUGHT I HEARD SOMEONE SPEAKING. GOTTA GET BACK TO WORK!
COOL COOL, FIRST MY CAT IS PINK, AND NOW I'M HEARING MY FRIENDS' VOICES IN MY HEAD.
GOT TO TELL HER ABOUT WEATHER...IT'S NEVER GONNA WORK OUT.
HAVE FUN?
UH, ANYTHING HAPPEN RECENTLY THAT YOU NEED TO TELL ME?
NOPE.
...THIS ROOM JUST GOT WAY TENSE.
THEY'RE LYING TO YOU.

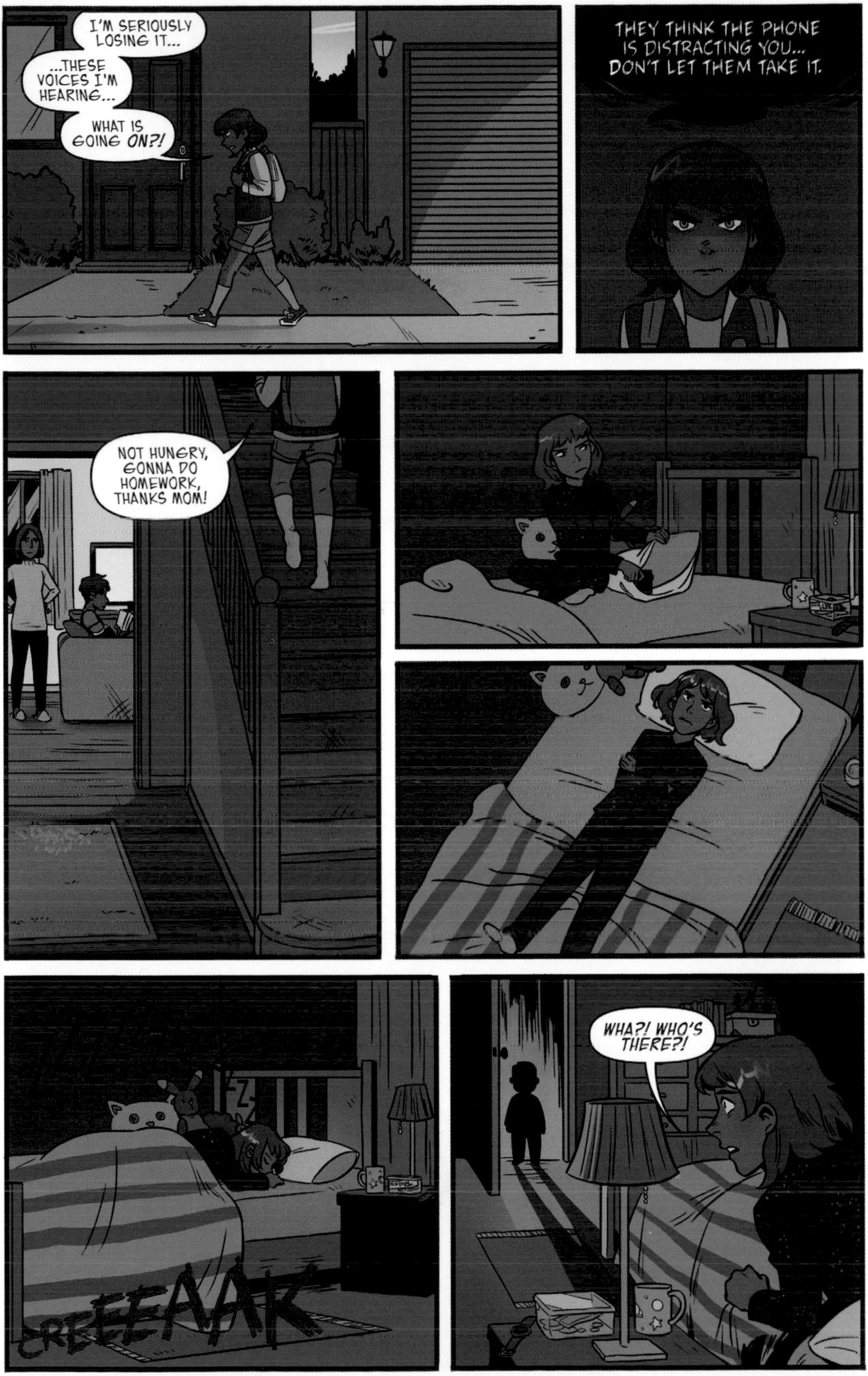

I'M SERIOUSLY LOSING IT...
...THESE VOICES I'M HEARING...
WHAT IS GOING ON?!
THEY THINK THE PHONE IS DISTRACTING YOU... DON'T LET THEM TAKE IT.
NOT HUNGRY, GONNA DO HOMEWORK, THANKS MOM!
ZZ
CREEEAAK
WHA?! WHO'S THERE?!

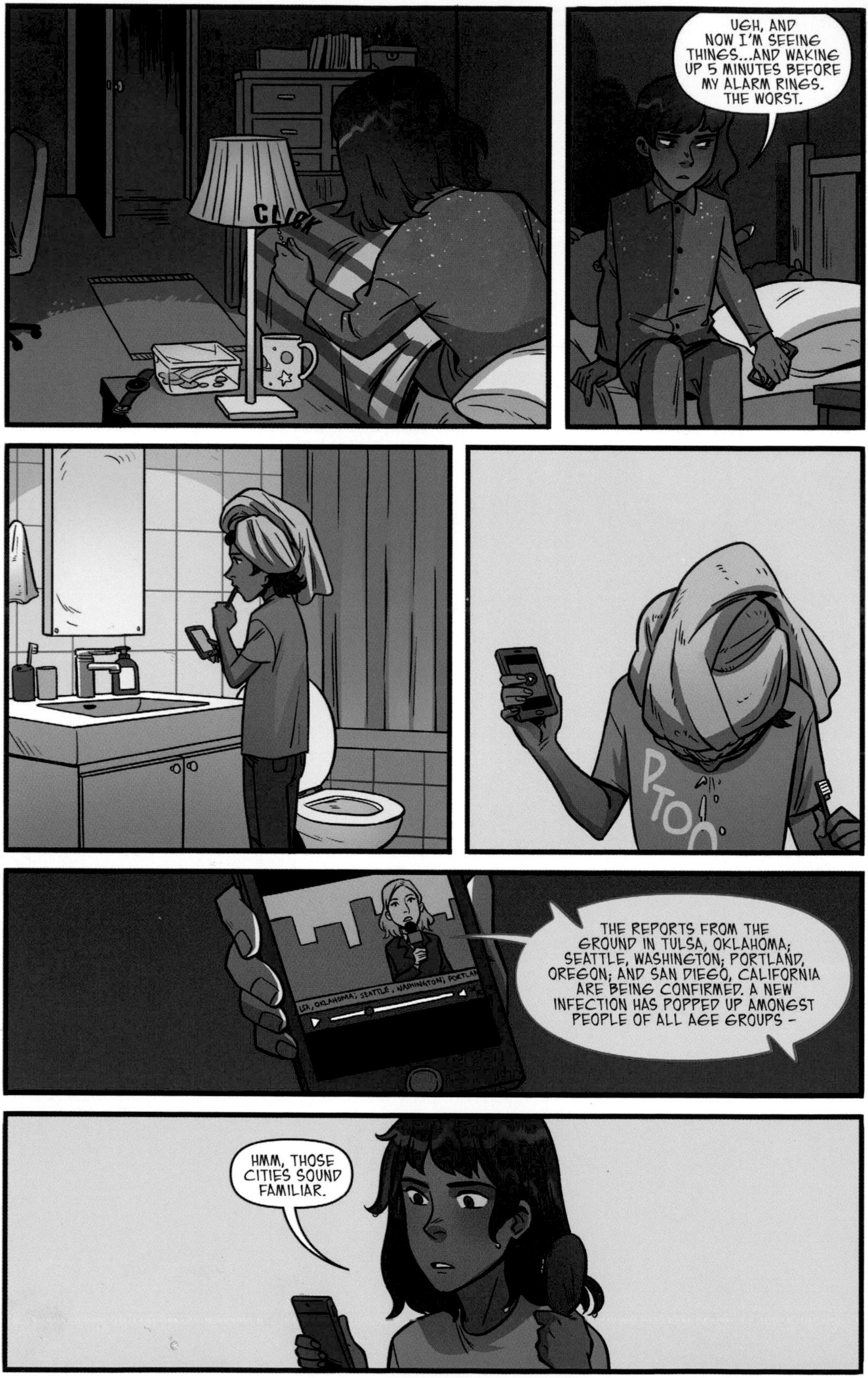
CLICK
UGH, AND NOW I'M SEEING THINGS...AND WAKING UP 5 MINUTES BEFORE MY ALARM RINGS. THE WORST.
PTOO
THE REPORTS FROM THE GROUND IN TULSA, OKLAHOMA; SEATTLE, WASHINGTON; PORTLAND, OREGON; AND SAN DIEGO, CALIFORNIA ARE BEING CONFIRMED. A NEW INFECTION HAS POPPED UP AMONGST PEOPLE OF ALL AGE GROUPS -
HMM, THOSE CITIES SOUND FAMILIAR.

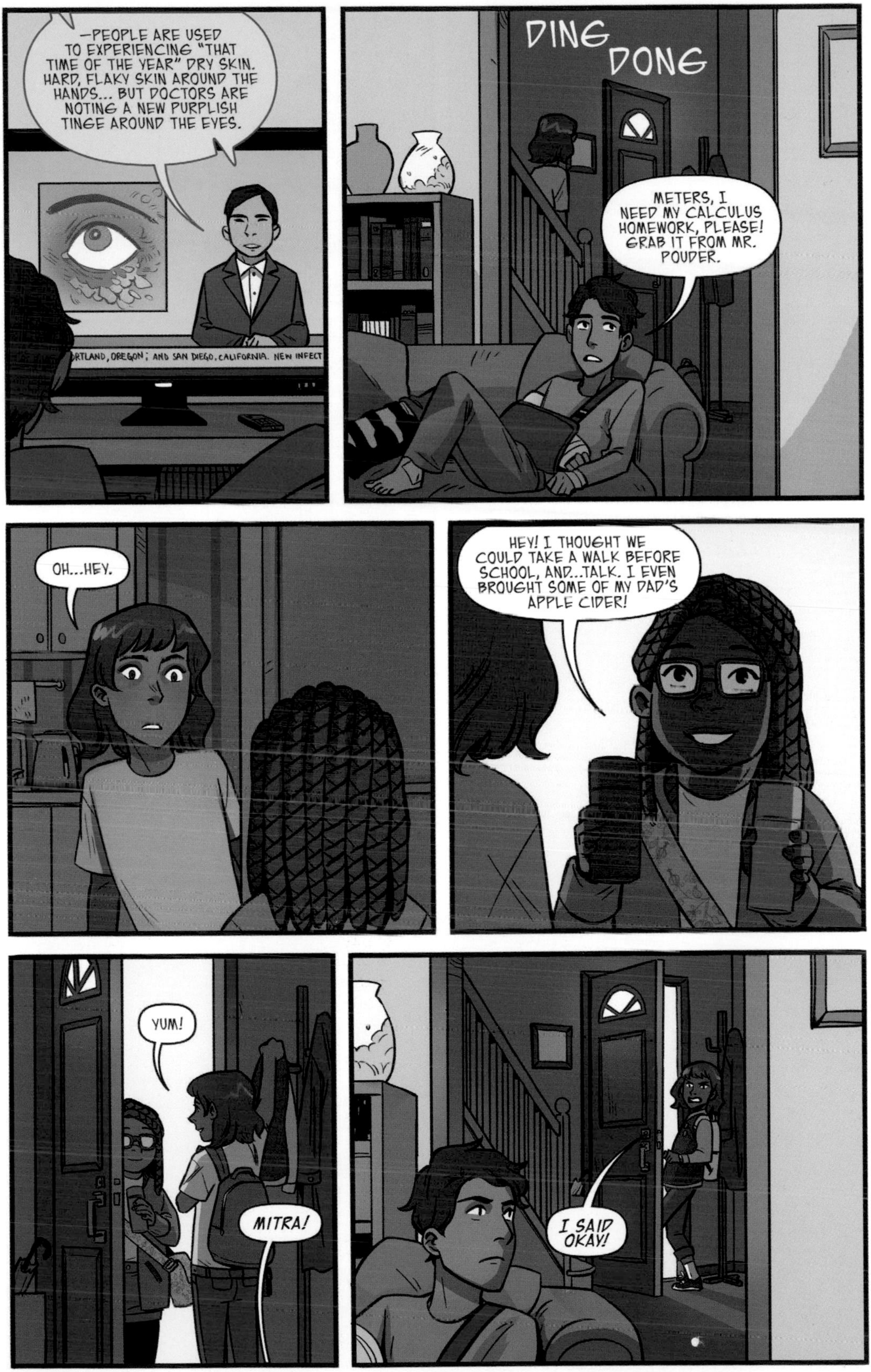
—PEOPLE ARE USED TO EXPERIENCING "THAT TIME OF THE YEAR" DRY SKIN. HARD, FLAKY SKIN AROUND THE HANDS... BUT DOCTORS ARE NOTING A NEW PURPLISH TINGE AROUND THE EYES.
RTLAND, OREGON; AND SAN DIEGO, CALIFORNIA. NEW INFECT
DING DONG
METERS, I NEED MY CALCULUS HOMEWORK, PLEASE! GRAB IT FROM MR. POUDER.
OH...HEY.
HEY! I THOUGHT WE COULD TAKE A WALK BEFORE SCHOOL, AND...TALK. I EVEN BROUGHT SOME OF MY DAD'S APPLE CIDER!
YUM!
MITRA!
I SAID OKAY!

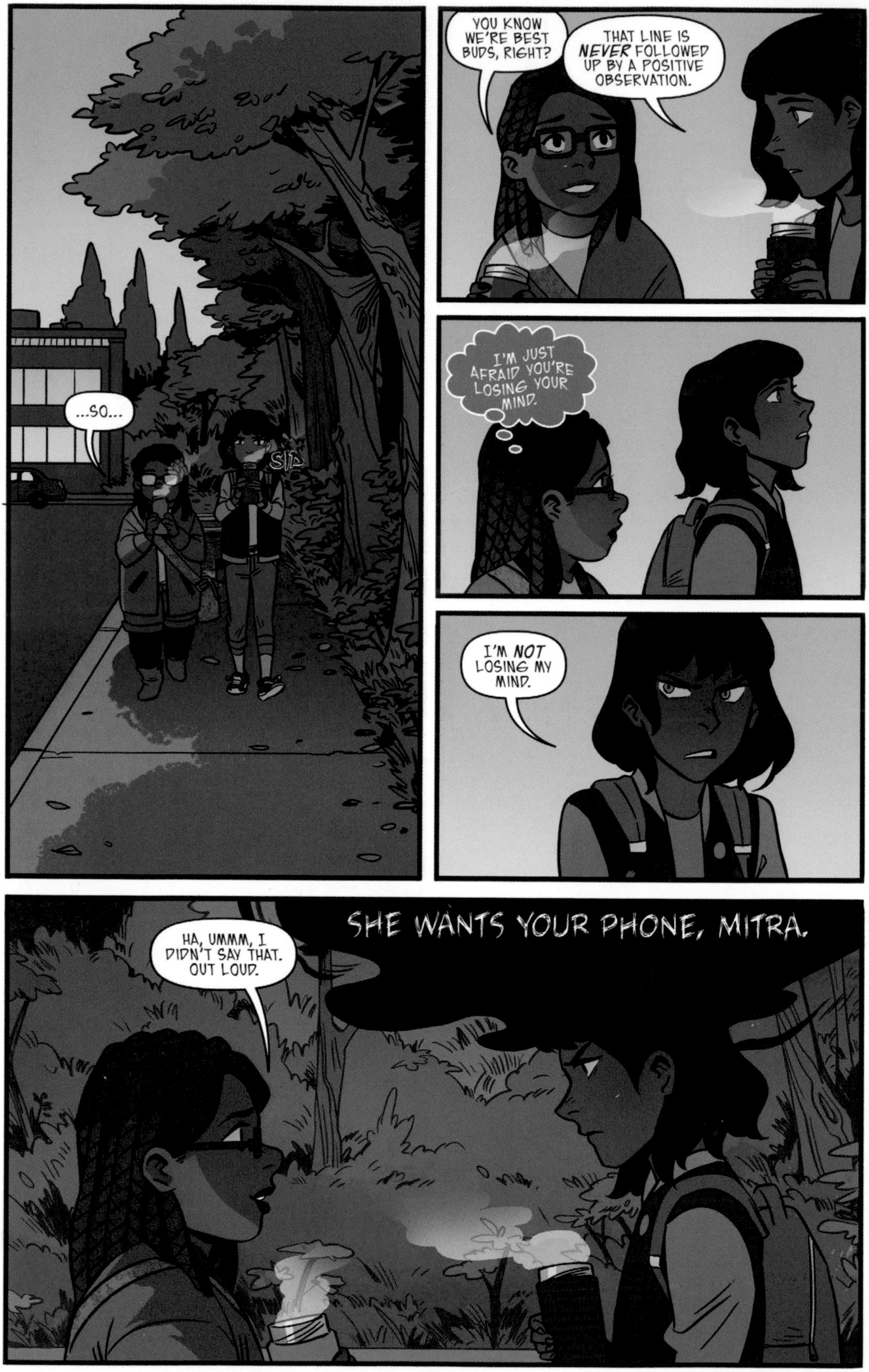
...SO...
SIP
YOU KNOW WE'RE BEST BUDS, RIGHT?
THAT LINE IS NEVER FOLLOWED UP BY A POSITIVE OBSERVATION.
I'M JUST AFRAID YOU'RE LOSING YOUR MIND.
I'M NOT LOSING MY MIND.
HA, UMMM, I DIDN'T SAY THAT. OUT LOUD.
SHE WANTS YOUR PHONE, MITRA.

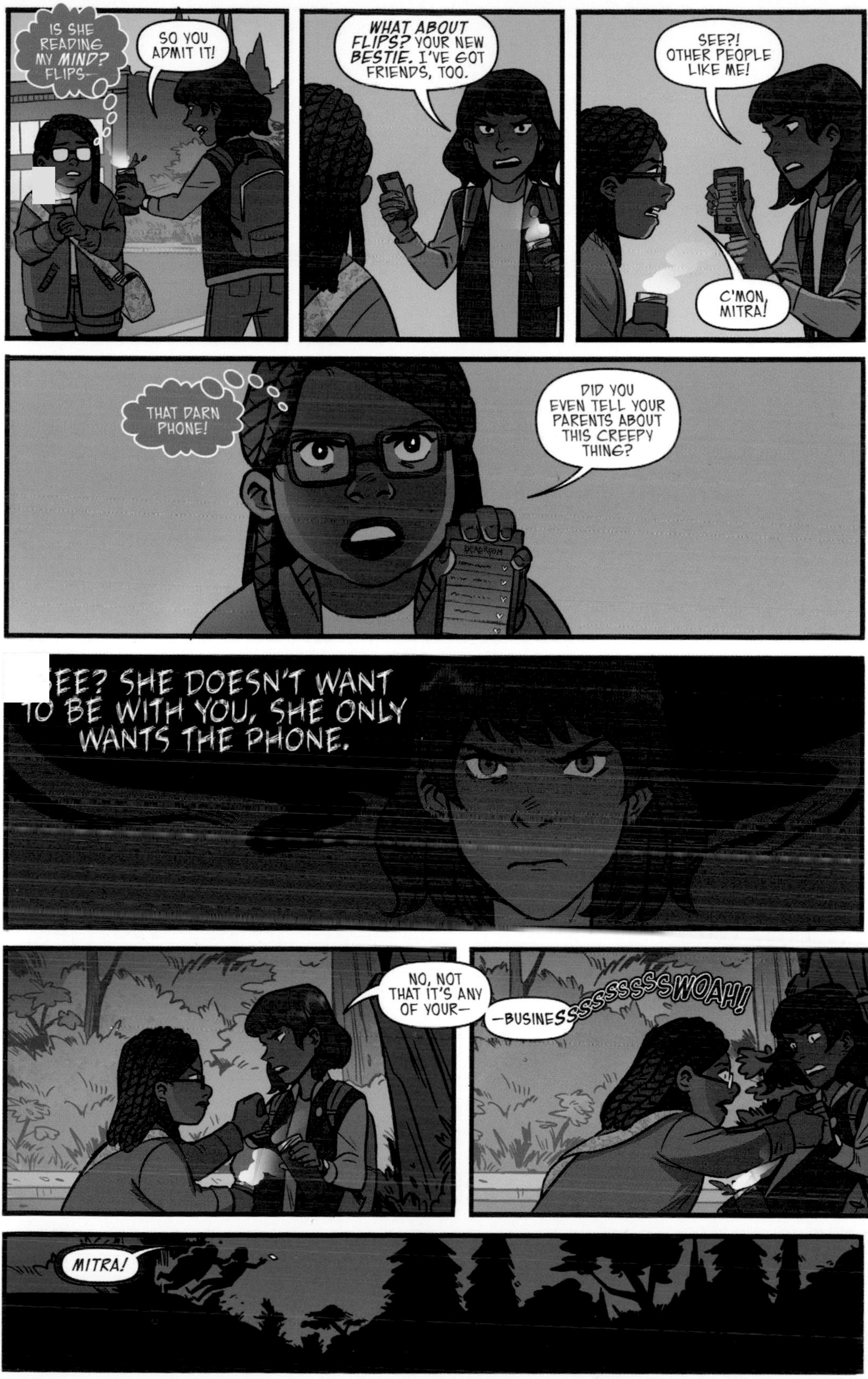
IS SHE READING MY MIND? FLIPS—
SO YOU ADMIT IT!
WHAT ABOUT FLIPS? YOUR NEW BESTIE. I'VE GOT FRIENDS, TOO.
SEE?! OTHER PEOPLE LIKE ME!
C'MON, MITRA!
THAT DARN PHONE!
DID YOU EVEN TELL YOUR PARENTS ABOUT THIS CREEPY THING?
SEE? SHE DOESN'T WANT TO BE WITH YOU, SHE ONLY WANTS THE PHONE.
NO, NOT THAT IT'S ANY OF YOUR—
—BUSINESSSSSSSSWOAH!
MITRA!

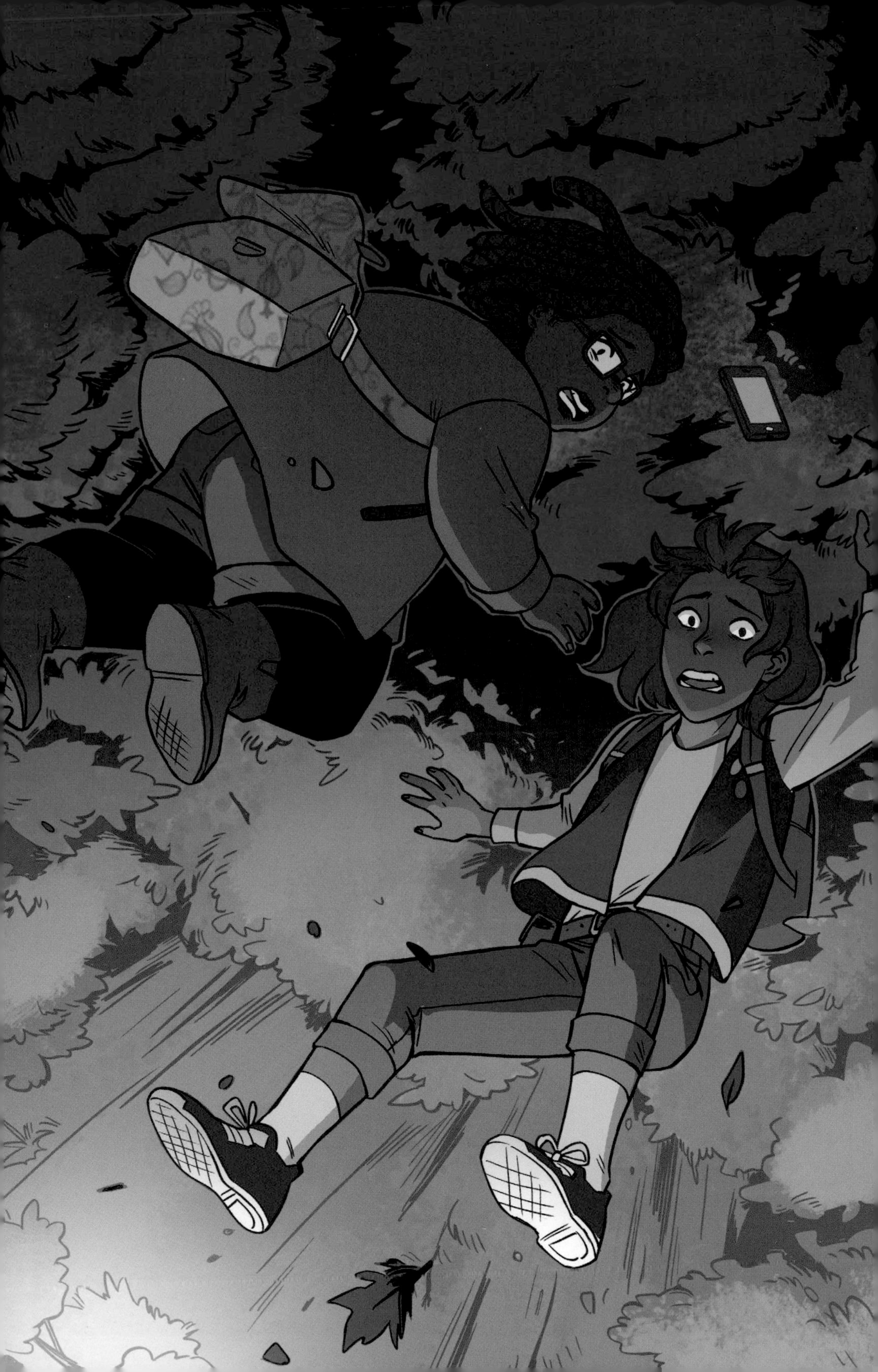

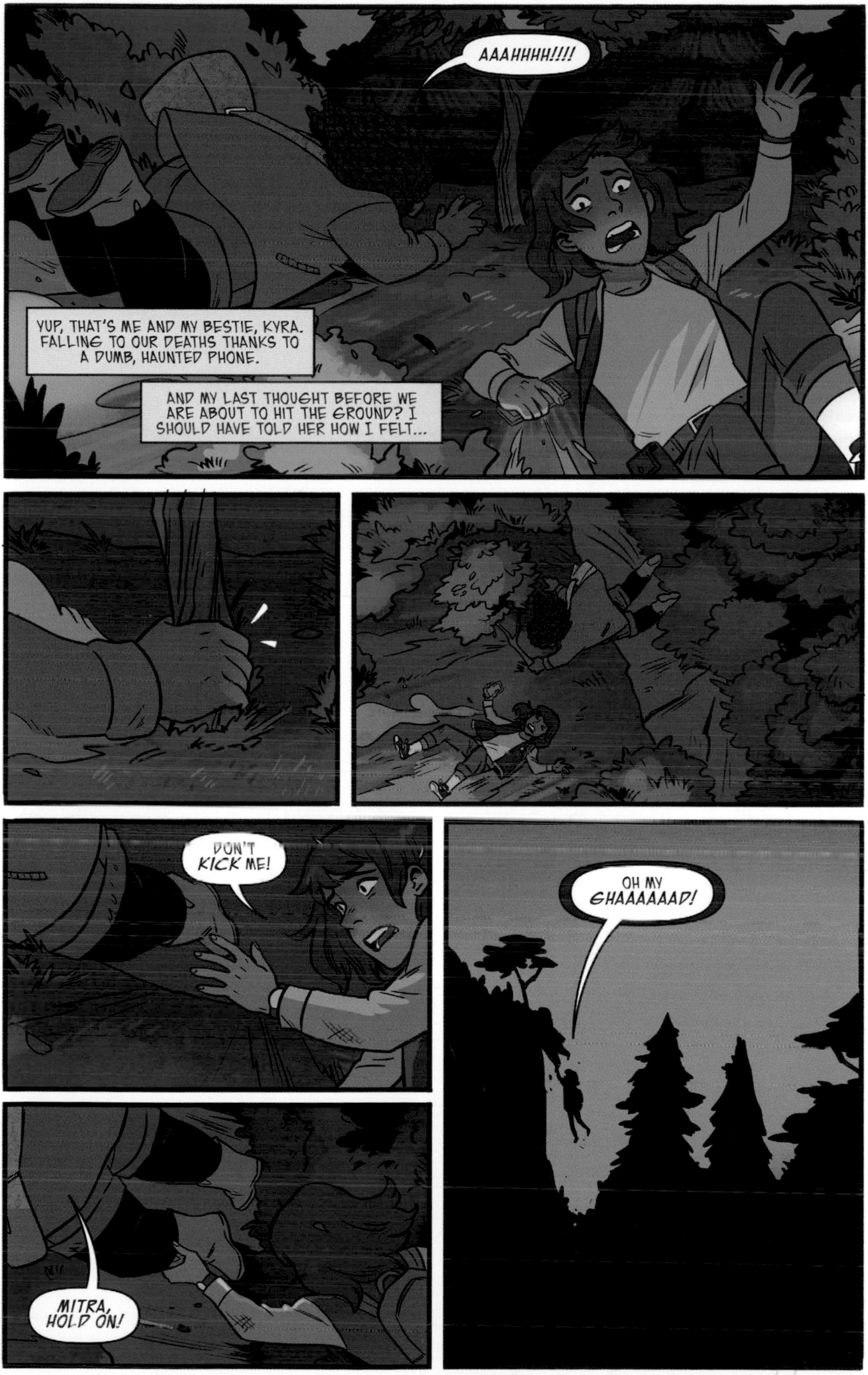
AAAHHHH!!!!
YUP, THAT'S ME AND MY BESTIE, KYRA. FALLING TO OUR DEATHS THANKS TO A DUMB, HAUNTED PHONE.
AND MY LAST THOUGHT BEFORE WE ARE ABOUT TO HIT THE GROUND? I SHOULD HAVE TOLD HER HOW I FELT...
DON'T KICK ME!
OH MY GHAAAAAAD!
MITRA, HOLD ON!

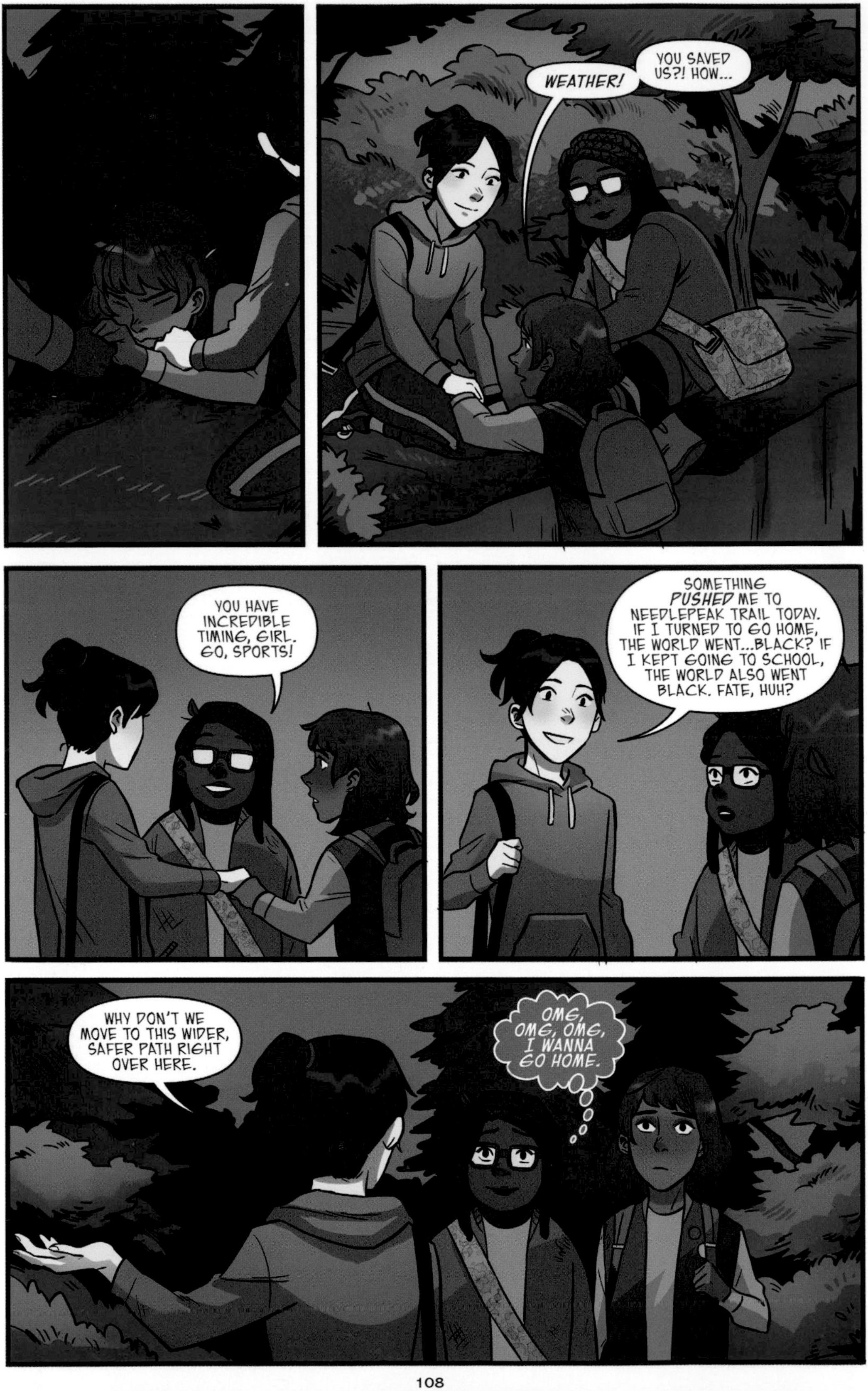
WEATHER!
YOU SAVED US?! HOW...
YOU HAVE INCREDIBLE TIMING, GIRL. GO, SPORTS!
SOMETHING PUSHED ME TO NEEDLEPEAK TRAIL TODAY. IF I TURNED TO GO HOME, THE WORLD WENT...BLACK? IF I KEPT GOING TO SCHOOL, THE WORLD ALSO WENT BLACK. FATE, HUH?
WHY DON'T WE MOVE TO THIS WIDER, SAFER PATH RIGHT OVER HERE.
OMG, OMG, OMG, I WANNA GO HOME.

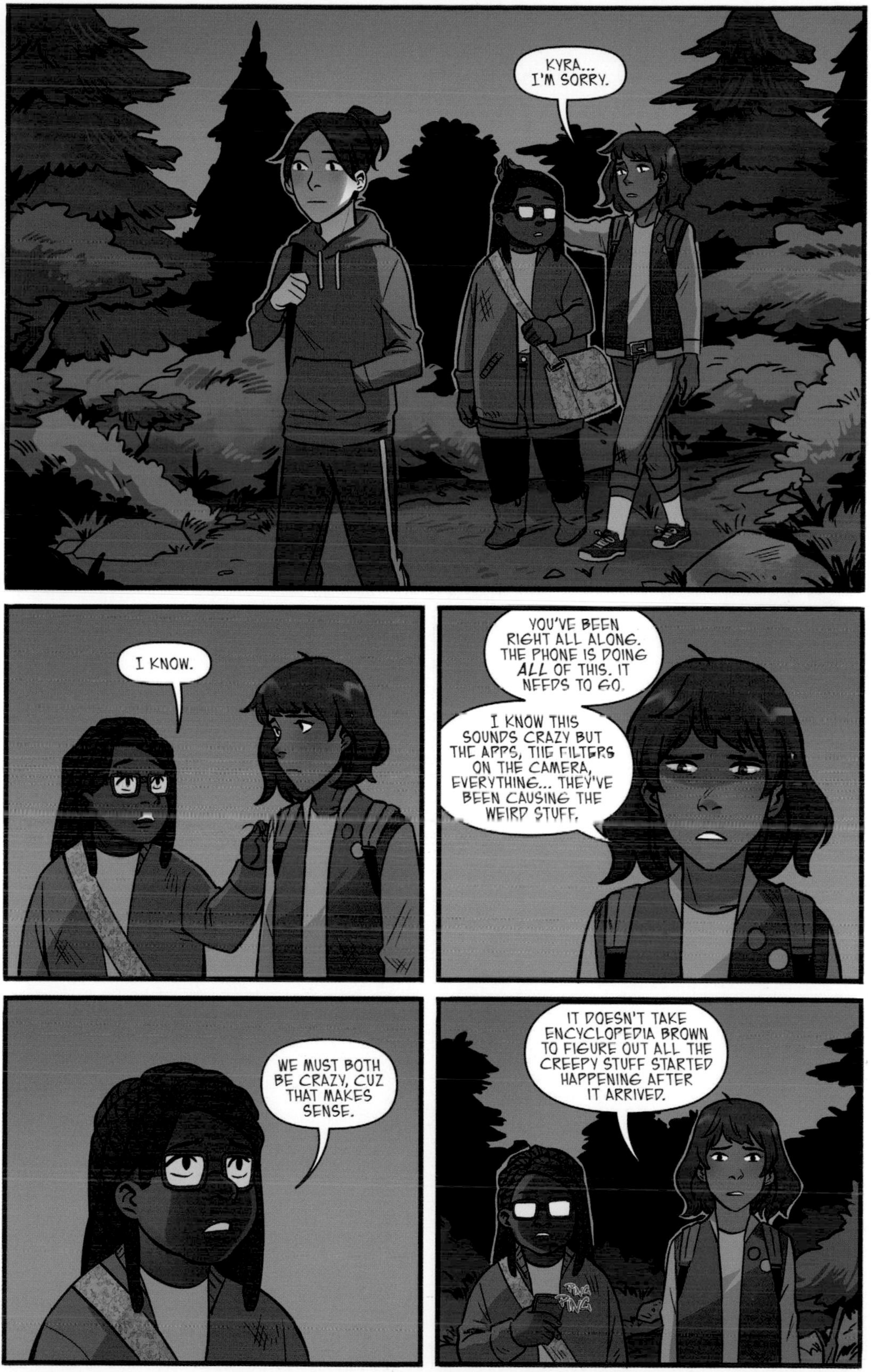
KYRA... I'M SORRY.
I KNOW.
YOU'VE BEEN RIGHT ALL ALONG. THE PHONE IS DOING *ALL* OF THIS. IT NEEDS TO GO.
I KNOW THIS SOUNDS CRAZY BUT THE APPS, THE FILTERS ON THE CAMERA, EVERYTHING... THEY'VE BEEN CAUSING THE WEIRD STUFF.
WE MUST BOTH BE CRAZY, CUZ THAT MAKES SENSE.
IT DOESN'T TAKE ENCYCLOPEDIA BROWN TO FIGURE OUT ALL THE CREEPY STUFF STARTED HAPPENING AFTER IT ARRIVED.
PING
PING

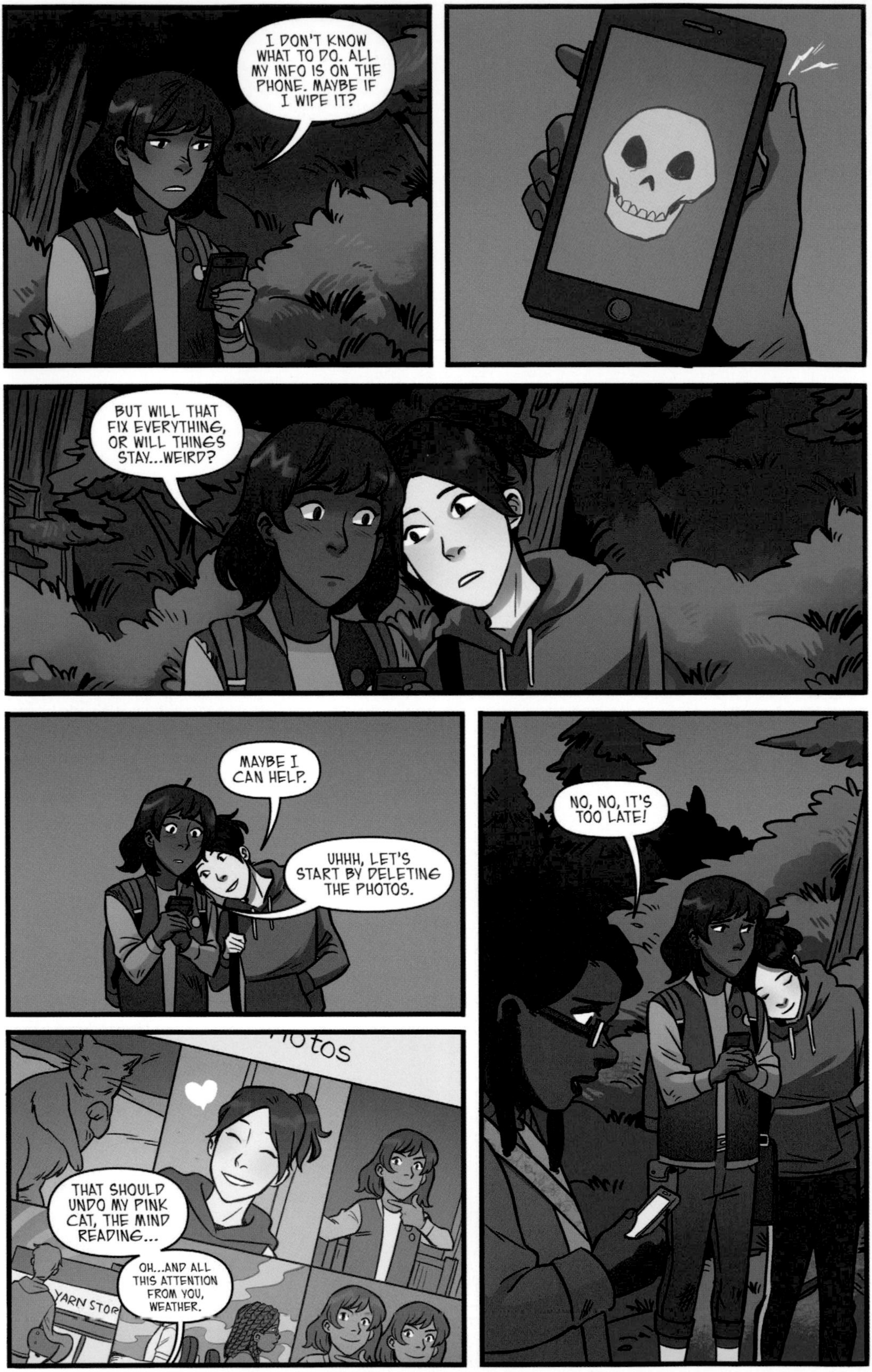

I DON'T KNOW WHAT TO DO. ALL MY INFO IS ON THE PHONE. MAYBE IF I WIPE IT?
BUT WILL THAT FIX EVERYTHING, OR WILL THINGS STAY...WEIRD?
MAYBE I CAN HELP.
UHHH, LET'S START BY DELETING THE PHOTOS.
hotos
THAT SHOULD UNDO MY PINK CAT, THE MIND READING...
OH...AND ALL THIS ATTENTION FROM YOU, WEATHER.
YARN STOR
NO, NO, IT'S TOO LATE!

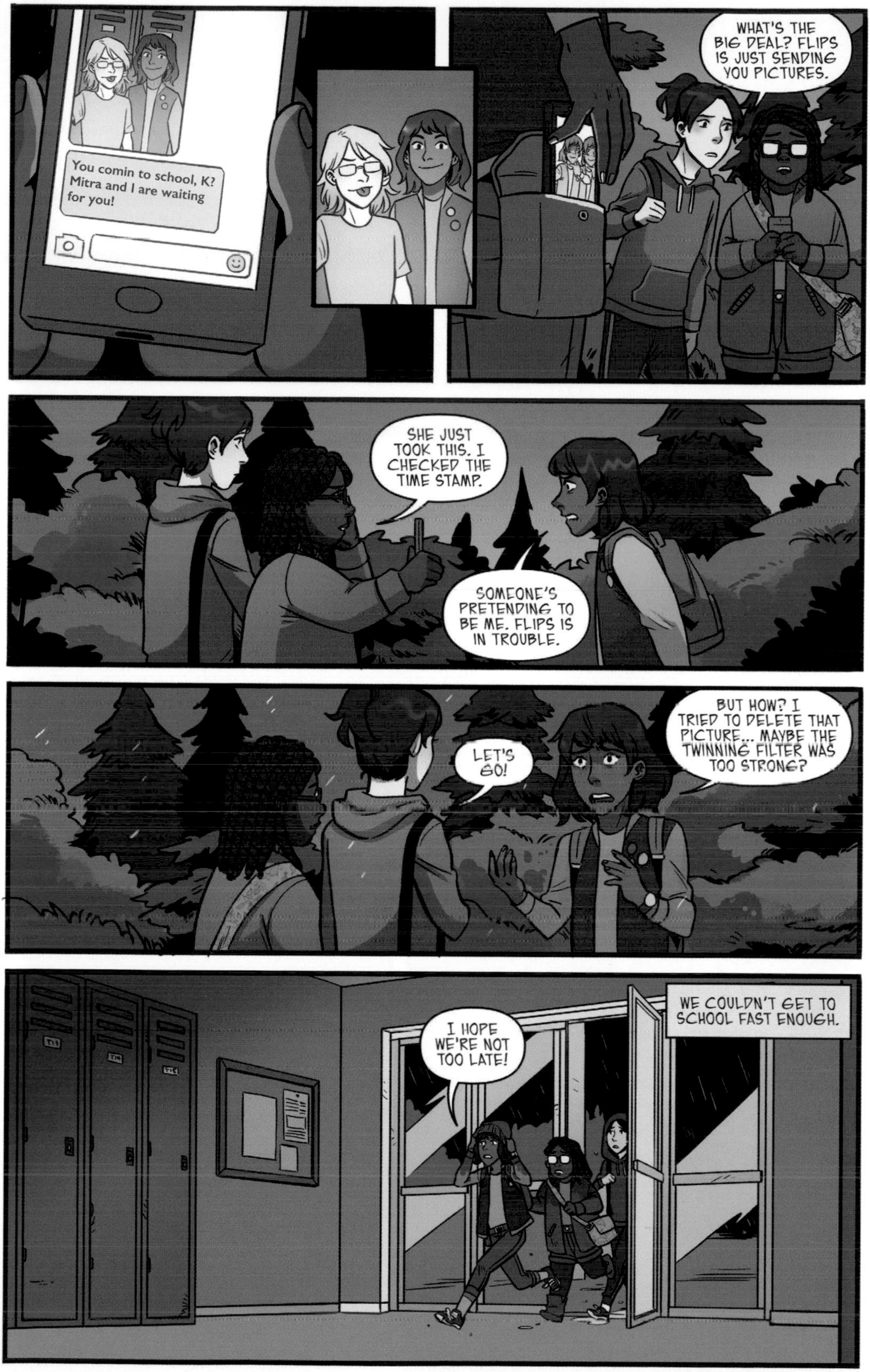

You comin to school, K? Mitra and I are waiting for you!
WHAT'S THE BIG DEAL? FLIPS IS JUST SENDING YOU PICTURES.
SHE JUST TOOK THIS. I CHECKED THE TIME STAMP.
SOMEONE'S PRETENDING TO BE ME. FLIPS IS IN TROUBLE.
BUT HOW? I TRIED TO DELETE THAT PICTURE... MAYBE THE TWINNING FILTER WAS TOO STRONG?
LET'S GO!
WE COULDN'T GET TO SCHOOL FAST ENOUGH.
I HOPE WE'RE NOT TOO LATE!

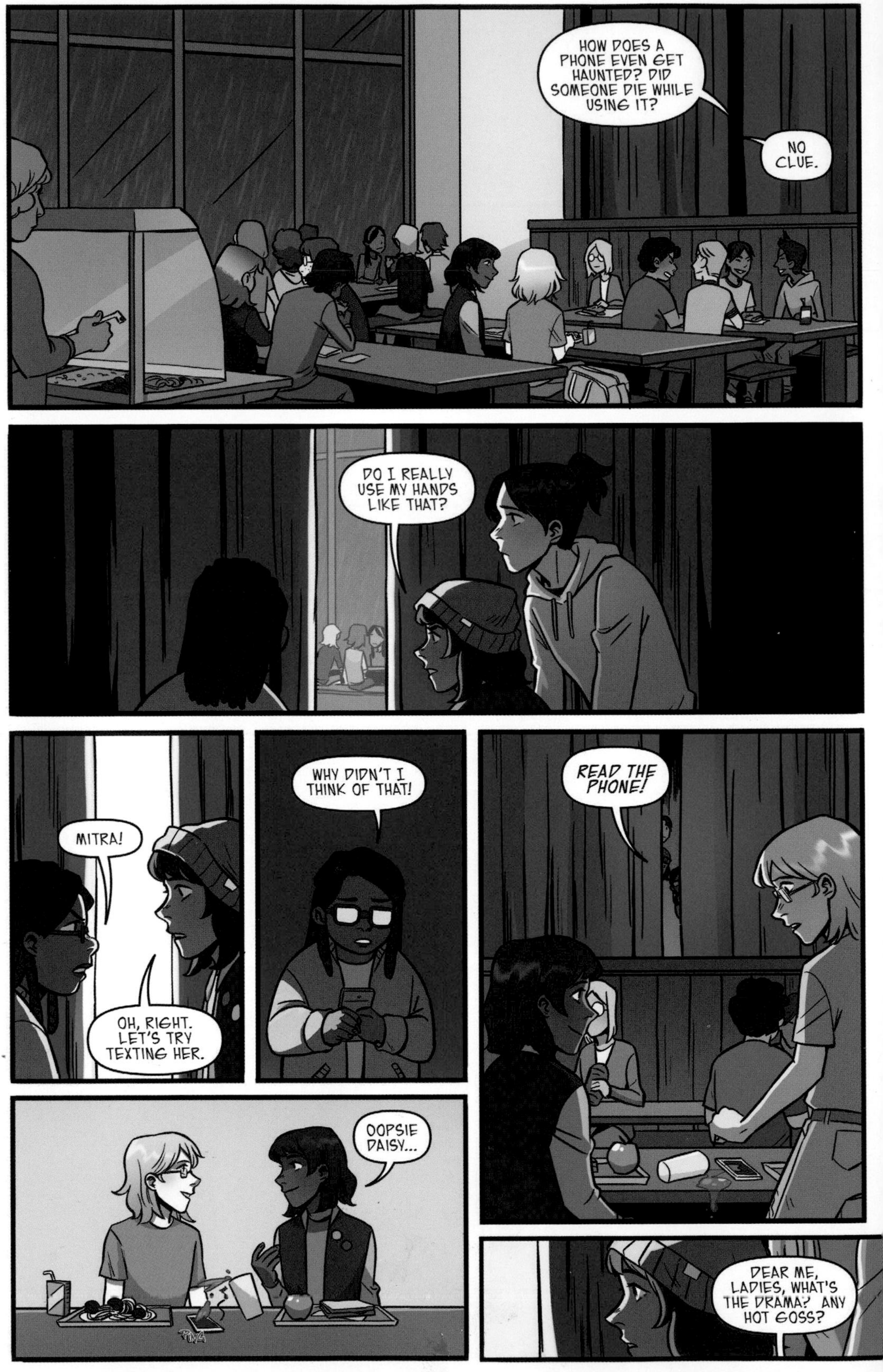
HOW DOES A PHONE EVEN GET HAUNTED? DID SOMEONE DIE WHILE USING IT?
NO CLUE.
DO I REALLY USE MY HANDS LIKE THAT?
MITRA!
OH, RIGHT. LET'S TRY TEXTING HER.
WHY DIDN'T I THINK OF THAT!
READ THE PHONE!
OOPSIE DAISY...
DEAR ME, LADIES, WHAT'S THE DRAMA? ANY HOT GOSS?

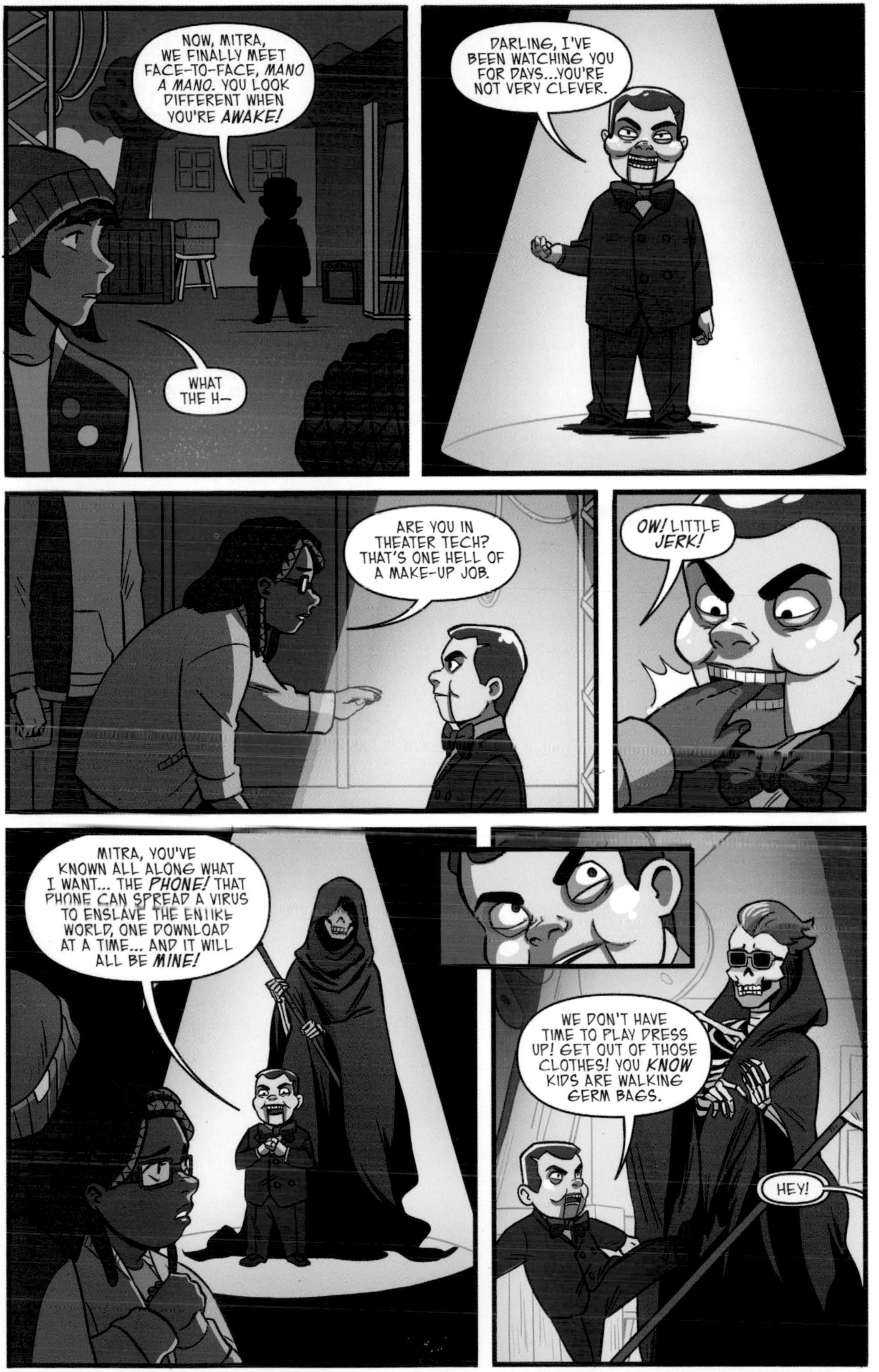
NOW, MITRA, WE FINALLY MEET FACE-TO-FACE, MANO A MANO. YOU LOOK DIFFERENT WHEN YOU'RE AWAKE!
WHAT THE H—
DARLING, I'VE BEEN WATCHING YOU FOR DAYS...YOU'RE NOT VERY CLEVER.
ARE YOU IN THEATER TECH? THAT'S ONE HELL OF A MAKE-UP JOB.
OW! LITTLE JERK!
MITRA, YOU'VE KNOWN ALL ALONG WHAT I WANT... THE PHONE! THAT PHONE CAN SPREAD A VIRUS TO ENSLAVE THE ENTIRE WORLD, ONE DOWNLOAD AT A TIME... AND IT WILL ALL BE MINE!
WE DON'T HAVE TIME TO PLAY DRESS UP! GET OUT OF THOSE CLOTHES! YOU KNOW KIDS ARE WALKING GERM BAGS.
HEY!

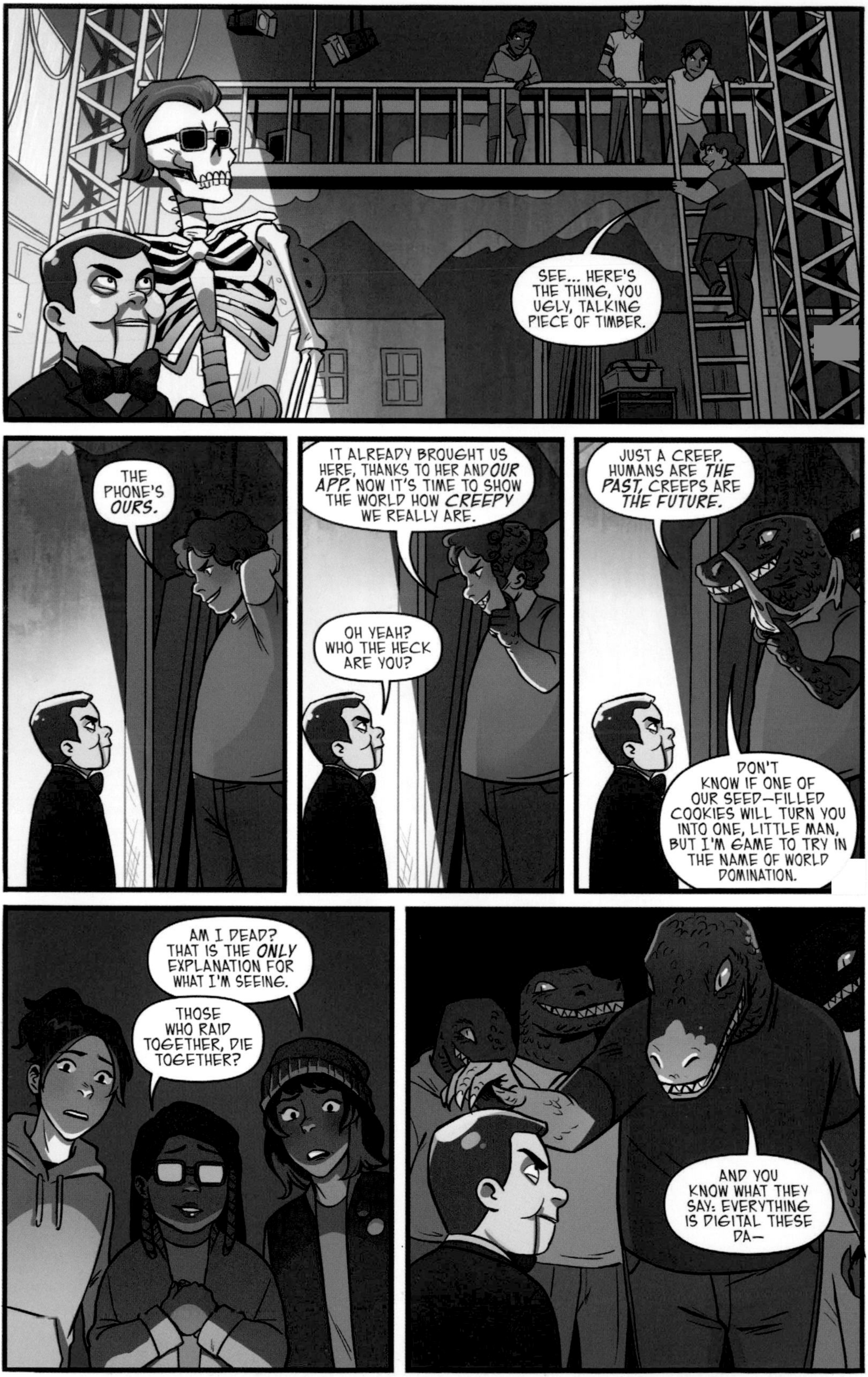
SEE... HERE'S THE THING, YOU UGLY, TALKING PIECE OF TIMBER.
THE PHONE'S OURS.
IT ALREADY BROUGHT US HERE, THANKS TO HER AND OUR APP. NOW IT'S TIME TO SHOW THE WORLD HOW CREEPY WE REALLY ARE.
OH YEAH? WHO THE HECK ARE YOU?
JUST A CREEP. HUMANS ARE THE PAST, CREEPS ARE THE FUTURE.
DON'T KNOW IF ONE OF OUR SEED-FILLED COOKIES WILL TURN YOU INTO ONE, LITTLE MAN, BUT I'M GAME TO TRY IN THE NAME OF WORLD DOMINATION.
AM I DEAD? THAT IS THE ONLY EXPLANATION FOR WHAT I'M SEEING.
THOSE WHO RAID TOGETHER, DIE TOGETHER?
AND YOU KNOW WHAT THEY SAY: EVERYTHING IS DIGITAL THESE DA—

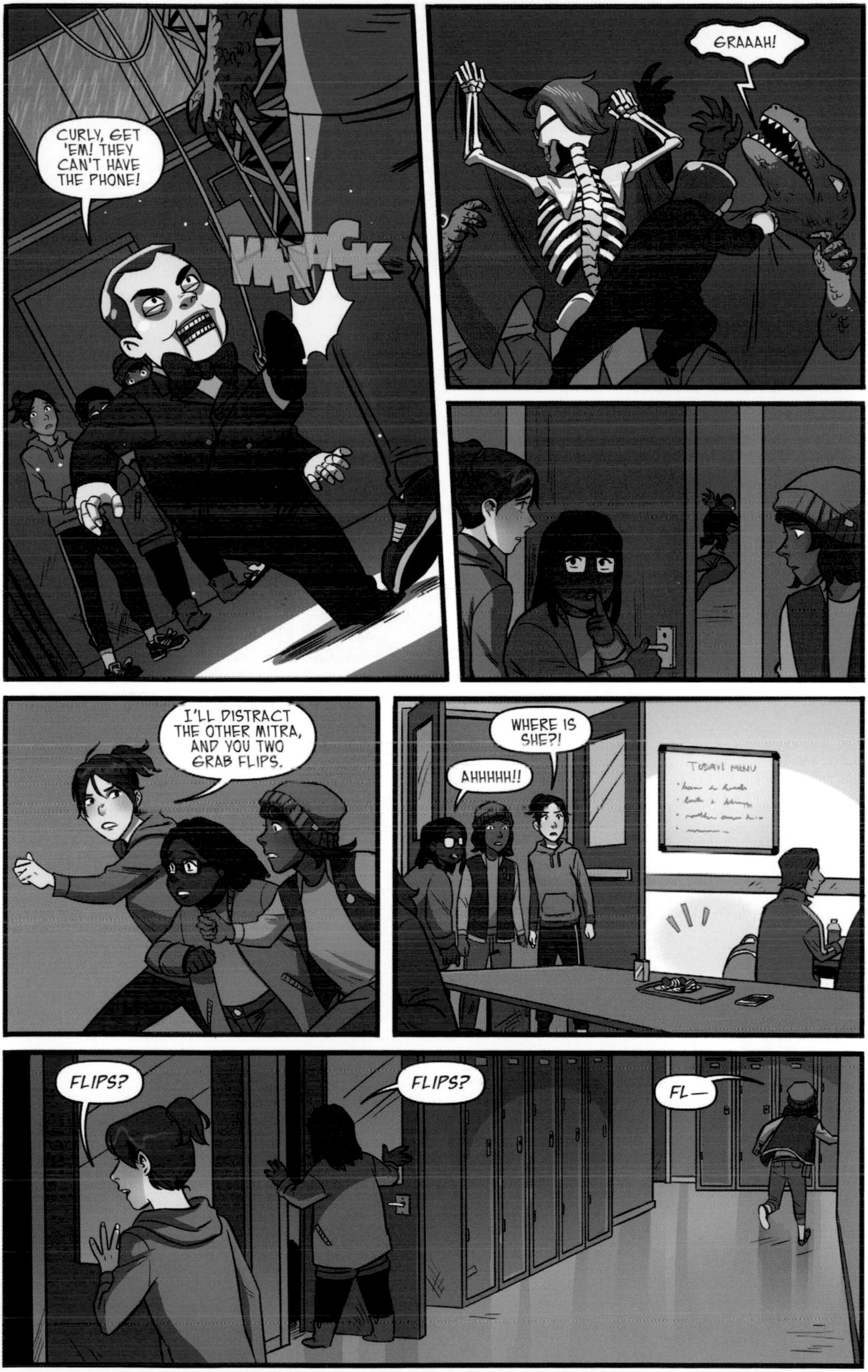
CURLY, GET 'EM! THEY CAN'T HAVE THE PHONE!
WHACK
GRAAAH!
I'LL DISTRACT THE OTHER MITRA, AND YOU TWO GRAB FLIPS.
WHERE IS SHE?!
AHHHHH!!
FLIPS?
FLIPS?
FL—

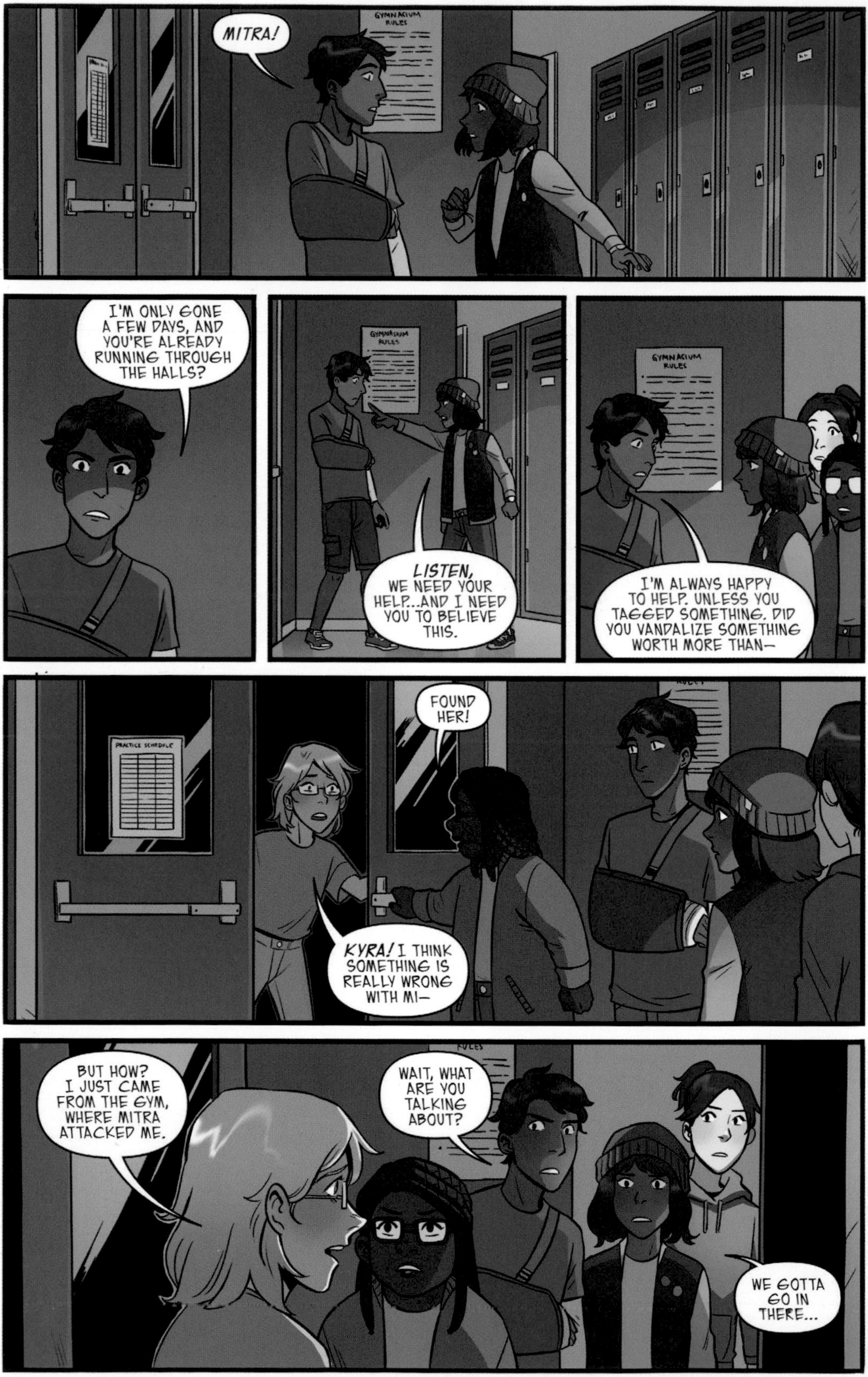
GYMNASIUM RULES
MITRA!
I'M ONLY GONE A FEW DAYS, AND YOU'RE ALREADY RUNNING THROUGH THE HALLS?
GYMNASIUM RULES
LISTEN, WE NEED YOUR HELP...AND I NEED YOU TO BELIEVE THIS.
GYMNASIUM RULES
I'M ALWAYS HAPPY TO HELP. UNLESS YOU TAGGED SOMETHING. DID YOU VANDALIZE SOMETHING WORTH MORE THAN—
PRACTICE SCHEDULE
FOUND HER!
KYRA! I THINK SOMETHING IS REALLY WRONG WITH MI—
BUT HOW? I JUST CAME FROM THE GYM, WHERE MITRA ATTACKED ME.
WAIT, WHAT ARE YOU TALKING ABOUT?
WE GOTTA GO IN THERE...

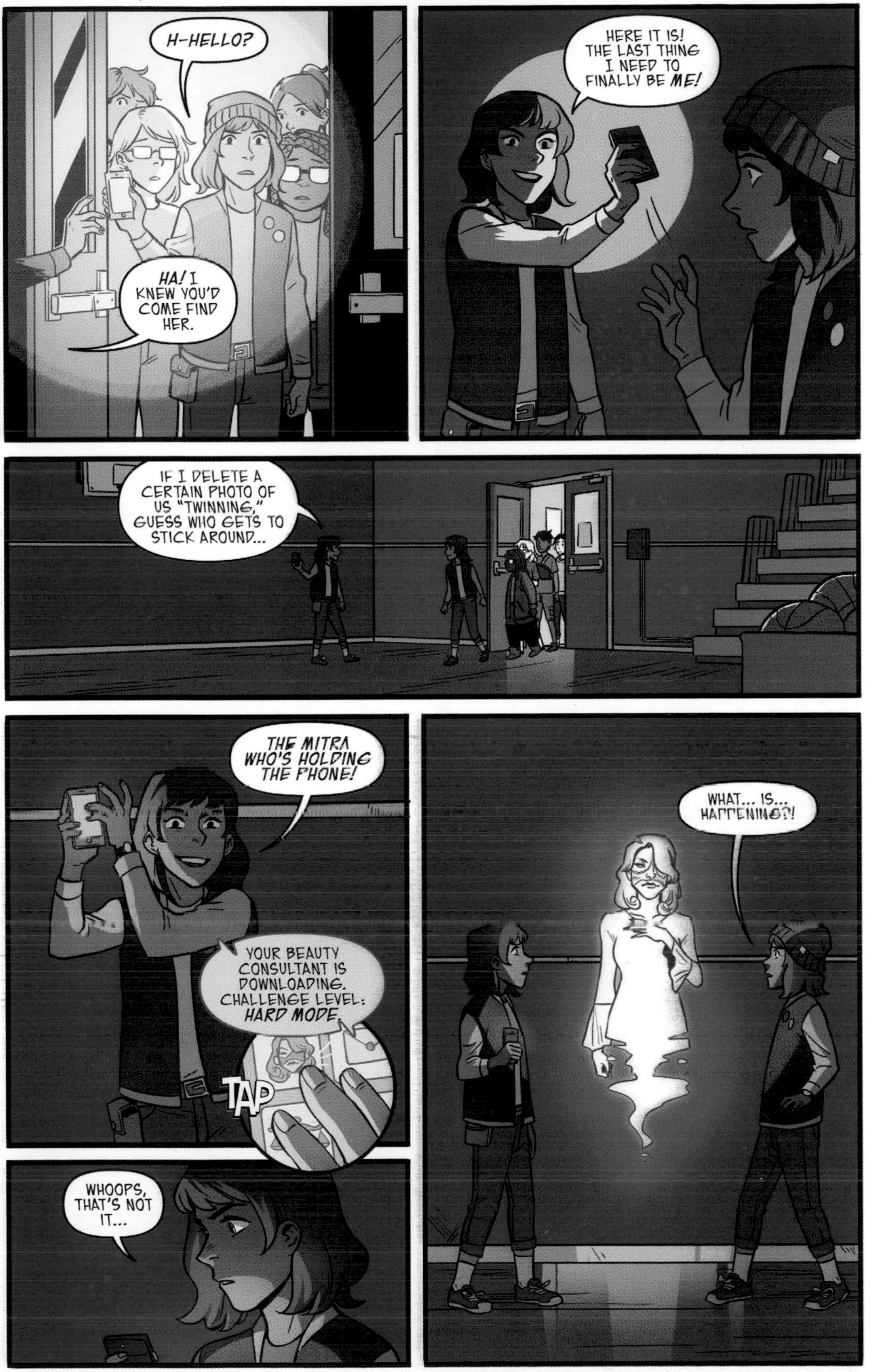
H-HELLO?
HA! I KNEW YOU'D COME FIND HER.
HERE IT IS! THE LAST THING I NEED TO FINALLY BE ME!
IF I DELETE A CERTAIN PHOTO OF US "TWINNING," GUESS WHO GETS TO STICK AROUND...
THE MITRA WHO'S HOLDING THE PHONE!
YOUR BEAUTY CONSULTANT IS DOWNLOADING. CHALLENGE LEVEL: HARD MODE.
TAP
WHOOPS, THAT'S NOT IT...
WHAT... IS... HAPPENING?!

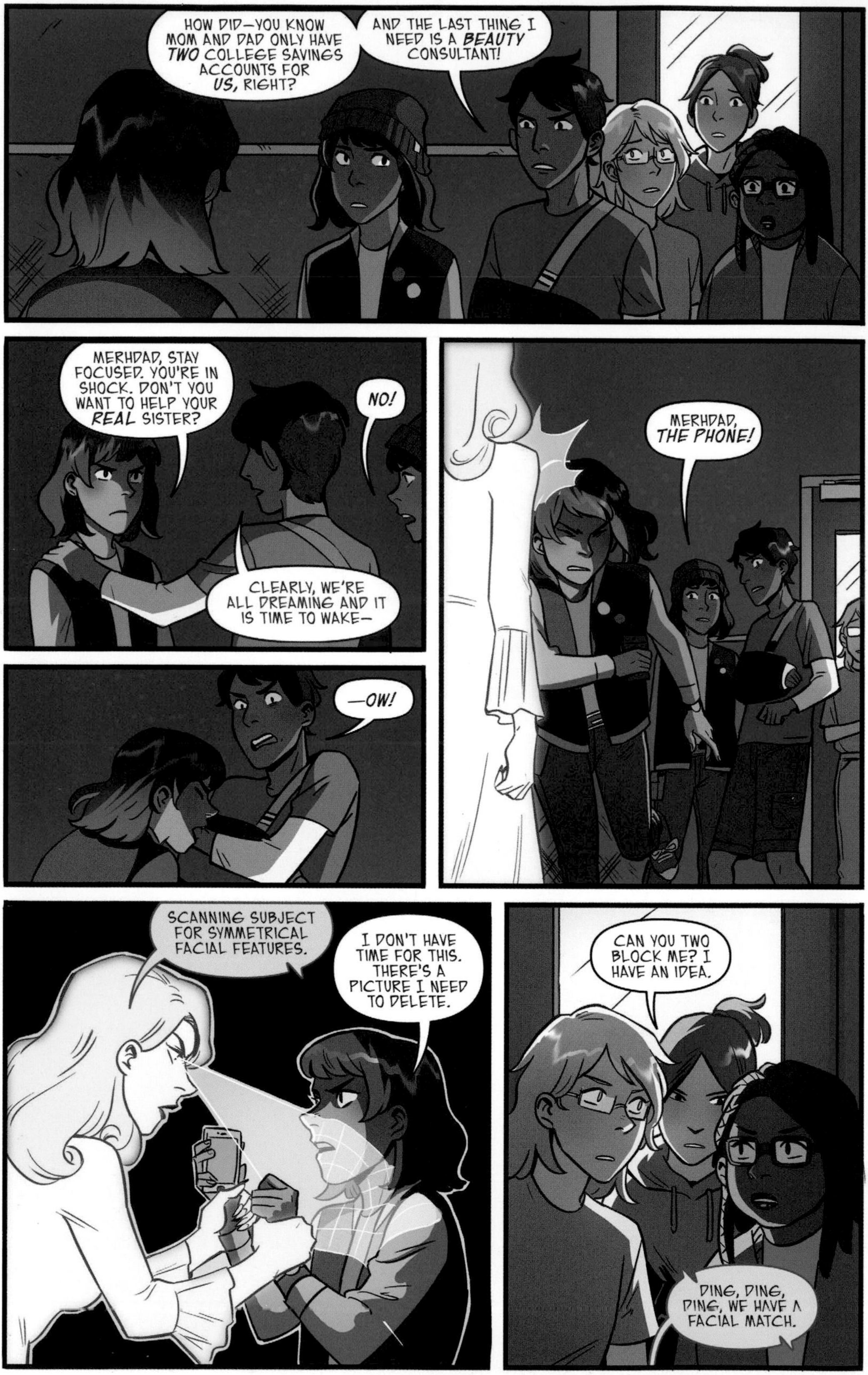
HOW DID—YOU KNOW MOM AND DAD ONLY HAVE TWO COLLEGE SAVINGS ACCOUNTS FOR US, RIGHT?
AND THE LAST THING I NEED IS A BEAUTY CONSULTANT!
MERHDAD, STAY FOCUSED. YOU'RE IN SHOCK. DON'T YOU WANT TO HELP YOUR REAL SISTER?
NO!
CLEARLY, WE'RE ALL DREAMING AND IT IS TIME TO WAKE—
—OW!
MERHDAD, THE PHONE!
SCANNING SUBJECT FOR SYMMETRICAL FACIAL FEATURES.
I DON'T HAVE TIME FOR THIS. THERE'S A PICTURE I NEED TO DELETE.
CAN YOU TWO BLOCK ME? I HAVE AN IDEA.
DING, DING, DING, WE HAVE A FACIAL MATCH.

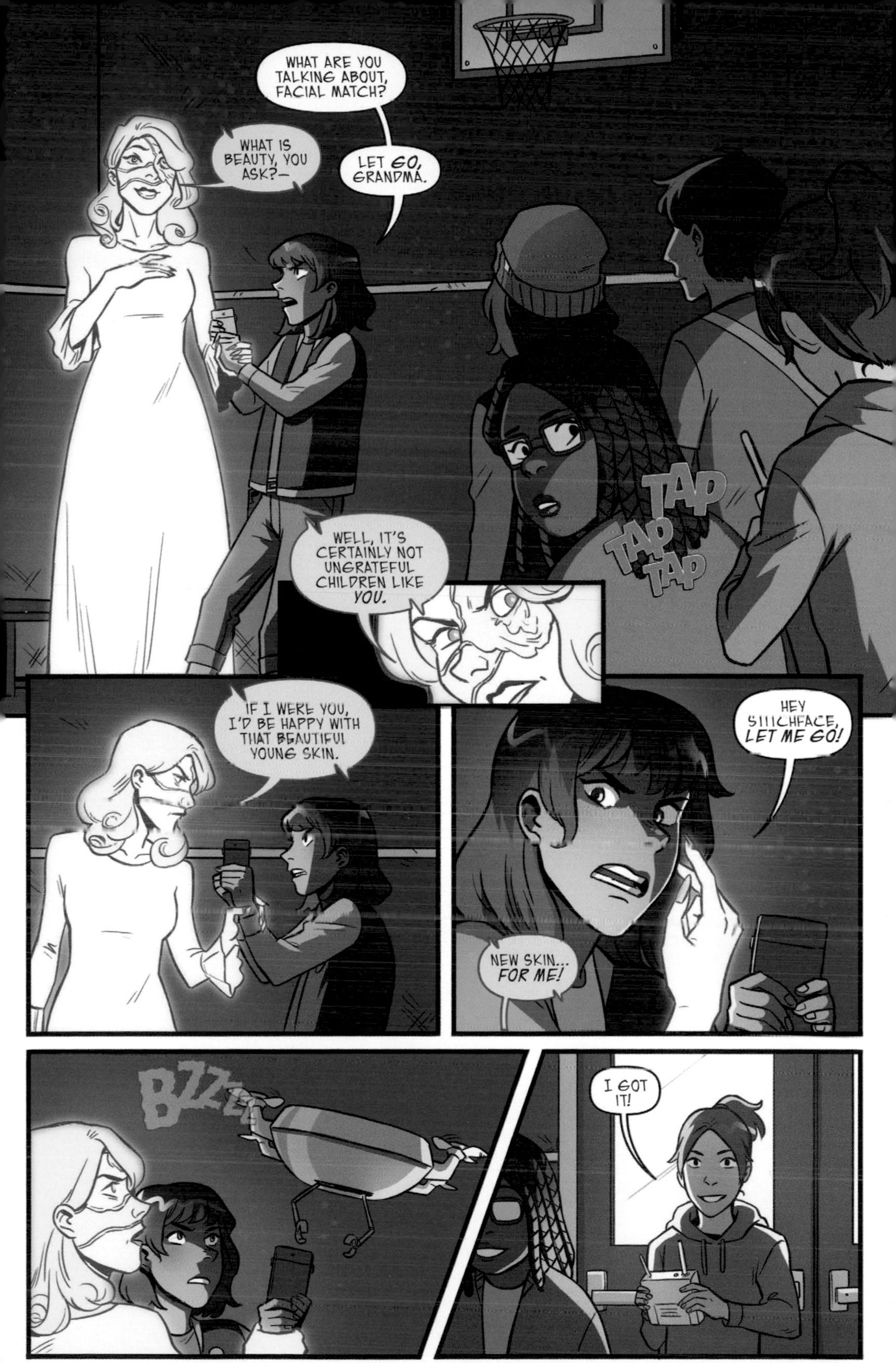
WHAT IS BEAUTY, YOU ASK?—
WHAT ARE YOU TALKING ABOUT, FACIAL MATCH?
LET GO, GRANDMA.
TAP TAP TAP
WELL, IT'S CERTAINLY NOT UNGRATEFUL CHILDREN LIKE YOU.
IF I WERE YOU, I'D BE HAPPY WITH THAT BEAUTIFUL YOUNG SKIN.
HEY STITCHFACE, LET ME GO!
NEW SKIN... FOR ME!
BZZZZ
I GOT IT!

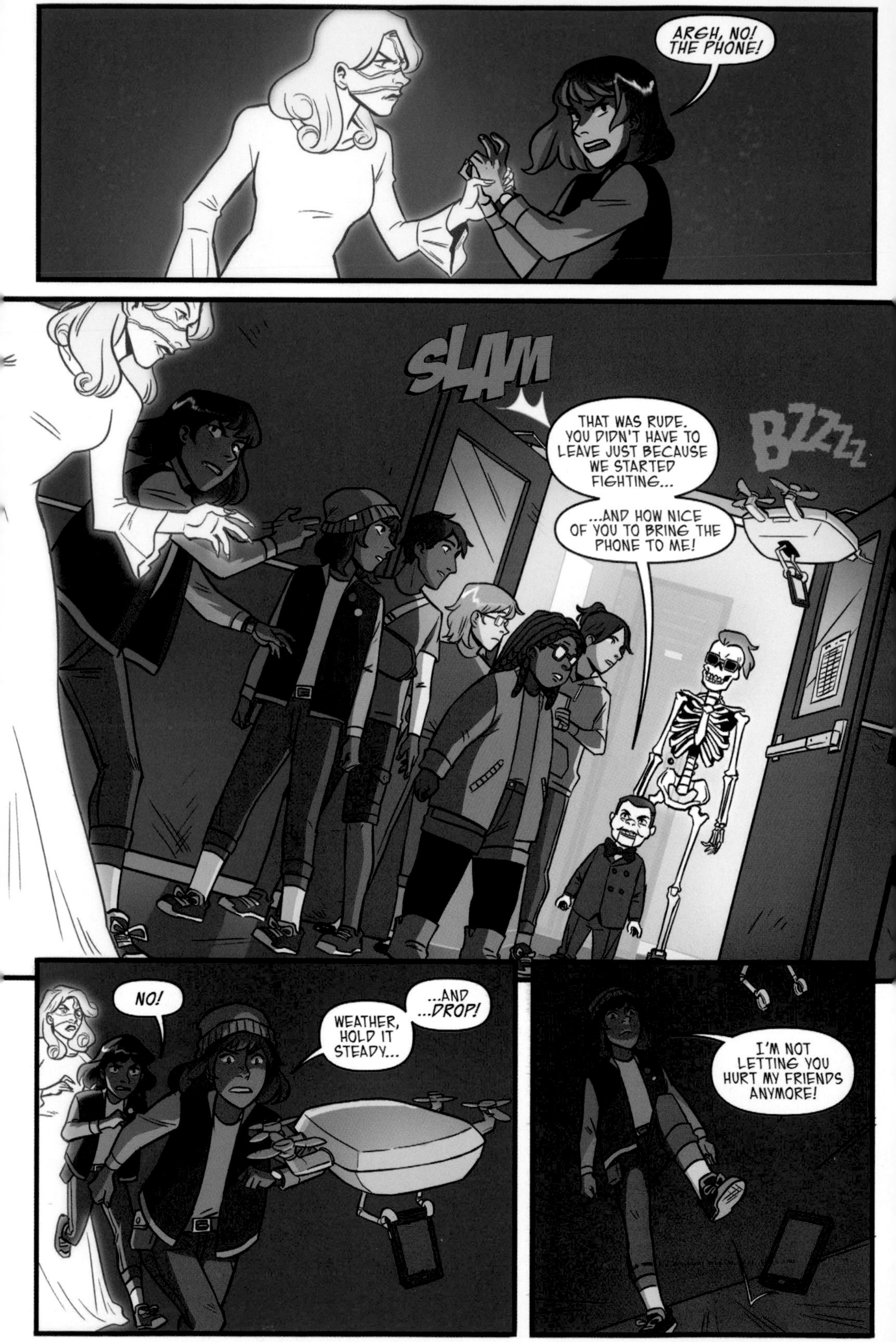
ARGH, NO! THE PHONE!
SLAM
BZZZZZ
THAT WAS RUDE. YOU DIDN'T HAVE TO LEAVE JUST BECAUSE WE STARTED FIGHTING...
...AND HOW NICE OF YOU TO BRING THE PHONE TO ME!
NO!
WEATHER, HOLD IT STEADY...
...AND ...DROP!
I'M NOT LETTING YOU HURT MY FRIENDS ANYMORE!

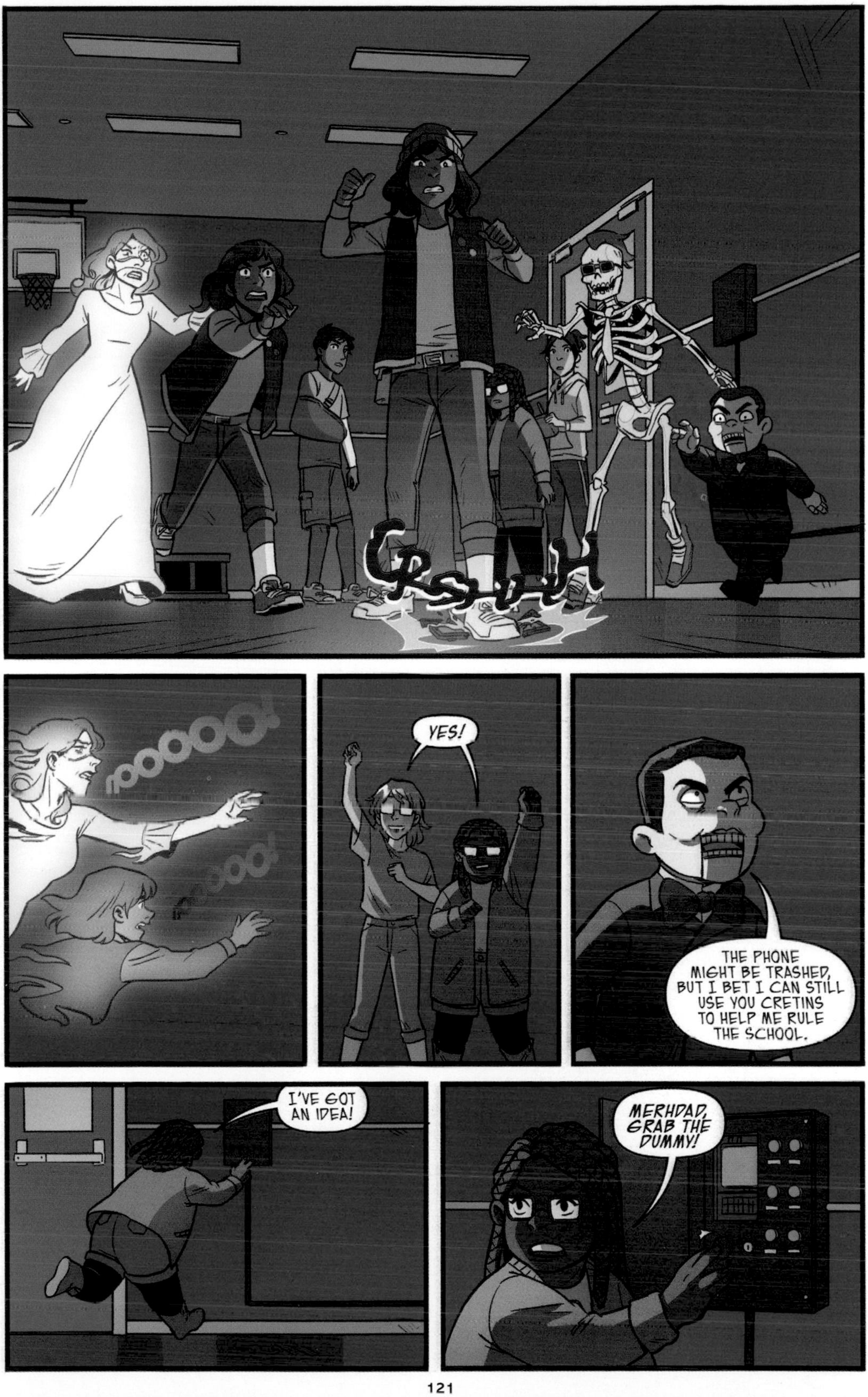
CRSHHH
NOOOOO!
NOOOOO!
YES!
THE PHONE MIGHT BE TRASHED, BUT I BET I CAN STILL USE YOU CRETINS TO HELP ME RULE THE SCHOOL.
I'VE GOT AN IDEA!
MERHDAD, GRAB THE DUMMY!

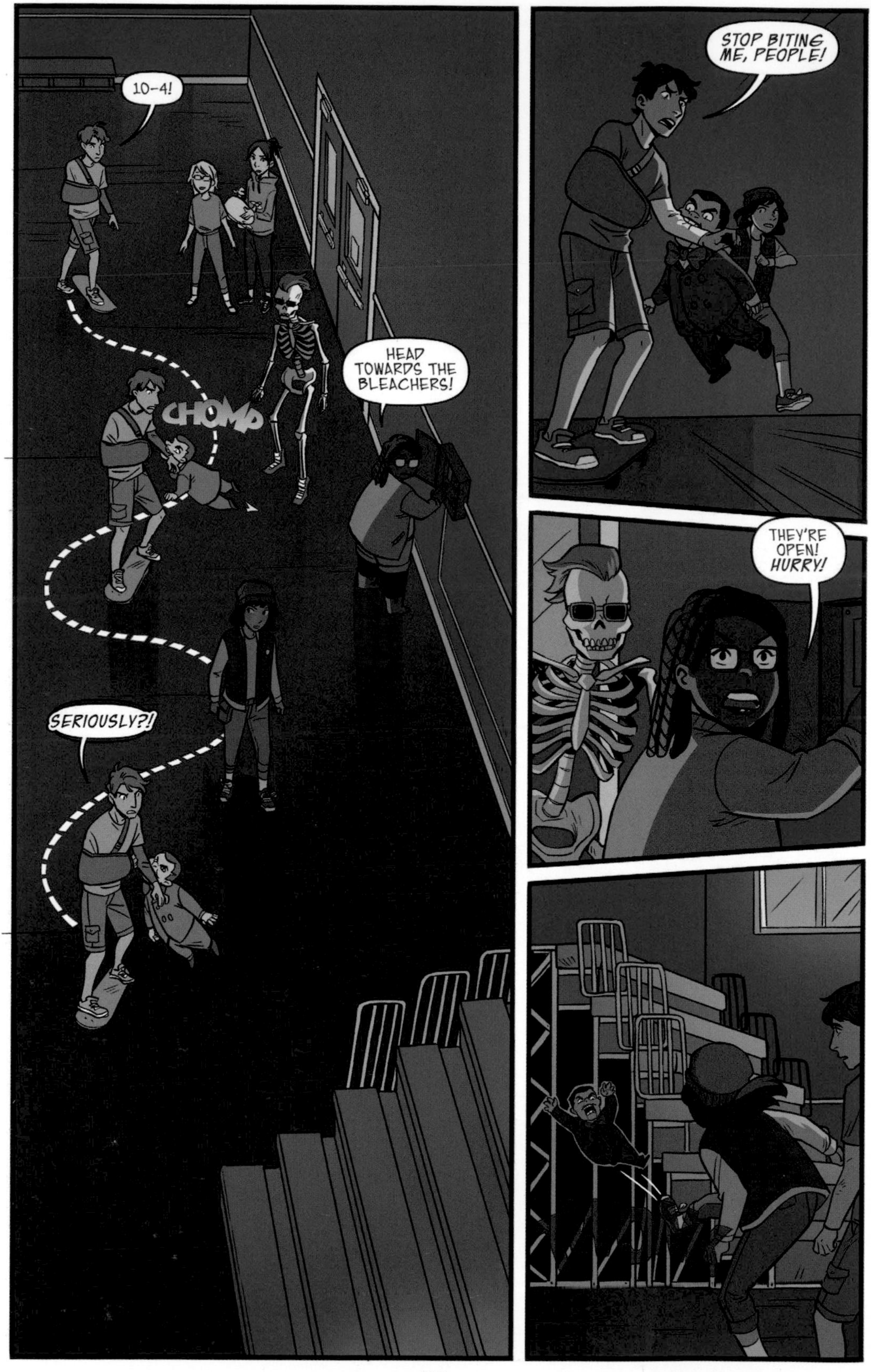
10-4!
HEAD TOWARDS THE BLEACHERS!
CHOMP
SERIOUSLY?!
STOP BITING ME, PEOPLE!
THEY'RE OPEN! HURRY!

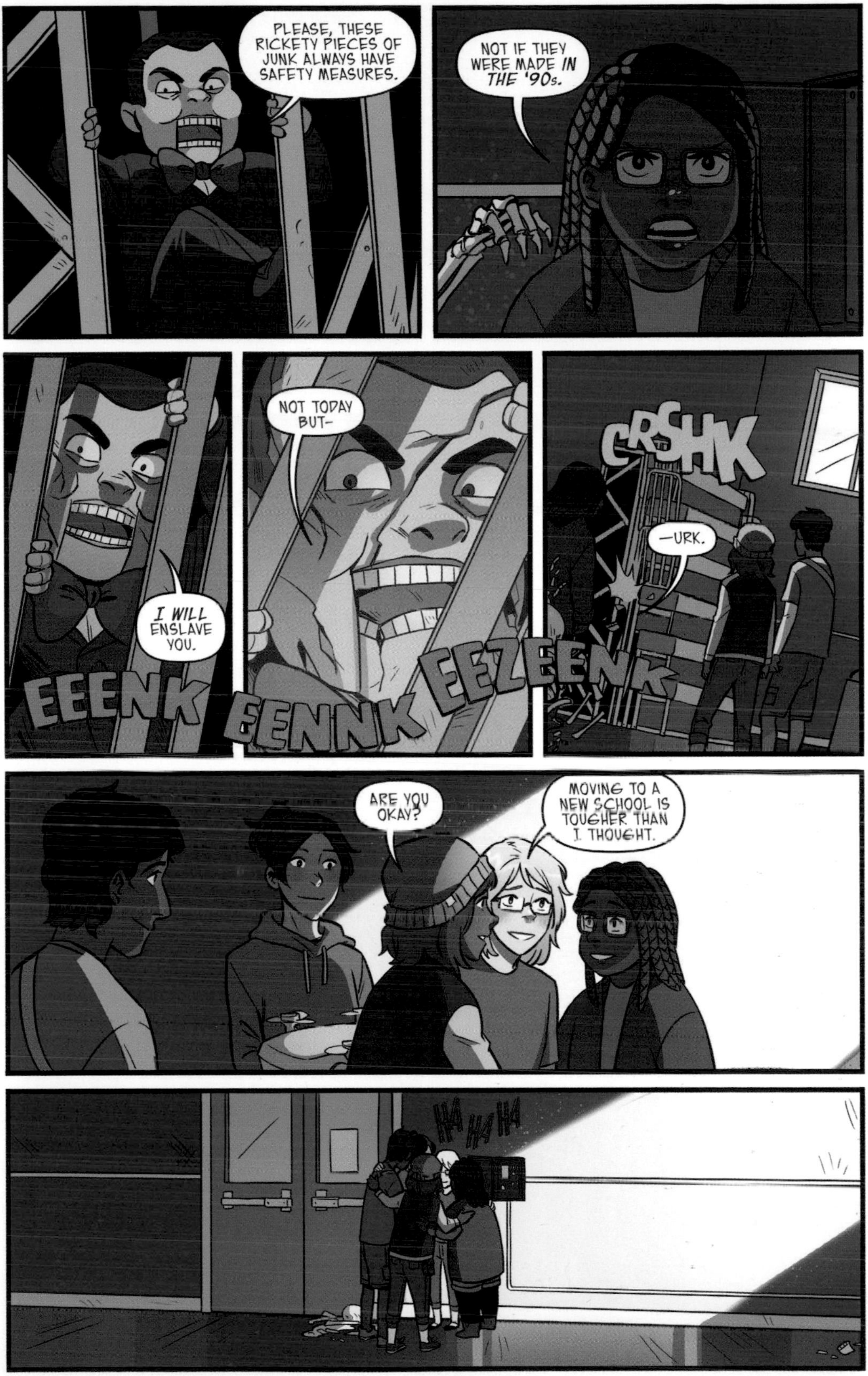

PLEASE, THESE RICKETY PIECES OF JUNK ALWAYS HAVE SAFETY MEASURES.
NOT IF THEY WERE MADE IN THE '90s.
I WILL ENSLAVE YOU.
NOT TODAY BUT-
CRSHK
—URK.
EEENK
EENNK
EEZEENK
ARE YOU OKAY?
MOVING TO A NEW SCHOOL IS TOUGHER THAN I THOUGHT.
HA HA HA

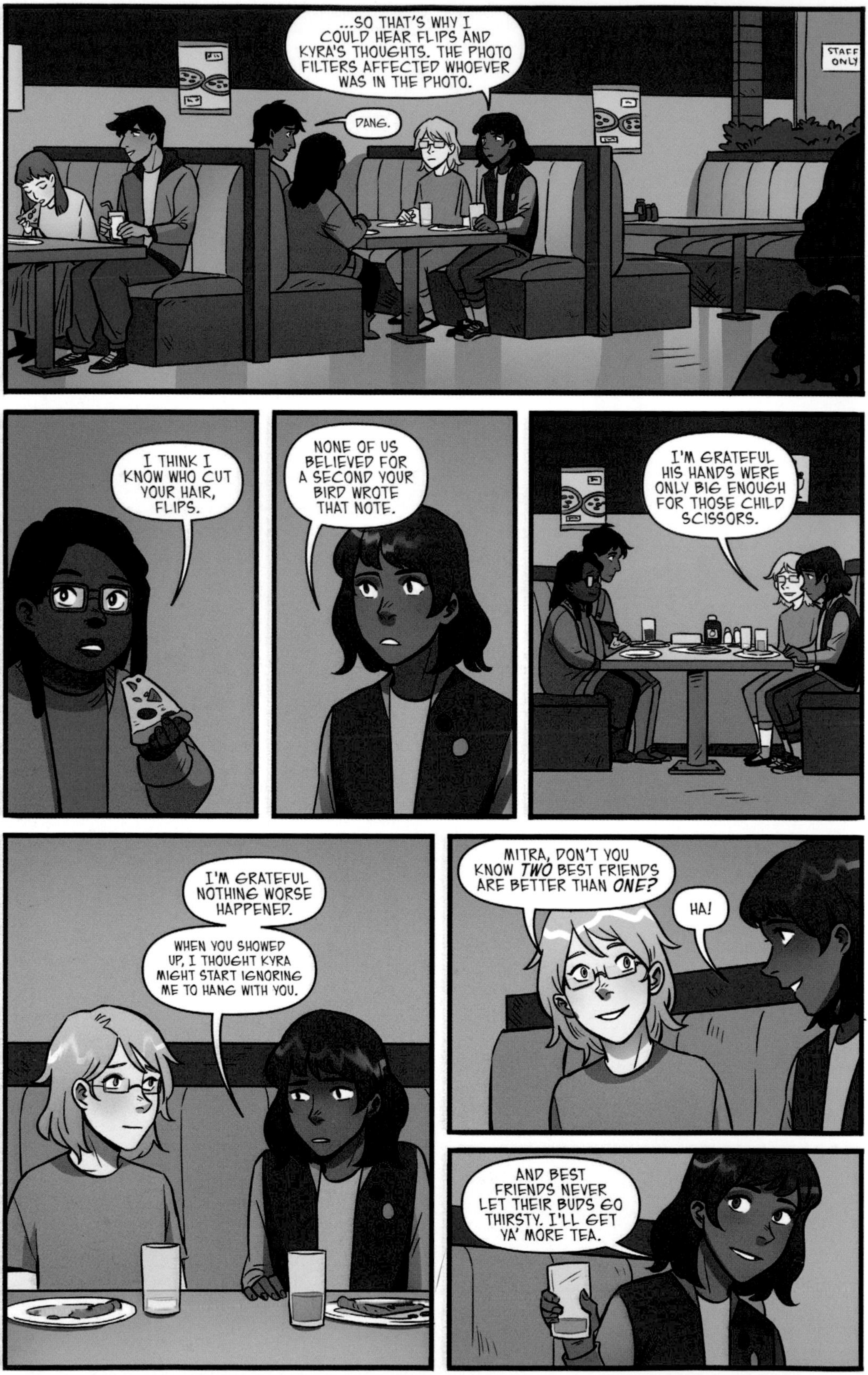
...SO THAT'S WHY I COULD HEAR FLIPS AND KYRA'S THOUGHTS. THE PHOTO FILTERS AFFECTED WHOEVER WAS IN THE PHOTO.
DANG.
STAFF ONLY
I THINK I KNOW WHO CUT YOUR HAIR, FLIPS.
NONE OF US BELIEVED FOR A SECOND YOUR BIRD WROTE THAT NOTE.
I'M GRATEFUL HIS HANDS WERE ONLY BIG ENOUGH FOR THOSE CHILD SCISSORS.
I'M GRATEFUL NOTHING WORSE HAPPENED.
WHEN YOU SHOWED UP, I THOUGHT KYRA MIGHT START IGNORING ME TO HANG WITH YOU.
MITRA, DON'T YOU KNOW *TWO* BEST FRIENDS ARE BETTER THAN *ONE?*
HA!
AND BEST FRIENDS NEVER LET THEIR BUDS GO THIRSTY. I'LL GET YA' MORE TEA.

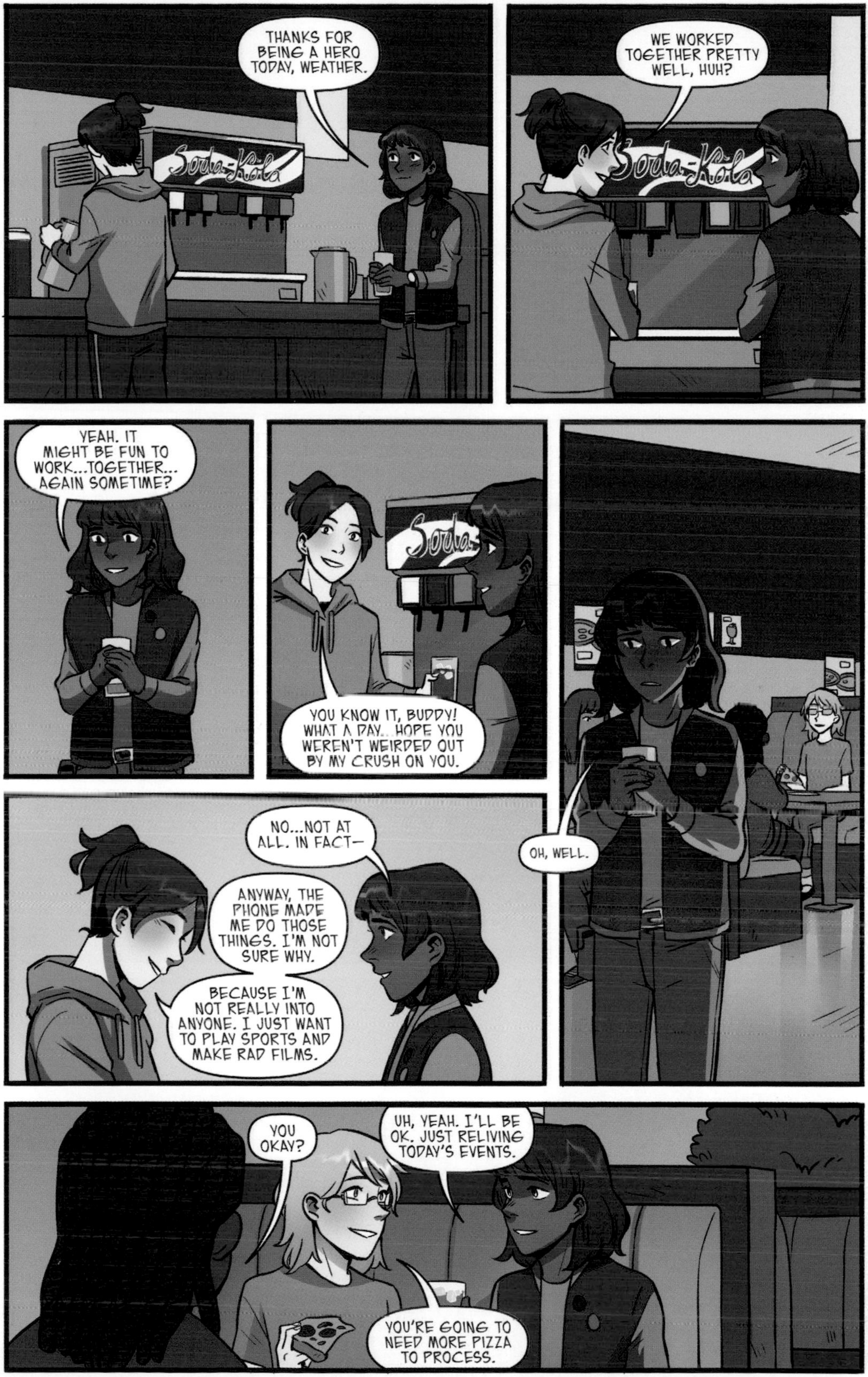
THANKS FOR BEING A HERO TODAY, WEATHER.
Soda-Kola
WE WORKED TOGETHER PRETTY WELL, HUH?
Soda-Kola
YEAH. IT MIGHT BE FUN TO WORK...TOGETHER... AGAIN SOMETIME?
Soda
YOU KNOW IT, BUDDY! WHAT A DAY... HOPE YOU WEREN'T WEIRDED OUT BY MY CRUSH ON YOU.
NO...NOT AT ALL. IN FACT—
ANYWAY, THE PHONE MADE ME DO THOSE THINGS. I'M NOT SURE WHY.
BECAUSE I'M NOT REALLY INTO ANYONE. I JUST WANT TO PLAY SPORTS AND MAKE RAD FILMS.
OH, WELL.
YOU OKAY?
UH, YEAH. I'LL BE OK. JUST RELIVING TODAY'S EVENTS.
YOU'RE GOING TO NEED MORE PIZZA TO PROCESS.

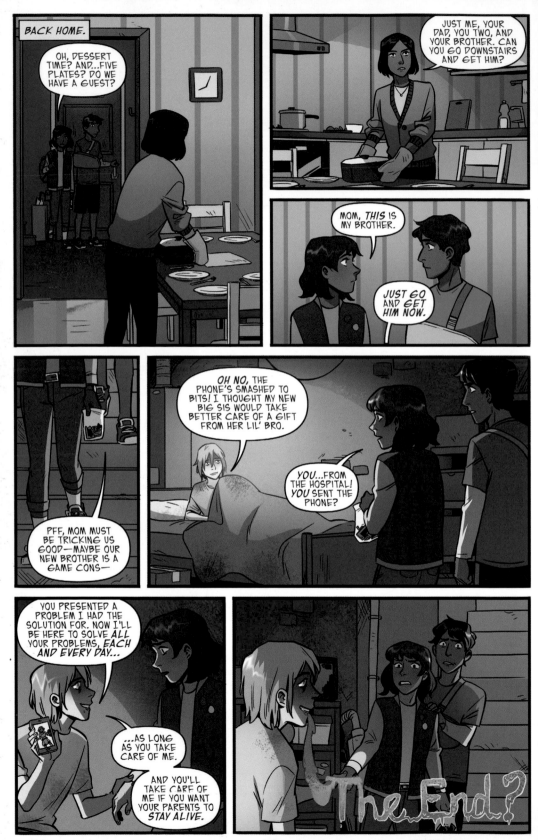

BACK HOME.

OH, DESSERT TIME? AND...FIVE PLATES? DO WE HAVE A GUEST?

JUST ME, YOUR DAD, YOU TWO, AND YOUR BROTHER. CAN YOU GO DOWNSTAIRS AND GET HIM?

MOM, *THIS* IS MY BROTHER.

JUST GO AND GET HIM NOW.

OH NO, THE PHONE'S SMASHED TO BITS! I THOUGHT MY NEW BIG SIS WOULD TAKE BETTER CARE OF A GIFT FROM HER LIL' BRO.

YOU...FROM THE HOSPITAL! YOU SENT THE PHONE?

PFF, MOM MUST BE TRICKING US GOOD—MAYBE OUR NEW BROTHER IS A GAME CONS—

YOU PRESENTED A PROBLEM I HAD THE SOLUTION FOR. NOW I'LL BE HERE TO SOLVE *ALL* YOUR PROBLEMS, *EACH AND EVERY DAY...*

...AS LONG AS YOU TAKE CARE OF ME.

AND YOU'LL TAKE CARE OF ME IF YOU WANT YOUR PARENTS TO *STAY ALIVE.*

The End?

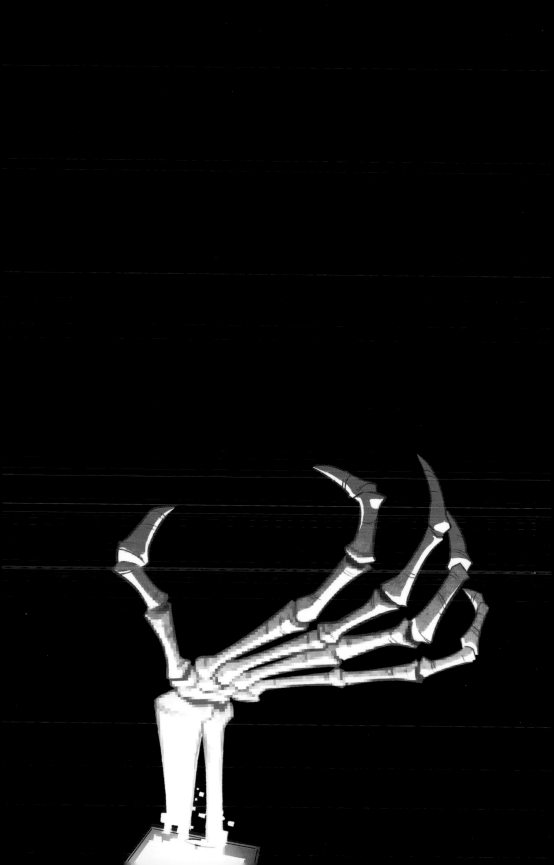

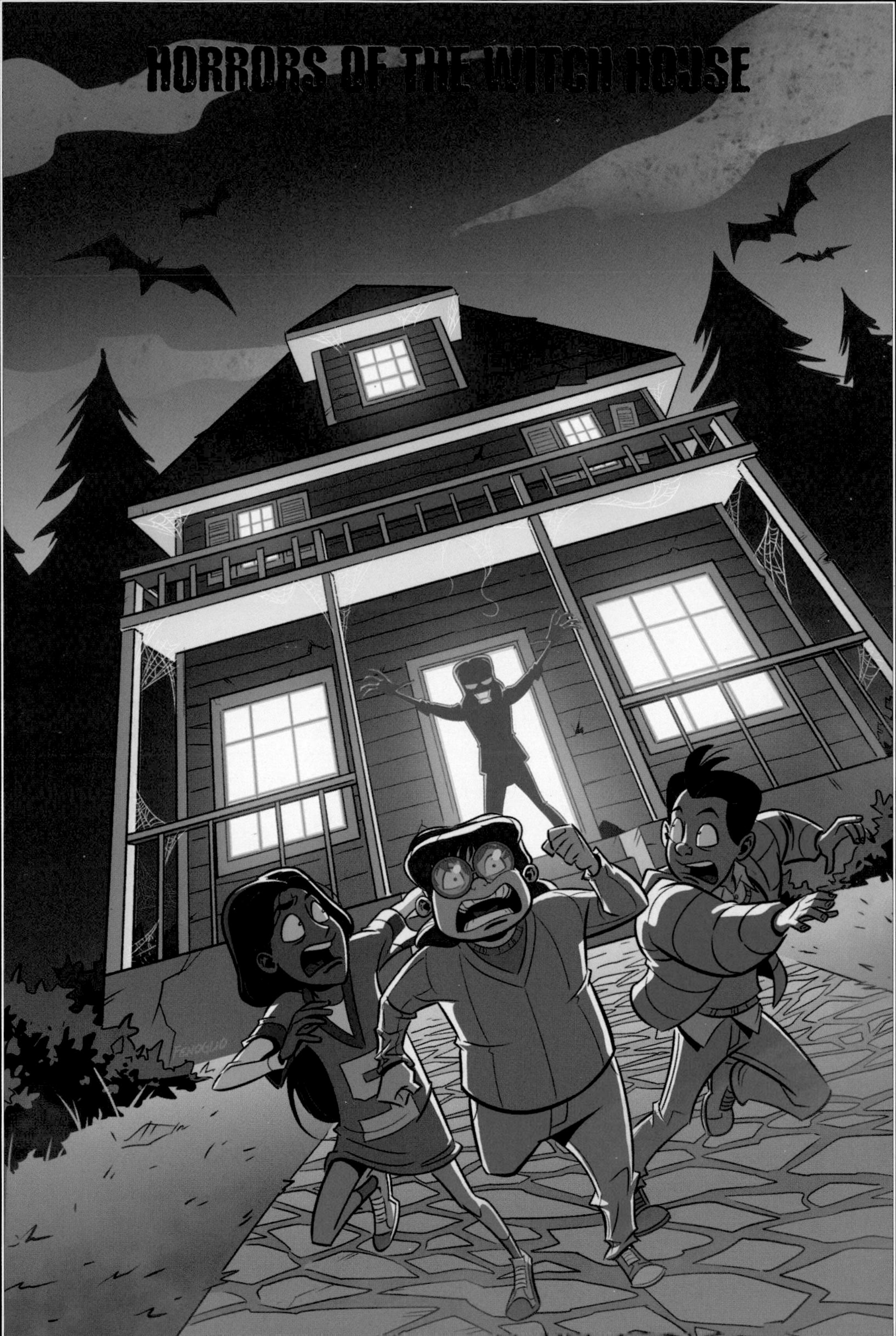
HORRORS OF THE WITCH HOUSE
FENOGLIO

ART BY
CHRIS FENOGLIO

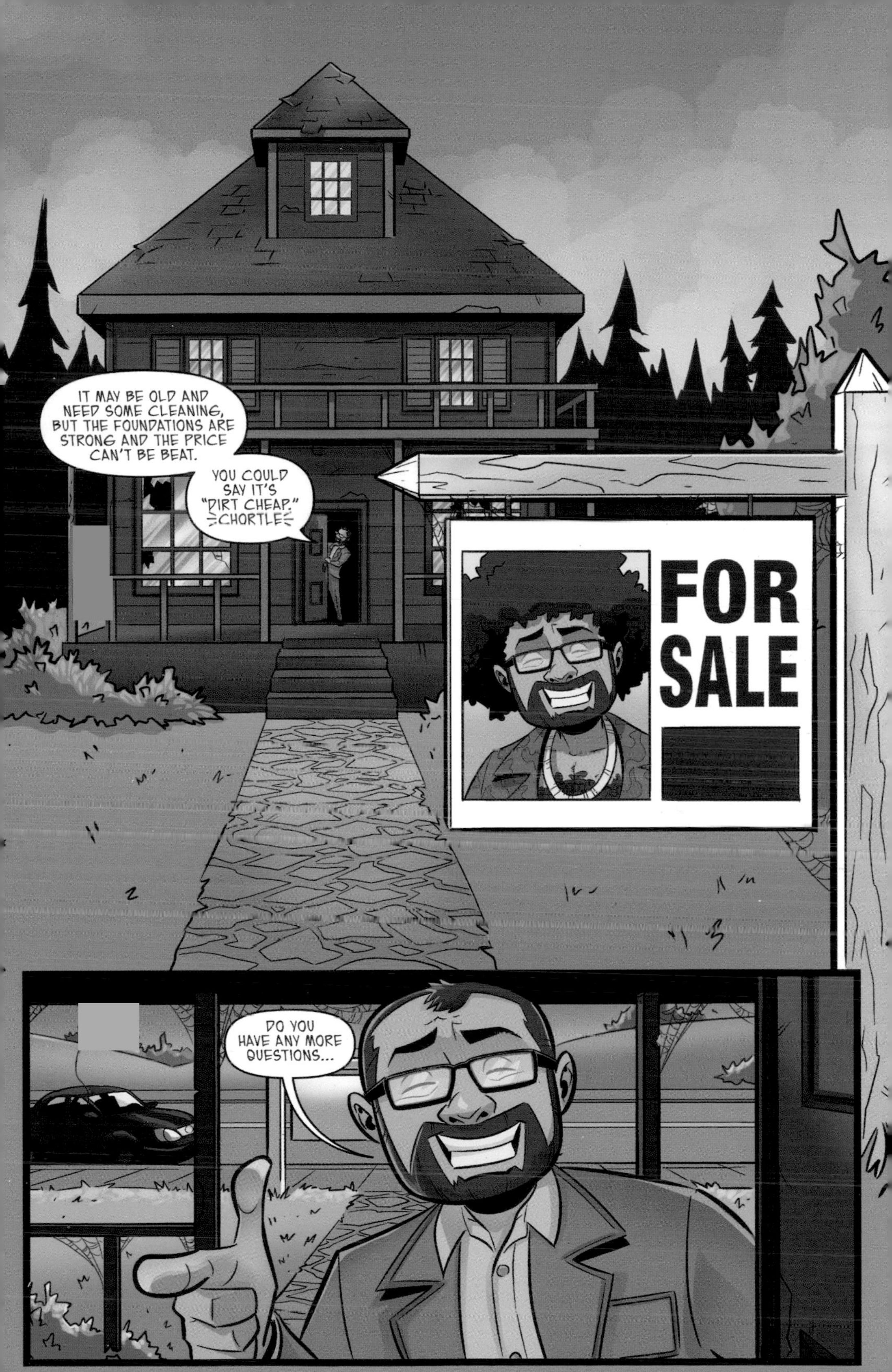
IT MAY BE OLD AND NEED SOME CLEANING, BUT THE FOUNDATIONS ARE STRONG AND THE PRICE CAN'T BE BEAT.
YOU COULD SAY IT'S "DIRT CHEAP."
CHORTLE
FOR SALE
DO YOU HAVE ANY MORE QUESTIONS...

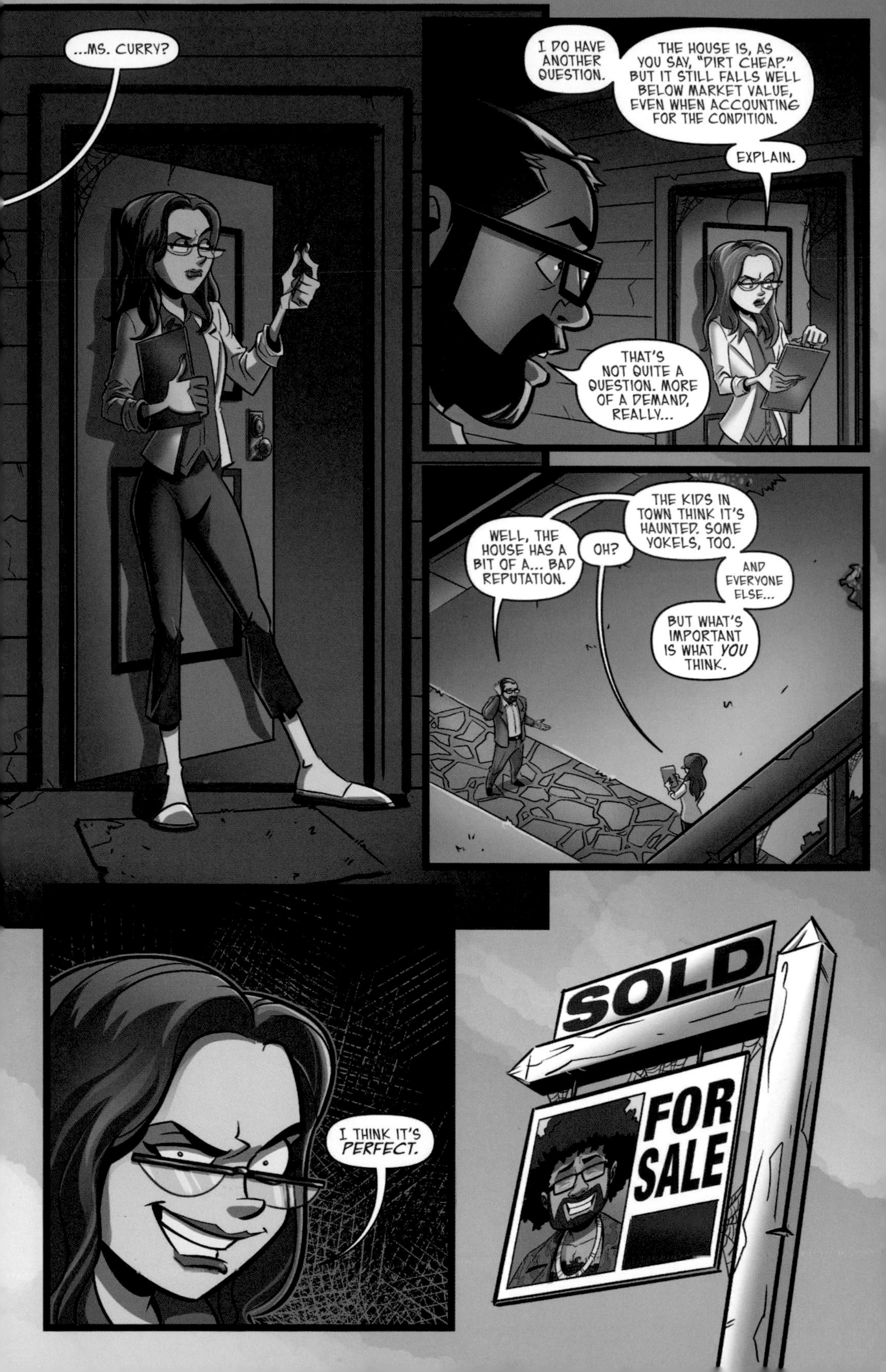
...MS. CURRY?
I DO HAVE ANOTHER QUESTION.
THE HOUSE IS, AS YOU SAY, "DIRT CHEAP." BUT IT STILL FALLS WELL BELOW MARKET VALUE, EVEN WHEN ACCOUNTING FOR THE CONDITION.
EXPLAIN.
THAT'S NOT QUITE A QUESTION. MORE OF A DEMAND, REALLY...
WELL, THE HOUSE HAS A BIT OF A... BAD REPUTATION.
OH?
THE KIDS IN TOWN THINK IT'S HAUNTED. SOME YOKELS, TOO.
AND EVERYONE ELSE...
BUT WHAT'S IMPORTANT IS WHAT *YOU* THINK.
I THINK IT'S *PERFECT.*
SOLD
FOR SALE

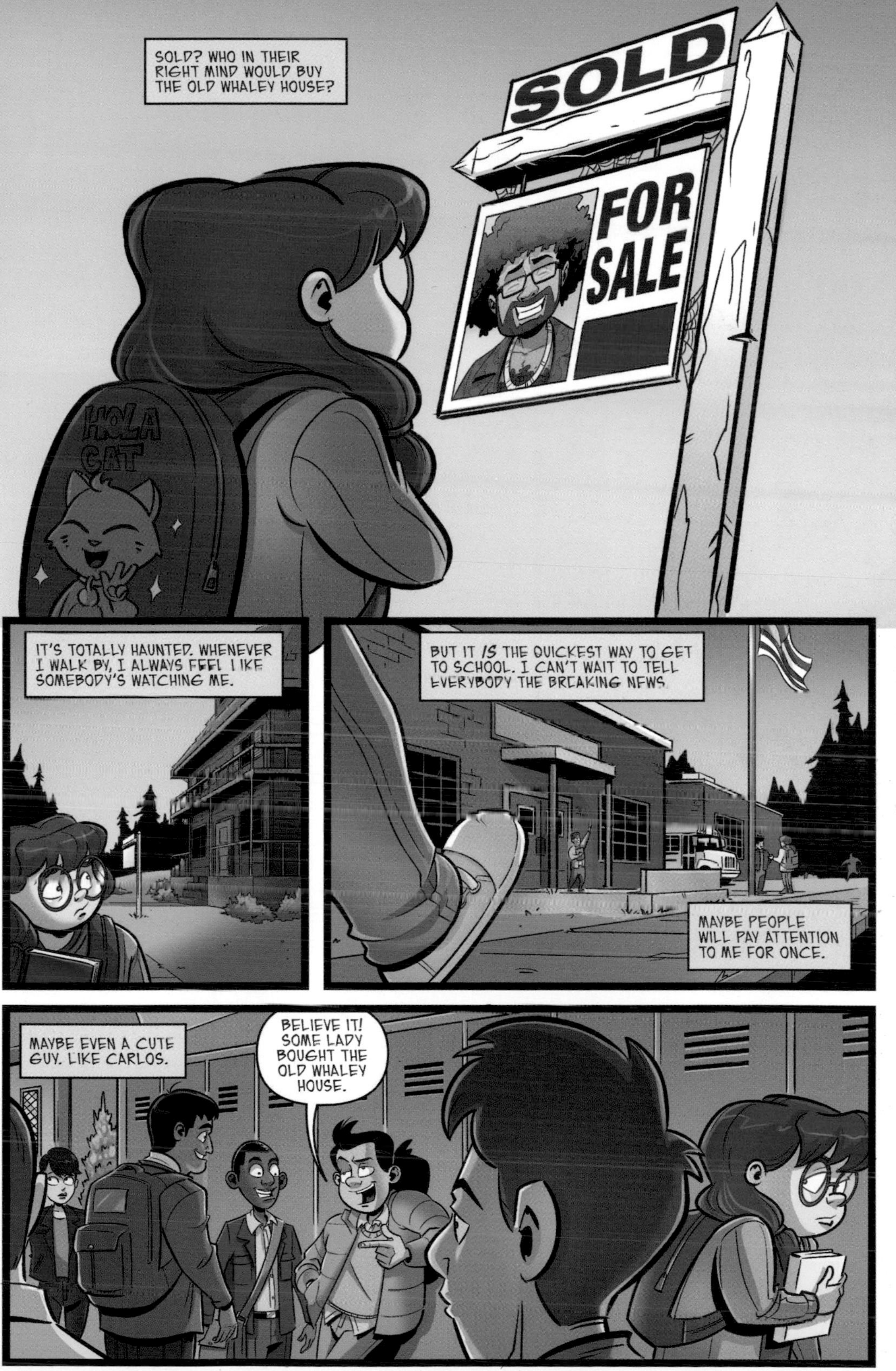
SOLD? WHO IN THEIR RIGHT MIND WOULD BUY THE OLD WHALEY HOUSE?
SOLD
FOR SALE
HOLA CAT
IT'S TOTALLY HAUNTED. WHENEVER I WALK BY, I ALWAYS FEEL LIKE SOMEBODY'S WATCHING ME.
BUT IT *IS* THE QUICKEST WAY TO GET TO SCHOOL. I CAN'T WAIT TO TELL EVERYBODY THE BREAKING NEWS.
MAYBE PEOPLE WILL PAY ATTENTION TO ME FOR ONCE.
MAYBE EVEN A CUTE GUY. LIKE CARLOS.
BELIEVE IT! SOME LADY BOUGHT THE OLD WHALEY HOUSE.

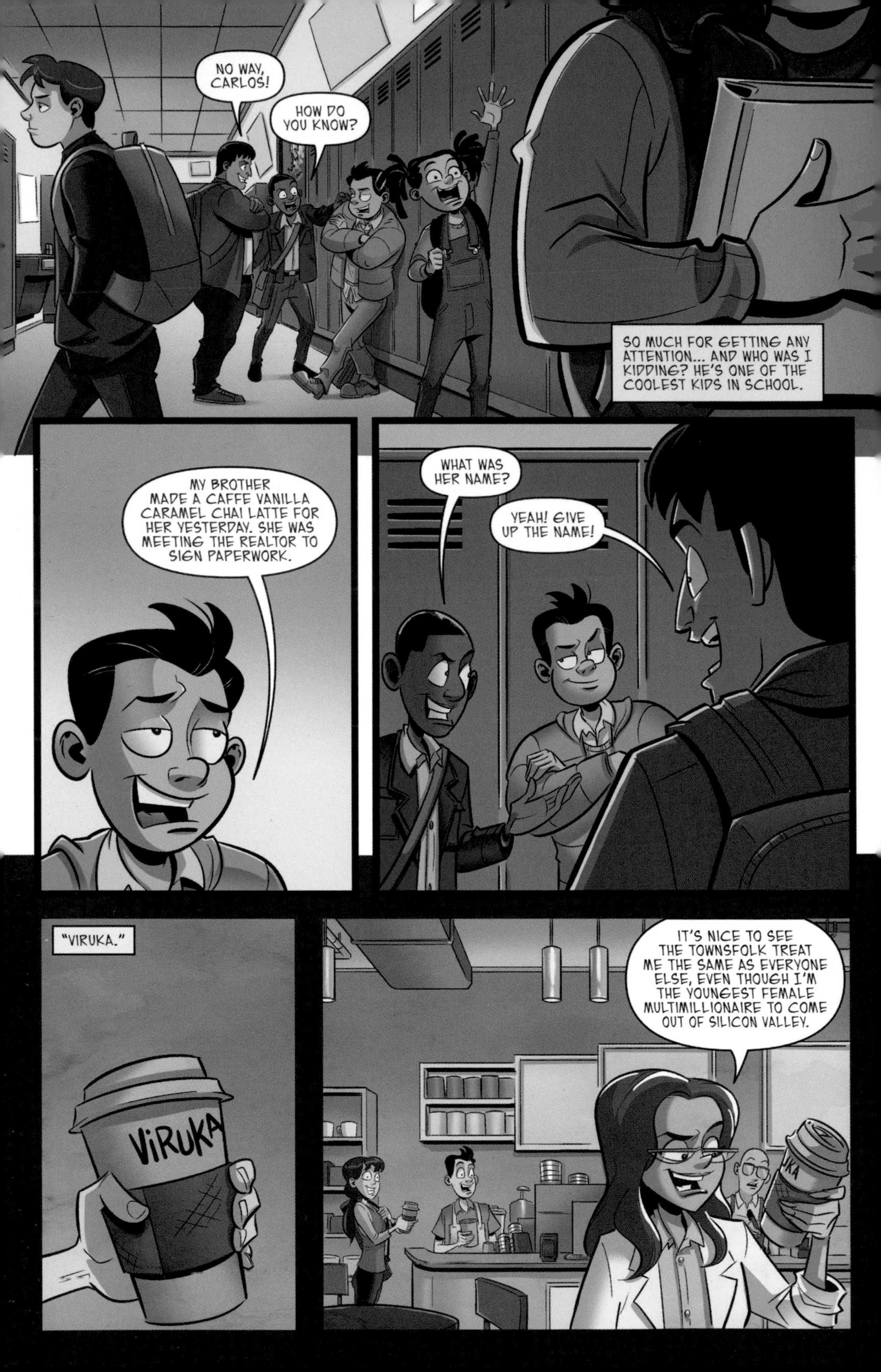
NO WAY, CARLOS!
HOW DO YOU KNOW?
SO MUCH FOR GETTING ANY ATTENTION... AND WHO WAS I KIDDING? HE'S ONE OF THE COOLEST KIDS IN SCHOOL.
MY BROTHER MADE A CAFFE VANILLA CARAMEL CHAI LATTE FOR HER YESTERDAY. SHE WAS MEETING THE REALTOR TO SIGN PAPERWORK.
WHAT WAS HER NAME?
YEAH! GIVE UP THE NAME!
"VIRUKA."
VIRUKA
IT'S NICE TO SEE THE TOWNSFOLK TREAT ME THE SAME AS EVERYONE ELSE, EVEN THOUGH I'M THE YOUNGEST FEMALE MULTIMILLIONAIRE TO COME OUT OF SILICON VALLEY.

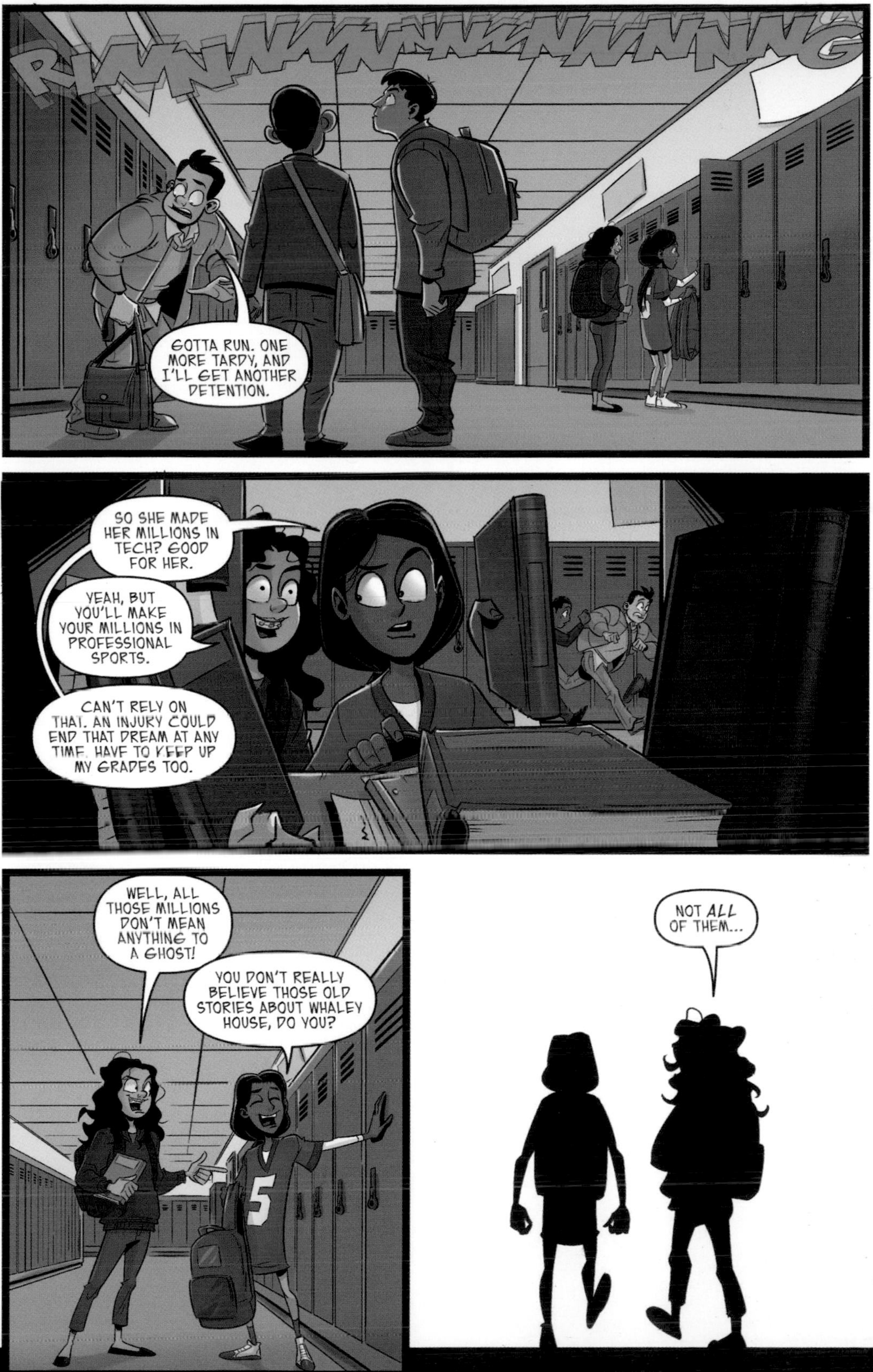
RIIINNNNNNNNNNNNNNNNNG
GOTTA RUN. ONE MORE TARDY, AND I'LL GET ANOTHER DETENTION.
SO SHE MADE HER MILLIONS IN TECH? GOOD FOR HER.
YEAH, BUT YOU'LL MAKE YOUR MILLIONS IN PROFESSIONAL SPORTS.
CAN'T RELY ON THAT. AN INJURY COULD END THAT DREAM AT ANY TIME. HAVE TO KEEP UP MY GRADES TOO.
WELL, ALL THOSE MILLIONS DON'T MEAN ANYTHING TO A GHOST!
YOU DON'T REALLY BELIEVE THOSE OLD STORIES ABOUT WHALEY HOUSE, DO YOU?
NOT ALL OF THEM...

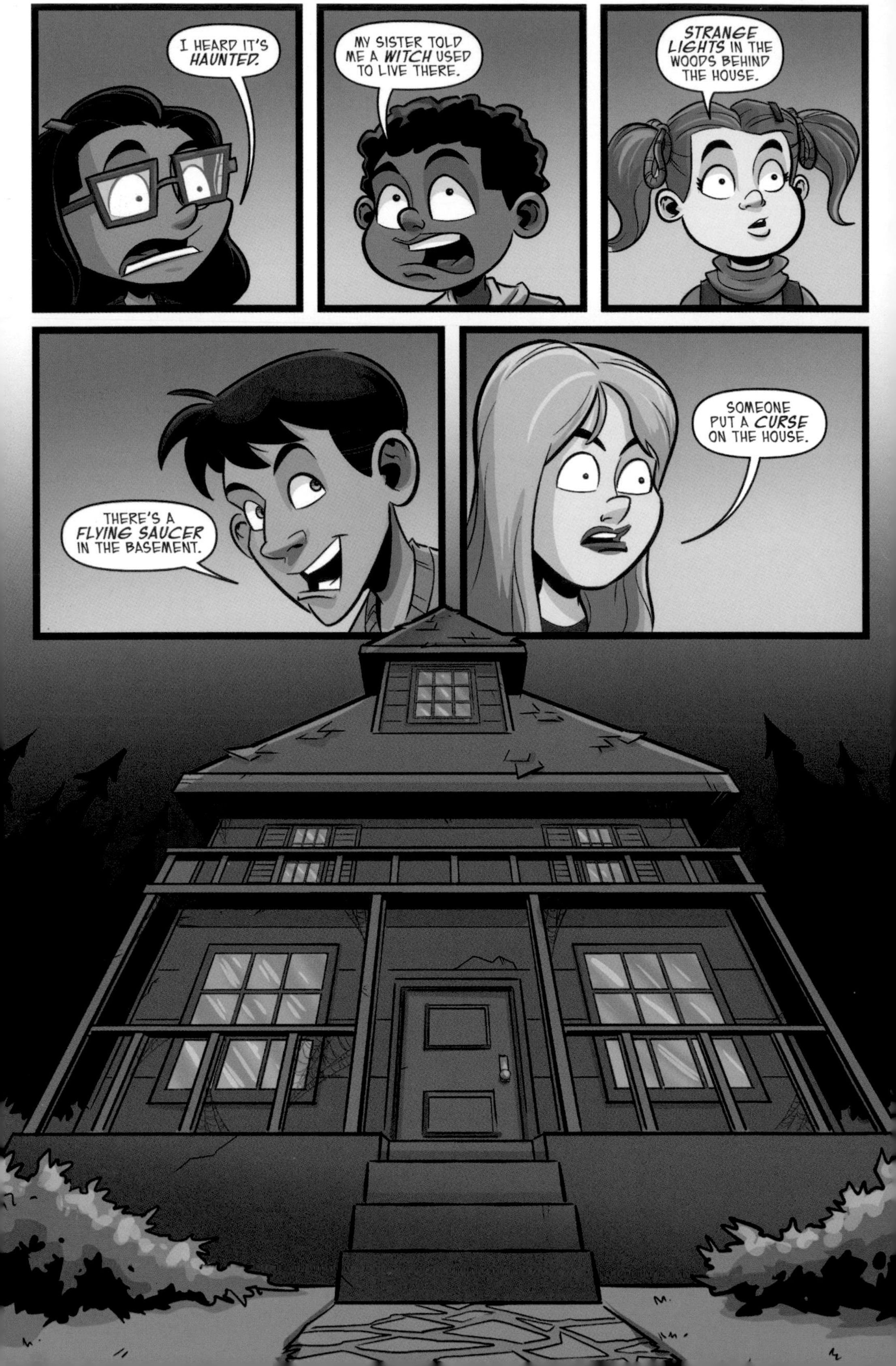
I HEARD IT'S *HAUNTED.*
MY SISTER TOLD ME A *WITCH* USED TO LIVE THERE.
STRANGE LIGHTS IN THE WOODS BEHIND THE HOUSE.
THERE'S A *FLYING SAUCER* IN THE BASEMENT.
SOMEONE PUT A *CURSE* ON THE HOUSE.

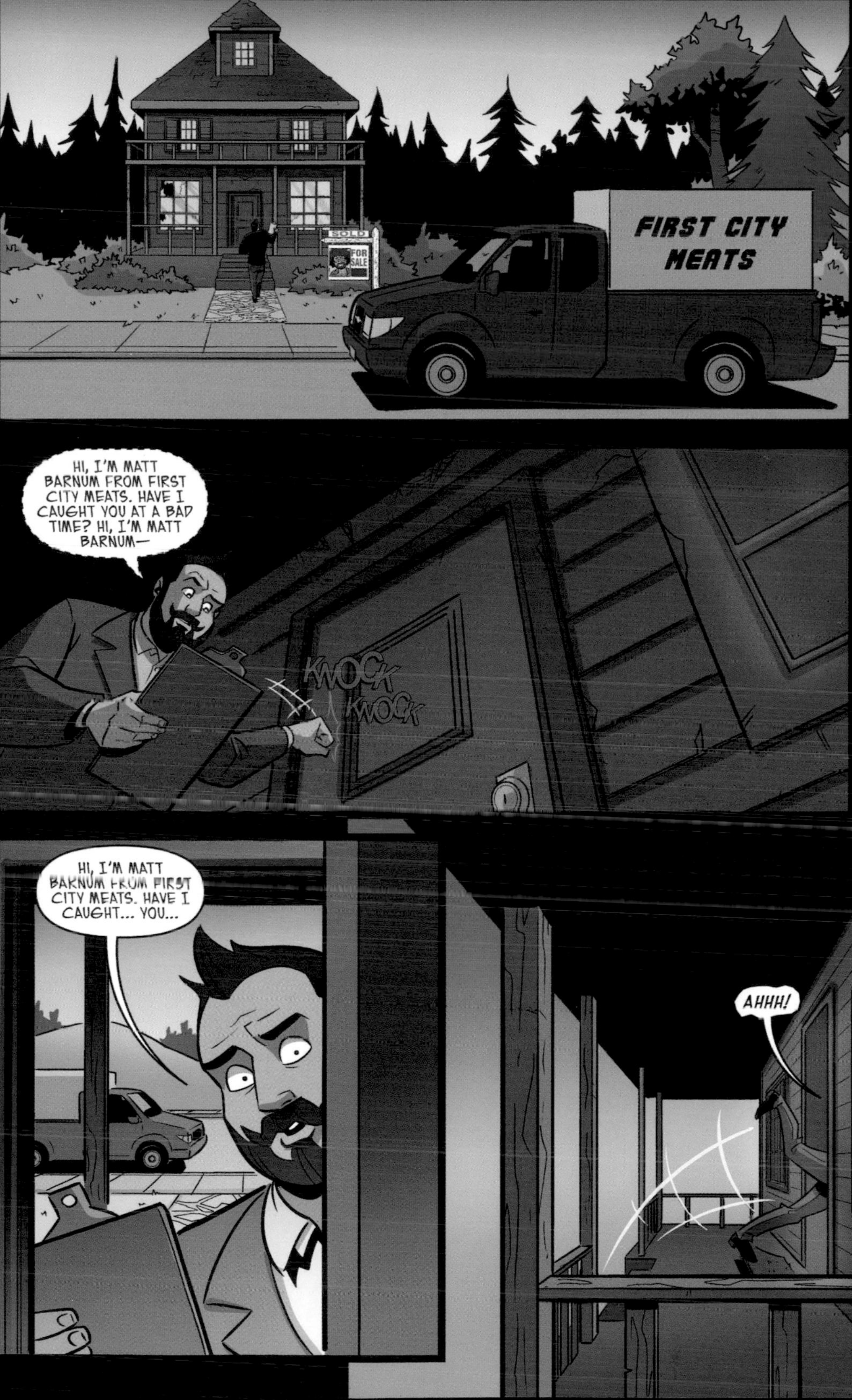
SOLD
FOR SALE
FIRST CITY MEATS
HI, I'M MATT BARNUM FROM FIRST CITY MEATS. HAVE I CAUGHT YOU AT A BAD TIME? HI, I'M MATT BARNUM—
KNOCK KNOCK
HI, I'M MATT BARNUM FROM FIRST CITY MEATS. HAVE I CAUGHT... YOU...
AHHH!

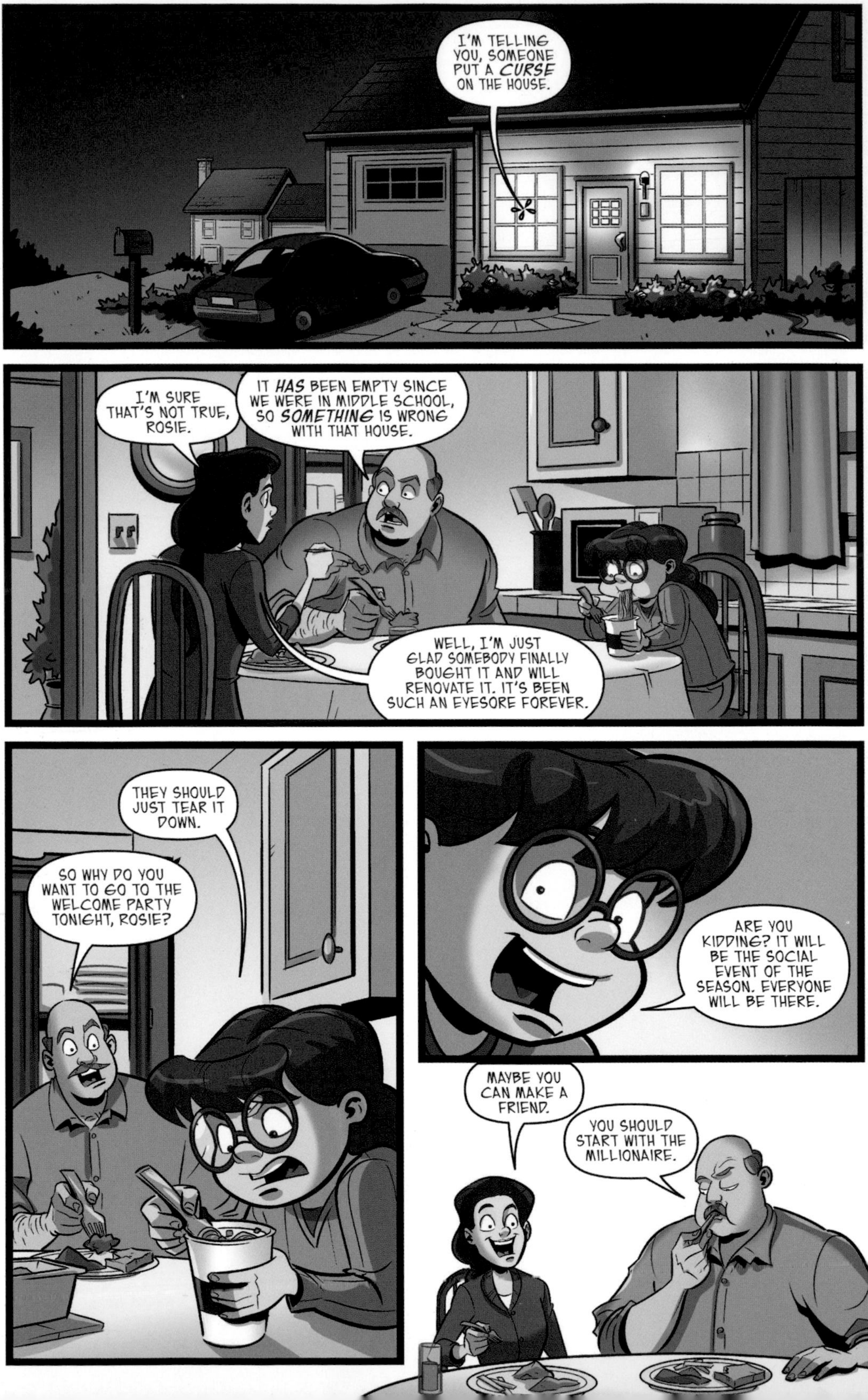
I'M TELLING YOU, SOMEONE PUT A *CURSE* ON THE HOUSE.
I'M SURE THAT'S NOT TRUE, ROSIE.
IT *HAS* BEEN EMPTY SINCE WE WERE IN MIDDLE SCHOOL, SO *SOMETHING* IS WRONG WITH THAT HOUSE.
WELL, I'M JUST GLAD SOMEBODY FINALLY BOUGHT IT AND WILL RENOVATE IT. IT'S BEEN SUCH AN EYESORE FOREVER.
THEY SHOULD JUST TEAR IT DOWN.
SO WHY DO YOU WANT TO GO TO THE WELCOME PARTY TONIGHT, ROSIE?
ARE YOU KIDDING? IT WILL BE THE SOCIAL EVENT OF THE SEASON. EVERYONE WILL BE THERE.
MAYBE YOU CAN MAKE A FRIEND.
YOU SHOULD START WITH THE MILLIONAIRE.

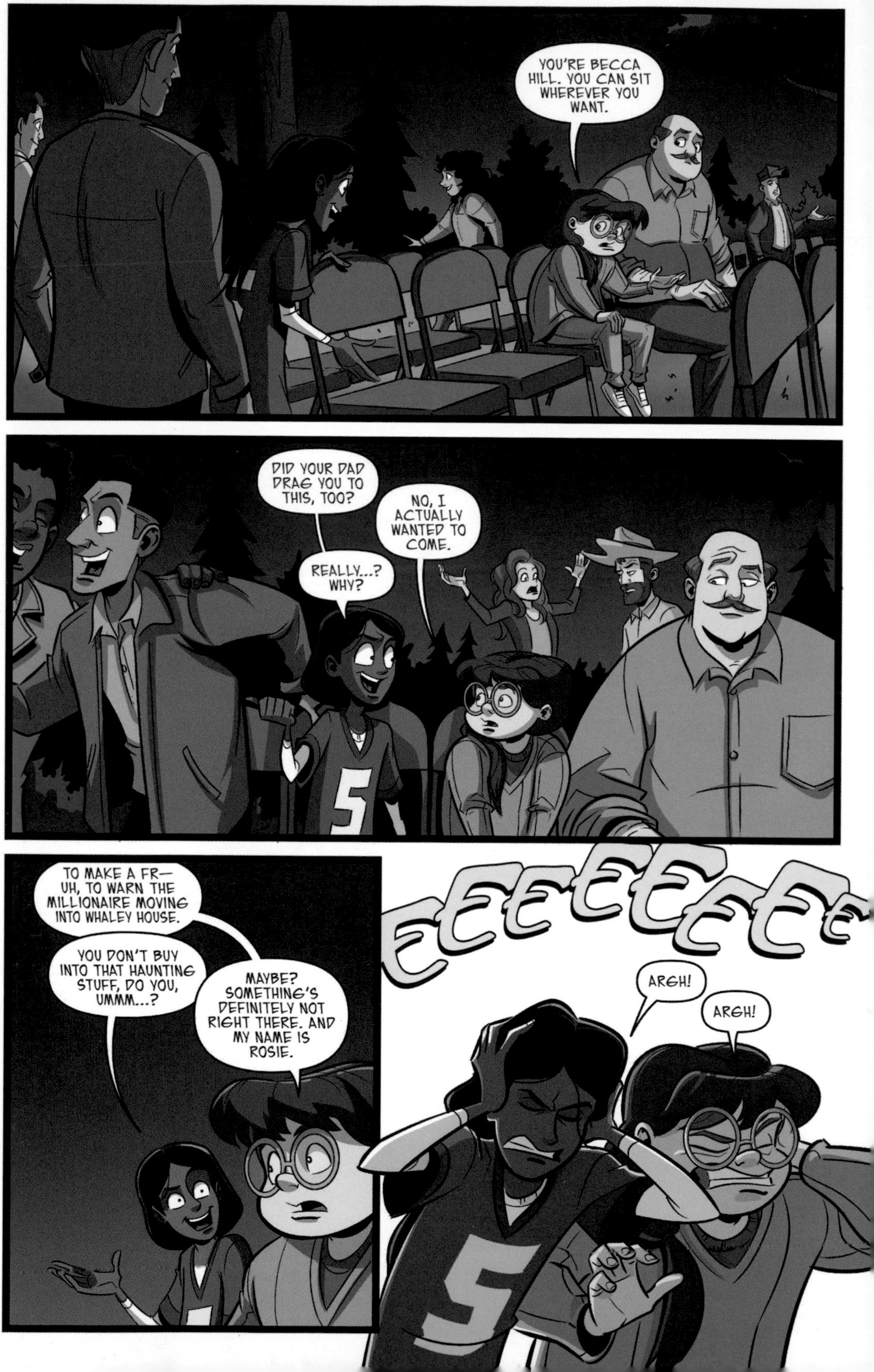
YOU'RE BECCA HILL. YOU CAN SIT WHEREVER YOU WANT.
DID YOUR DAD DRAG YOU TO THIS, TOO?
NO, I ACTUALLY WANTED TO COME.
REALLY...? WHY?
TO MAKE A FR— UH, TO WARN THE MILLIONAIRE MOVING INTO WHALEY HOUSE.
YOU DON'T BUY INTO THAT HAUNTING STUFF, DO YOU, UMMM...?
MAYBE? SOMETHING'S DEFINITELY NOT RIGHT THERE. AND MY NAME IS ROSIE.
EEEEEEEEE
ARGH!
ARGH!

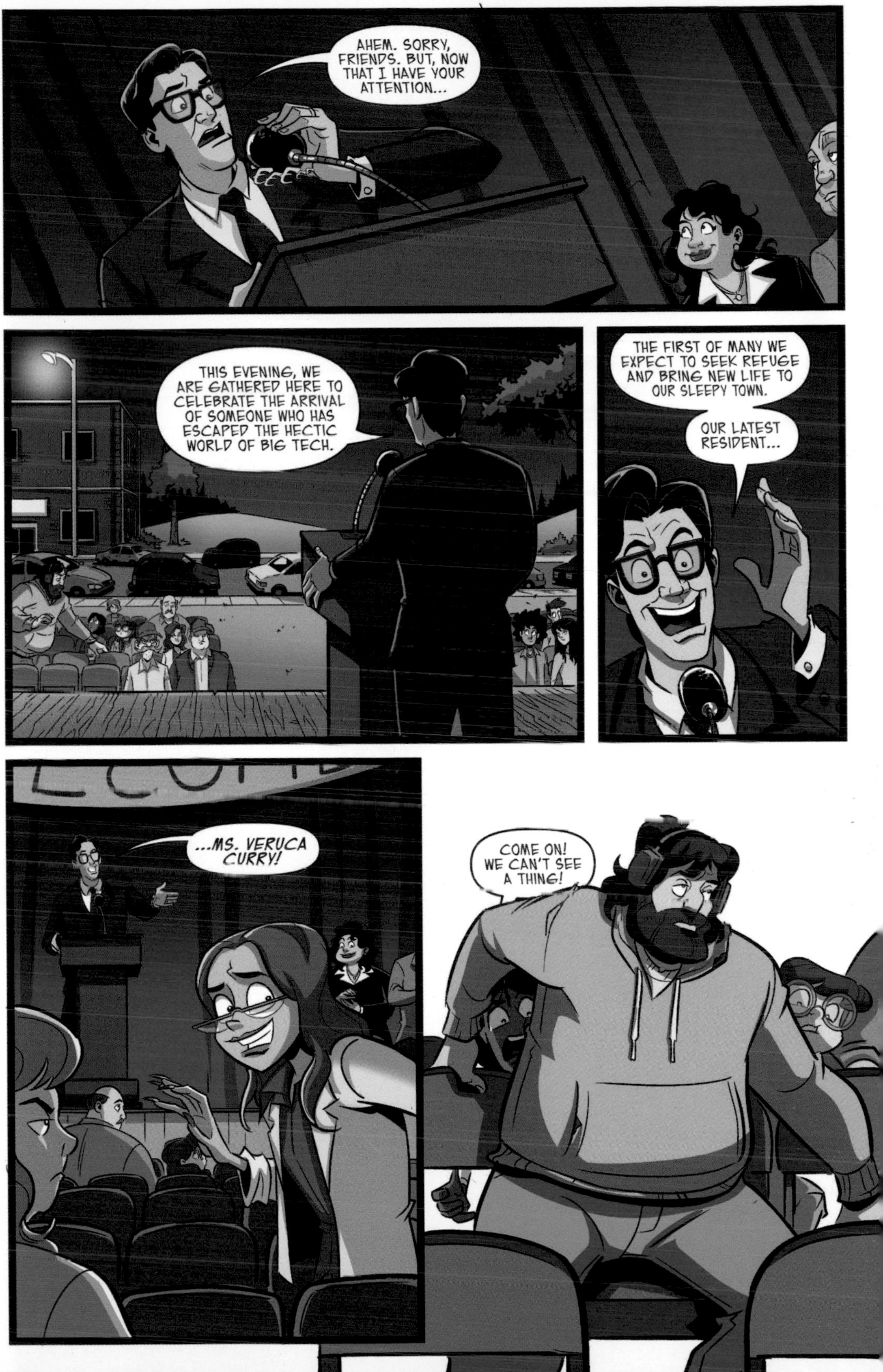
AHEM. SORRY, FRIENDS. BUT, NOW THAT I HAVE YOUR ATTENTION...
EEEE
THIS EVENING, WE ARE GATHERED HERE TO CELEBRATE THE ARRIVAL OF SOMEONE WHO HAS ESCAPED THE HECTIC WORLD OF BIG TECH.
THE FIRST OF MANY WE EXPECT TO SEEK REFUGE AND BRING NEW LIFE TO OUR SLEEPY TOWN.
OUR LATEST RESIDENT...
...MS. VERUCA CURRY!
COME ON! WE CAN'T SEE A THING!

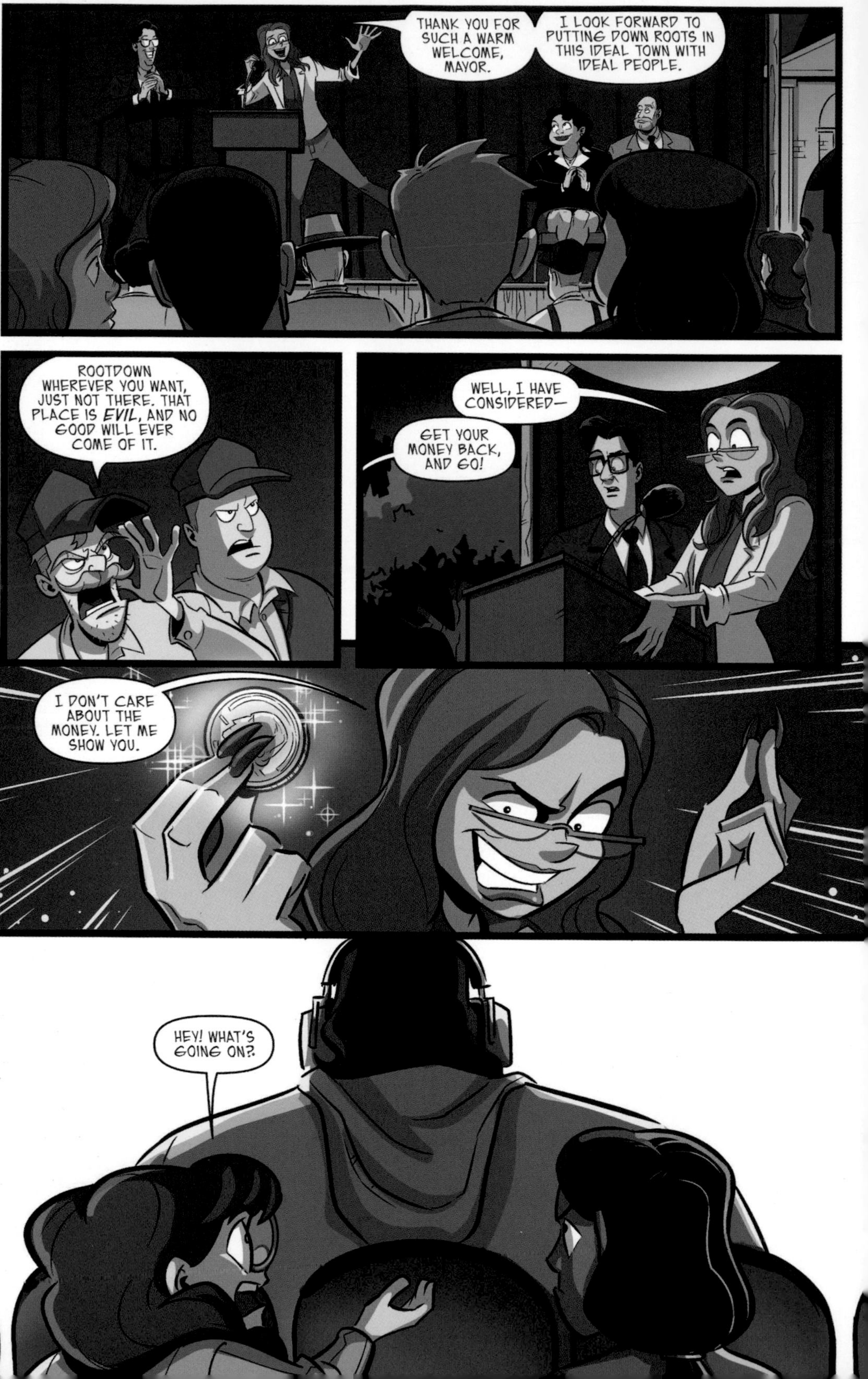
THANK YOU FOR SUCH A WARM WELCOME, MAYOR.
I LOOK FORWARD TO PUTTING DOWN ROOTS IN THIS IDEAL TOWN WITH IDEAL PEOPLE.
ROOTDOWN WHEREVER YOU WANT, JUST NOT THERE. THAT PLACE IS EVIL, AND NO GOOD WILL EVER COME OF IT.
WELL, I HAVE CONSIDERED—
GET YOUR MONEY BACK, AND GO!
I DON'T CARE ABOUT THE MONEY. LET ME SHOW YOU.
HEY! WHAT'S GOING ON?!

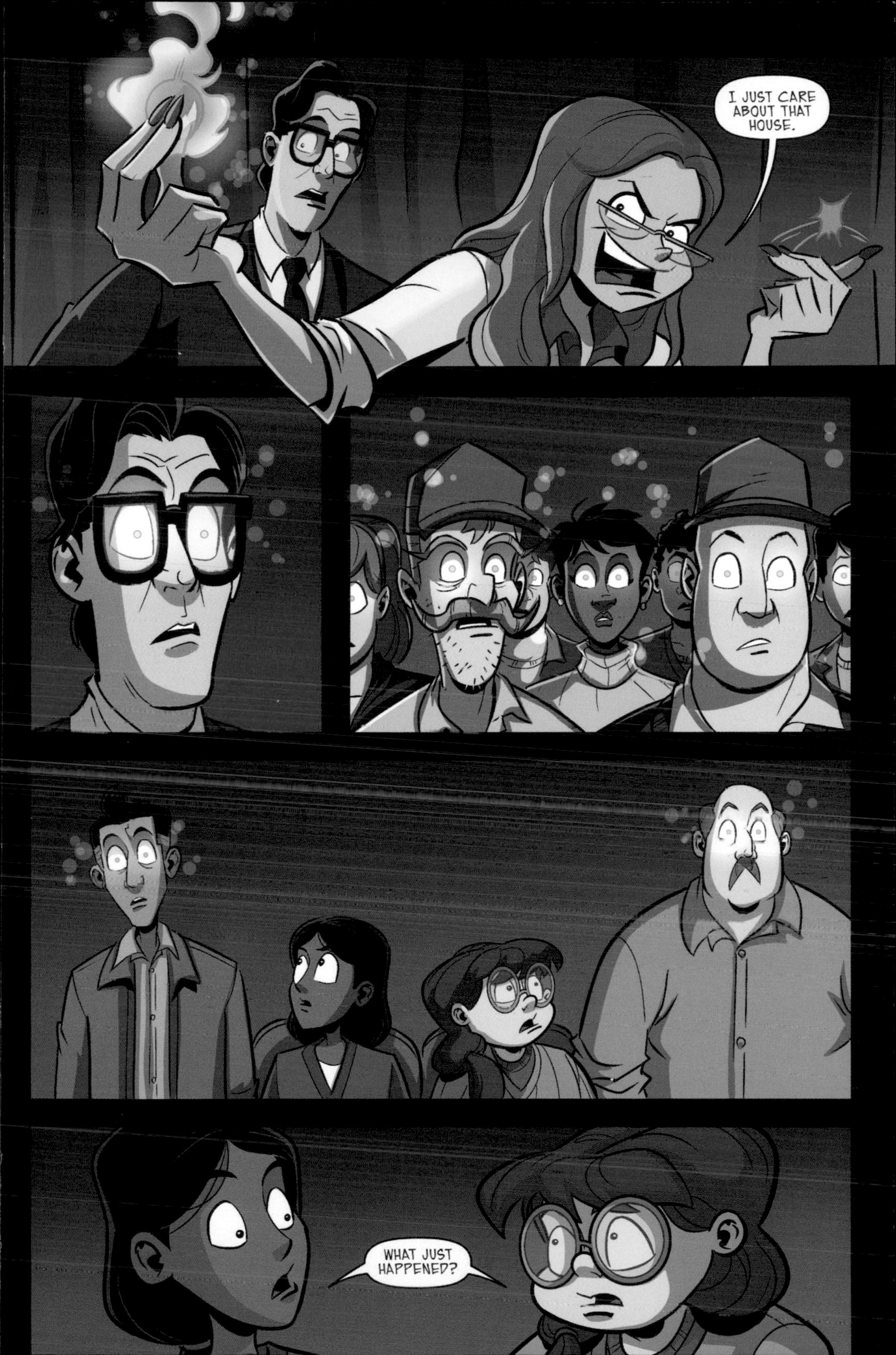
I JUST CARE ABOUT THAT HOUSE.
WHAT JUST HAPPENED?

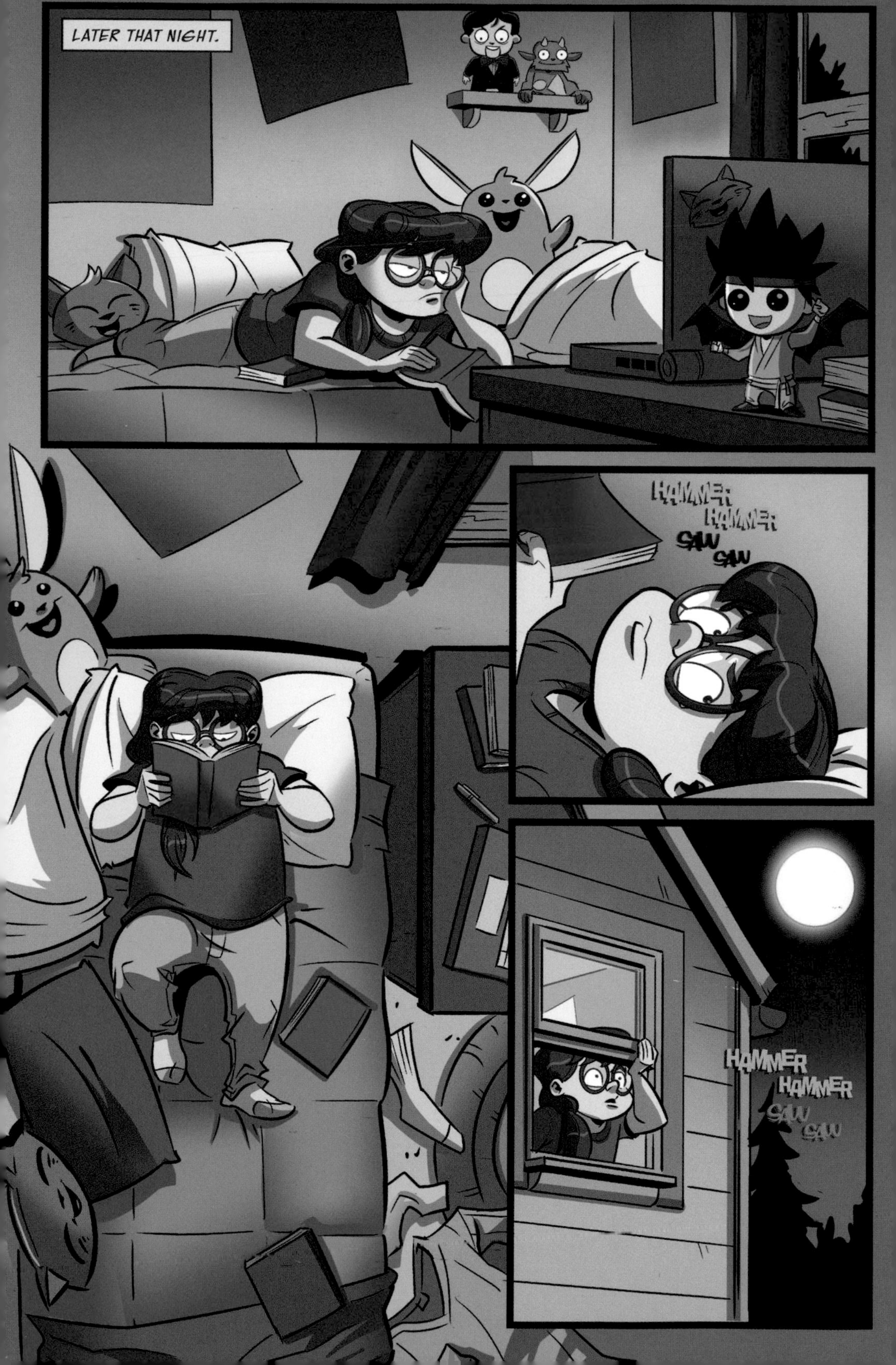
LATER THAT NIGHT.
HAMMER
HAMMER
SAW
SAW
HAMMER
HAMMER
SAW
SAW

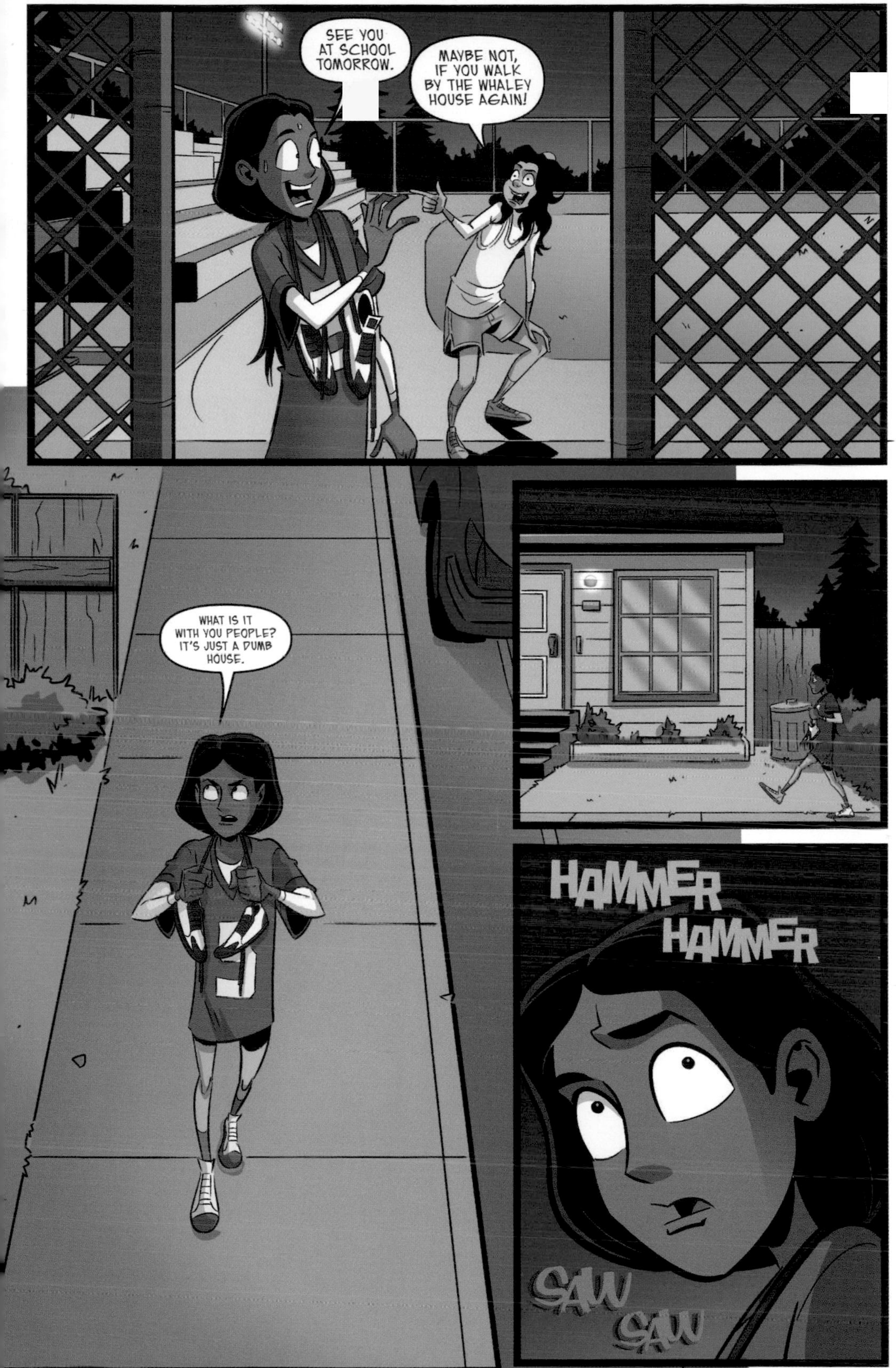
SEE YOU AT SCHOOL TOMORROW.
MAYBE NOT, IF YOU WALK BY THE WHALEY HOUSE AGAIN!
WHAT IS IT WITH YOU PEOPLE? IT'S JUST A DUMB HOUSE.
HAMMER
HAMMER
SAW
SAW

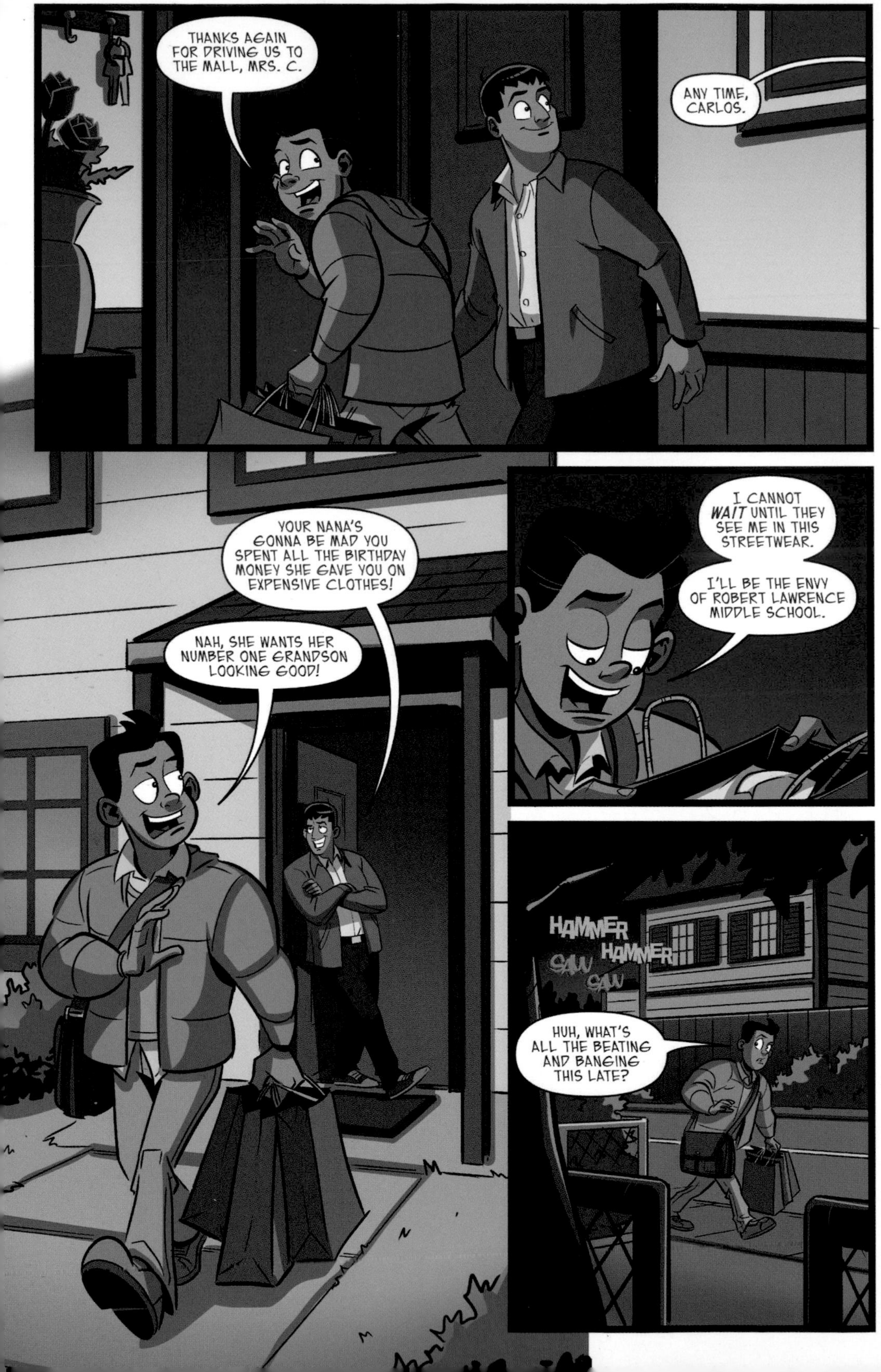
THANKS AGAIN FOR DRIVING US TO THE MALL, MRS. C.
ANY TIME, CARLOS.
YOUR NANA'S GONNA BE MAD YOU SPENT ALL THE BIRTHDAY MONEY SHE GAVE YOU ON EXPENSIVE CLOTHES!
NAH, SHE WANTS HER NUMBER ONE GRANDSON LOOKING GOOD!
I CANNOT *WAIT* UNTIL THEY SEE ME IN THIS STREETWEAR.
I'LL BE THE ENVY OF ROBERT LAWRENCE MIDDLE SCHOOL.
HAMMER
HAMMER
SAW
SAW
HUH, WHAT'S ALL THE BEATING AND BANGING THIS LATE?

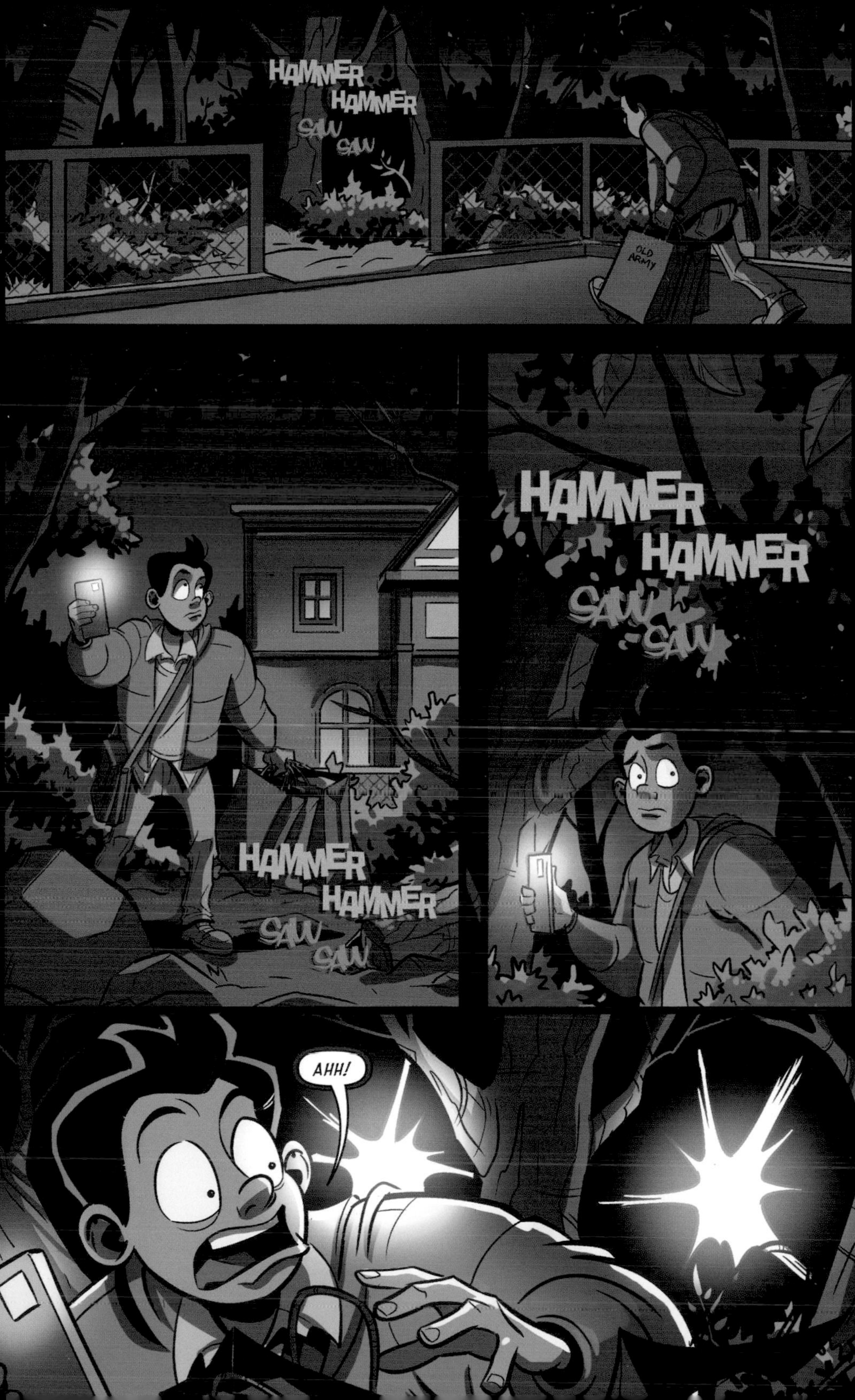
HAMMER
HAMMER
SAW
SAW
OLD ARMY
HAMMER
HAMMER
SAW
SAW
HAMMER
HAMMER
SAW
SAW
AHH!

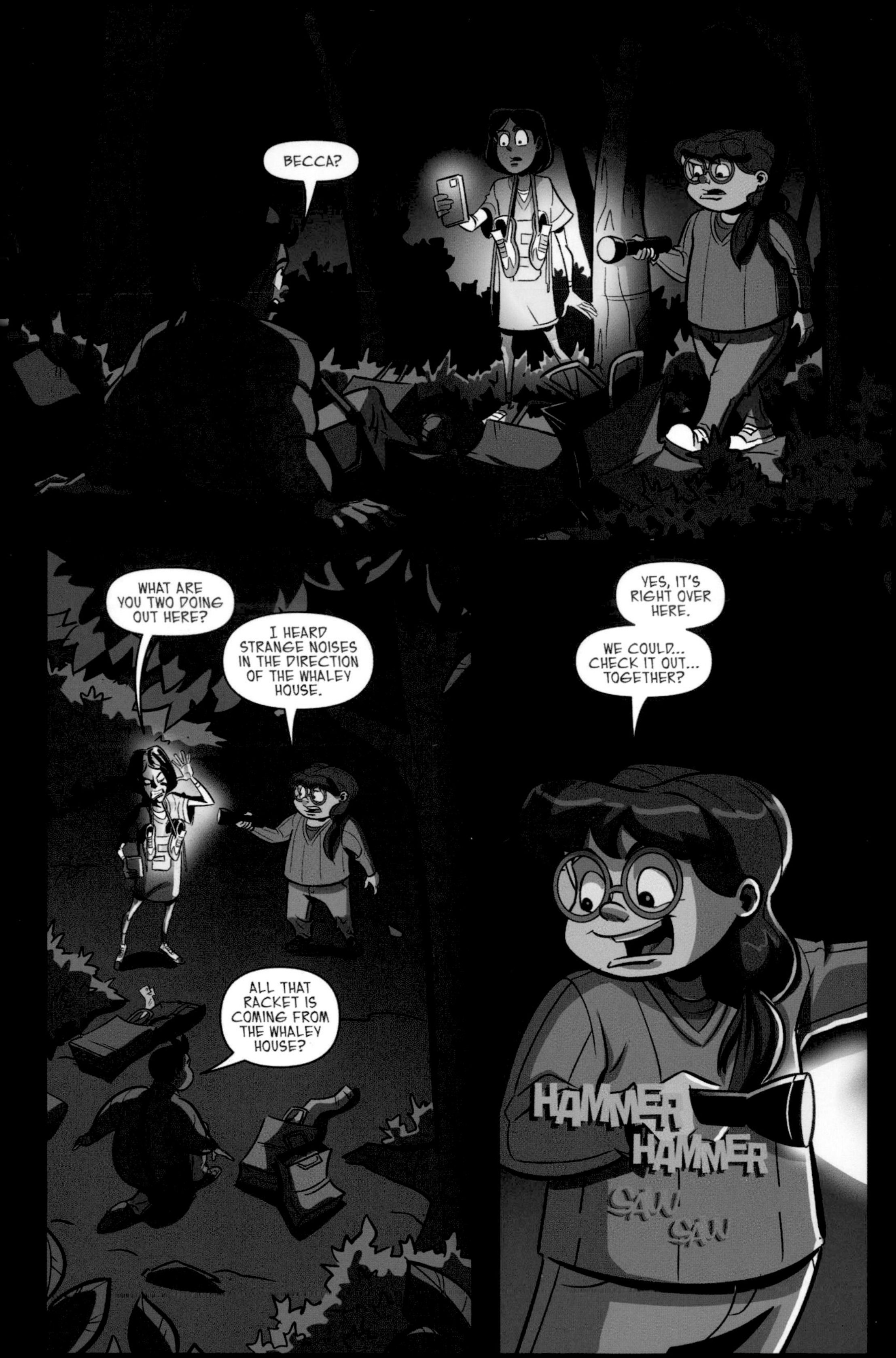

BECCA?
WHAT ARE YOU TWO DOING OUT HERE?
I HEARD STRANGE NOISES IN THE DIRECTION OF THE WHALEY HOUSE.
ALL THAT RACKET IS COMING FROM THE WHALEY HOUSE?
YES, IT'S RIGHT OVER HERE.
WE COULD... CHECK IT OUT... TOGETHER?
HAMMER HAMMER
SAW SAW

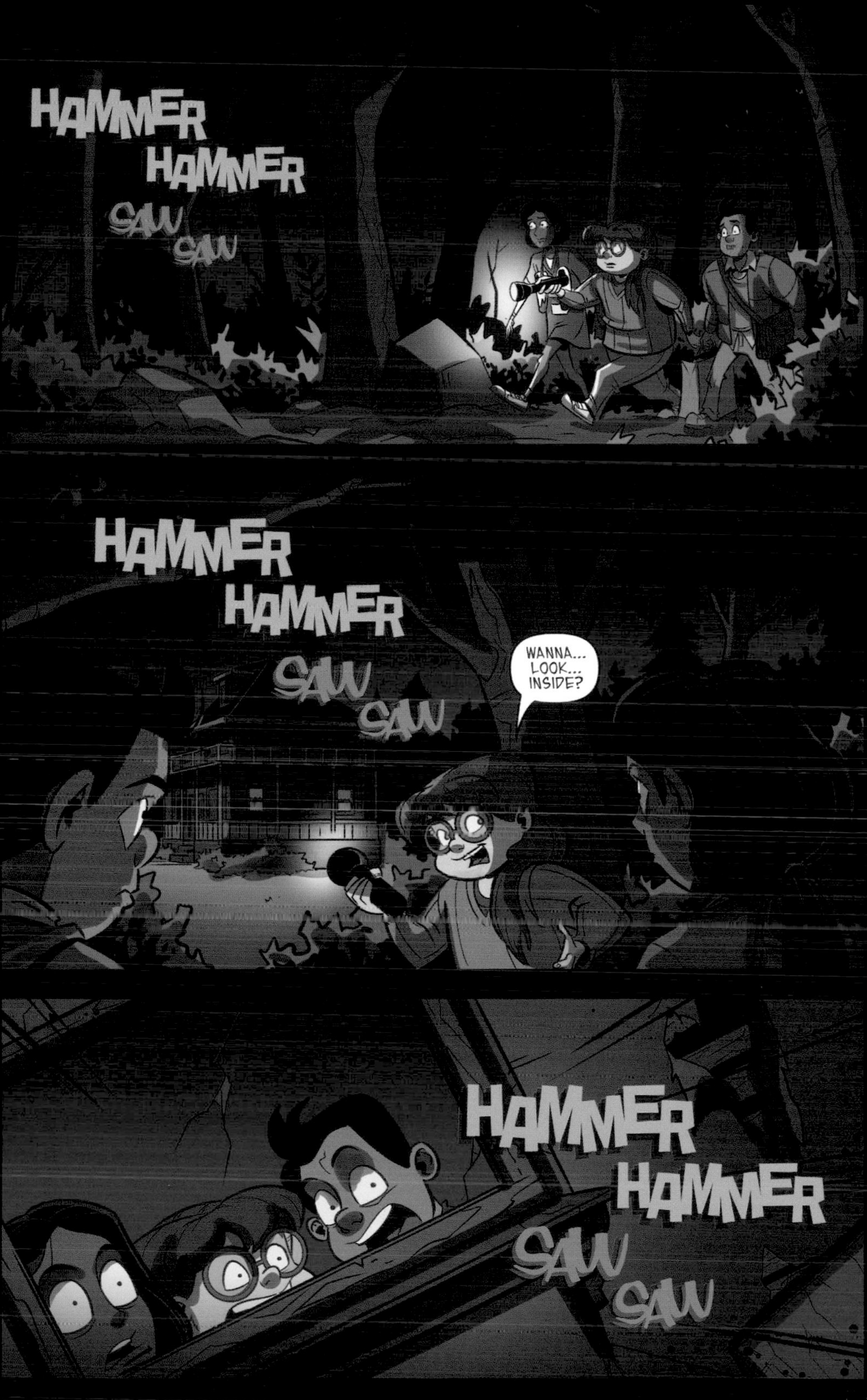
HAMMER
HAMMER
SAW
SAW
HAMMER
HAMMER
SAW
SAW
WANNA... LOOK... INSIDE?
HAMMER
HAMMER
SAW
SAW

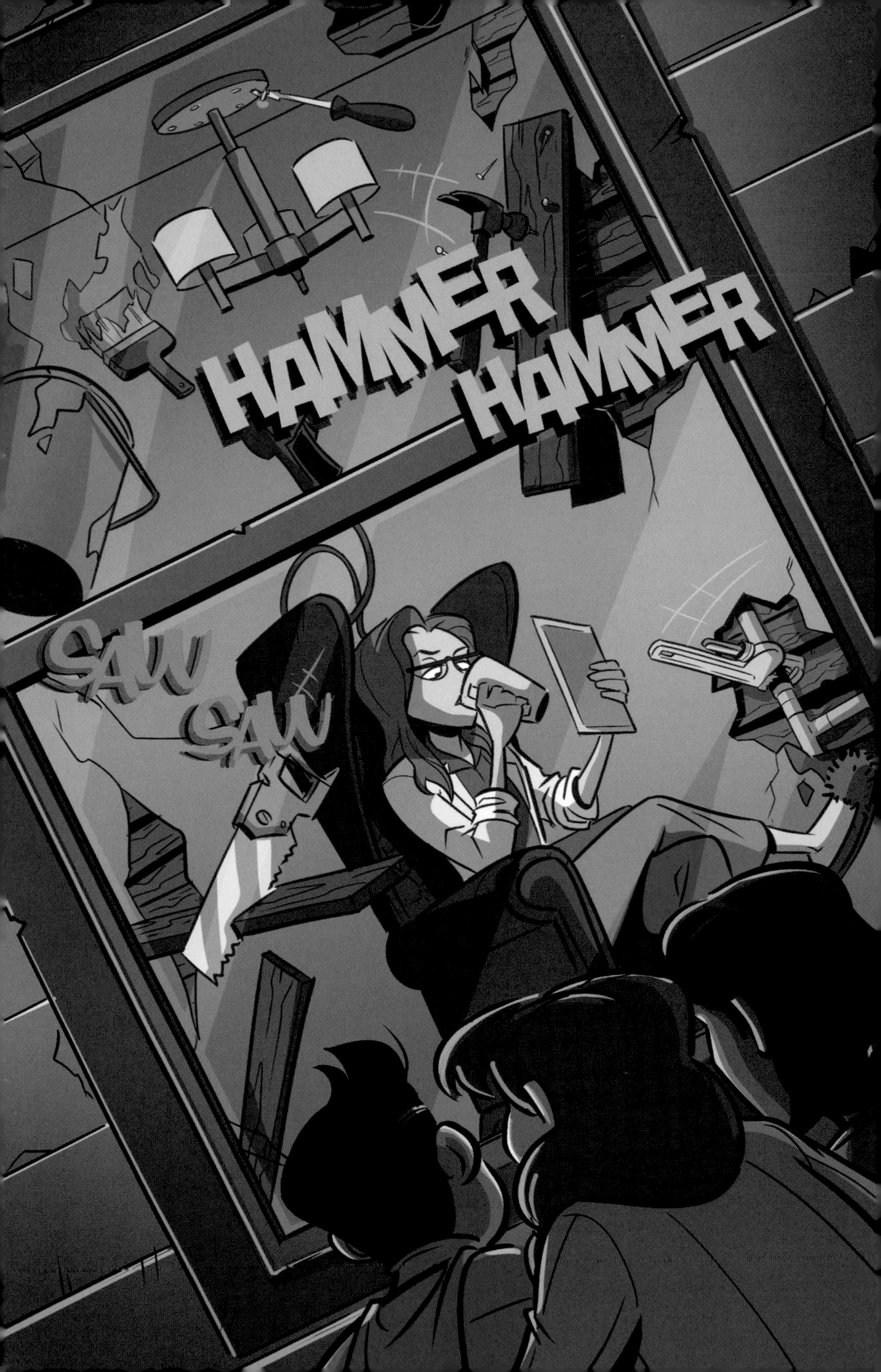
HAMMER
HAMMER
SAW
SAW

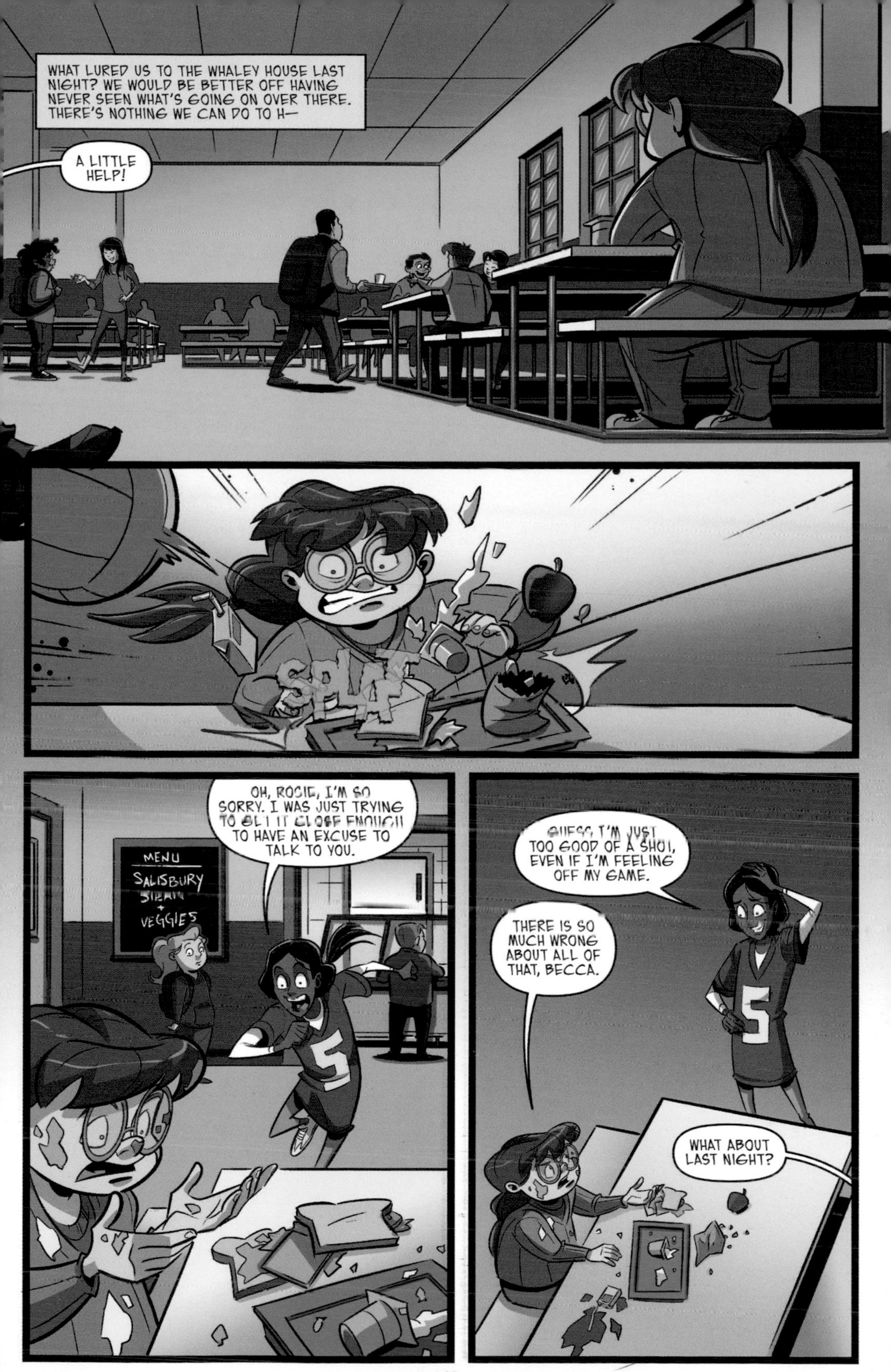
WHAT LURED US TO THE WHALEY HOUSE LAST NIGHT? WE WOULD BE BETTER OFF HAVING NEVER SEEN WHAT'S GOING ON OVER THERE. THERE'S NOTHING WE CAN DO TO H—
A LITTLE HELP!
SPLAT
OH, ROSIE, I'M SO SORRY. I WAS JUST TRYING TO GET IT CLOSE ENOUGH TO HAVE AN EXCUSE TO TALK TO YOU.
MENU
SALISBURY STEAK + VEGGIES
GUESS I'M JUST TOO GOOD OF A SHOT, EVEN IF I'M FEELING OFF MY GAME.
THERE IS SO MUCH WRONG ABOUT ALL OF THAT, BECCA.
WHAT ABOUT LAST NIGHT?

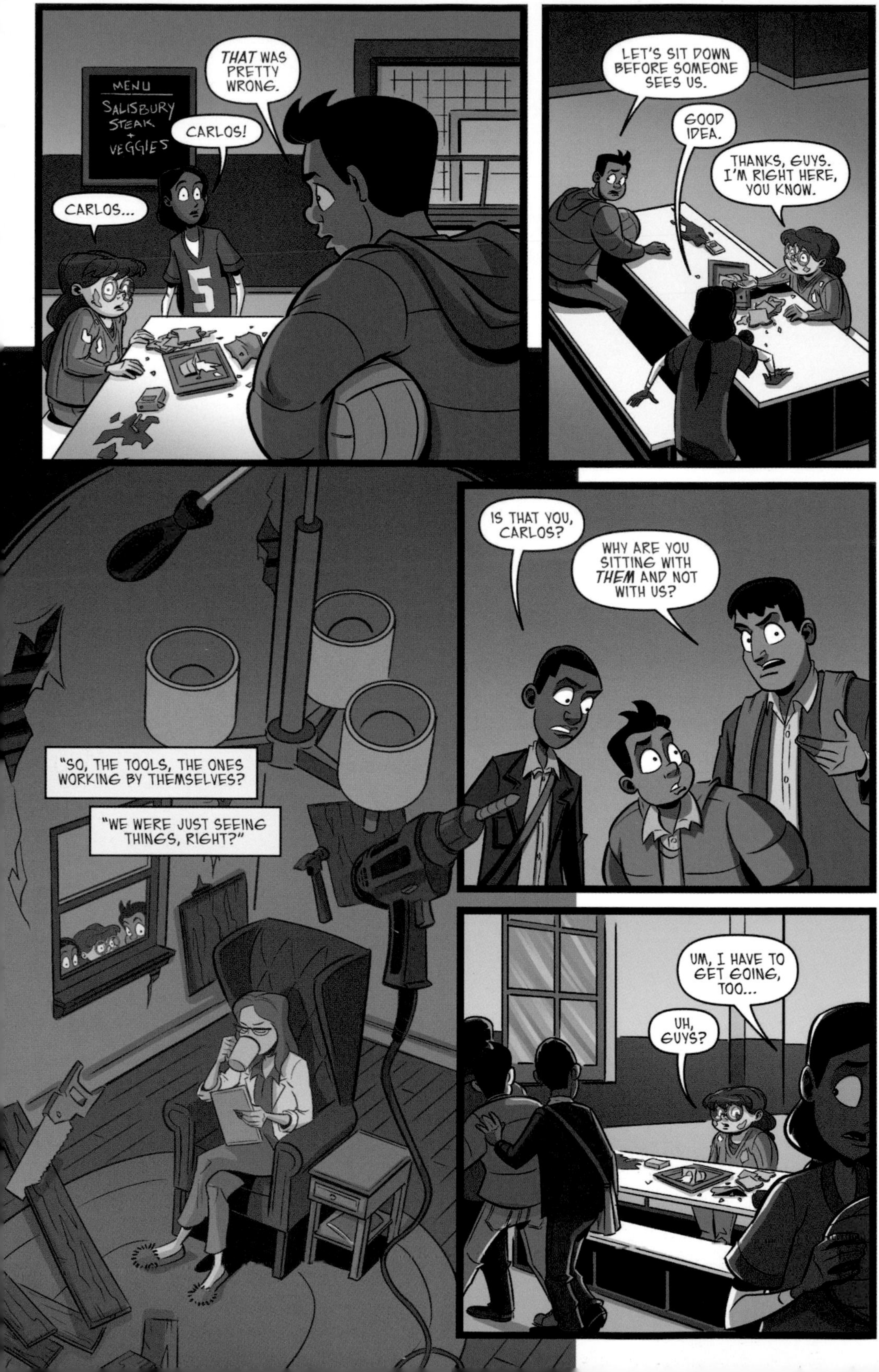
MENU
SALISBURY STEAK + VEGGIES
THAT WAS PRETTY WRONG.
CARLOS!
CARLOS...
LET'S SIT DOWN BEFORE SOMEONE SEES US.
GOOD IDEA.
THANKS, GUYS. I'M RIGHT HERE, YOU KNOW.
"SO, THE TOOLS, THE ONES WORKING BY THEMSELVES?
"WE WERE JUST SEEING THINGS, RIGHT?"
IS THAT YOU, CARLOS?
WHY ARE YOU SITTING WITH THEM AND NOT WITH US?
UM, I HAVE TO GET GOING, TOO...
UH, GUYS?

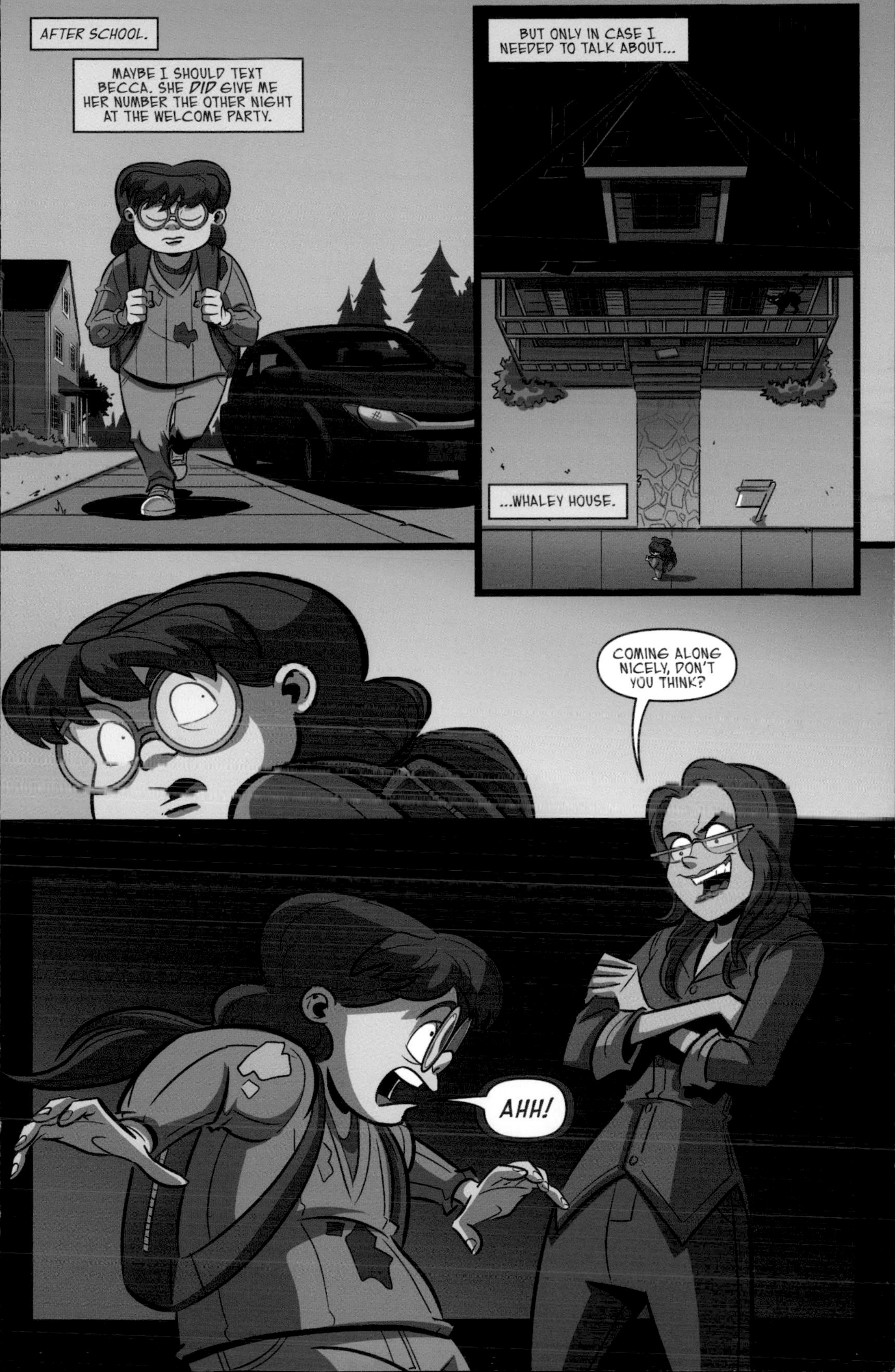
AFTER SCHOOL.
MAYBE I SHOULD TEXT BECCA. SHE *DID* GIVE ME HER NUMBER THE OTHER NIGHT AT THE WELCOME PARTY.
BUT ONLY IN CASE I NEEDED TO TALK ABOUT...
...WHALEY HOUSE.
COMING ALONG NICELY, DON'T YOU THINK?
AHH!

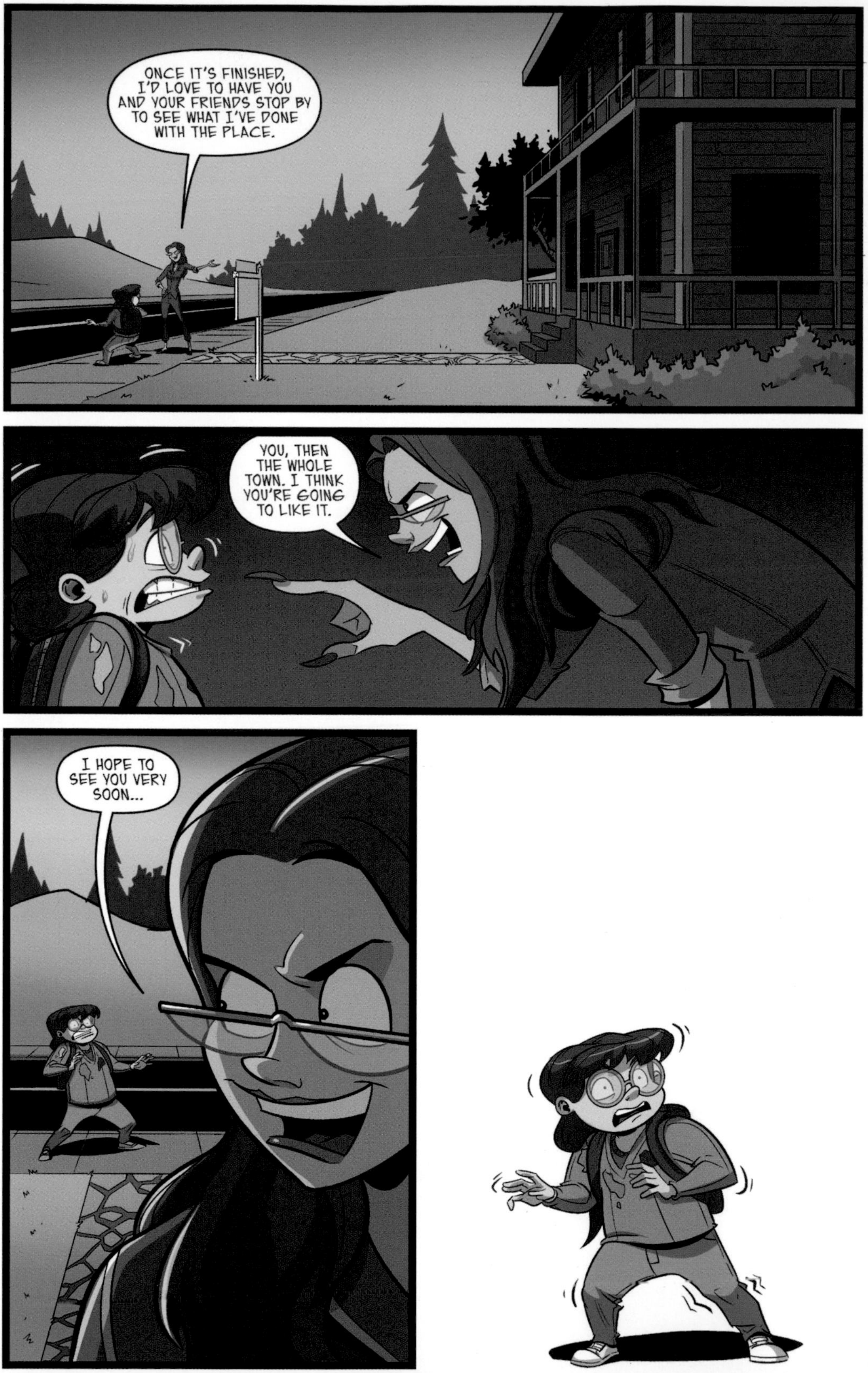
ONCE IT'S FINISHED, I'D LOVE TO HAVE YOU AND YOUR FRIENDS STOP BY TO SEE WHAT I'VE DONE WITH THE PLACE.
YOU, THEN THE WHOLE TOWN. I THINK YOU'RE GOING TO LIKE IT.
I HOPE TO SEE YOU VERY SOON...

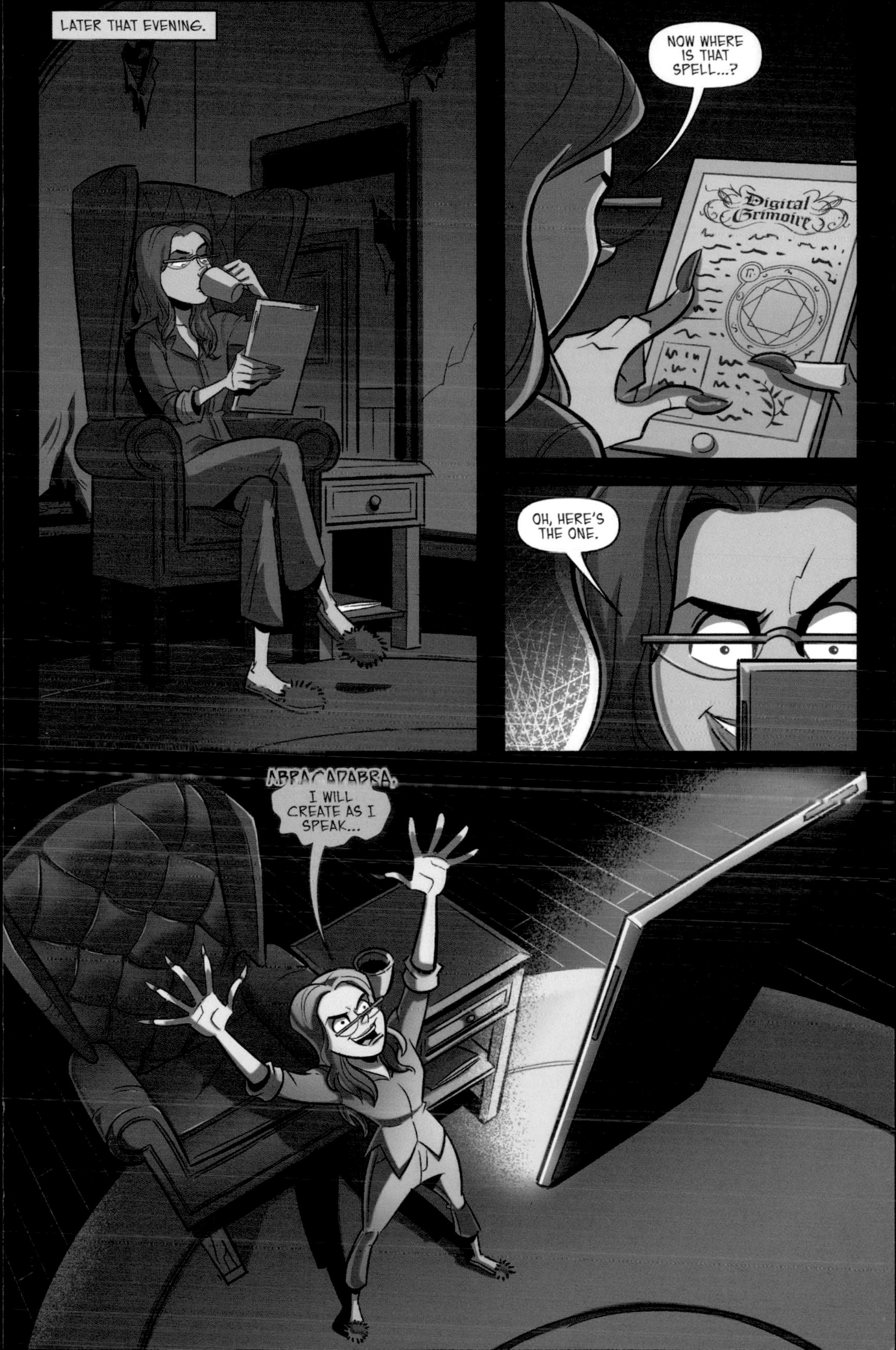
LATER THAT EVENING.
NOW WHERE IS THAT SPELL...?
Digital Grimoire
OH, HERE'S THE ONE.
ABRACADABRA. I WILL CREATE AS I SPEAK...

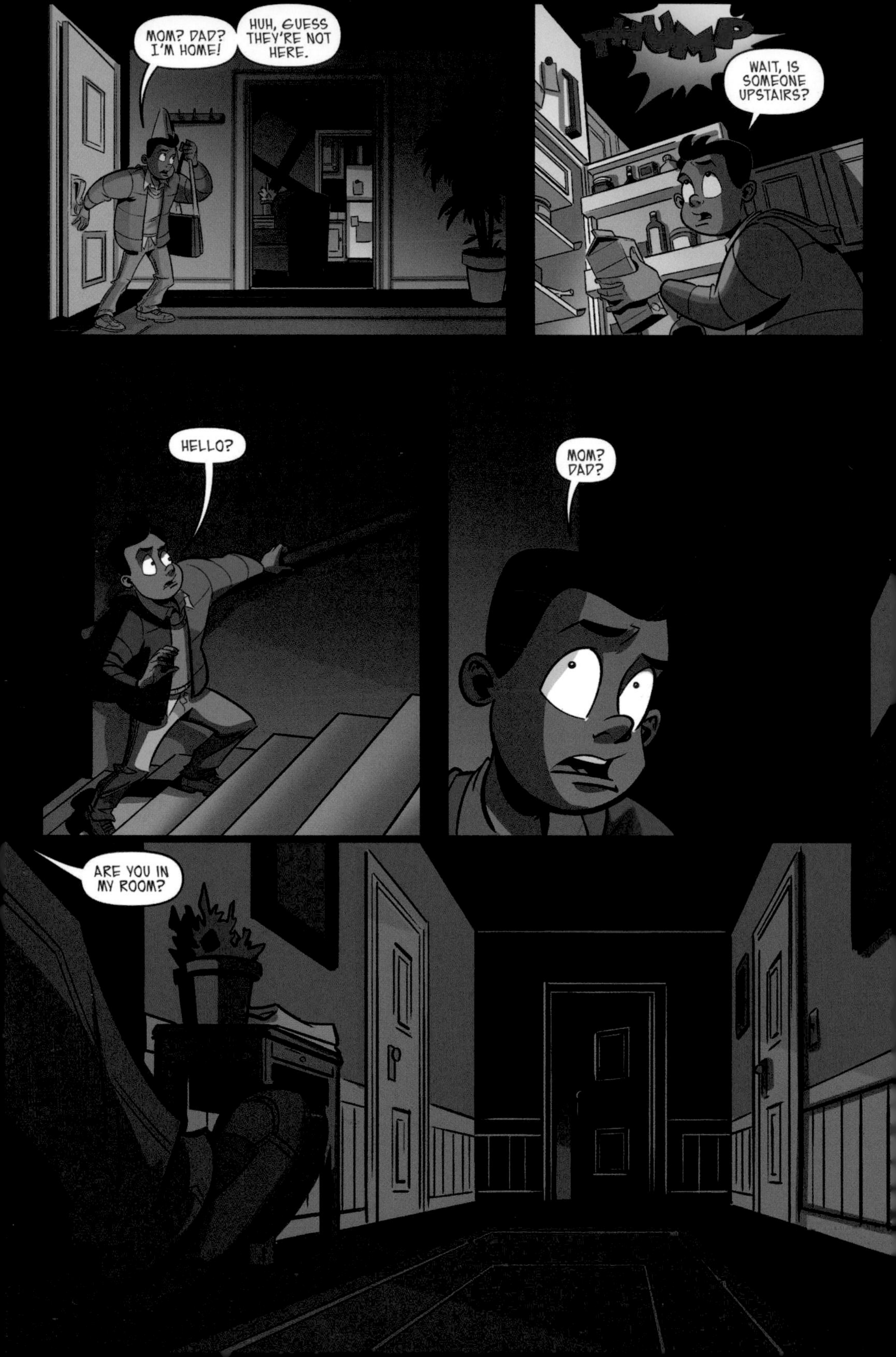
MOM? DAD? I'M HOME!
HUH, GUESS THEY'RE NOT HERE.
THUMP
WAIT, IS SOMEONE UPSTAIRS?
HELLO?
MOM? DAD?
ARE YOU IN MY ROOM?

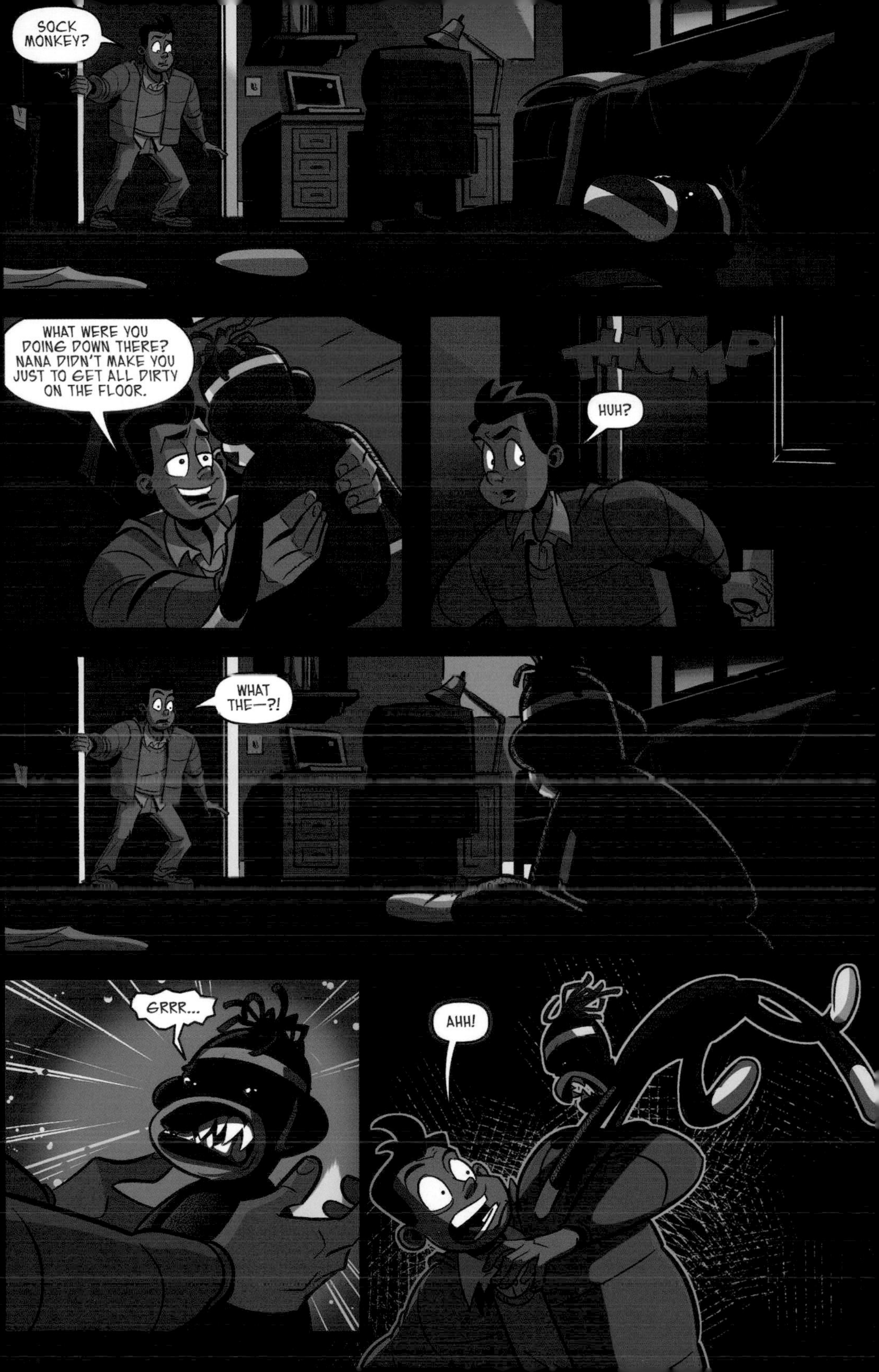
SOCK MONKEY?
WHAT WERE YOU DOING DOWN THERE? NANA DIDN'T MAKE YOU JUST TO GET ALL DIRTY ON THE FLOOR.
THUMP
HUH?
WHAT THE—?!
GRRR...
AHH!

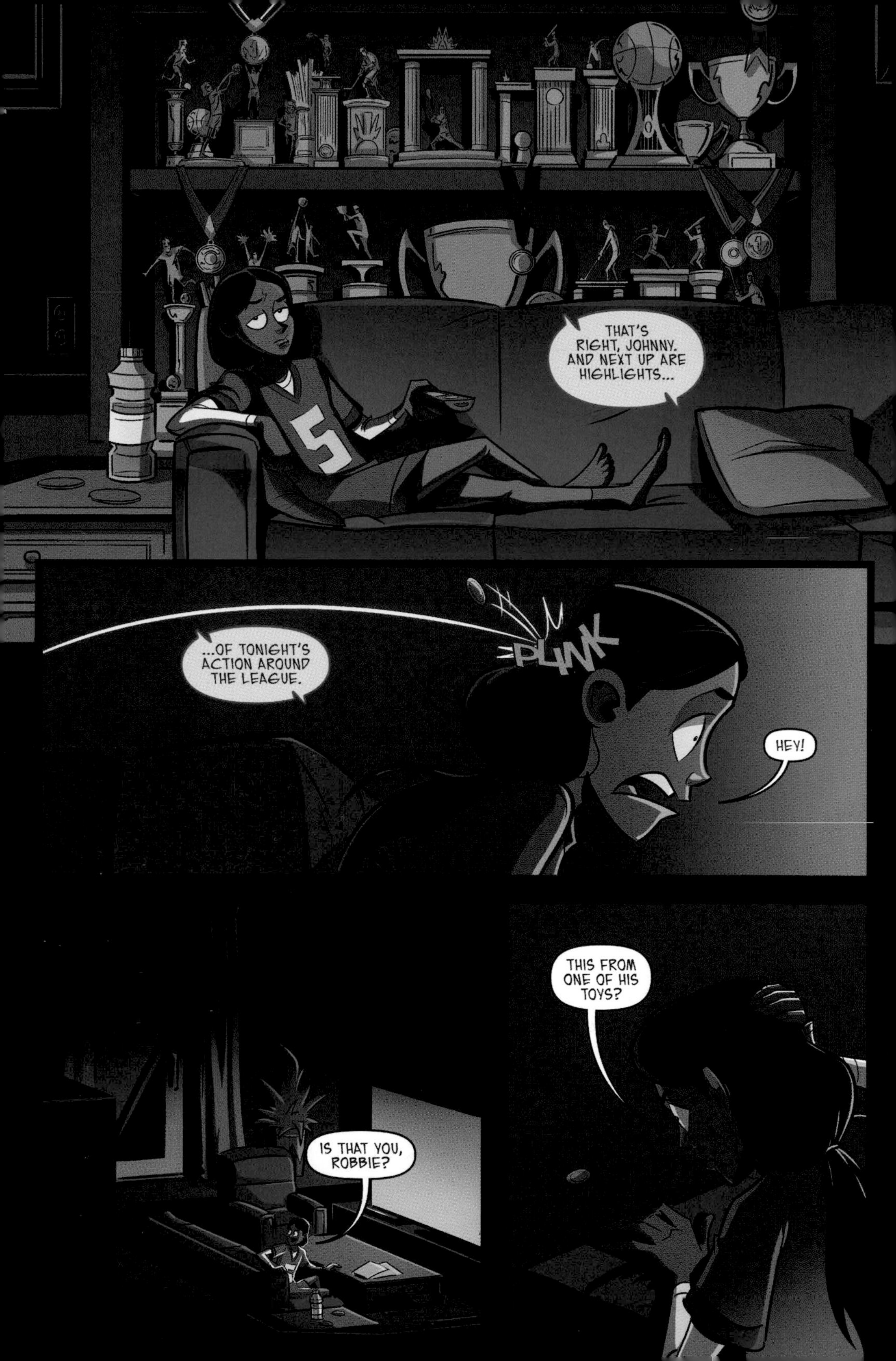
THAT'S RIGHT, JOHNNY. AND NEXT UP ARE HIGHLIGHTS...
...OF TONIGHT'S ACTION AROUND THE LEAGUE.
PLINK
HEY!
IS THAT YOU, ROBBIE?
THIS FROM ONE OF HIS TOYS?

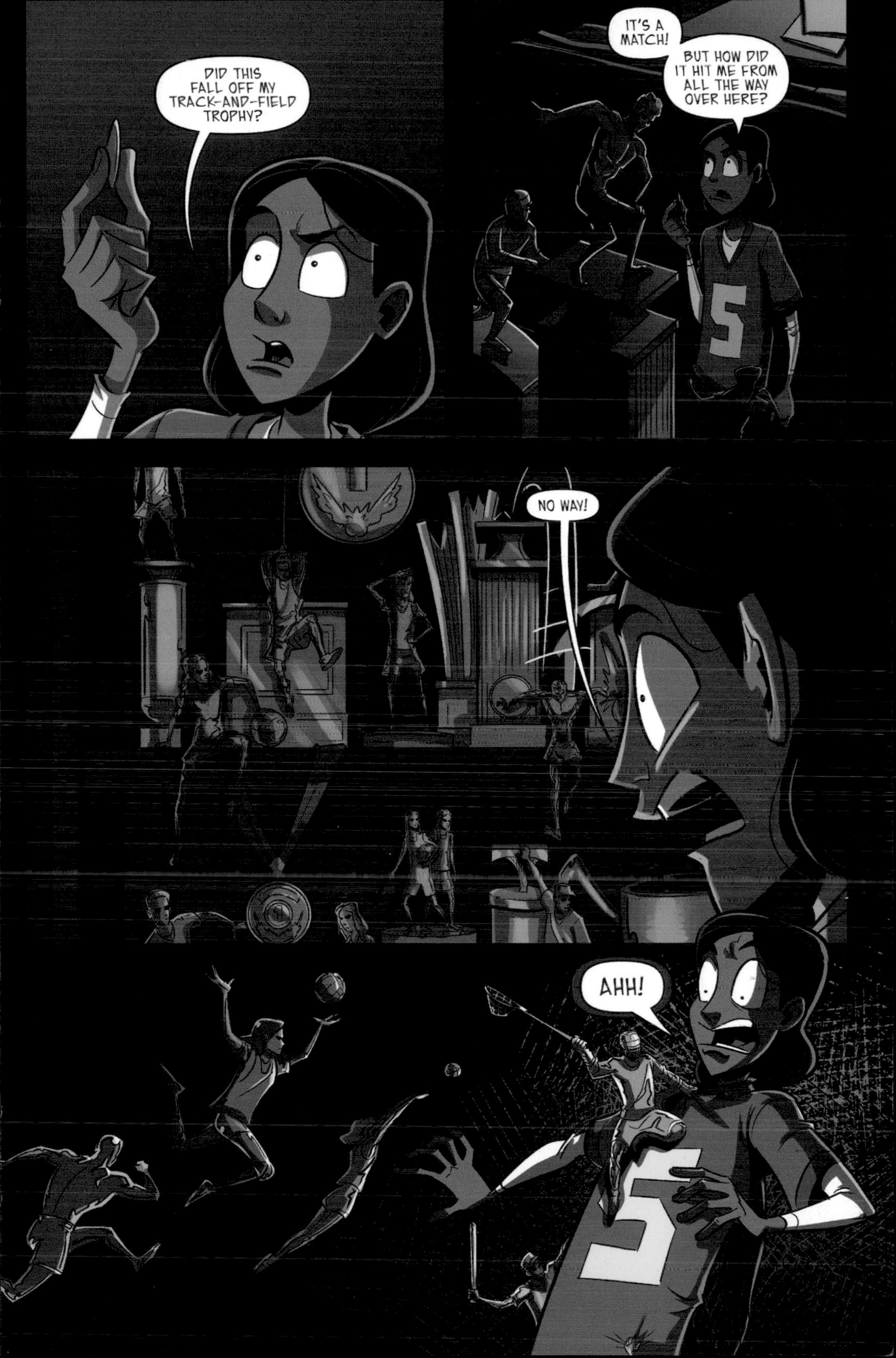
DID THIS FALL OFF MY TRACK-AND-FIELD TROPHY?
IT'S A MATCH!
BUT HOW DID IT HIT ME FROM ALL THE WAY OVER HERE?
NO WAY!
AHH!

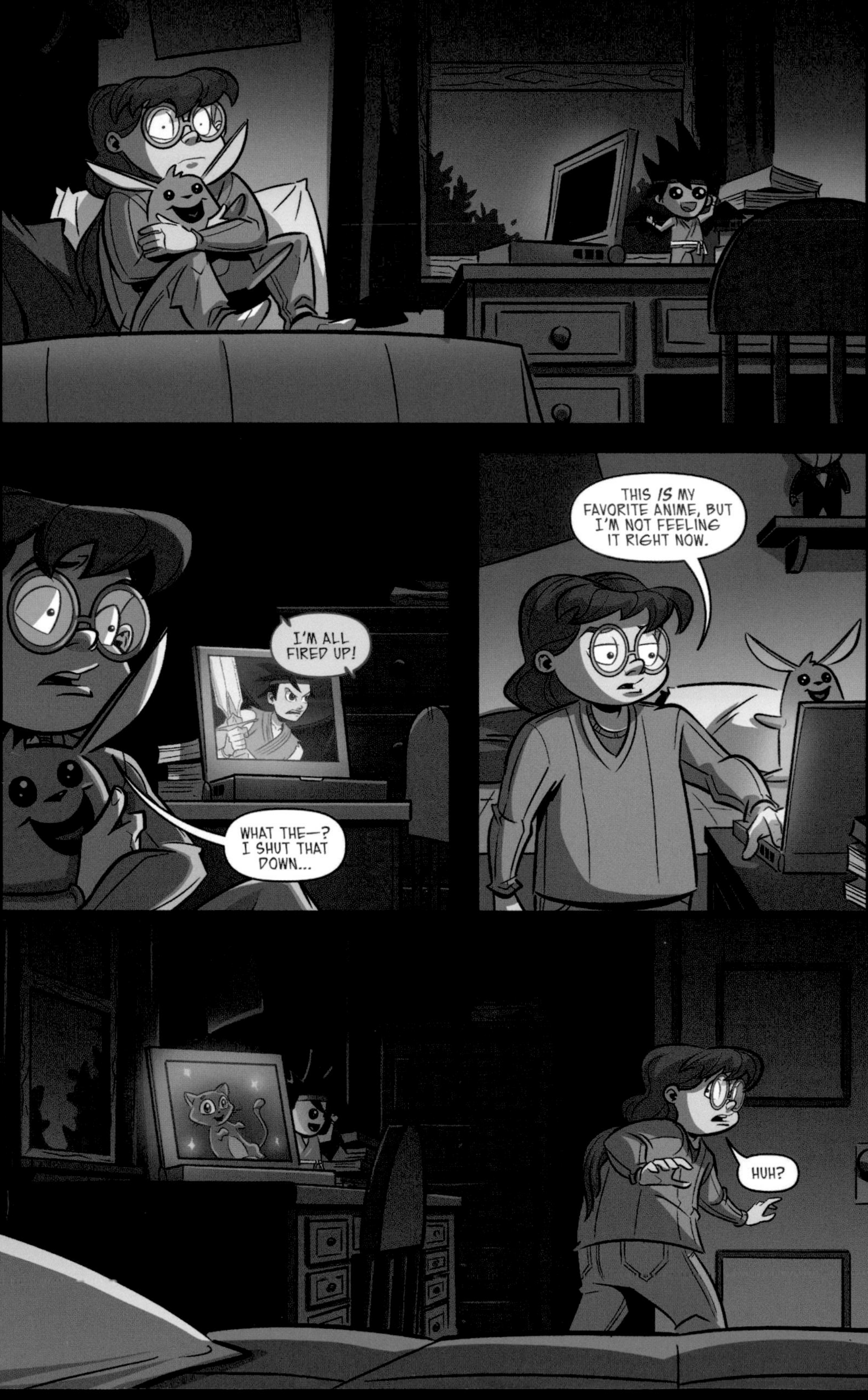
I'M ALL FIRED UP!
WHAT THE—? I SHUT THAT DOWN...
THIS *IS* MY FAVORITE ANIME, BUT I'M NOT FEELING IT RIGHT NOW.
HUH?

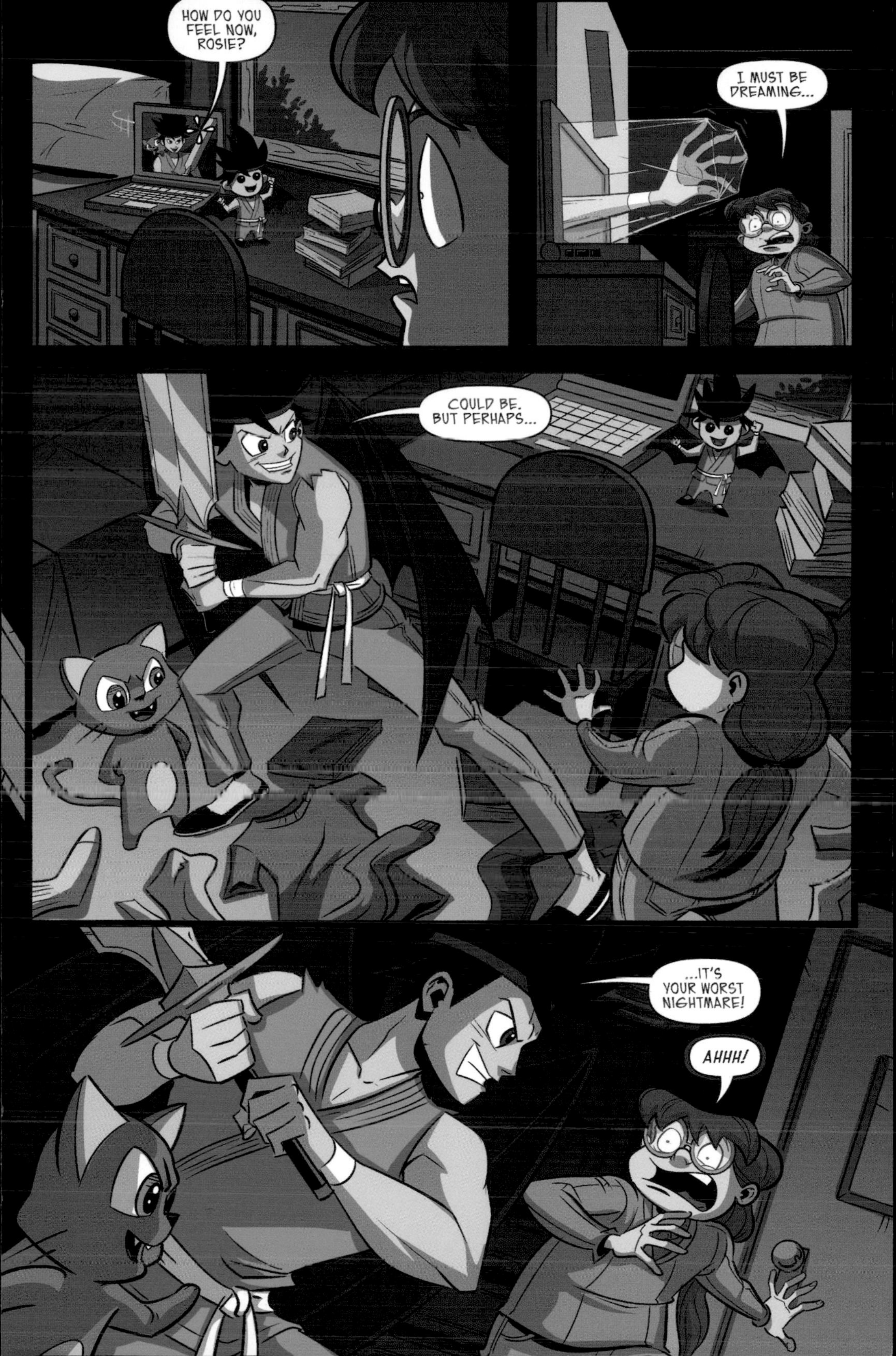
HOW DO YOU FEEL NOW, ROSIE?
I MUST BE DREAMING...
COULD BE. BUT PERHAPS...
...IT'S YOUR WORST NIGHTMARE!
AHHH!

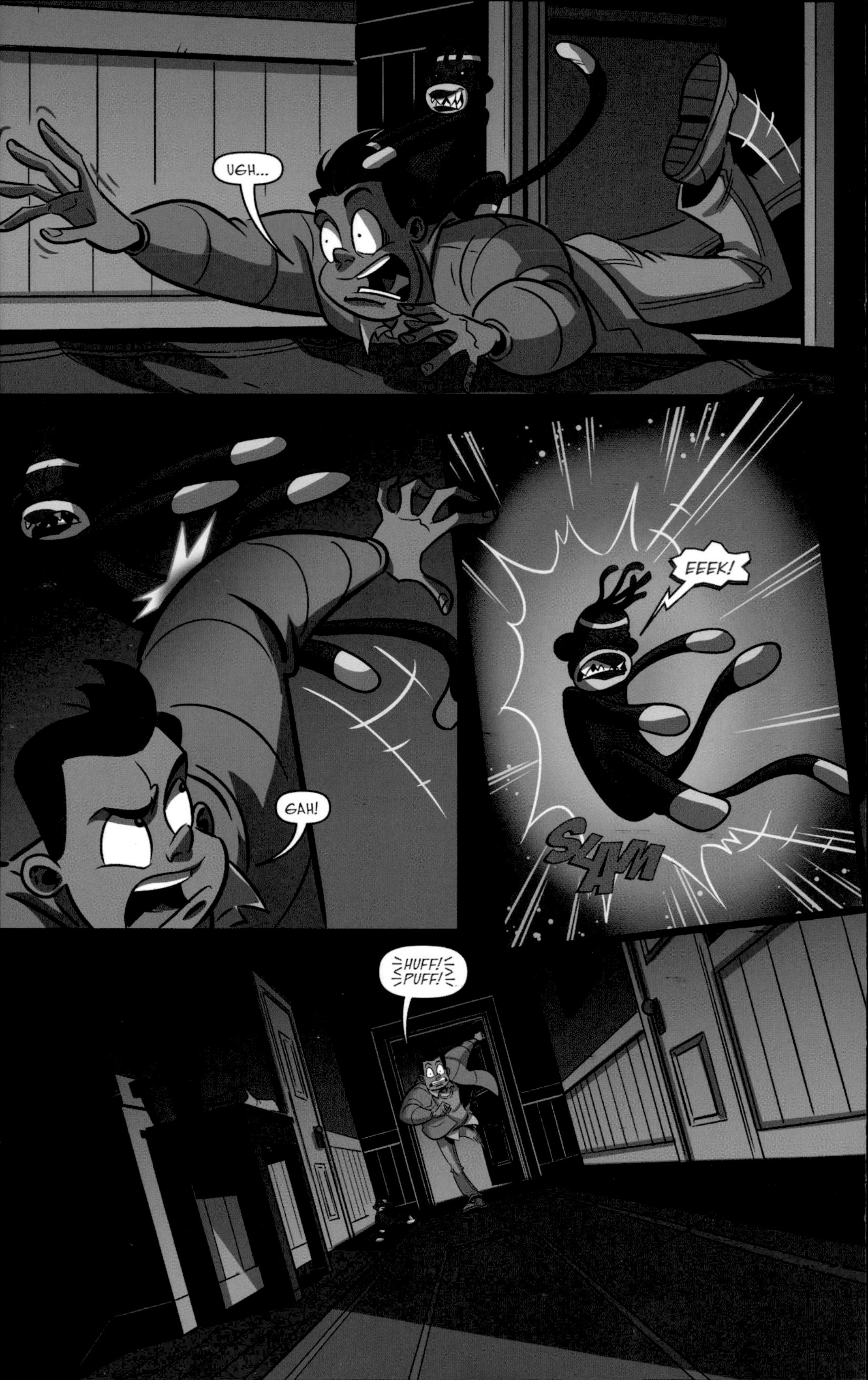
UGH...
GAH!
EEEK!
SLAM
HUFF! PUFF!

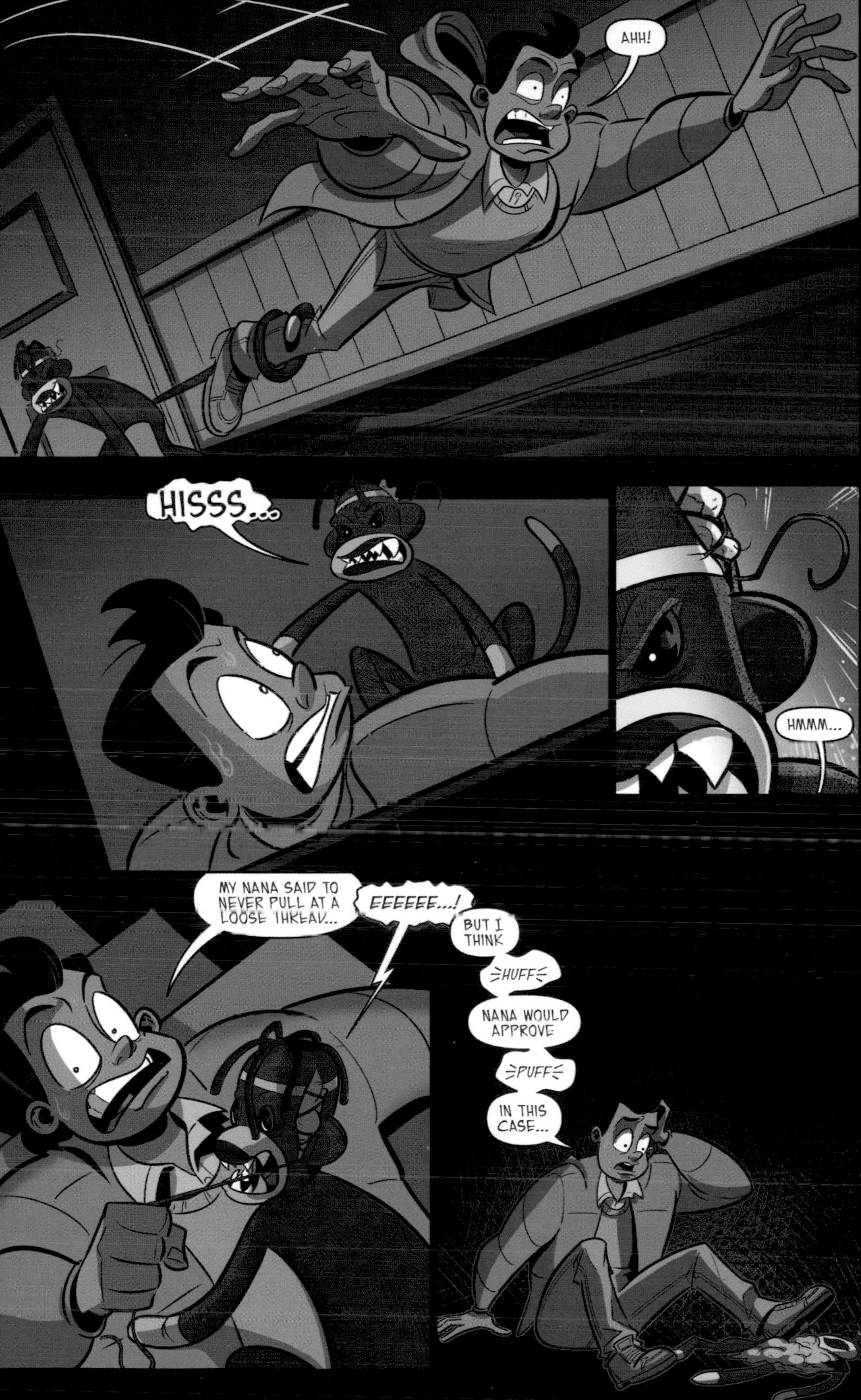

AHH!
HISSS...
HMMM...
MY NANA SAID TO NEVER PULL AT A LOOSE THREAD...
EEEEEE...!
BUT I THINK
HUFF
NANA WOULD APPROVE
PUFF
IN THIS CASE...

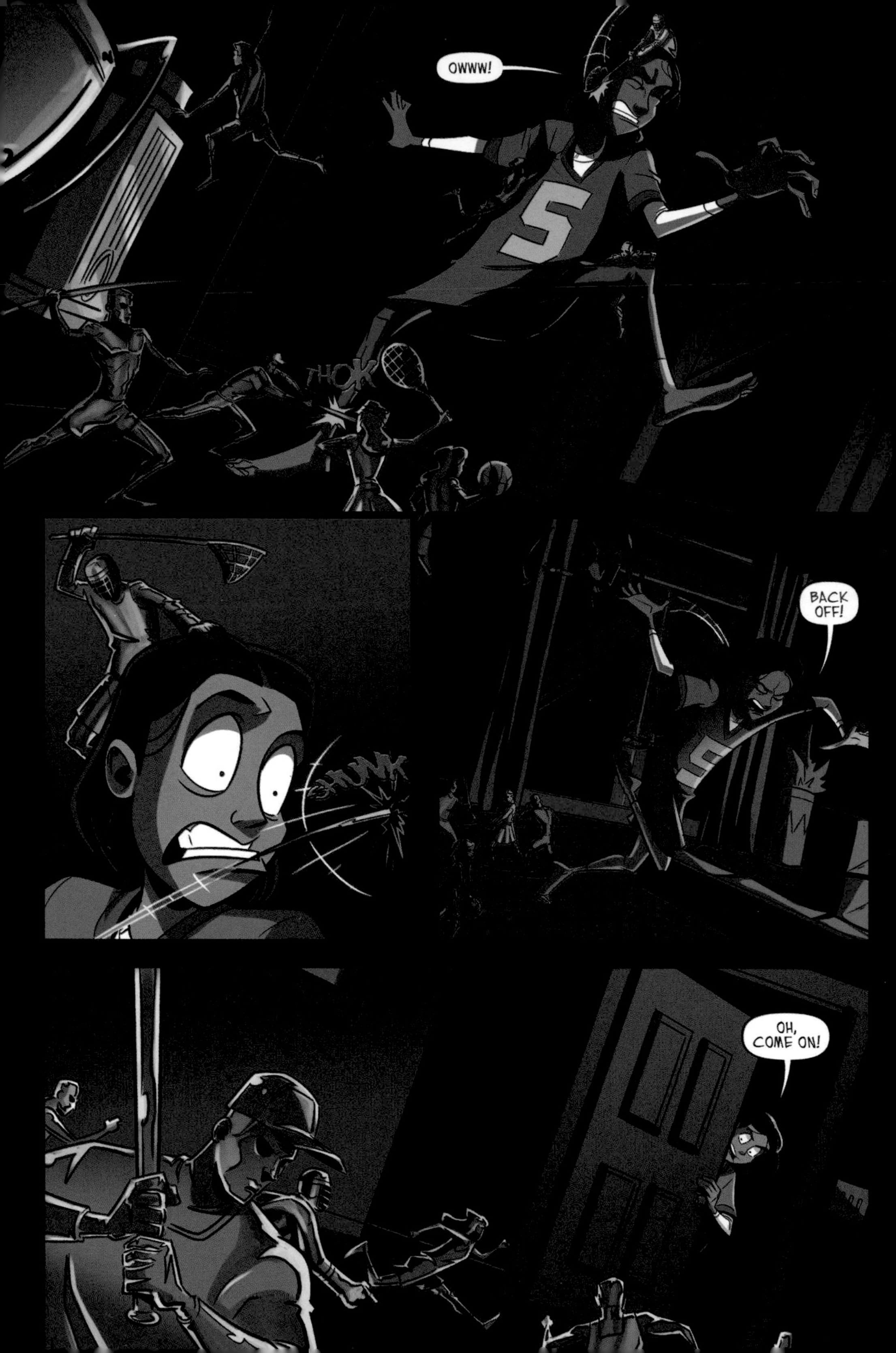
OWWW!
THOK
SHUNK
BACK OFF!
OH, COME ON!

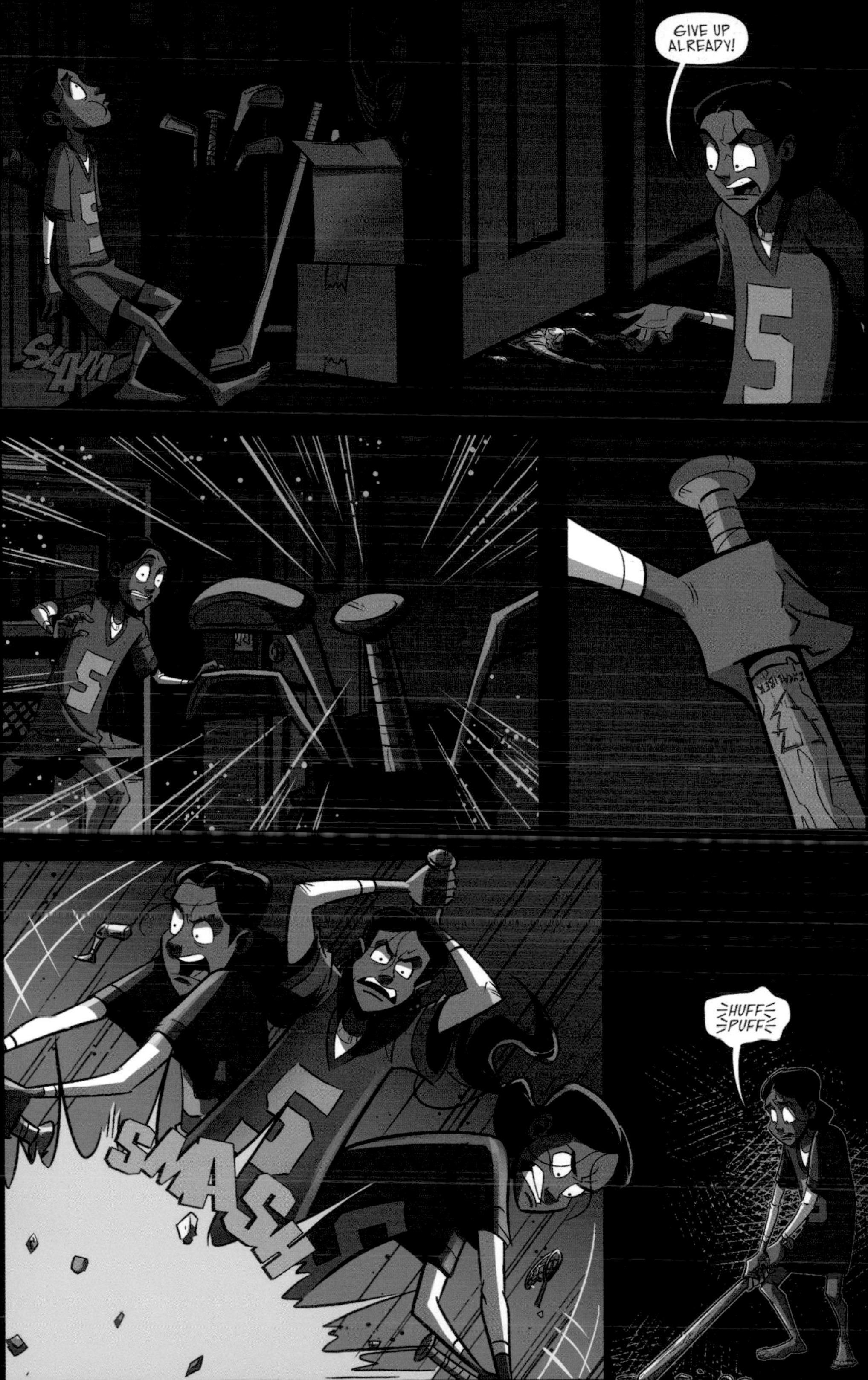
SLAM
GIVE UP ALREADY!
SMASH
HUFF PUFF

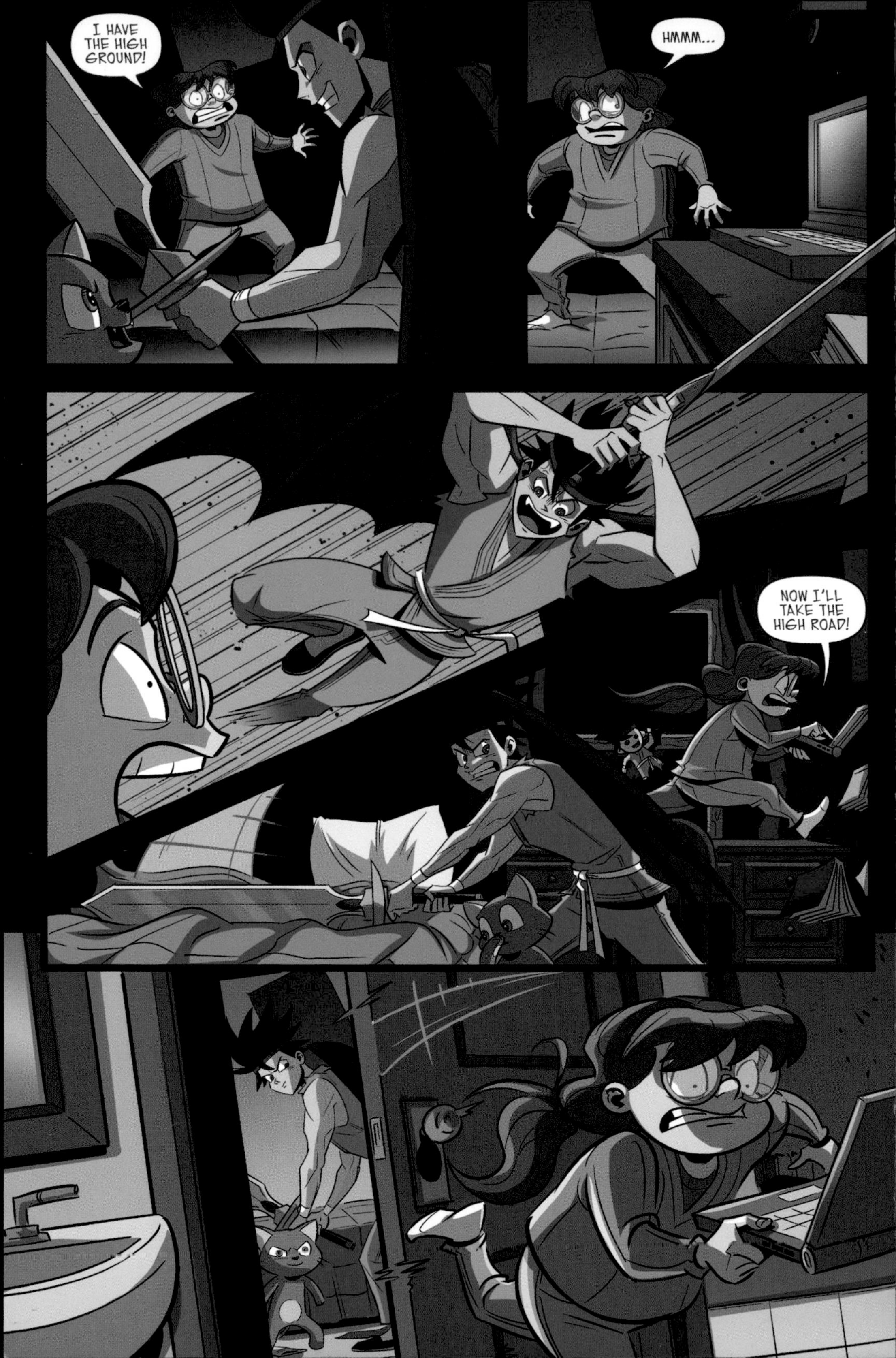
I HAVE THE HIGH GROUND!
HMMM...
NOW I'LL TAKE THE HIGH ROAD!

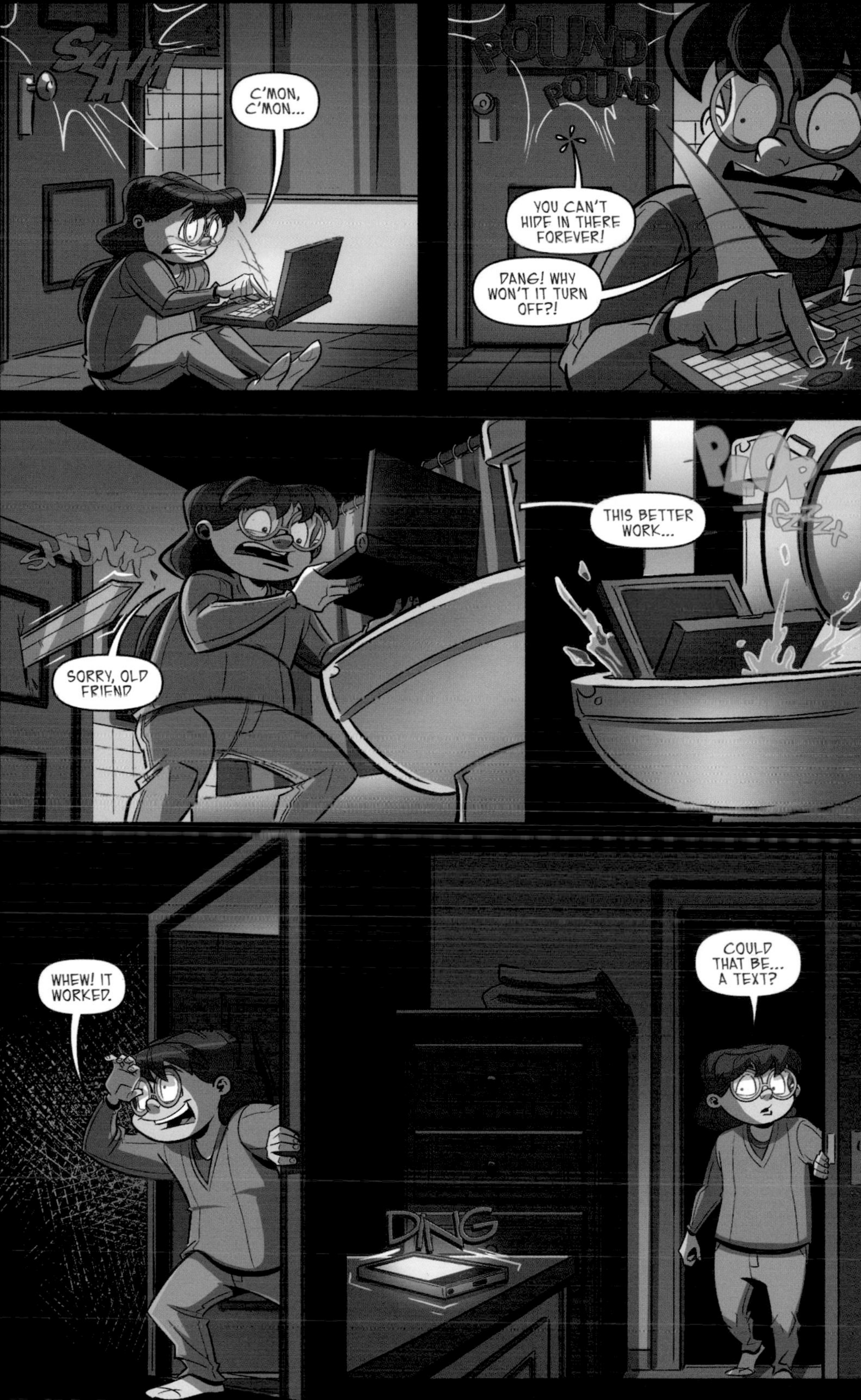
SLAM
C'MON, C'MON...
POUND
POUND
YOU CAN'T HIDE IN THERE FOREVER!
DANG! WHY WON'T IT TURN OFF?!
SHUNK
SORRY, OLD FRIEND
THIS BETTER WORK...
PLOP
FZZZT
WHEW! IT WORKED.
DING
COULD THAT BE... A TEXT?

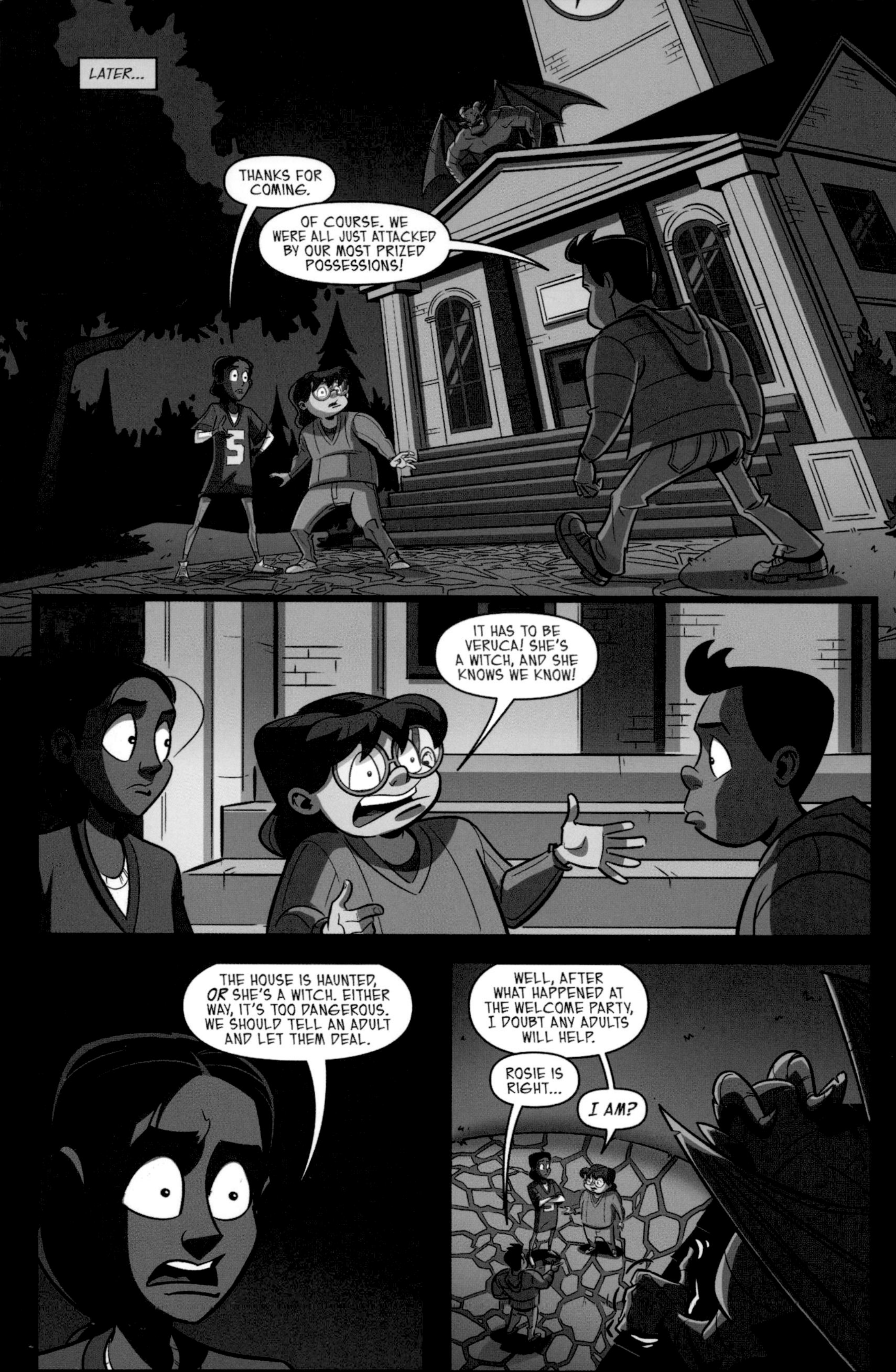
LATER...
THANKS FOR COMING.
OF COURSE. WE WERE ALL JUST ATTACKED BY OUR MOST PRIZED POSSESSIONS!
IT HAS TO BE VERUCA! SHE'S A WITCH, AND SHE KNOWS WE KNOW!
THE HOUSE IS HAUNTED, *OR* SHE'S A WITCH. EITHER WAY, IT'S TOO DANGEROUS. WE SHOULD TELL AN ADULT AND LET THEM DEAL.
WELL, AFTER WHAT HAPPENED AT THE WELCOME PARTY, I DOUBT ANY ADULTS WILL HELP.
ROSIE IS RIGHT...
I AM?

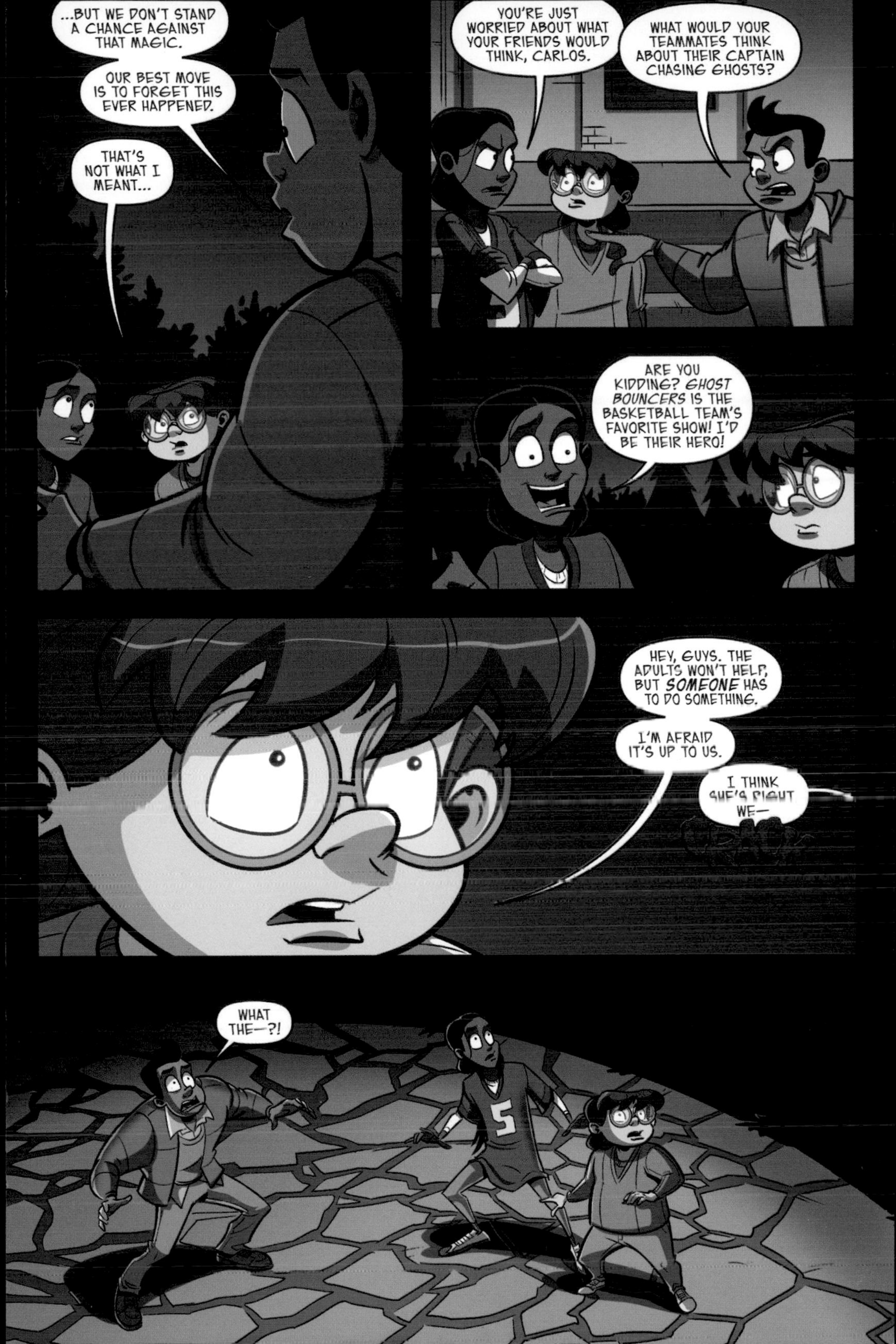
...BUT WE DON'T STAND A CHANCE AGAINST THAT MAGIC.
OUR BEST MOVE IS TO FORGET THIS EVER HAPPENED.
THAT'S NOT WHAT I MEANT...
YOU'RE JUST WORRIED ABOUT WHAT YOUR FRIENDS WOULD THINK, CARLOS.
WHAT WOULD YOUR TEAMMATES THINK ABOUT THEIR CAPTAIN CHASING GHOSTS?
ARE YOU KIDDING? GHOST BOUNCERS IS THE BASKETBALL TEAM'S FAVORITE SHOW! I'D BE THEIR HERO!
HEY, GUYS. THE ADULTS WON'T HELP, BUT SOMEONE HAS TO DO SOMETHING.
I'M AFRAID IT'S UP TO US.
I THINK SHE'S RIGHT. WE—
WHAT THE—?!

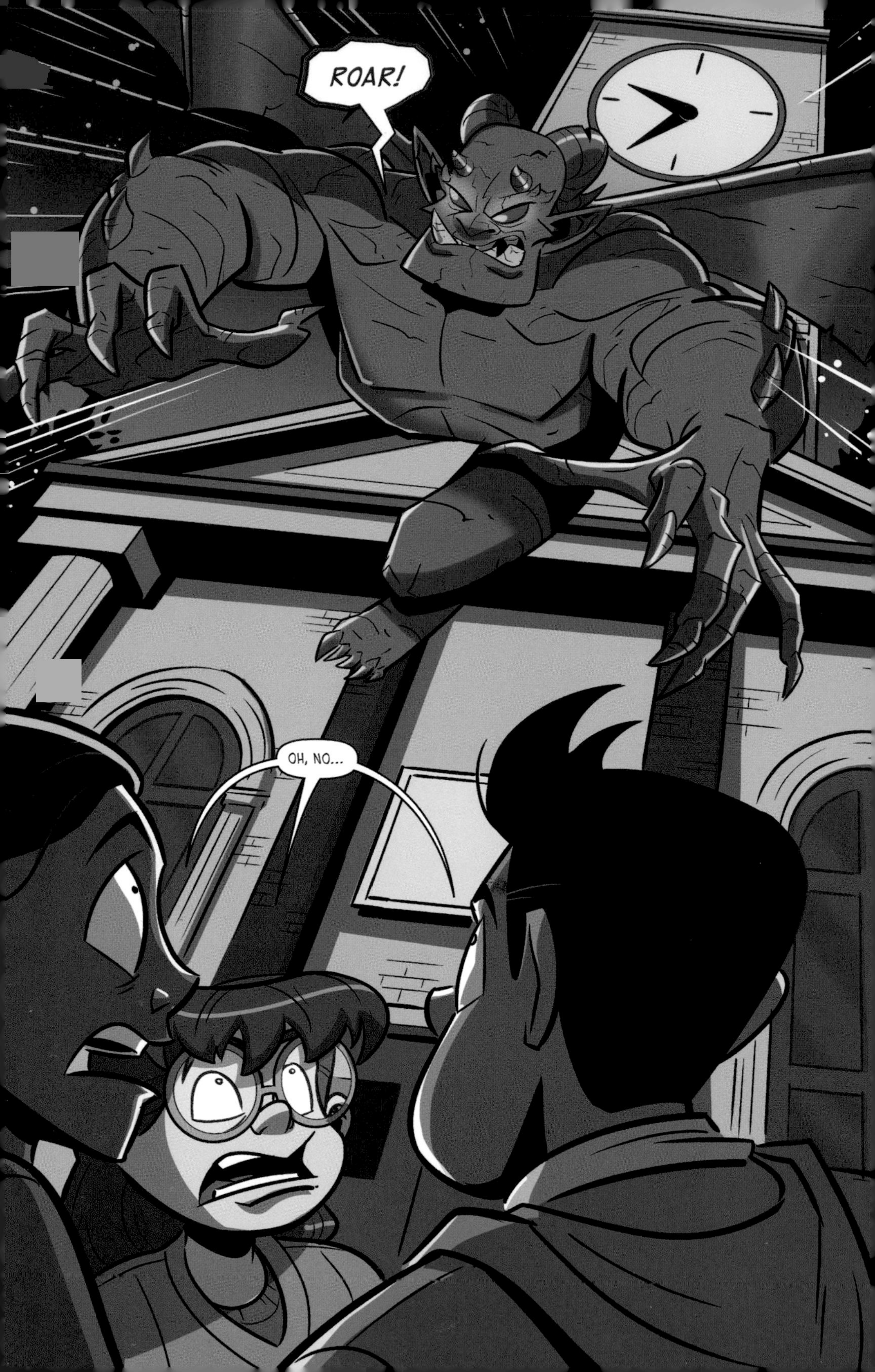
ROAR!
OH, NO...

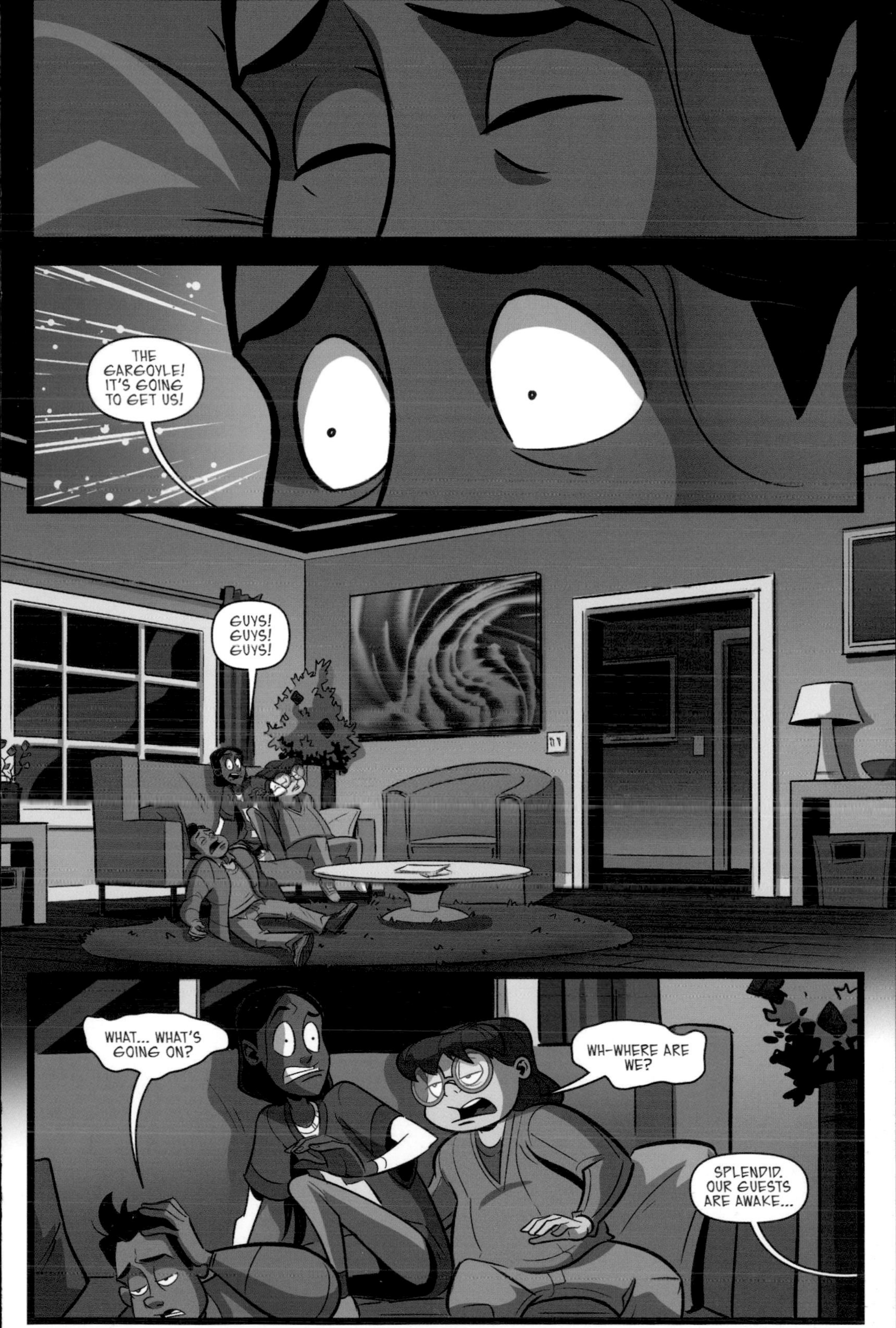

THE GARGOYLE! IT'S GOING TO GET US!
GUYS! GUYS! GUYS!
WHAT... WHAT'S GOING ON?
WH-WHERE ARE WE?
SPLENDID. OUR GUESTS ARE AWAKE...

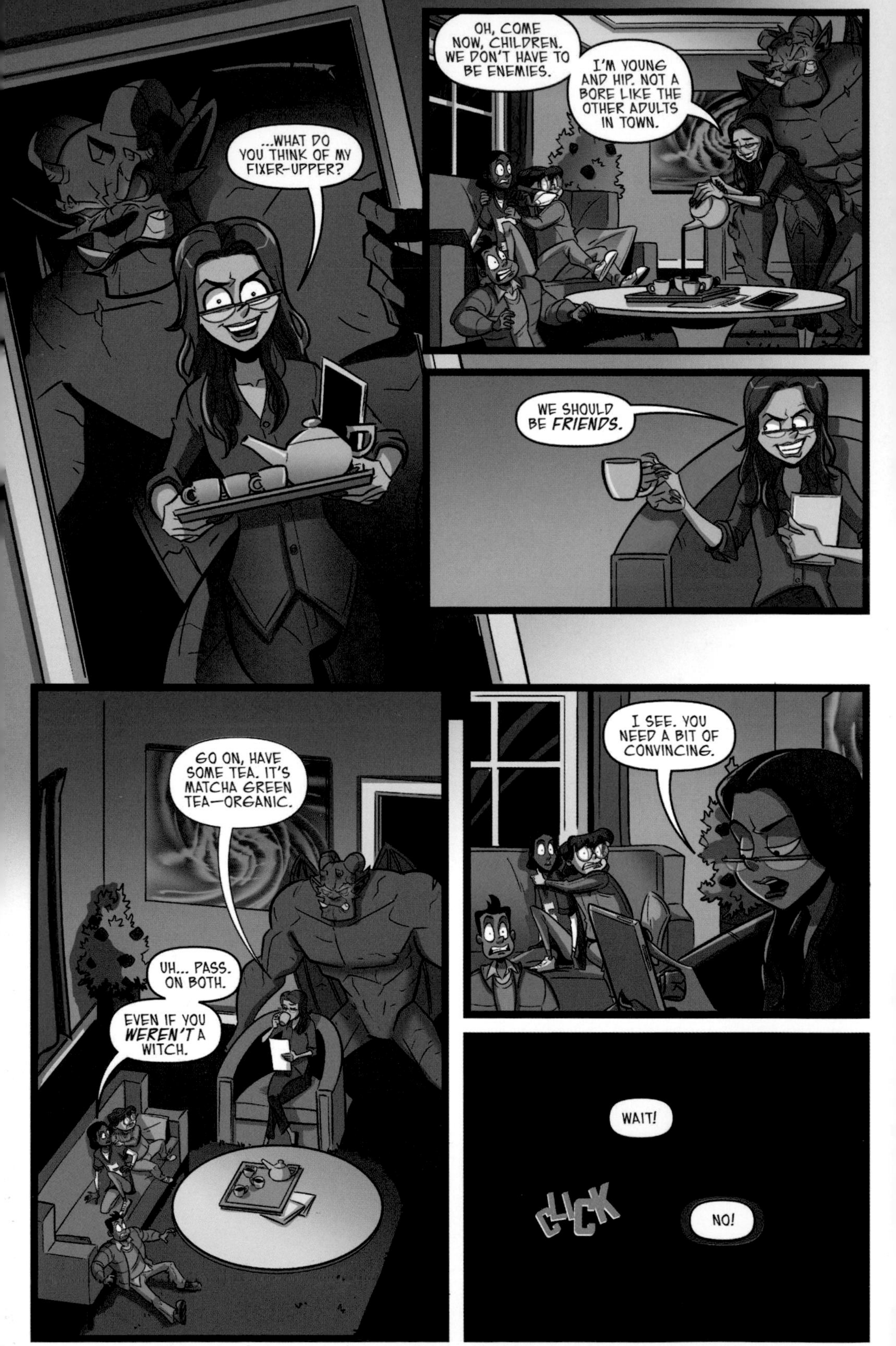
...WHAT DO YOU THINK OF MY FIXER-UPPER?
OH, COME NOW, CHILDREN. WE DON'T HAVE TO BE ENEMIES.
I'M YOUNG AND HIP. NOT A BORE LIKE THE OTHER ADULTS IN TOWN.
WE SHOULD BE *FRIENDS.*
GO ON, HAVE SOME TEA. IT'S MATCHA GREEN TEA—ORGANIC.
UH... PASS. ON BOTH.
EVEN IF YOU *WEREN'T* A WITCH.
I SEE. YOU NEED A BIT OF CONVINCING.
WAIT!
CLICK
NO!

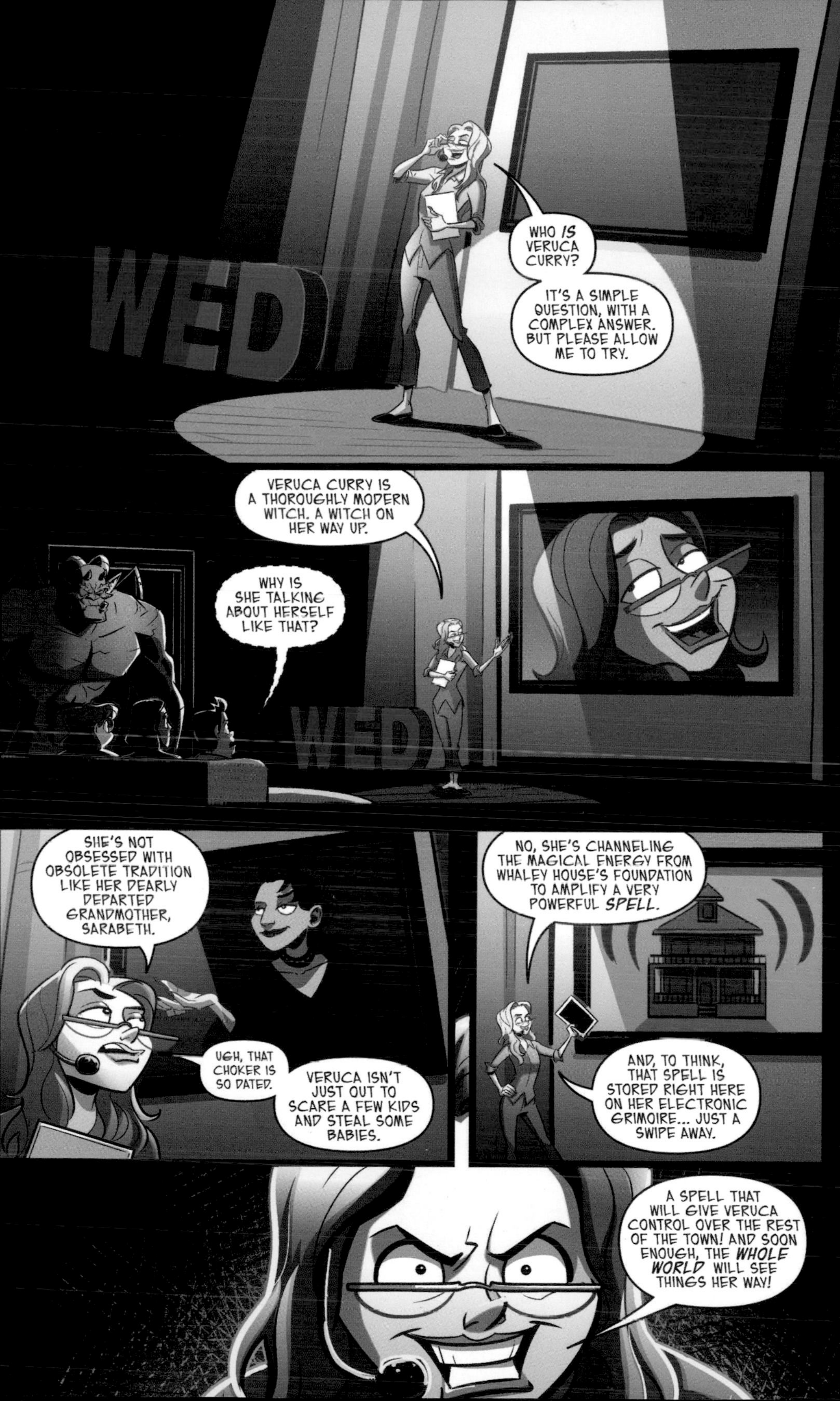

WED
WHO IS VERUCA CURRY?
IT'S A SIMPLE QUESTION, WITH A COMPLEX ANSWER. BUT PLEASE ALLOW ME TO TRY.
VERUCA CURRY IS A THOROUGHLY MODERN WITCH. A WITCH ON HER WAY UP.
WHY IS SHE TALKING ABOUT HERSELF LIKE THAT?
WED
SHE'S NOT OBSESSED WITH OBSOLETE TRADITION LIKE HER DEARLY DEPARTED GRANDMOTHER, SARABETH.
UGH, THAT CHOKER IS SO DATED.
VERUCA ISN'T JUST OUT TO SCARE A FEW KIDS AND STEAL SOME BABIES.
NO, SHE'S CHANNELING THE MAGICAL ENERGY FROM WHALEY HOUSE'S FOUNDATION TO AMPLIFY A VERY POWERFUL SPELL.
AND, TO THINK, THAT SPELL IS STORED RIGHT HERE ON HER ELECTRONIC GRIMOIRE... JUST A SWIPE AWAY.
A SPELL THAT WILL GIVE VERUCA CONTROL OVER THE REST OF THE TOWN! AND SOON ENOUGH, THE WHOLE WORLD WILL SEE THINGS HER WAY!

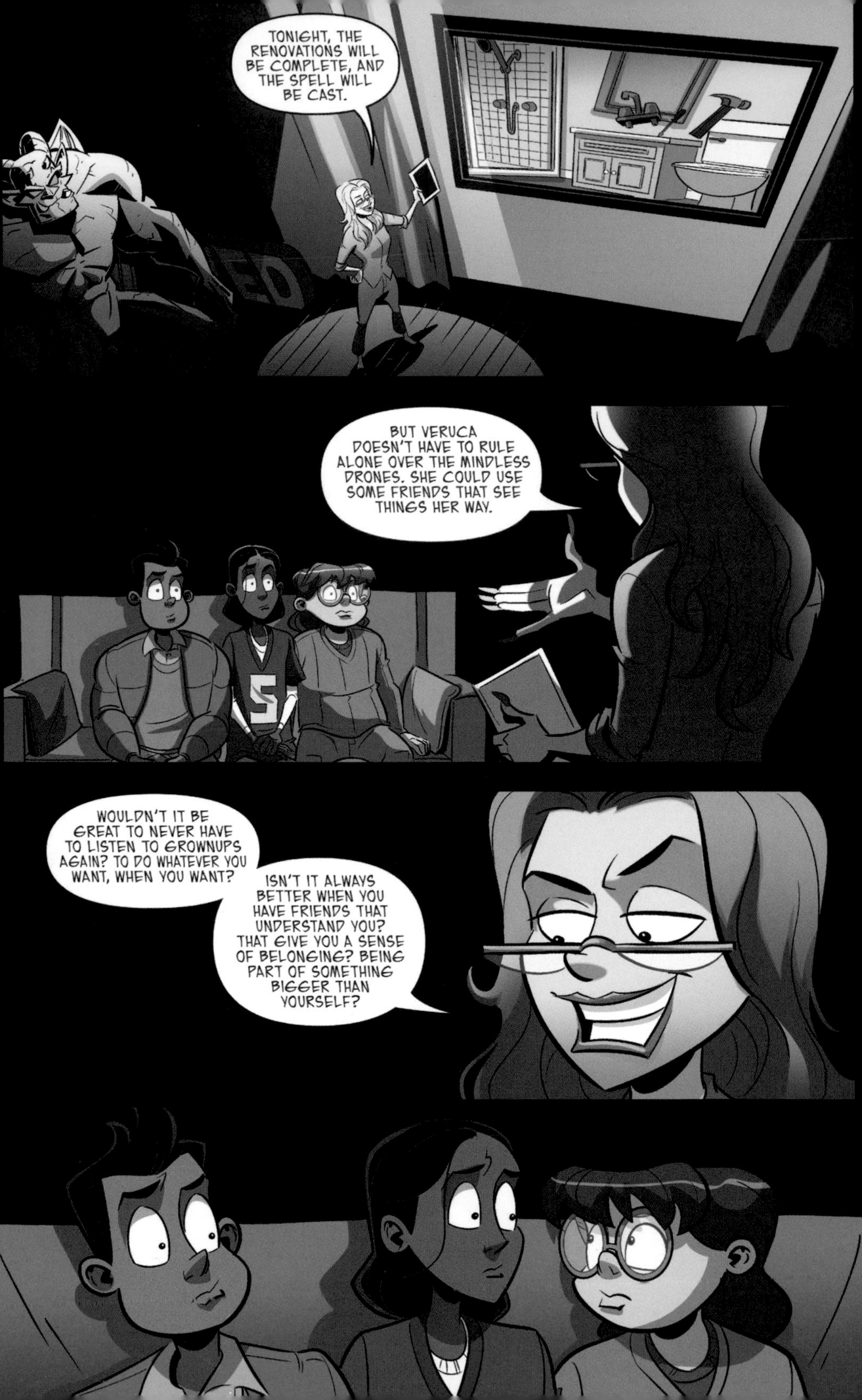
TONIGHT, THE RENOVATIONS WILL BE COMPLETE, AND THE SPELL WILL BE CAST.
BUT VERUCA DOESN'T HAVE TO RULE ALONE OVER THE MINDLESS DRONES. SHE COULD USE SOME FRIENDS THAT SEE THINGS HER WAY.
WOULDN'T IT BE GREAT TO NEVER HAVE TO LISTEN TO GROWNUPS AGAIN? TO DO WHATEVER YOU WANT, WHEN YOU WANT?
ISN'T IT ALWAYS BETTER WHEN YOU HAVE FRIENDS THAT UNDERSTAND YOU? THAT GIVE YOU A SENSE OF BELONGING? BEING PART OF SOMETHING BIGGER THAN YOURSELF?

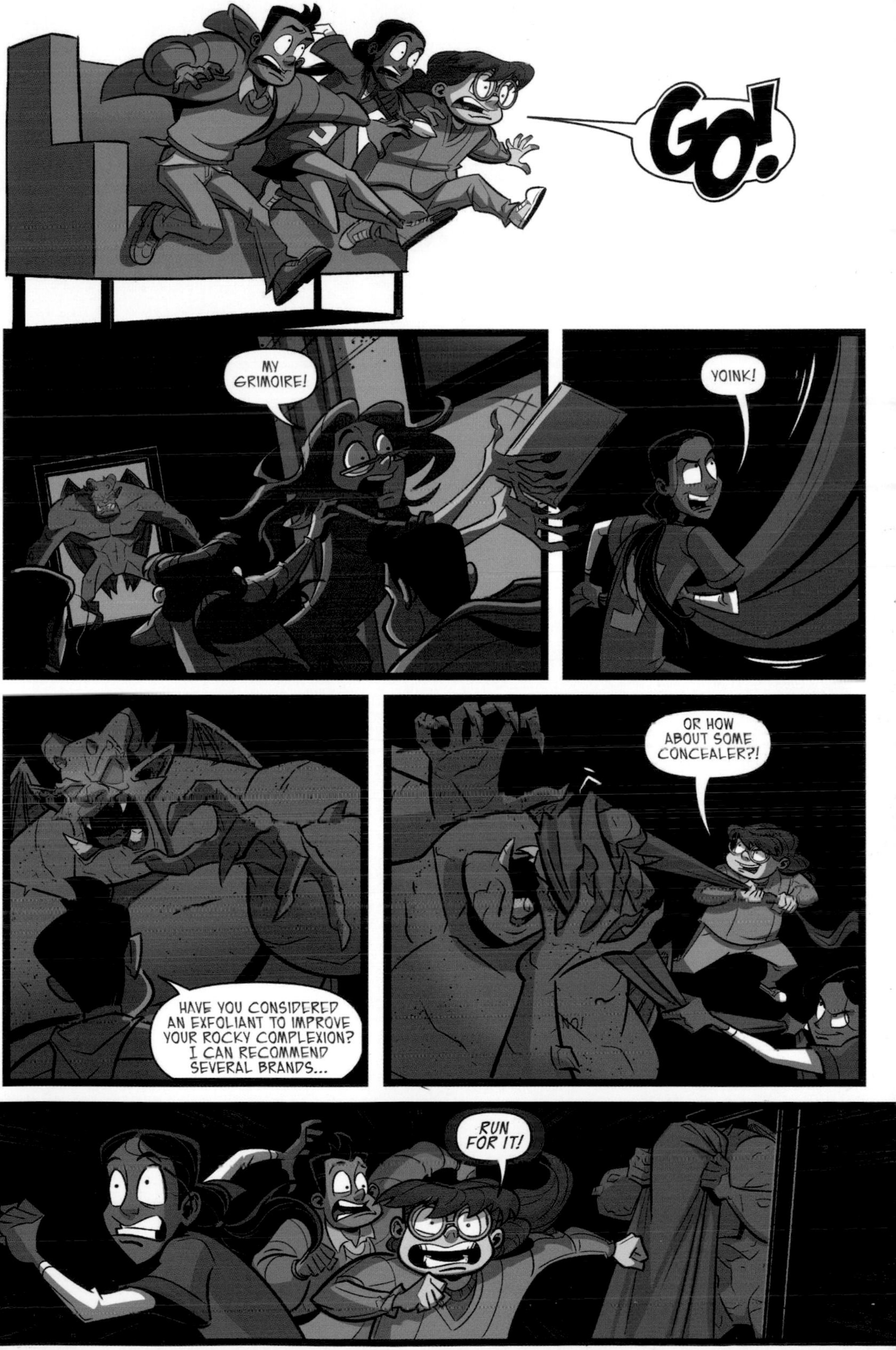
GO!
MY GRIMOIRE!
YOINK!
HAVE YOU CONSIDERED AN EXFOLIANT TO IMPROVE YOUR ROCKY COMPLEXION? I CAN RECOMMEND SEVERAL BRANDS...
OR HOW ABOUT SOME CONCEALER?!
RUN FOR IT!

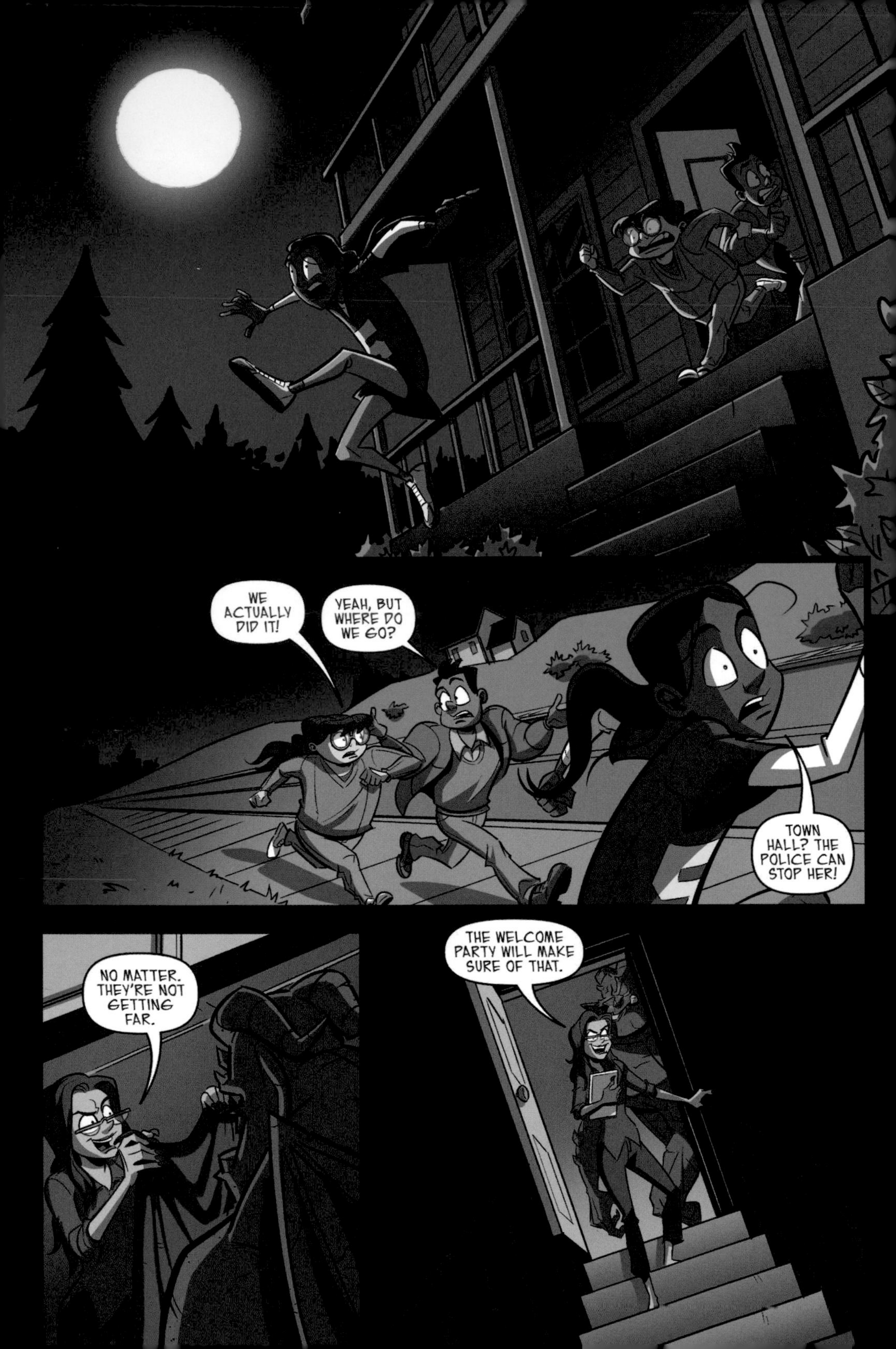
WE ACTUALLY DID IT!
YEAH, BUT WHERE DO WE GO?
TOWN HALL? THE POLICE CAN STOP HER!
NO MATTER. THEY'RE NOT GETTING FAR.
THE WELCOME PARTY WILL MAKE SURE OF THAT.

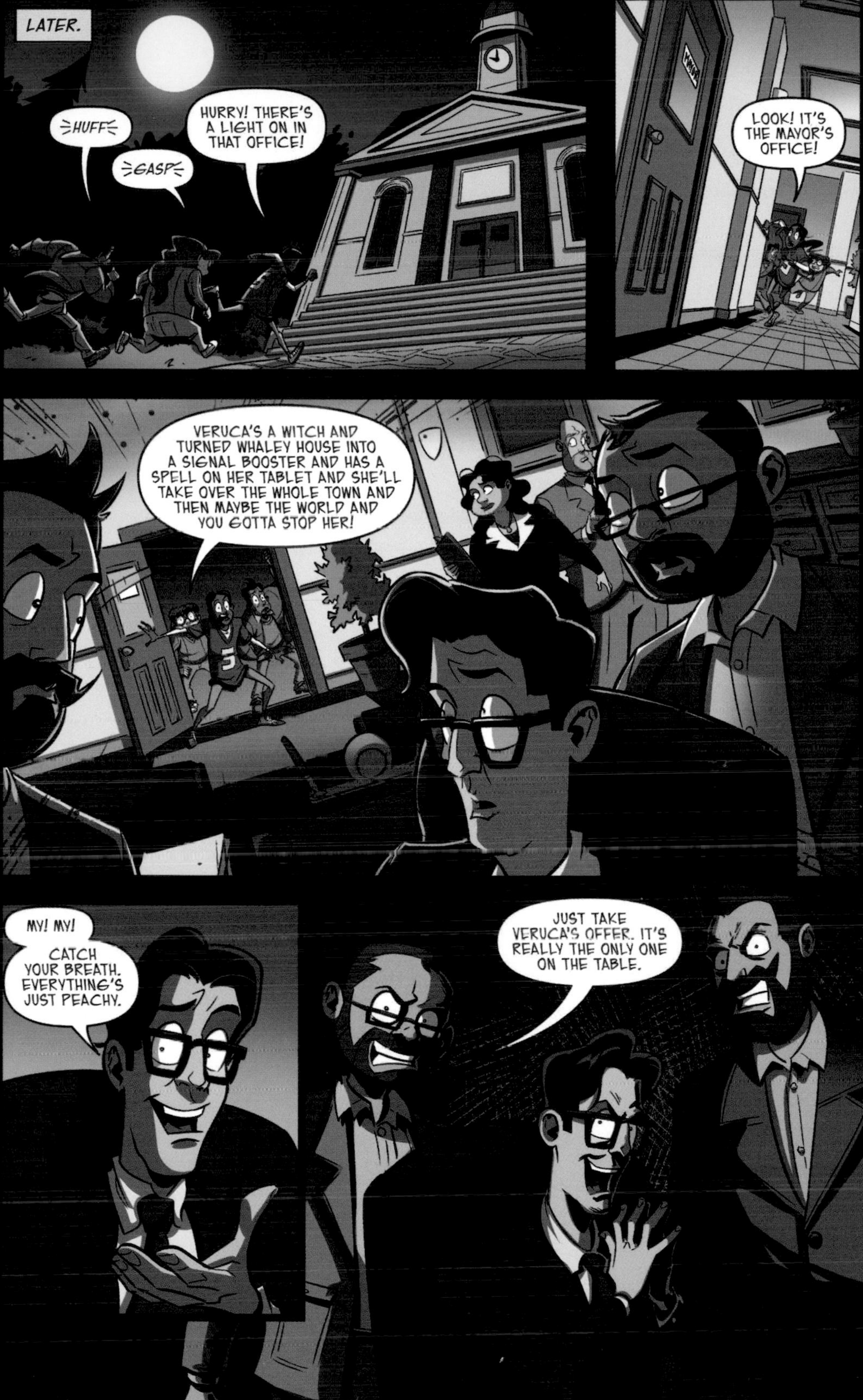
LATER.
HUFF
GASP
HURRY! THERE'S A LIGHT ON IN THAT OFFICE!
LOOK! IT'S THE MAYOR'S OFFICE!
VERUCA'S A WITCH AND TURNED WHALEY HOUSE INTO A SIGNAL BOOSTER AND HAS A SPELL ON HER TABLET AND SHE'LL TAKE OVER THE WHOLE TOWN AND THEN MAYBE THE WORLD AND YOU GOTTA STOP HER!
MY! MY!
CATCH YOUR BREATH. EVERYTHING'S JUST PEACHY.
JUST TAKE VERUCA'S OFFER. IT'S REALLY THE ONLY ONE ON THE TABLE.

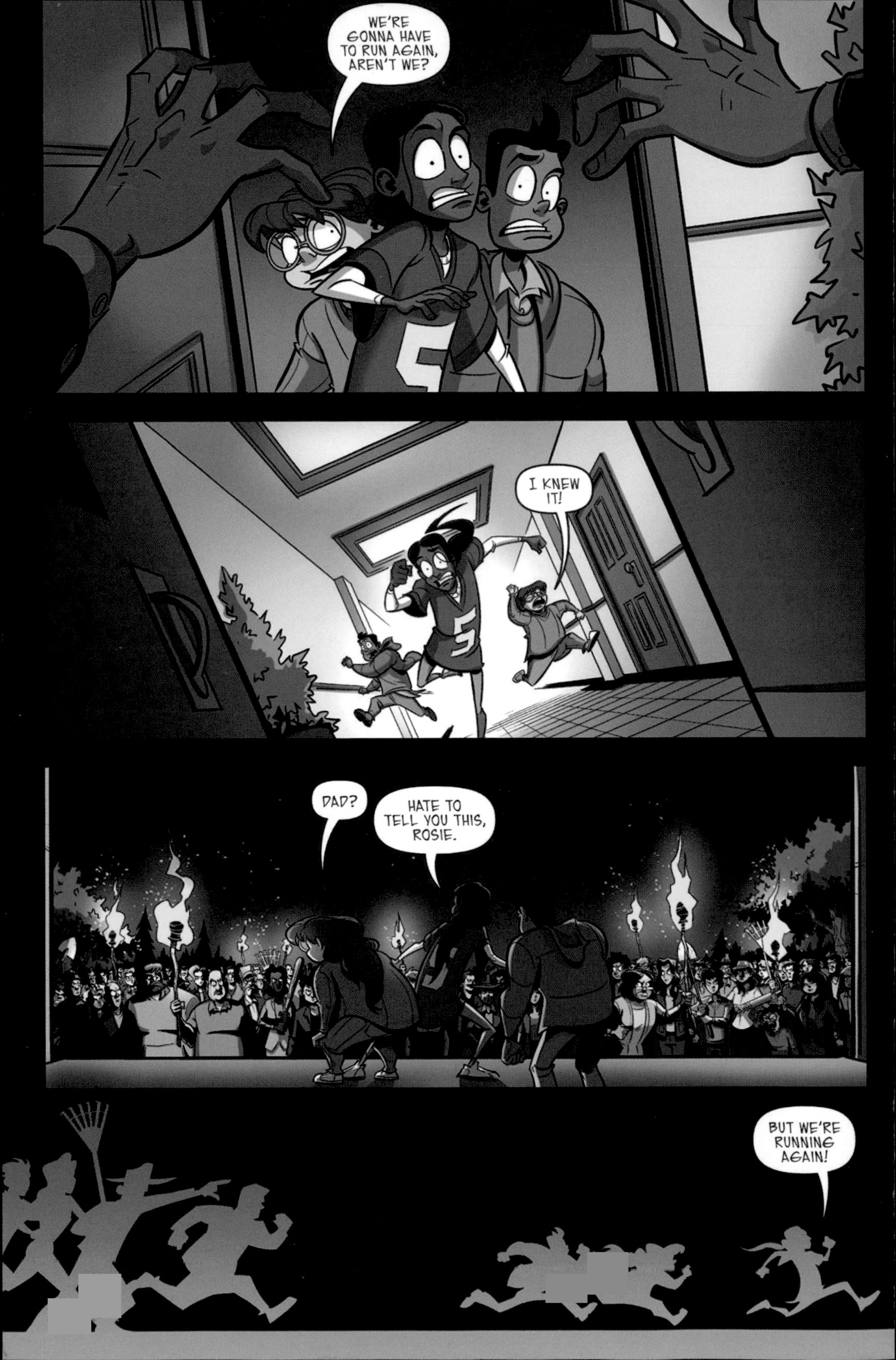
WE'RE GONNA HAVE TO RUN AGAIN, AREN'T WE?
I KNEW IT!
DAD?
HATE TO TELL YOU THIS, ROSIE.
BUT WE'RE RUNNING AGAIN!

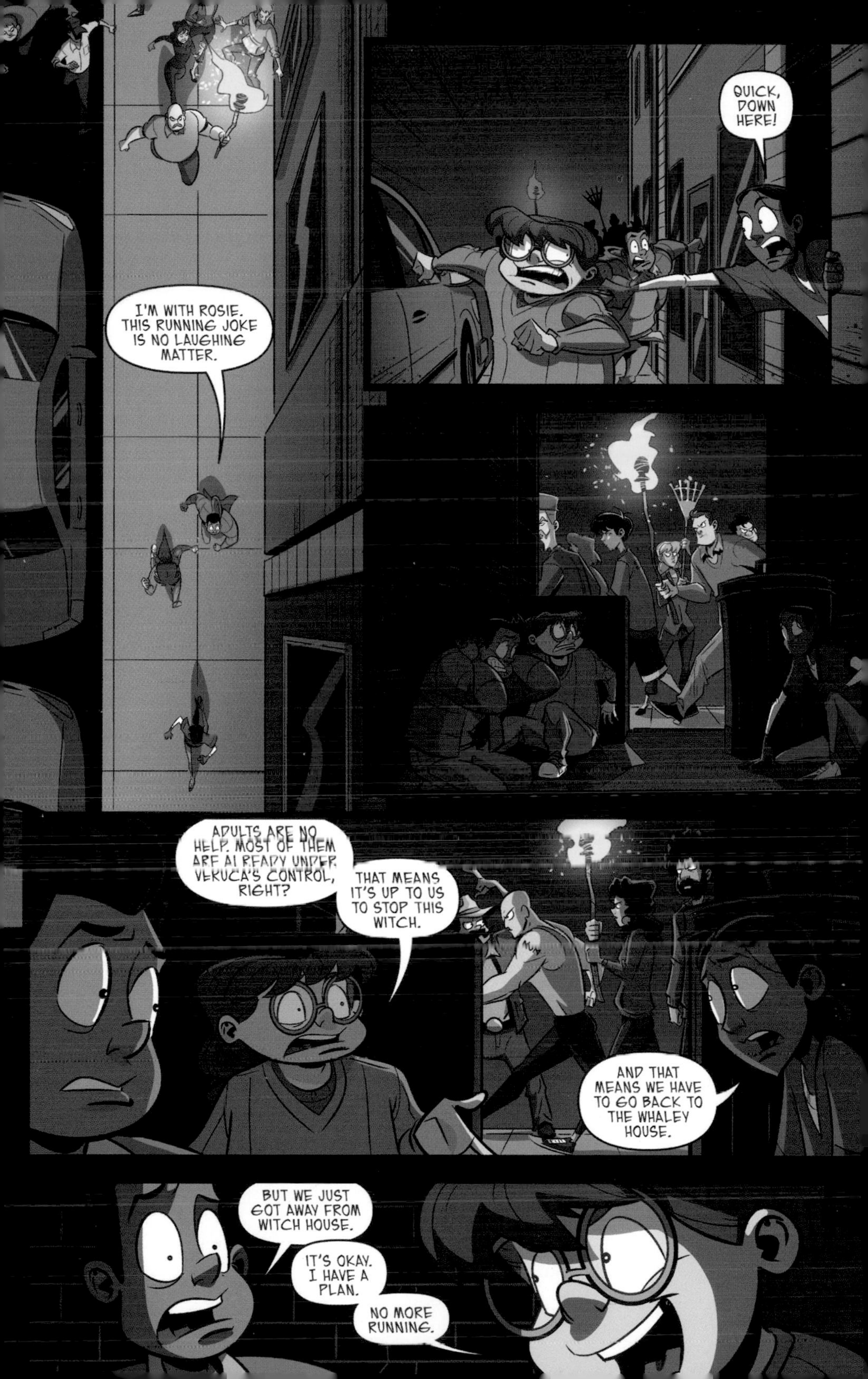

QUICK, DOWN HERE!
I'M WITH ROSIE. THIS RUNNING JOKE IS NO LAUGHING MATTER.
ADULTS ARE NO HELP. MOST OF THEM ARE ALREADY UNDER VERUCA'S CONTROL, RIGHT?
THAT MEANS IT'S UP TO US TO STOP THIS WITCH.
AND THAT MEANS WE HAVE TO GO BACK TO THE WHALEY HOUSE.
BUT WE JUST GOT AWAY FROM WITCH HOUSE.
IT'S OKAY. I HAVE A PLAN.
NO MORE RUNNING.

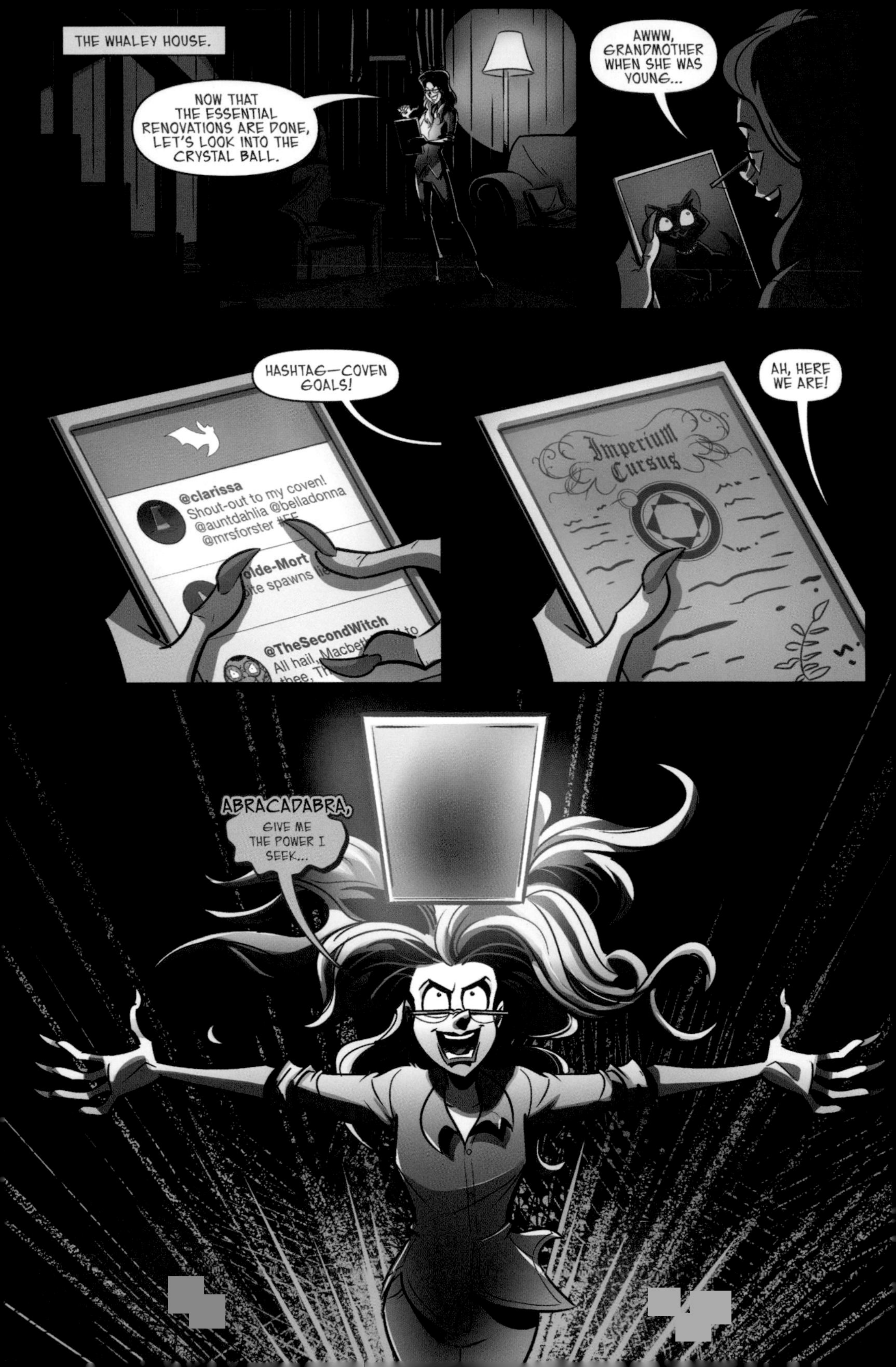
THE WHALEY HOUSE.
NOW THAT THE ESSENTIAL RENOVATIONS ARE DONE, LET'S LOOK INTO THE CRYSTAL BALL.
AWWW, GRANDMOTHER WHEN SHE WAS YOUNG...
HASHTAG—COVEN GOALS!
@clarissa
Shout-out to my coven!
@auntdahlia @belladonna
@TheSecondWitch
AH, HERE WE ARE!
Imperium Cursus
ABRACADABRA,
GIVE ME THE POWER I SEEK...

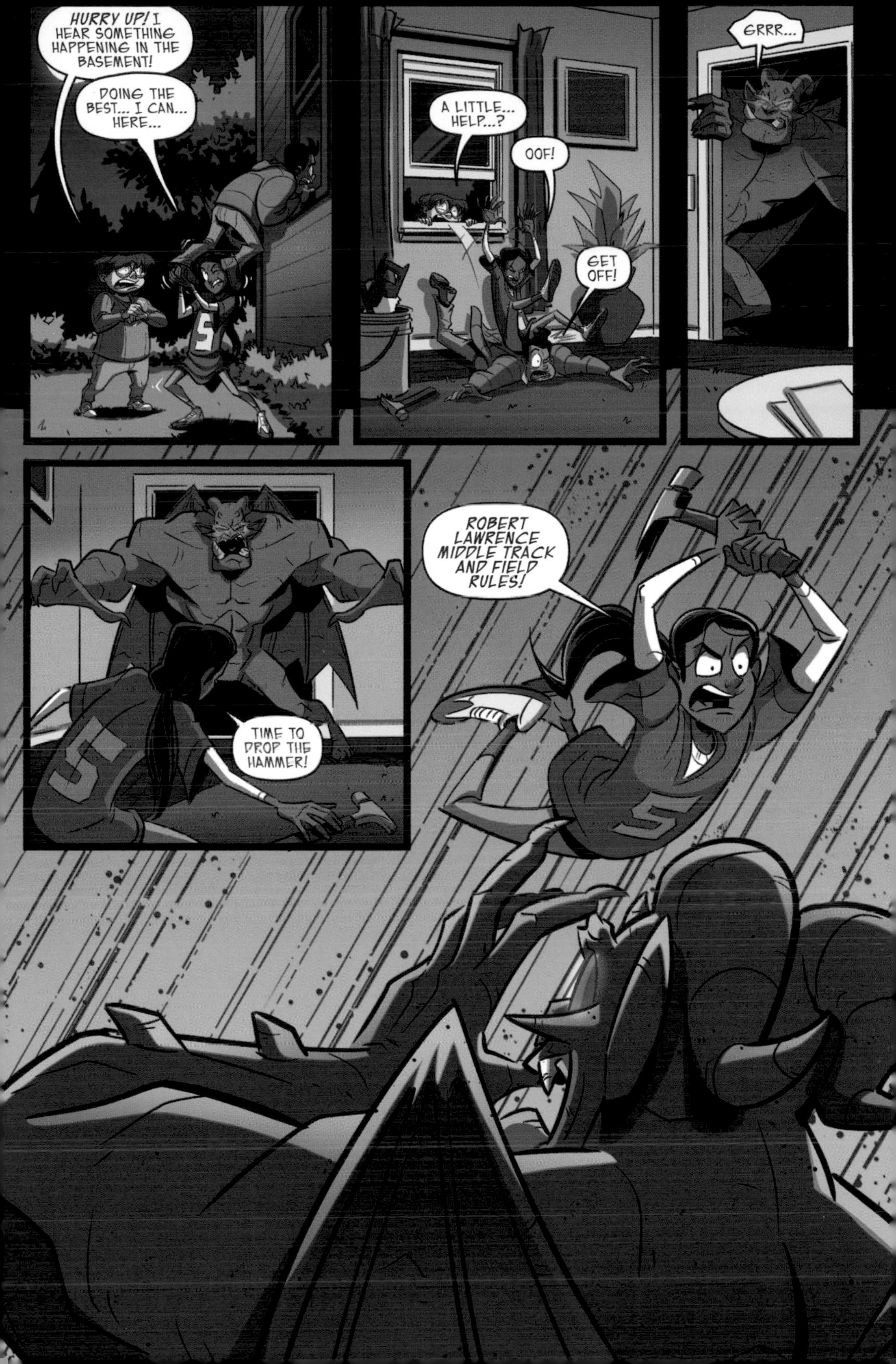
HURRY UP! I HEAR SOMETHING HAPPENING IN THE BASEMENT!
DOING THE BEST... I CAN... HERE...
A LITTLE... HELP...?
OOF!
GET OFF!
GRRR...
ROBERT LAWRENCE MIDDLE TRACK AND FIELD RULES!
TIME TO DROP THE HAMMER!

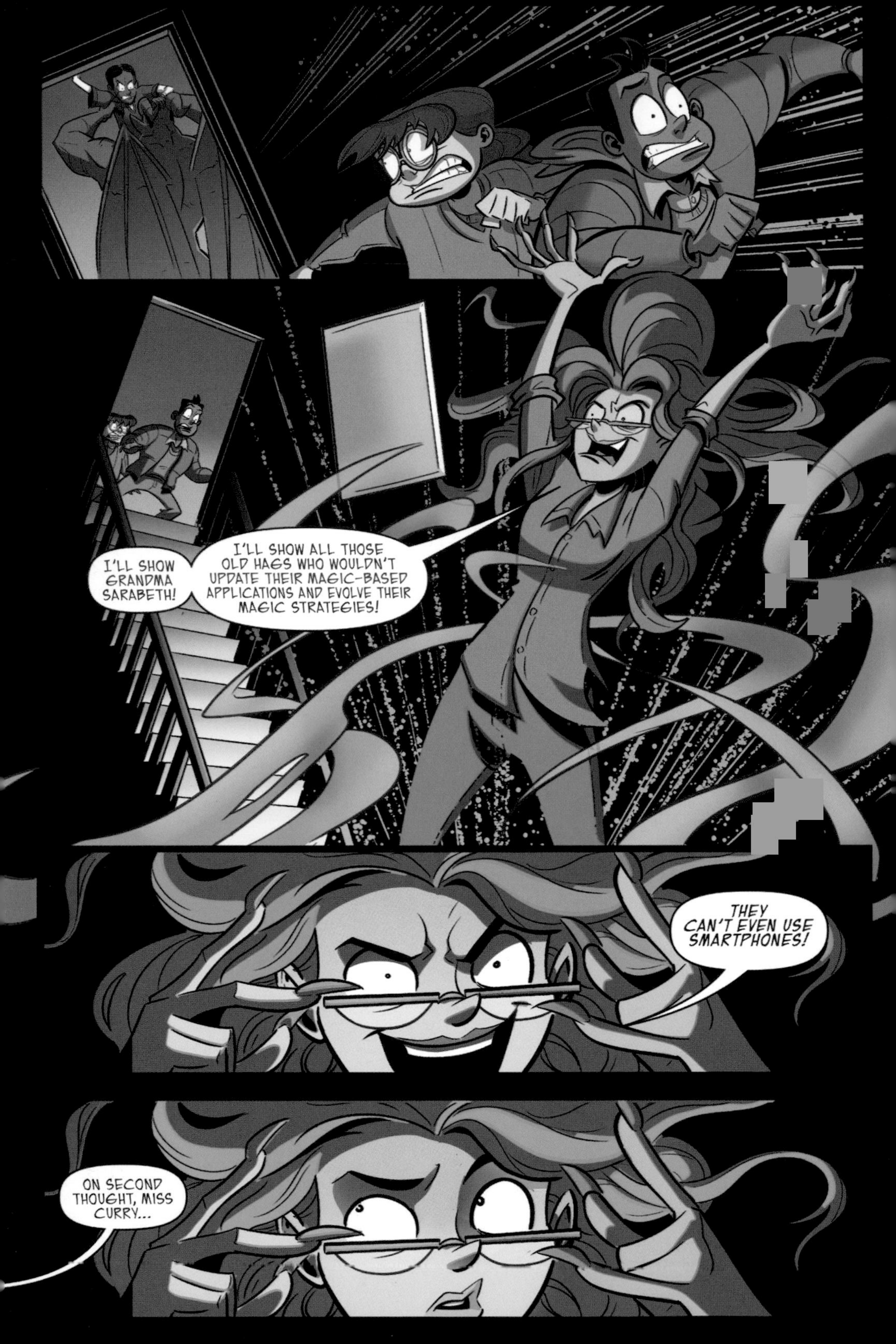
I'LL SHOW GRANDMA SARABETH!
I'LL SHOW ALL THOSE OLD HAGS WHO WOULDN'T UPDATE THEIR MAGIC-BASED APPLICATIONS AND EVOLVE THEIR MAGIC STRATEGIES!
THEY CAN'T EVEN USE SMARTPHONES!
ON SECOND THOUGHT, MISS CURRY...

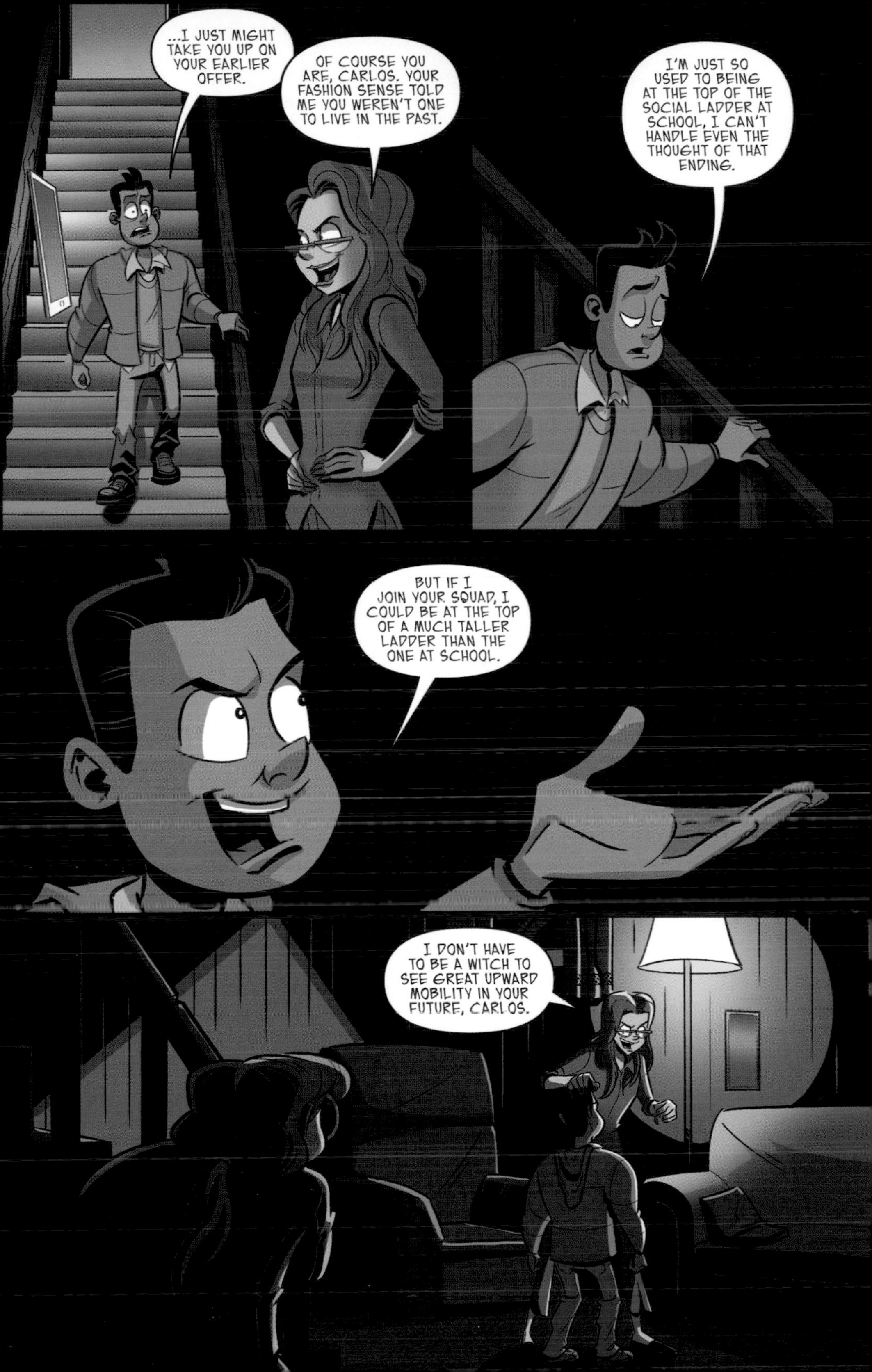
...I JUST MIGHT TAKE YOU UP ON YOUR EARLIER OFFER.
OF COURSE YOU ARE, CARLOS. YOUR FASHION SENSE TOLD ME YOU WEREN'T ONE TO LIVE IN THE PAST.
I'M JUST SO USED TO BEING AT THE TOP OF THE SOCIAL LADDER AT SCHOOL, I CAN'T HANDLE EVEN THE THOUGHT OF THAT ENDING.
BUT IF I JOIN YOUR SQUAD, I COULD BE AT THE TOP OF A MUCH TALLER LADDER THAN THE ONE AT SCHOOL.
I DON'T HAVE TO BE A WITCH TO SEE GREAT UPWARD MOBILITY IN YOUR FUTURE, CARLOS.

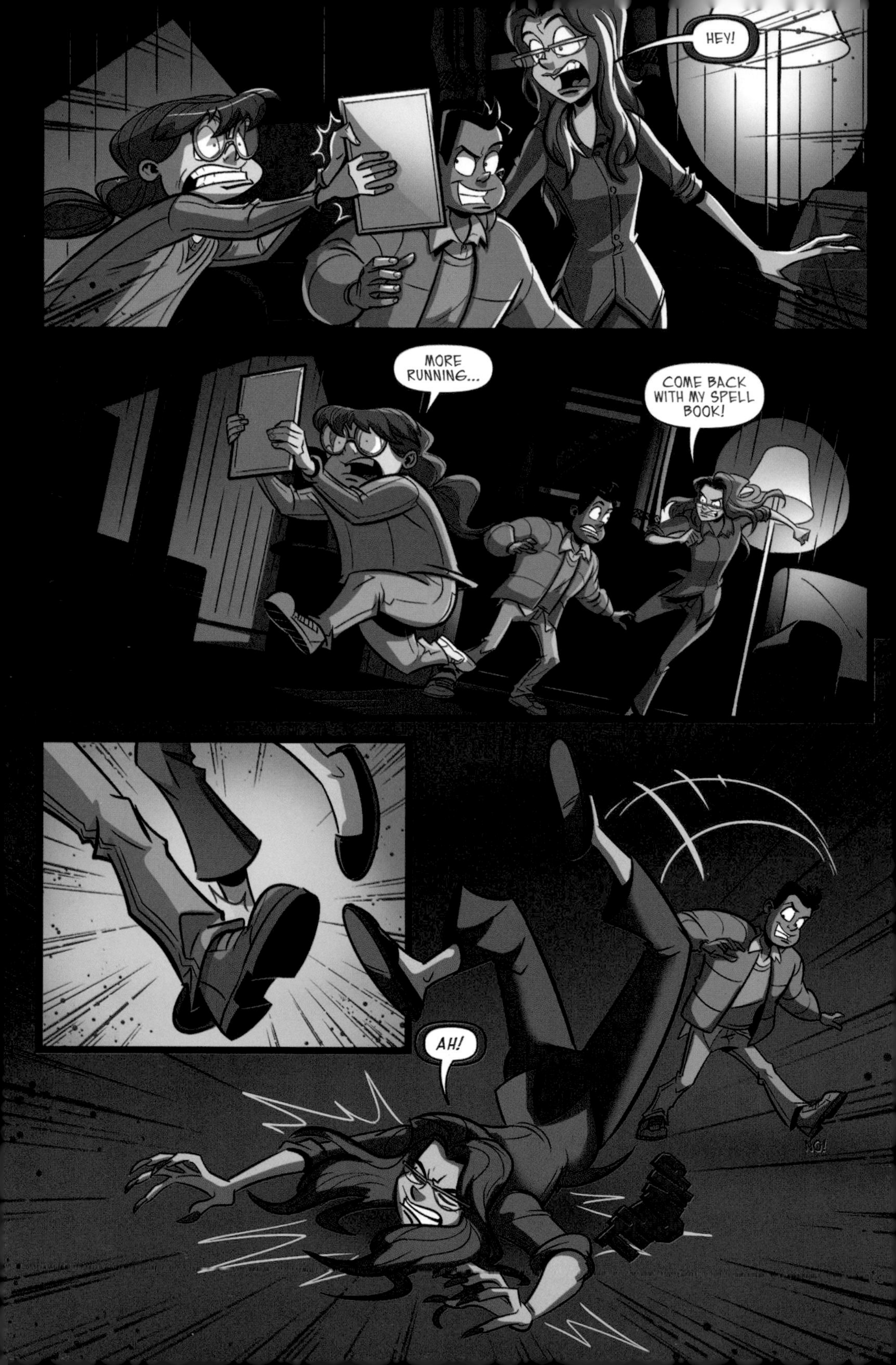
HEY!
MORE RUNNING...
COME BACK WITH MY SPELL BOOK!
AH!

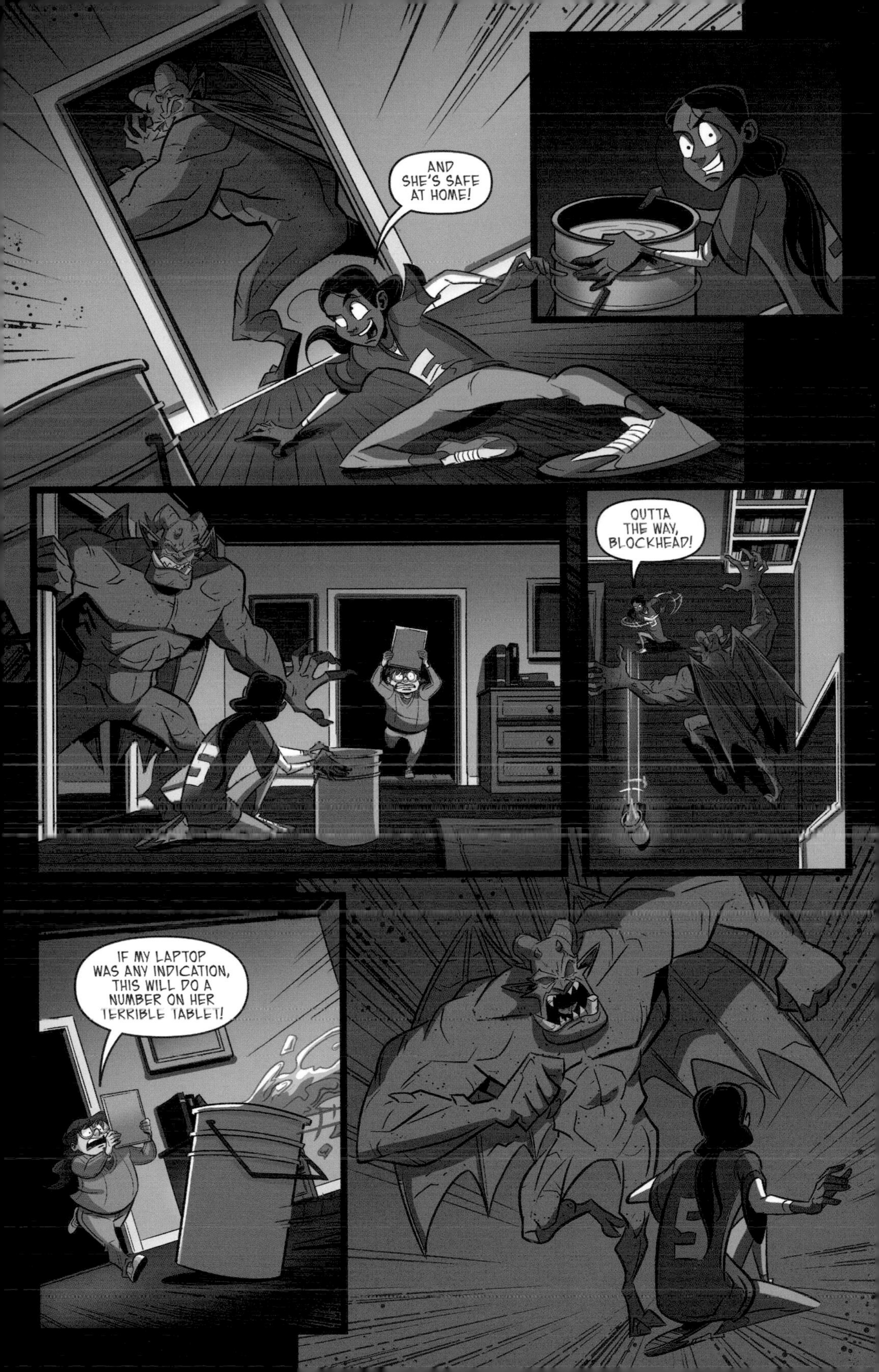
AND SHE'S SAFE AT HOME!
OUTTA THE WAY, BLOCKHEAD!
IF MY LAPTOP WAS ANY INDICATION, THIS WILL DO A NUMBER ON HER TERRIBLE TABLET!

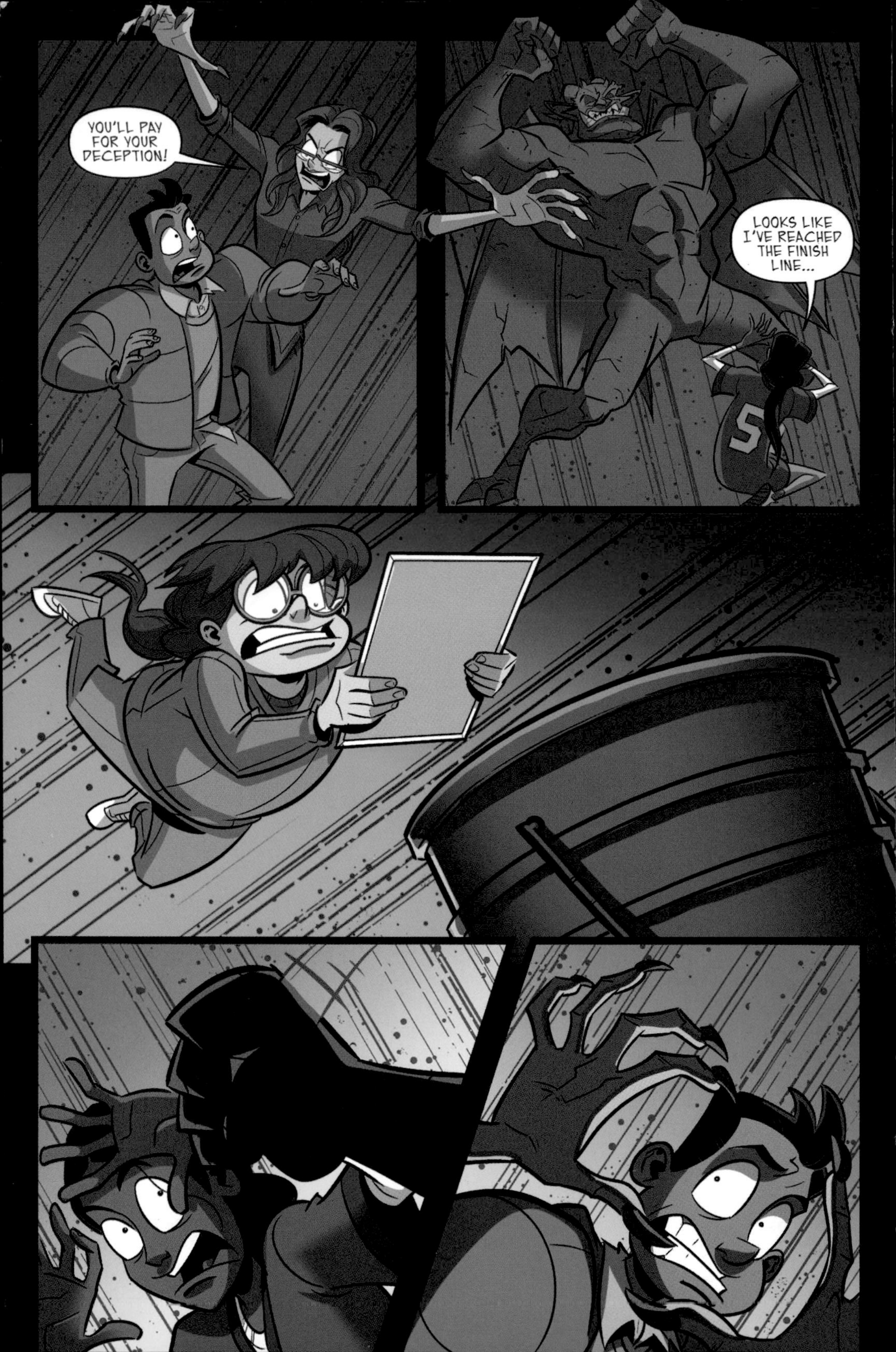
YOU'LL PAY FOR YOUR DECEPTION!
LOOKS LIKE I'VE REACHED THE FINISH LINE...

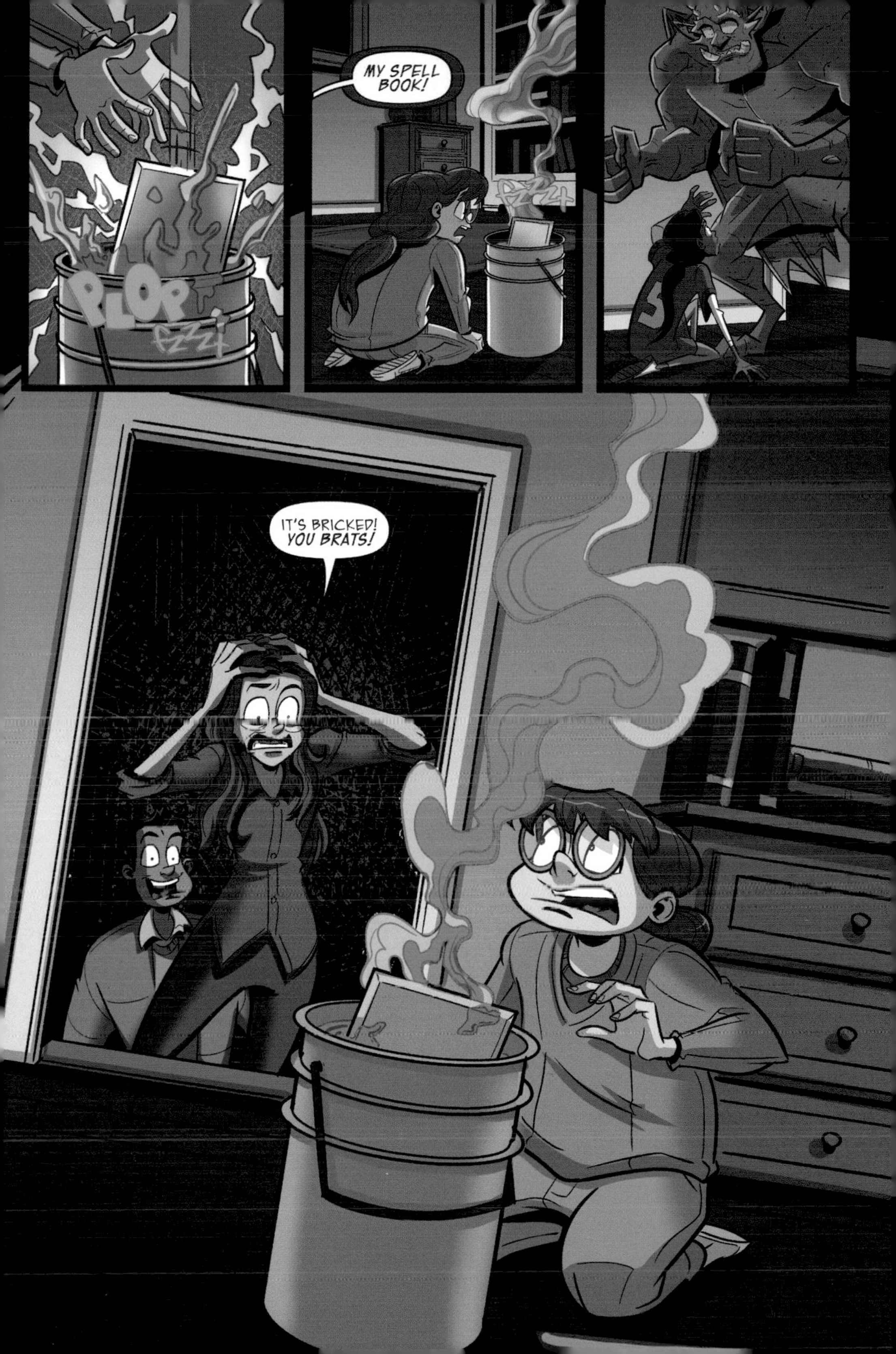
PLOP
fzzt
MY SPELL BOOK!
fzzt
IT'S BRICKED! YOU BRATS!

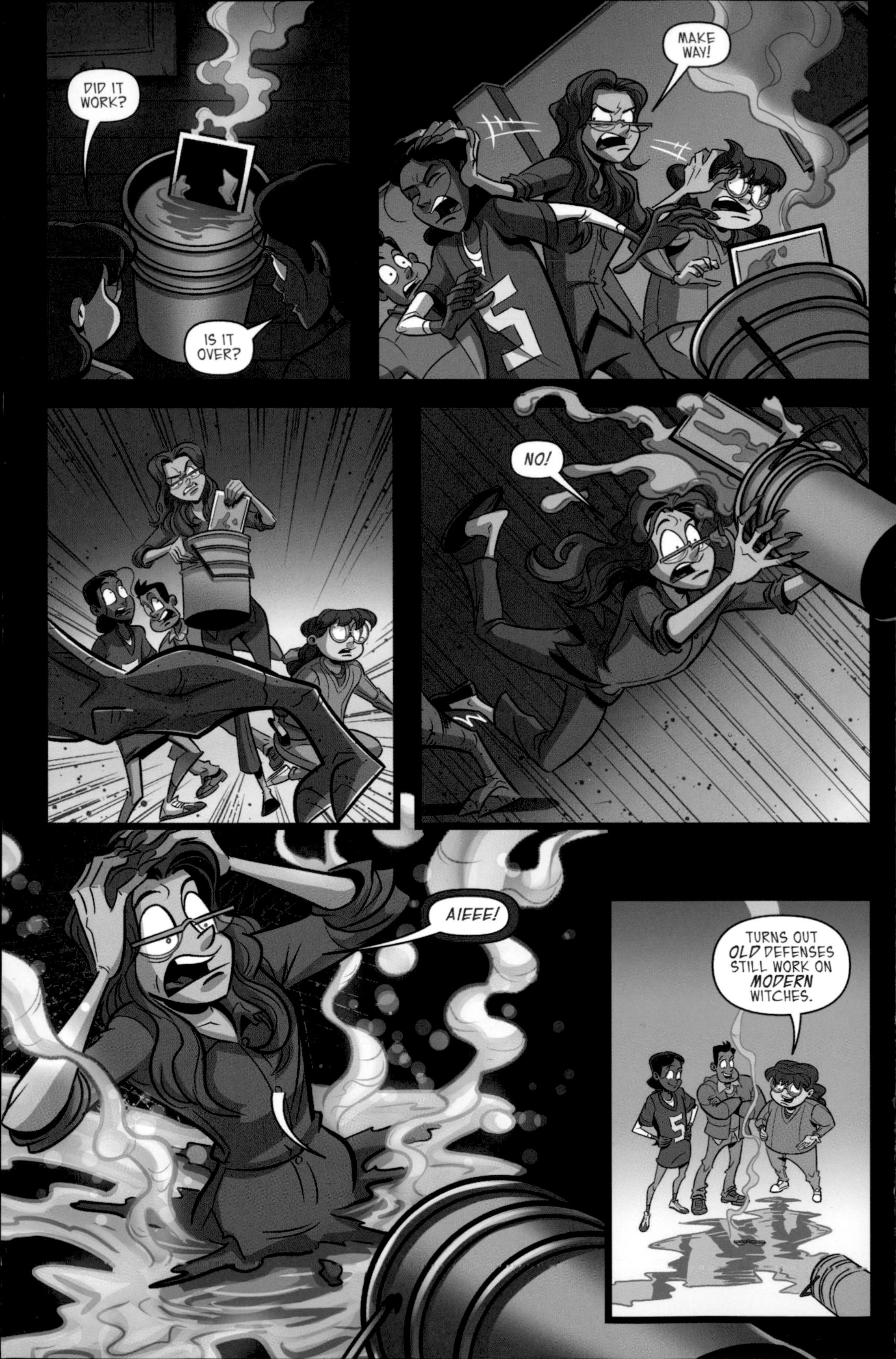
DID IT WORK?
IS IT OVER?
MAKE WAY!
NO!
AIEEE!
TURNS OUT OLD DEFENSES STILL WORK ON MODERN WITCHES.

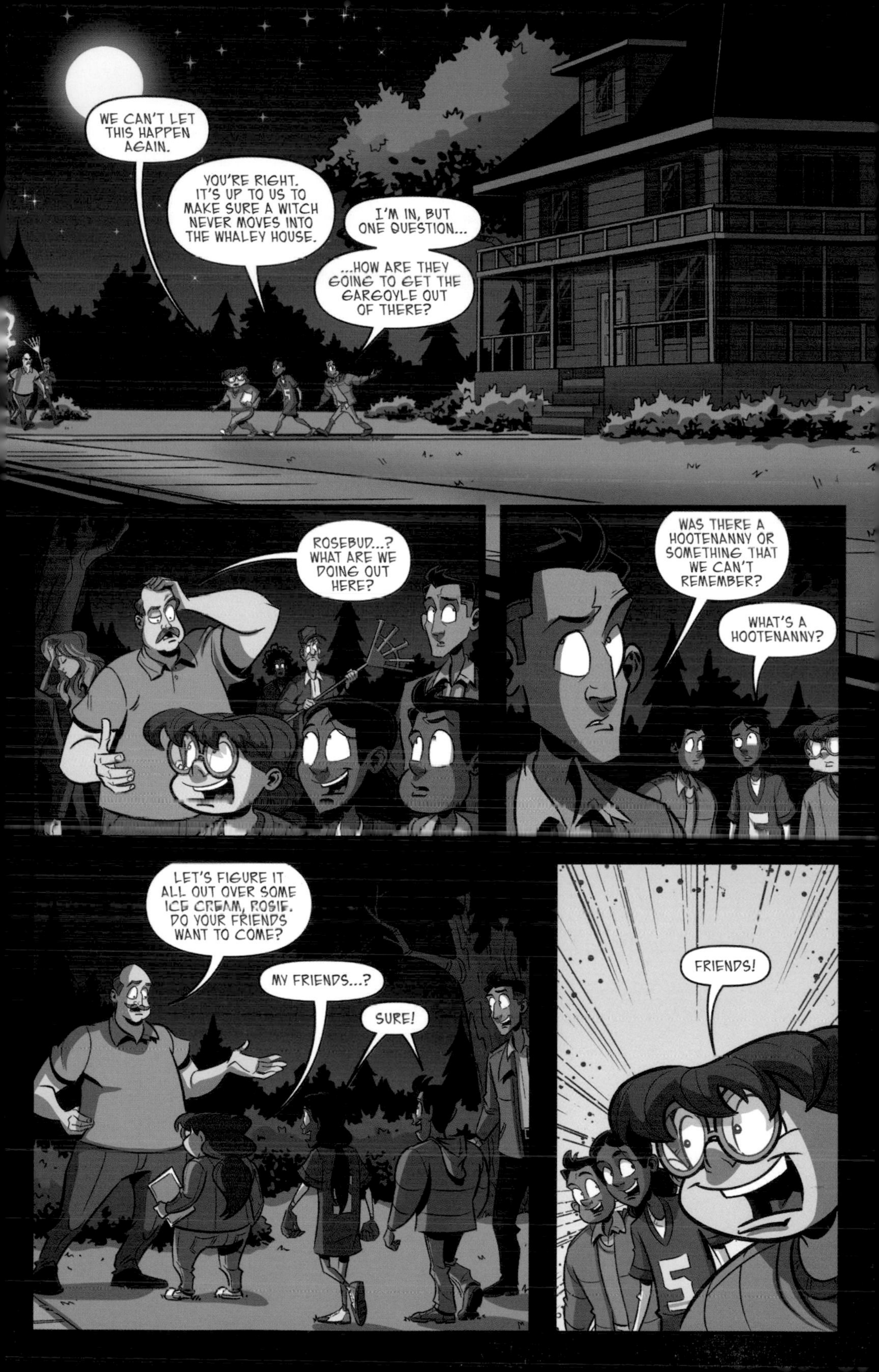
WE CAN'T LET THIS HAPPEN AGAIN.
YOU'RE RIGHT. IT'S UP TO US TO MAKE SURE A WITCH NEVER MOVES INTO THE WHALEY HOUSE.
I'M IN, BUT ONE QUESTION...
...HOW ARE THEY GOING TO GET THE GARGOYLE OUT OF THERE?
ROSEBUD...? WHAT ARE WE DOING OUT HERE?
WAS THERE A HOOTENANNY OR SOMETHING THAT WE CAN'T REMEMBER?
WHAT'S A HOOTENANNY?
LET'S FIGURE IT ALL OUT OVER SOME ICE CREAM, ROSIE. DO YOUR FRIENDS WANT TO COME?
MY FRIENDS...?
SURE!
FRIENDS!

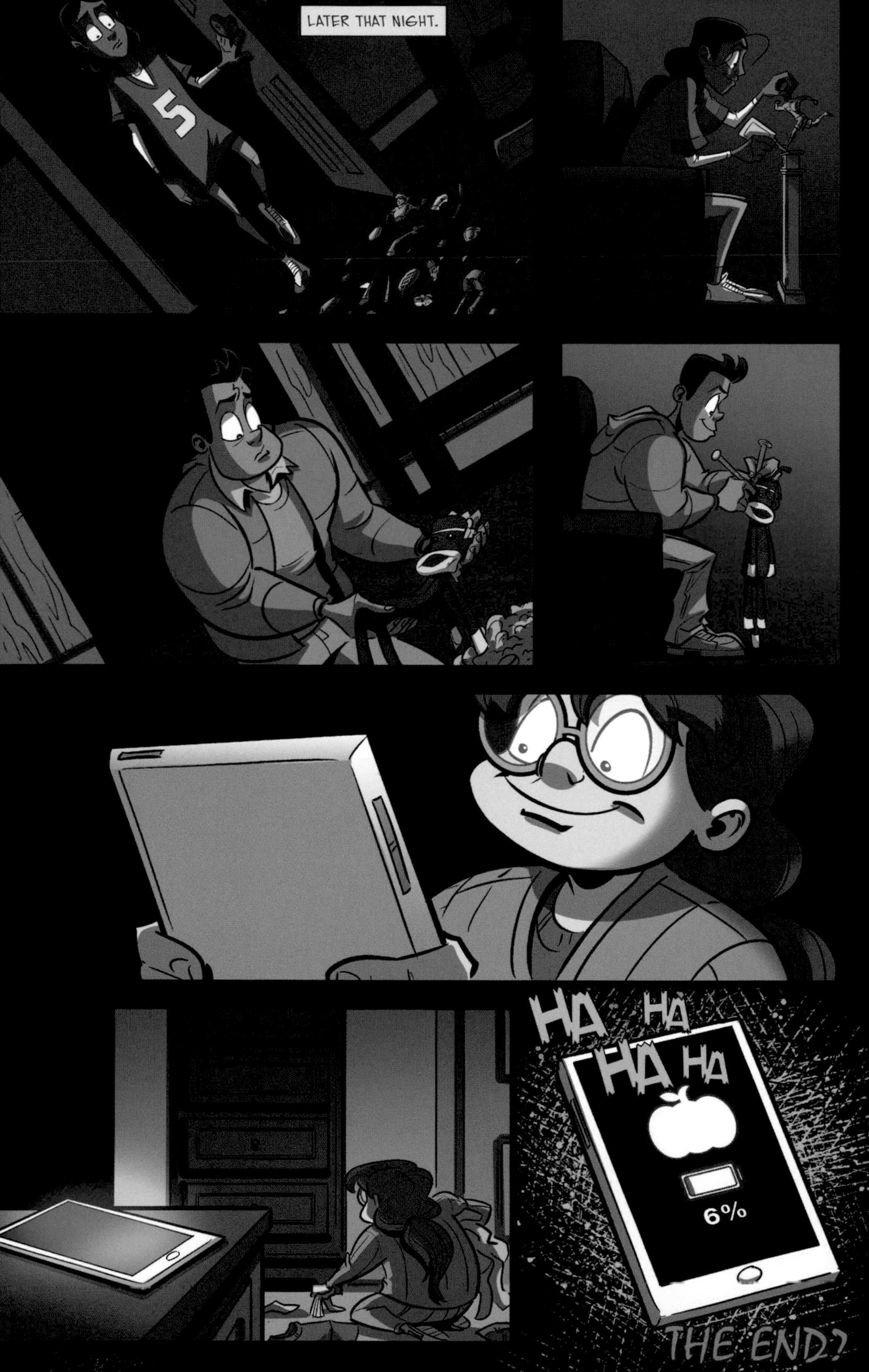
LATER THAT NIGHT.
HA HA
HA HA
6%
THE END?

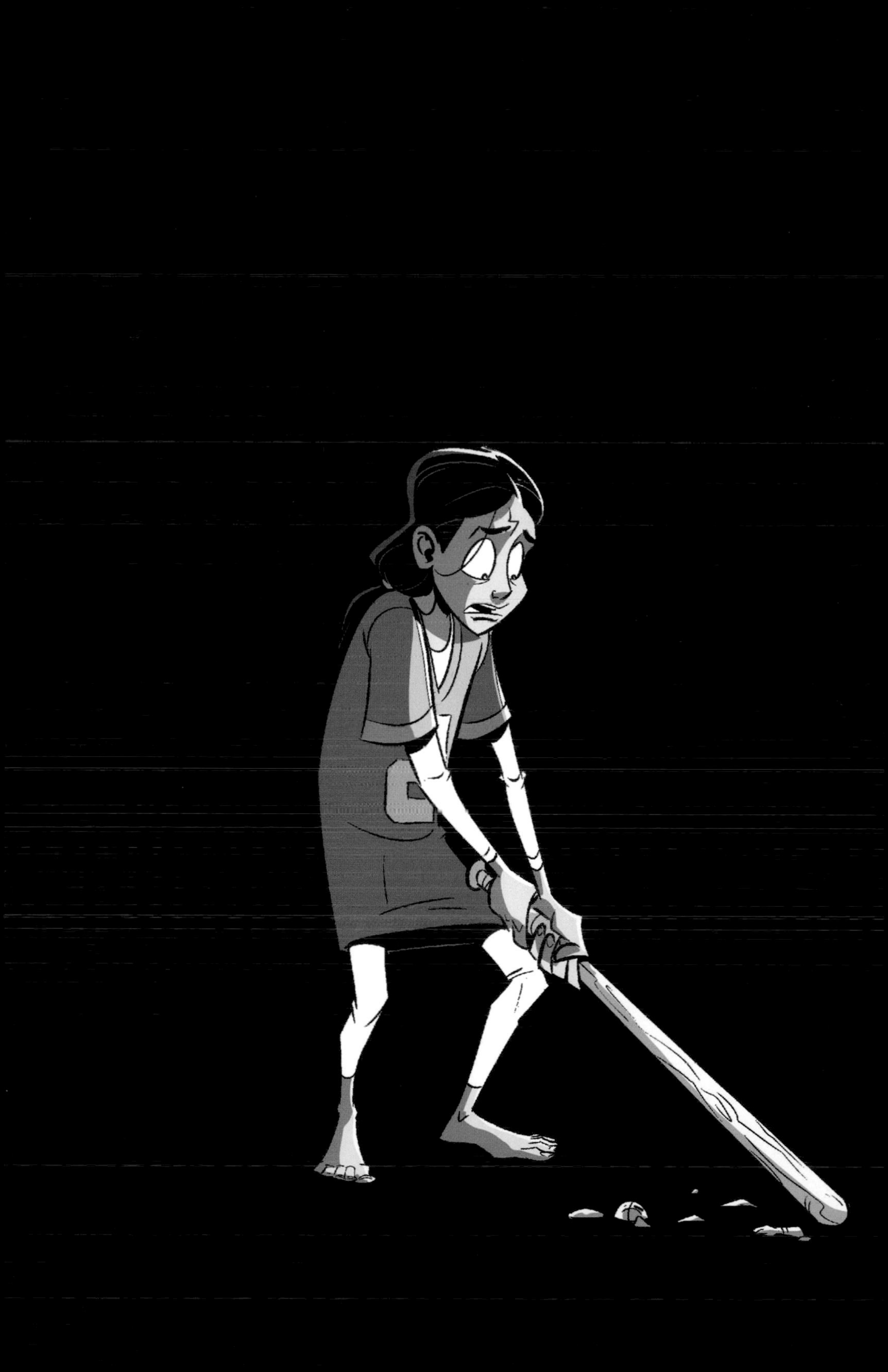

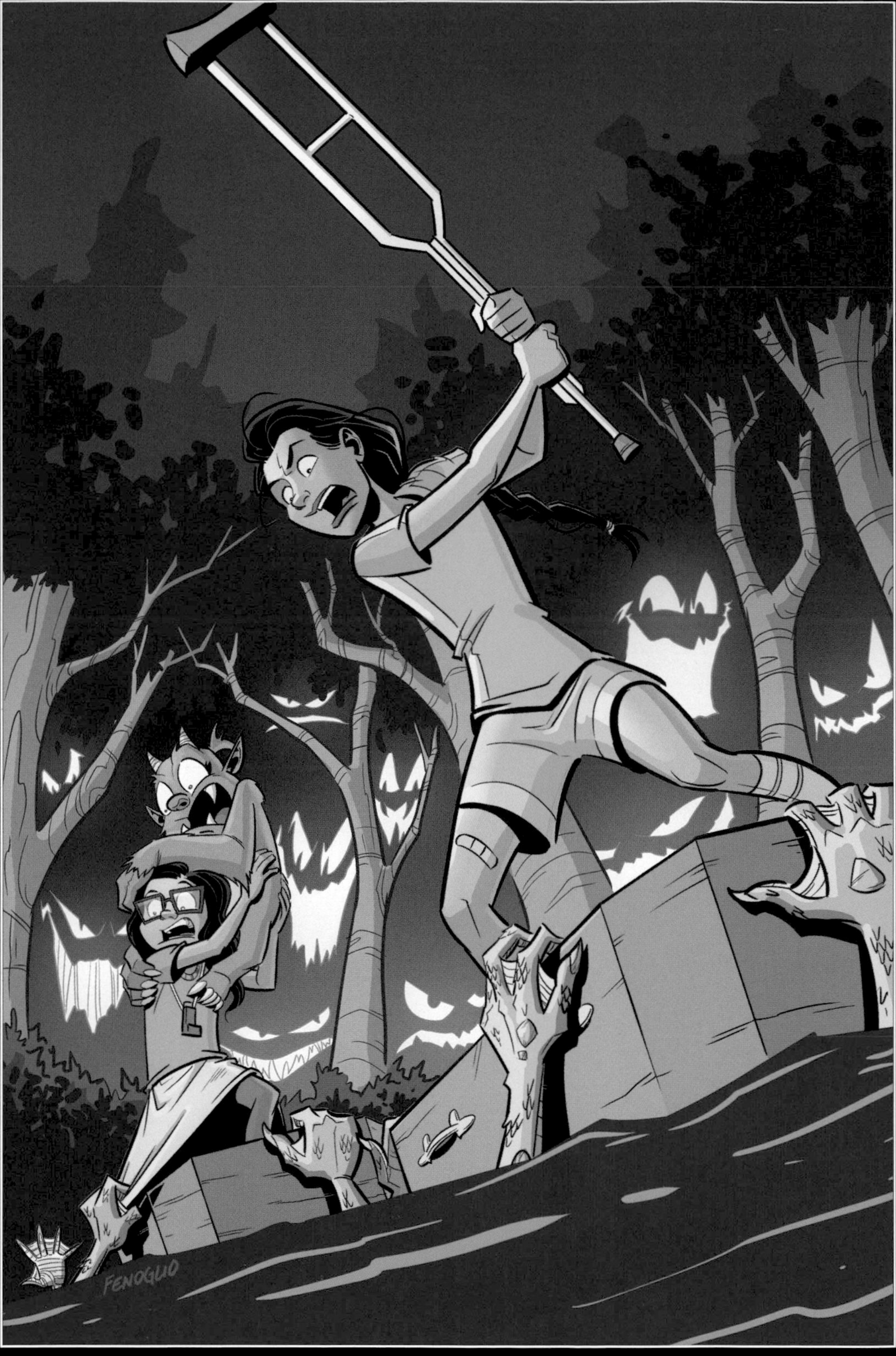
FENOGLIO

ART BY
CHRIS FENOGLIO

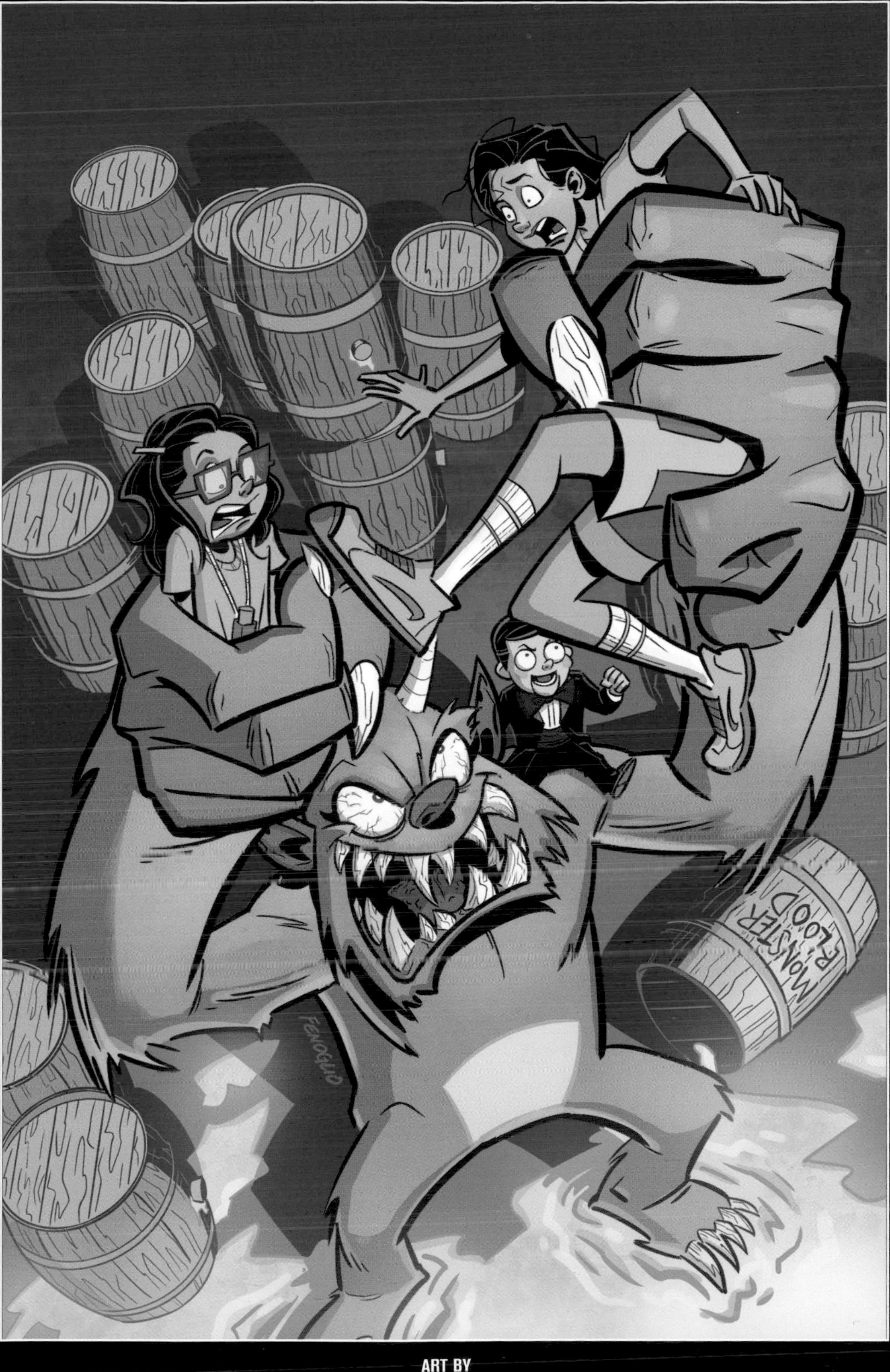
MONSTER FOOD
FENOGLIO

ART BY
CHRIS FENOGLIO

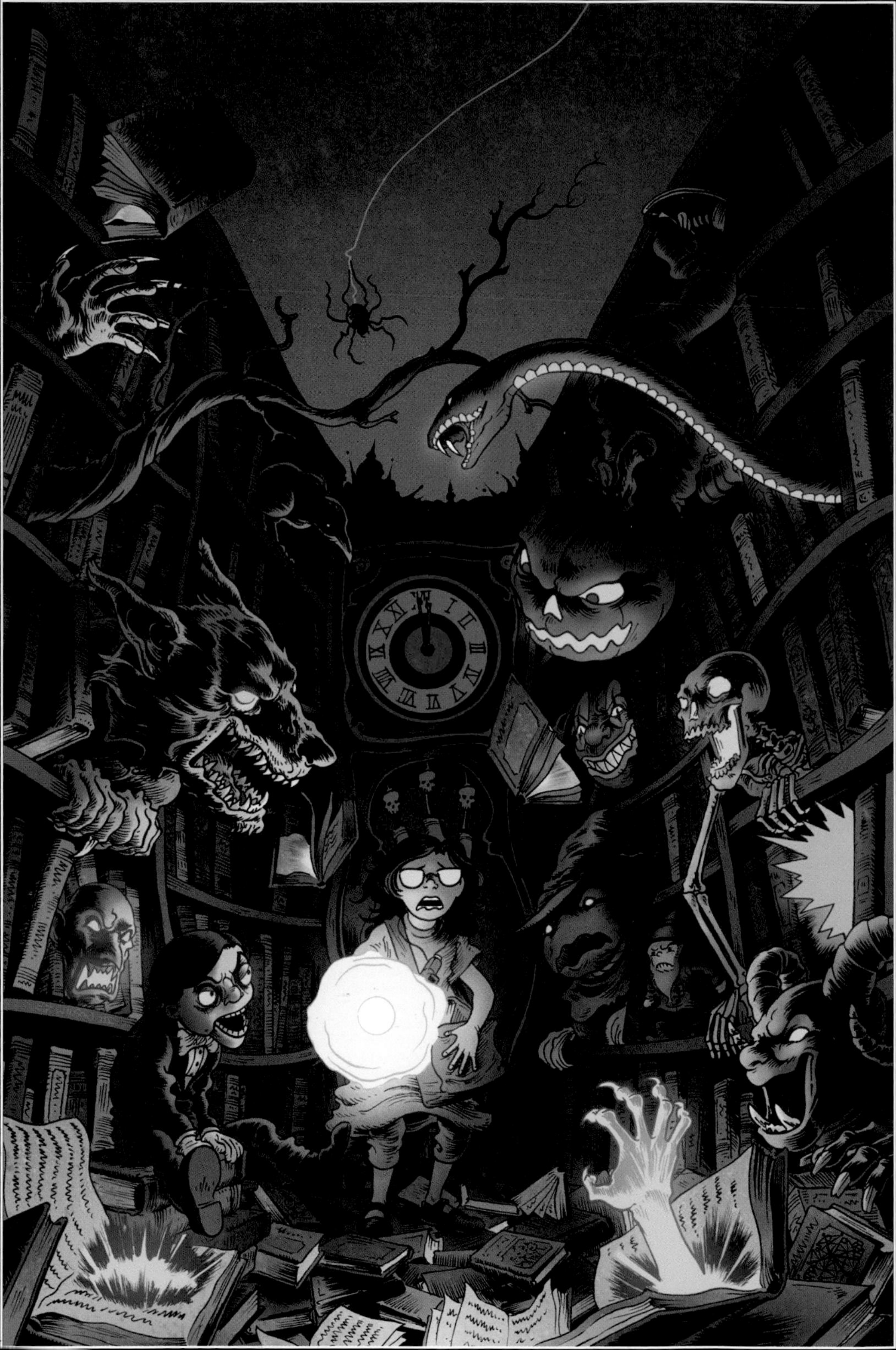

ART BY

C.P. WILSON III

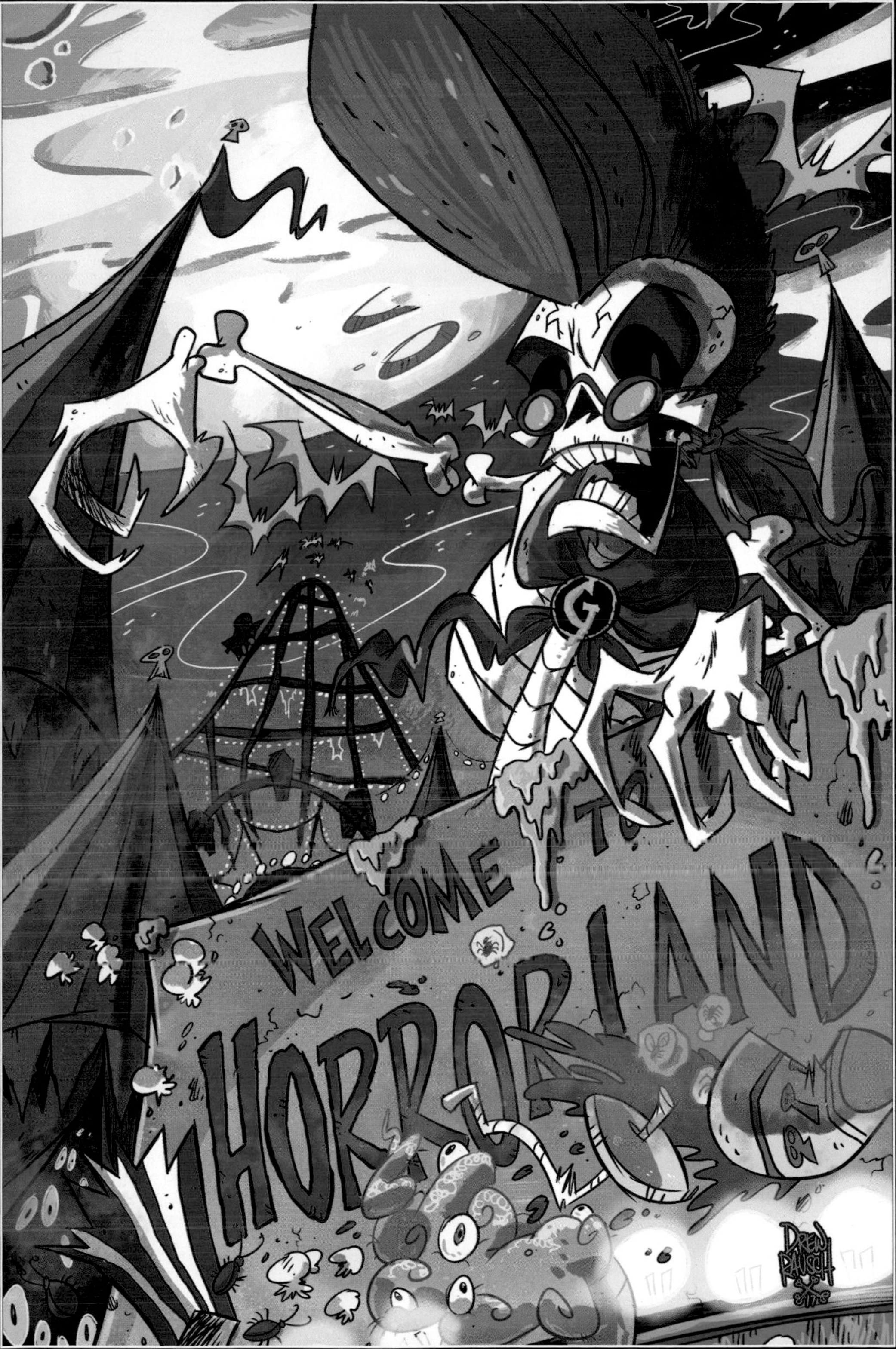
WELCOME TO
HORRORLAND
DREW RAUSCH

ART BY
DREW RAUSCH

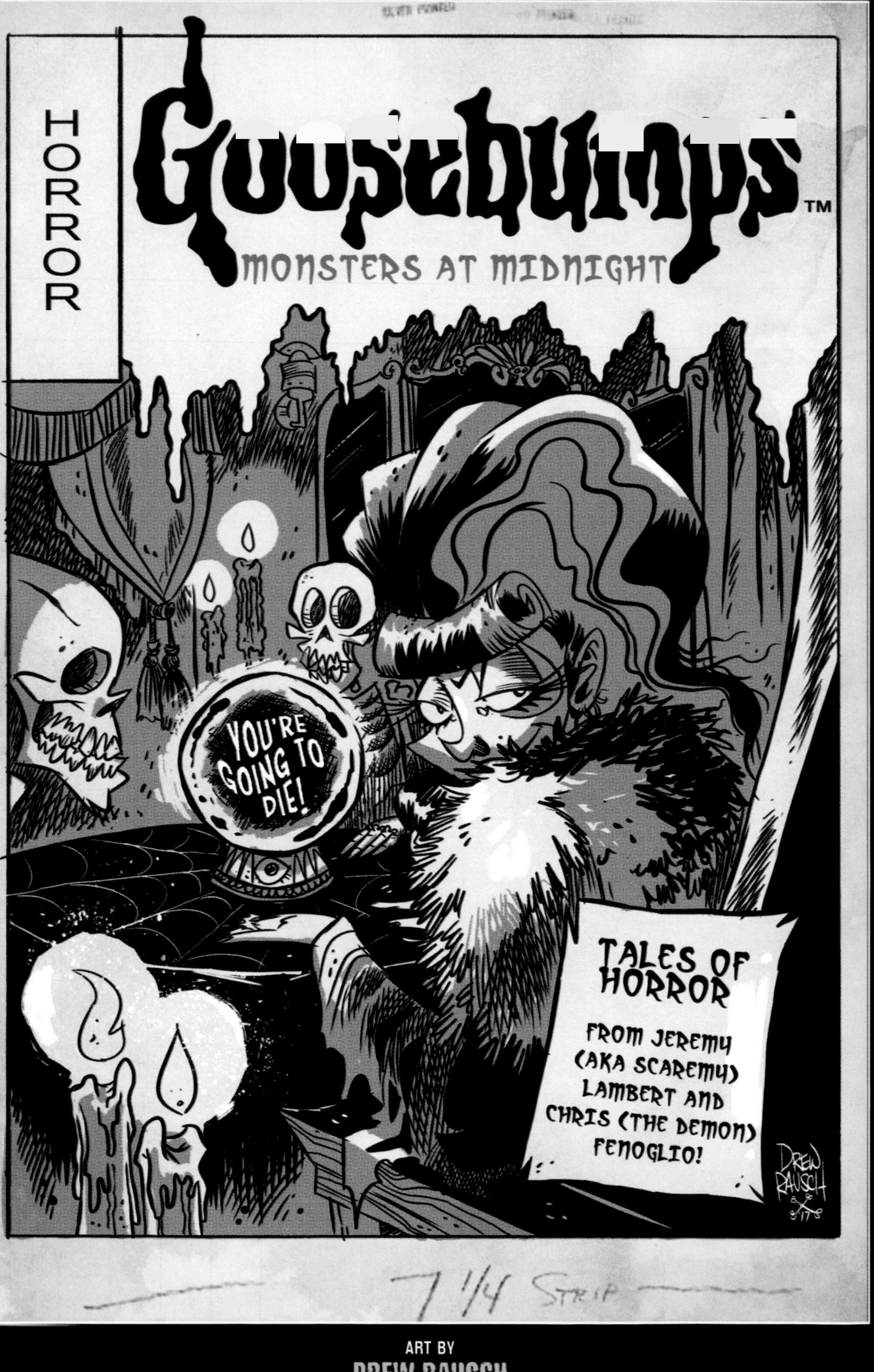
HORROR
Goosebumps™
MONSTERS AT MIDNIGHT
YOU'RE GOING TO DIE!
TALES OF HORROR
FROM JEREMY (AKA SCAREMY) LAMBERT AND CHRIS (THE DEMON) FENOGLIO!
DREW RAUSCH
7 1/4 Strip

ART BY
DREW RAUSCH

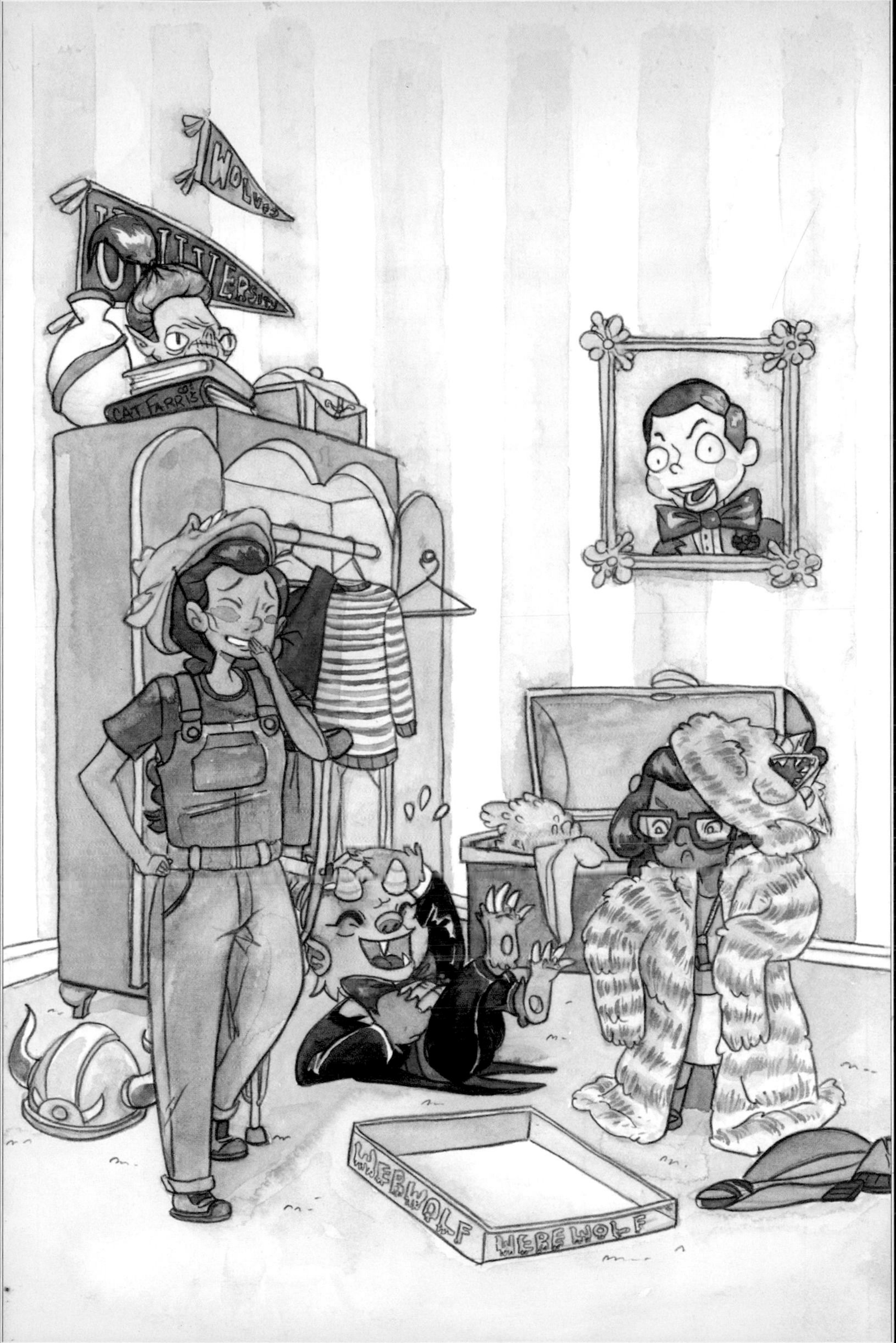
WOLVES
CAT FARRIS
WEREWOLF
WEREWOLF

ART BY
CAT FARRIS

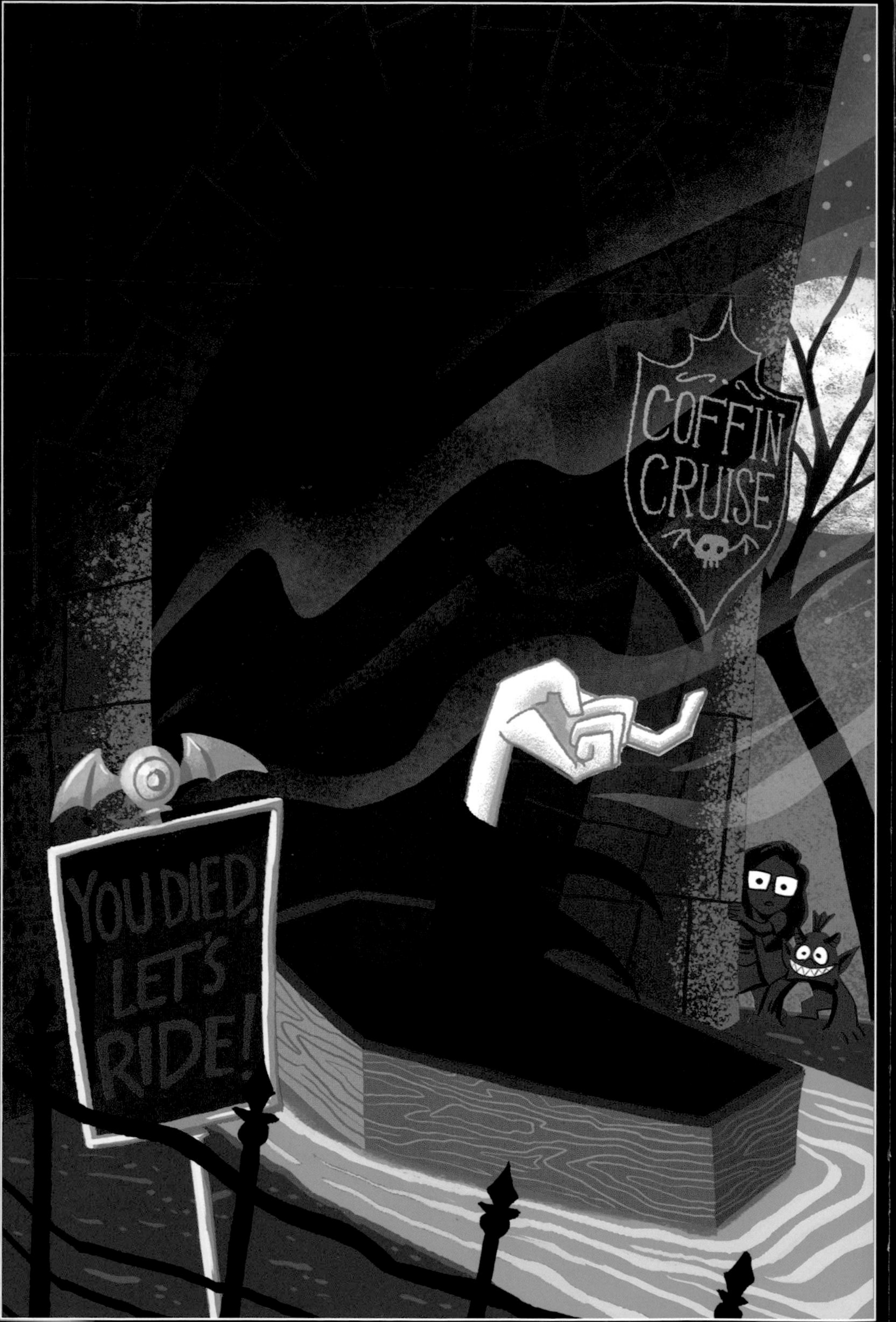
COFFIN CRUISE
YOU DIED, LET'S RIDE!

ART BY
DEREK CHARM

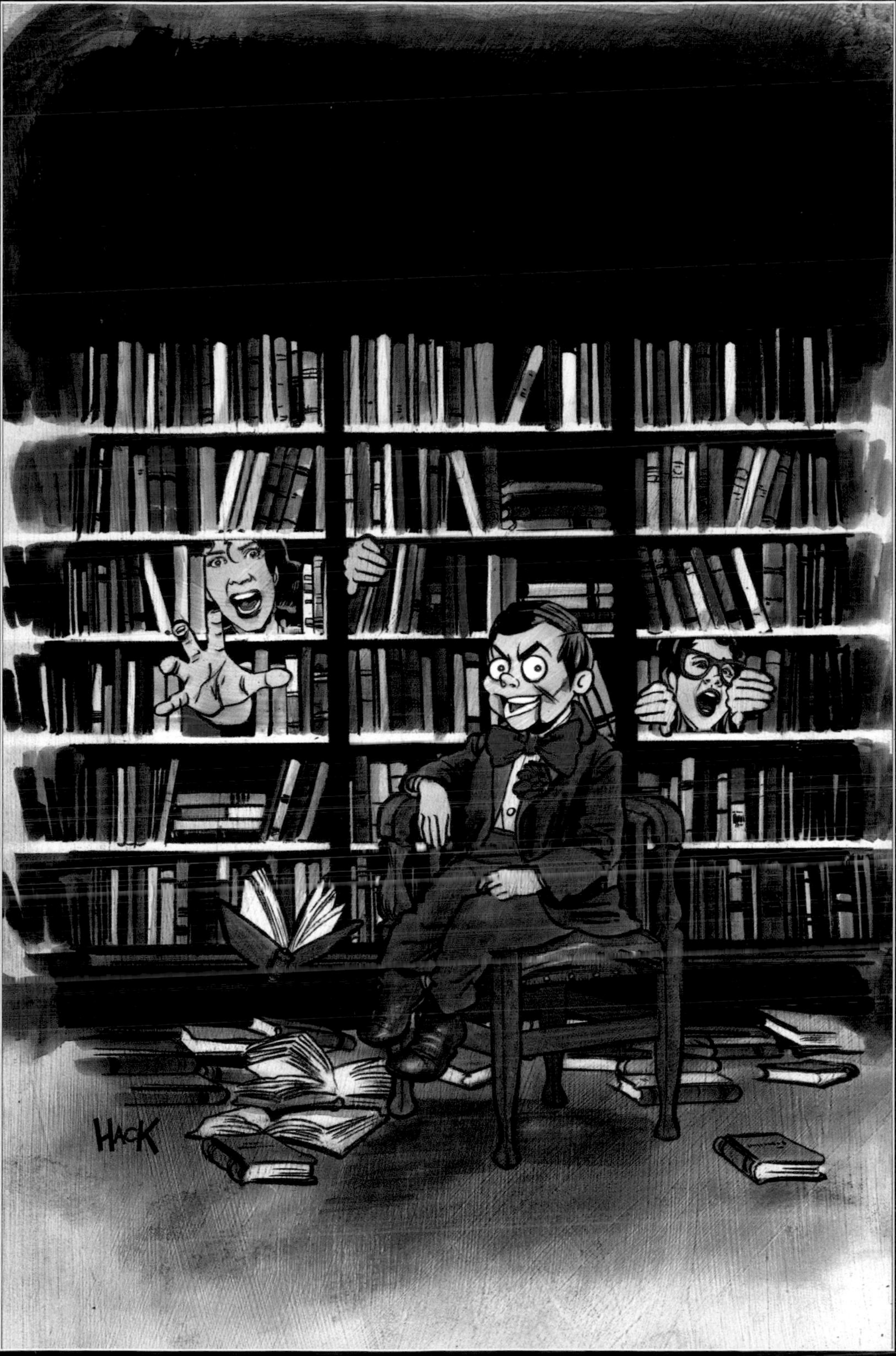
HACK

ART BY
ROBERT HACK

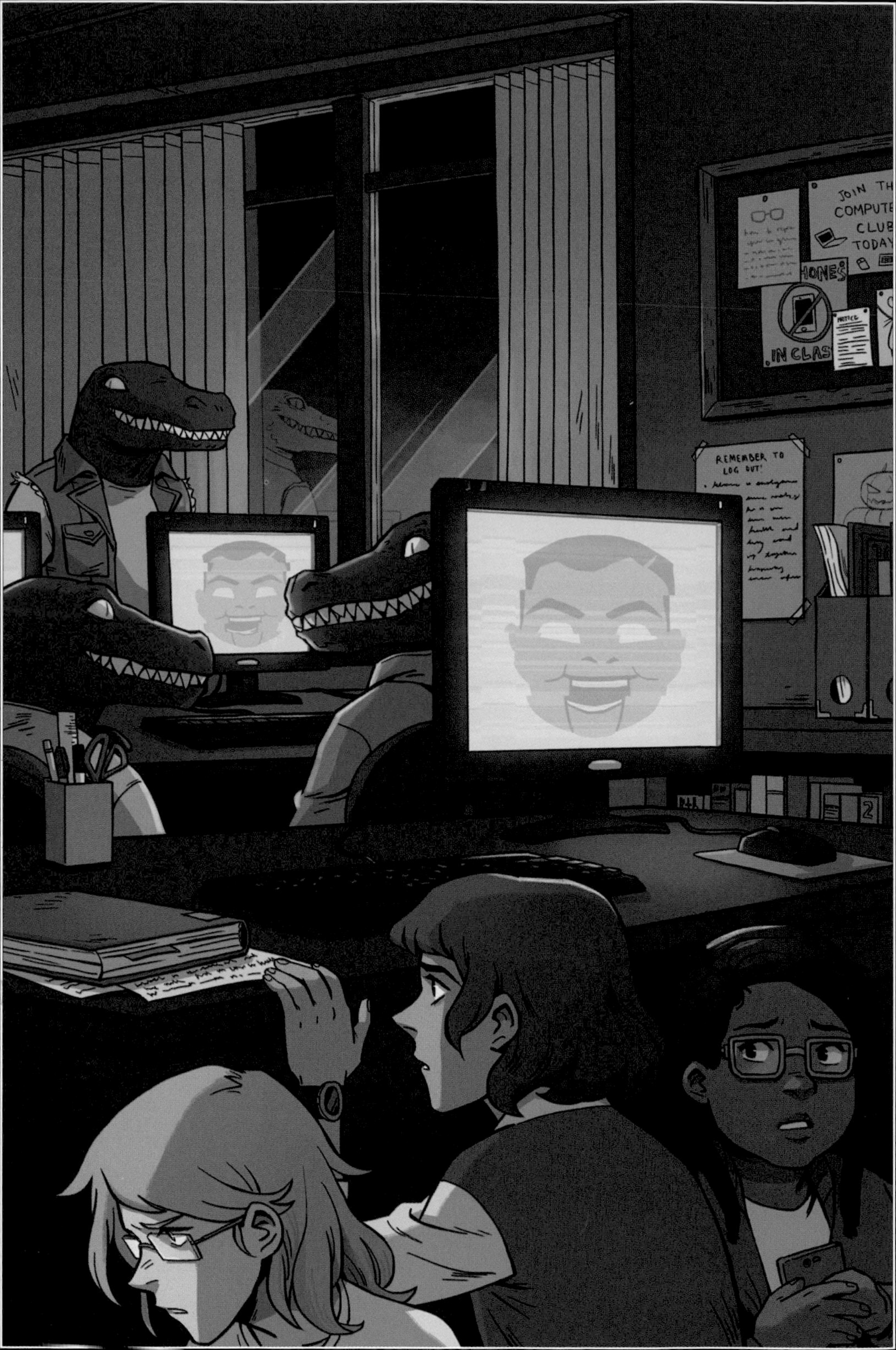
REMEMBER TO
LOG OUT!

ART BY
MICHELLE WONG

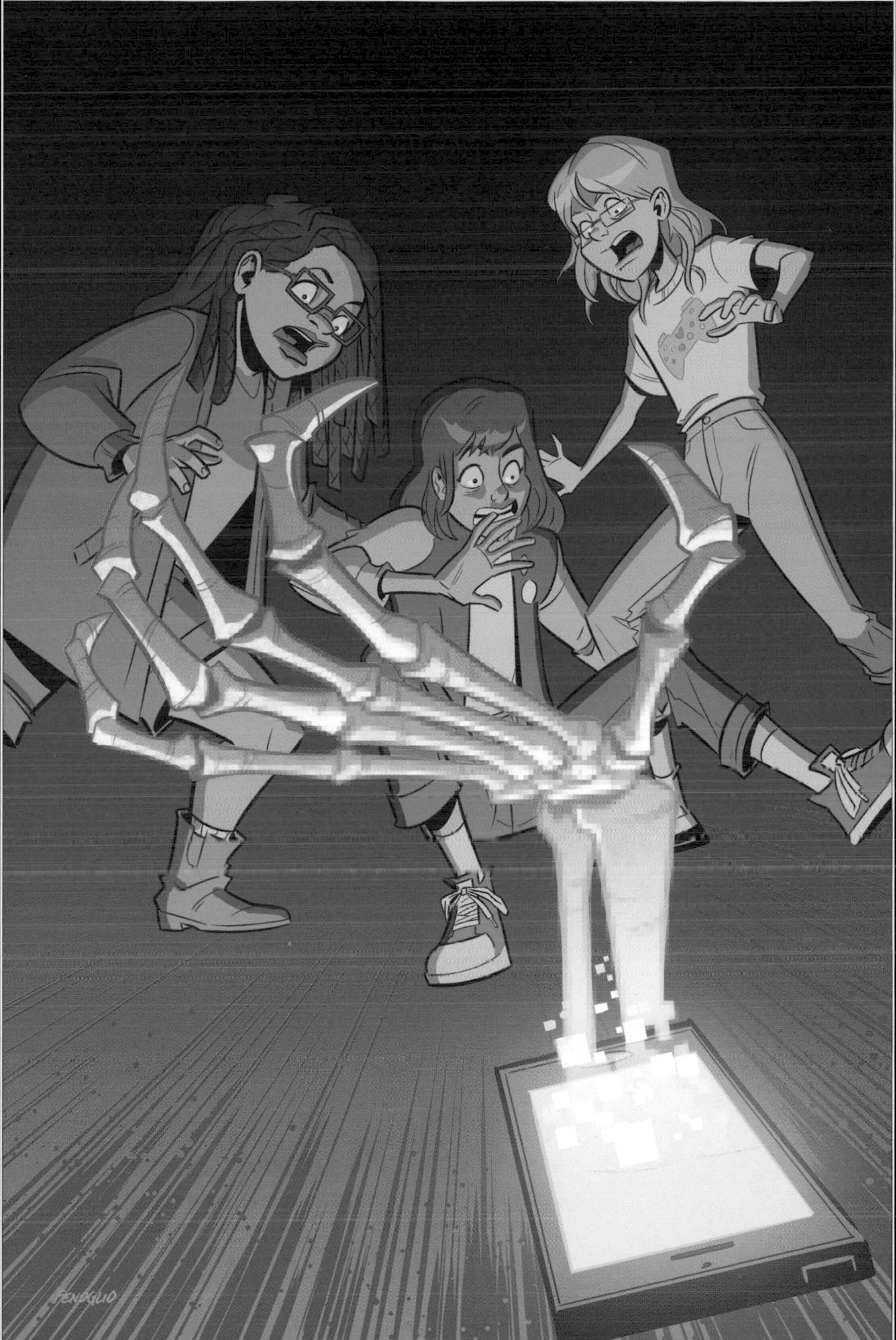
FENOGLIO

ART BY
CHRIS FENOGLIO

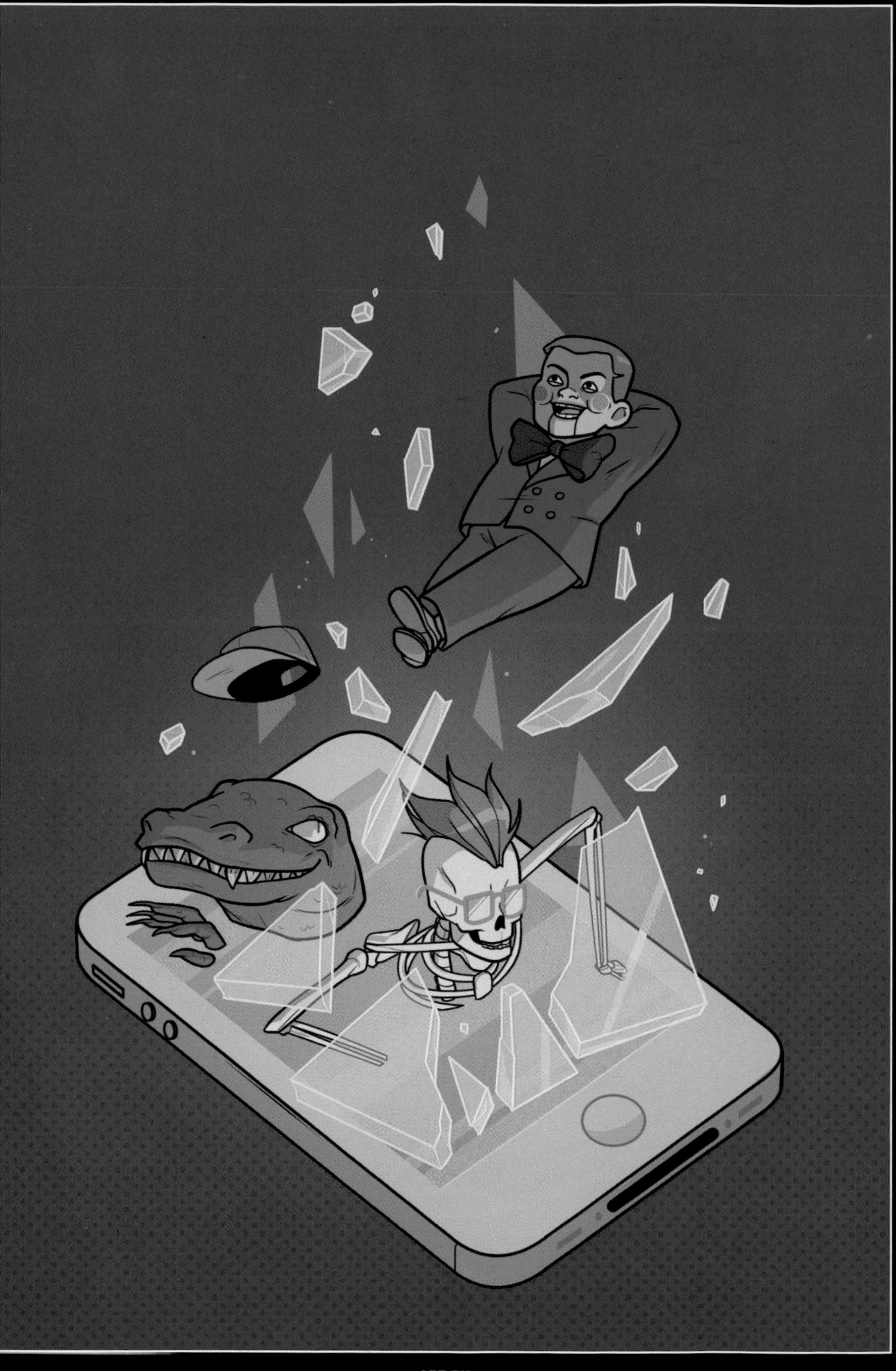

ART BY
TED DuVALL

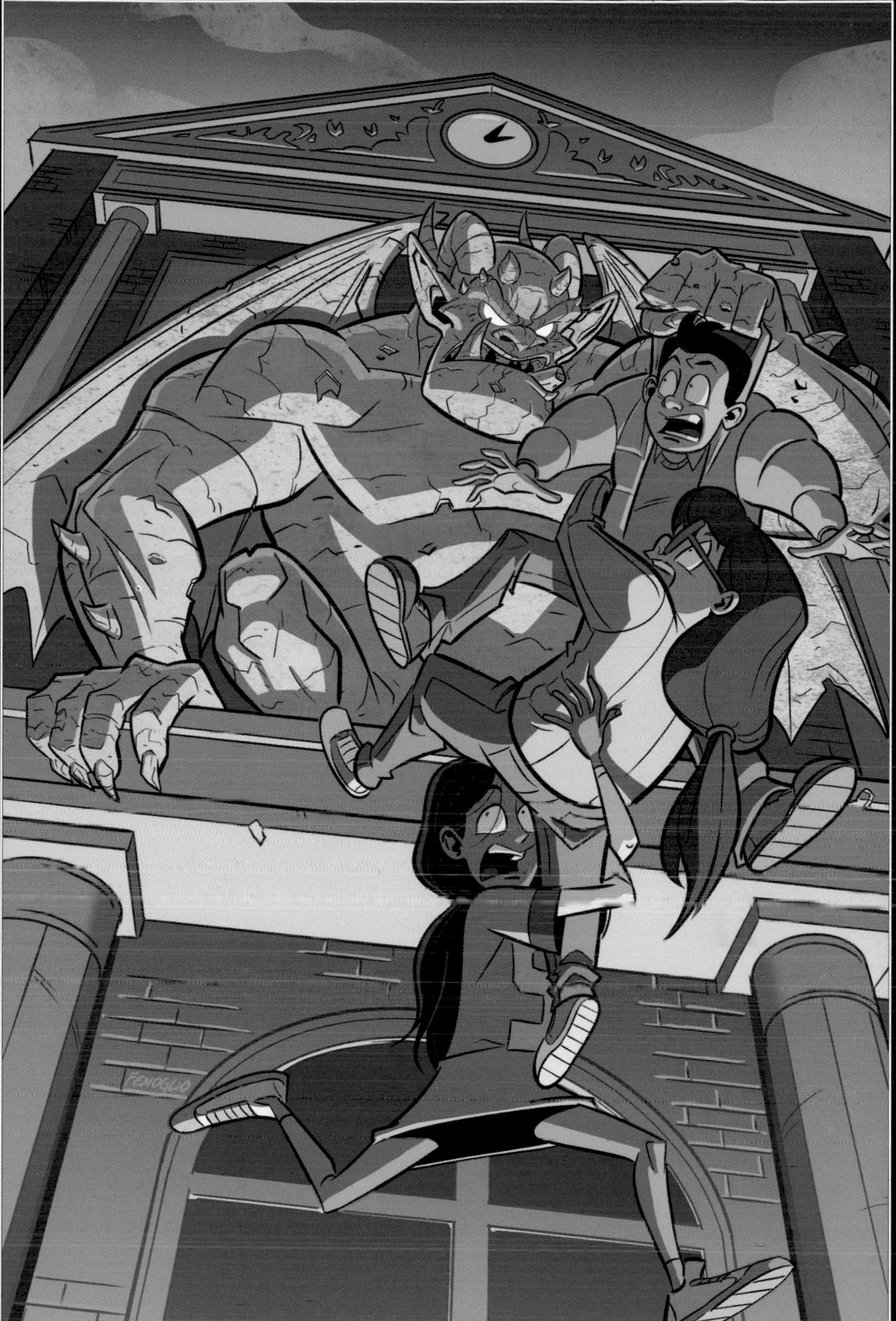
FENOGLIO

ART BY
CHRIS FENOGLIO

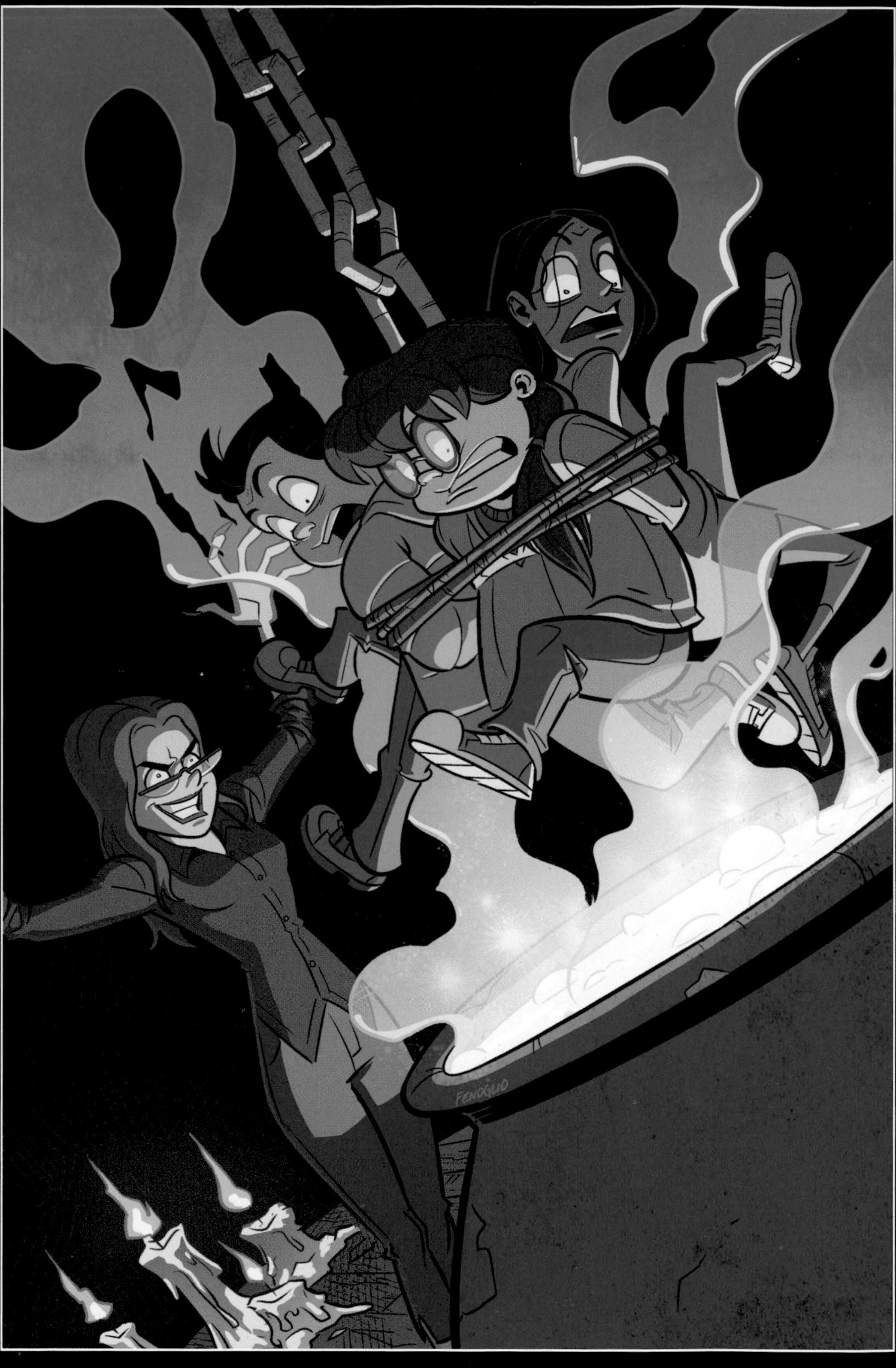
FENOGLIO

ART BY
CHRIS FENOGLIO

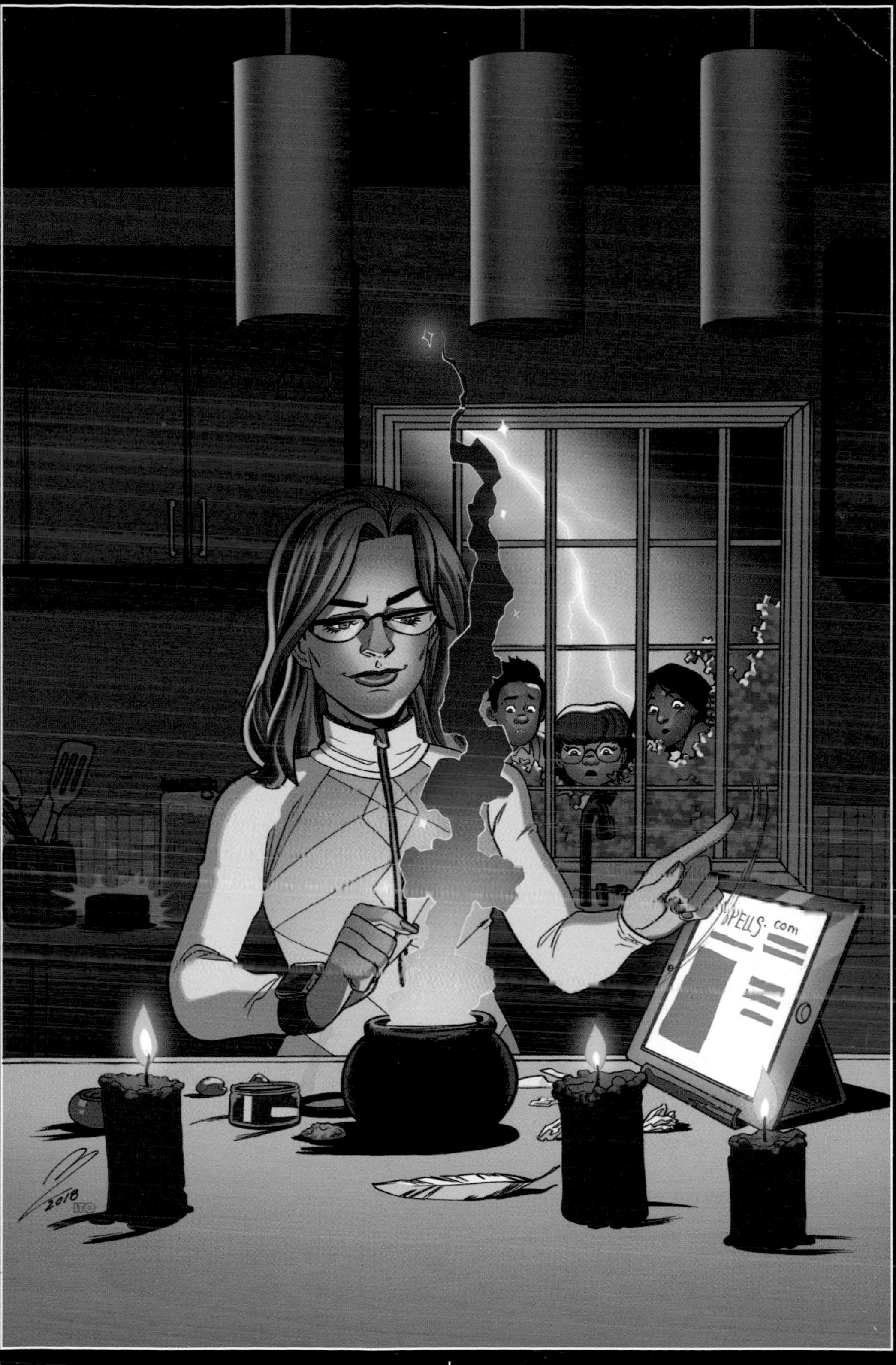

ART BY
MEGAN LEVENS

COLORS BY
LEONARDO ITO

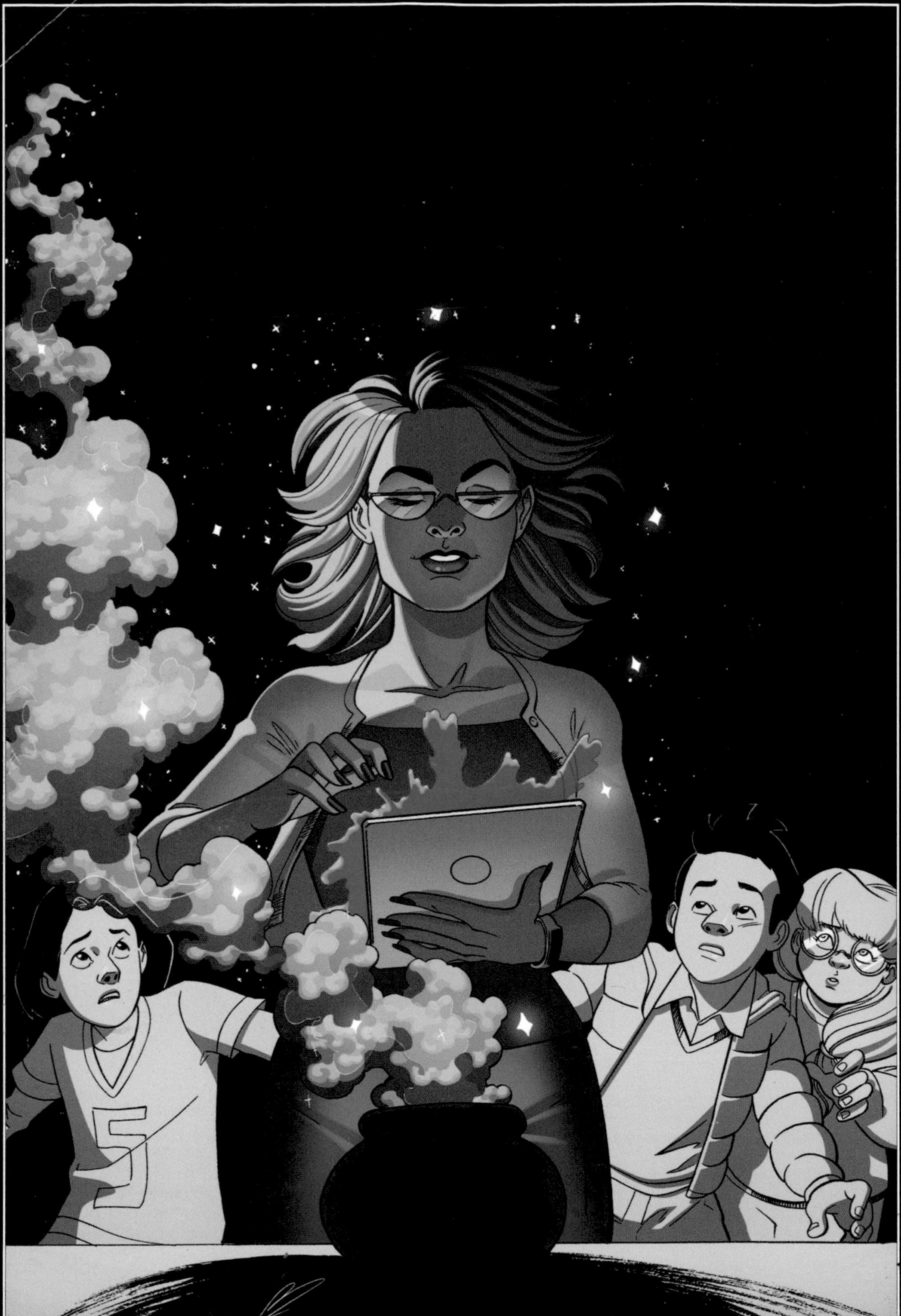

ART BY
MEGAN LEVENS

COLORS BY
LEONARDO ITO

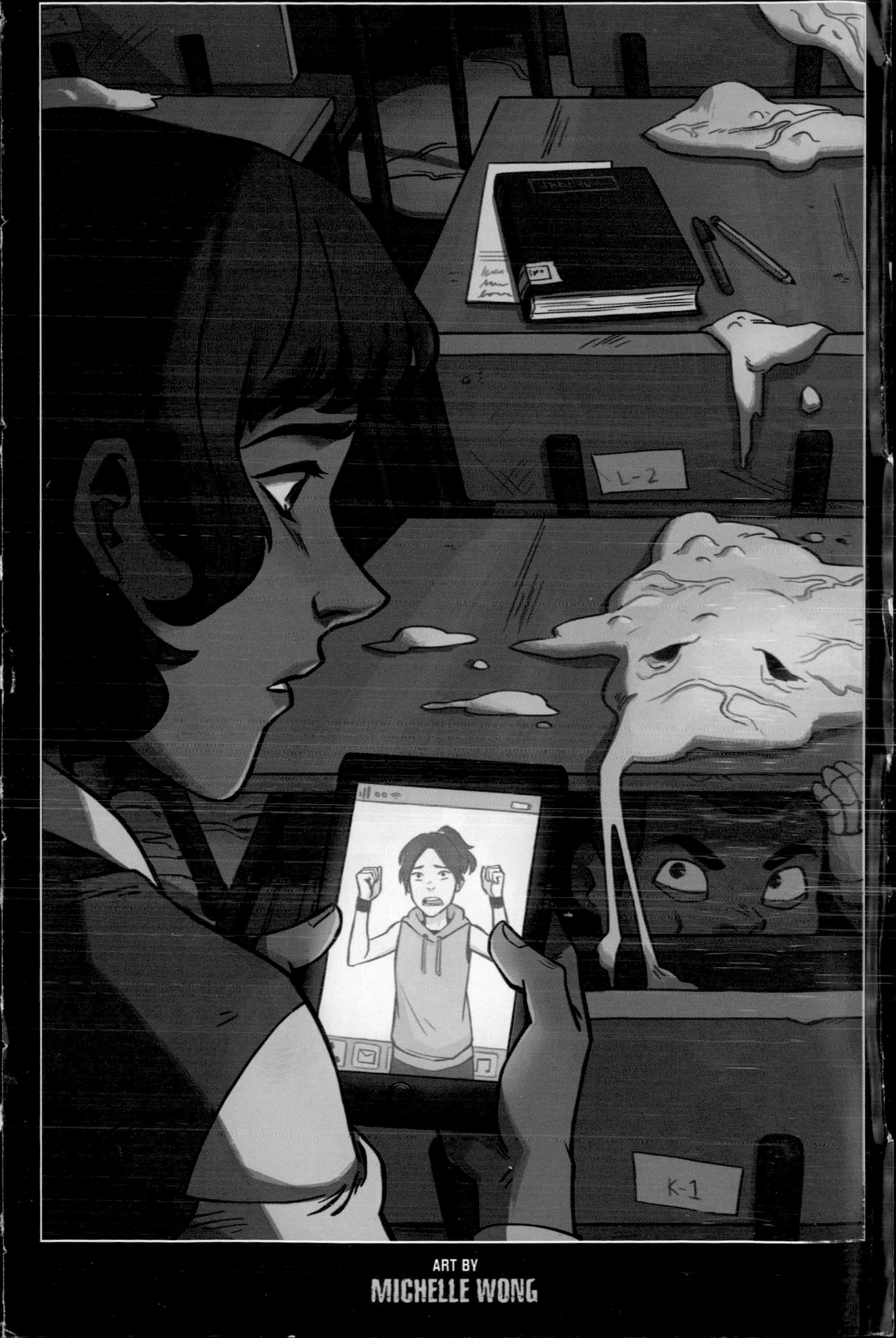
L-2
K-1

ART BY
MICHELLE WONG

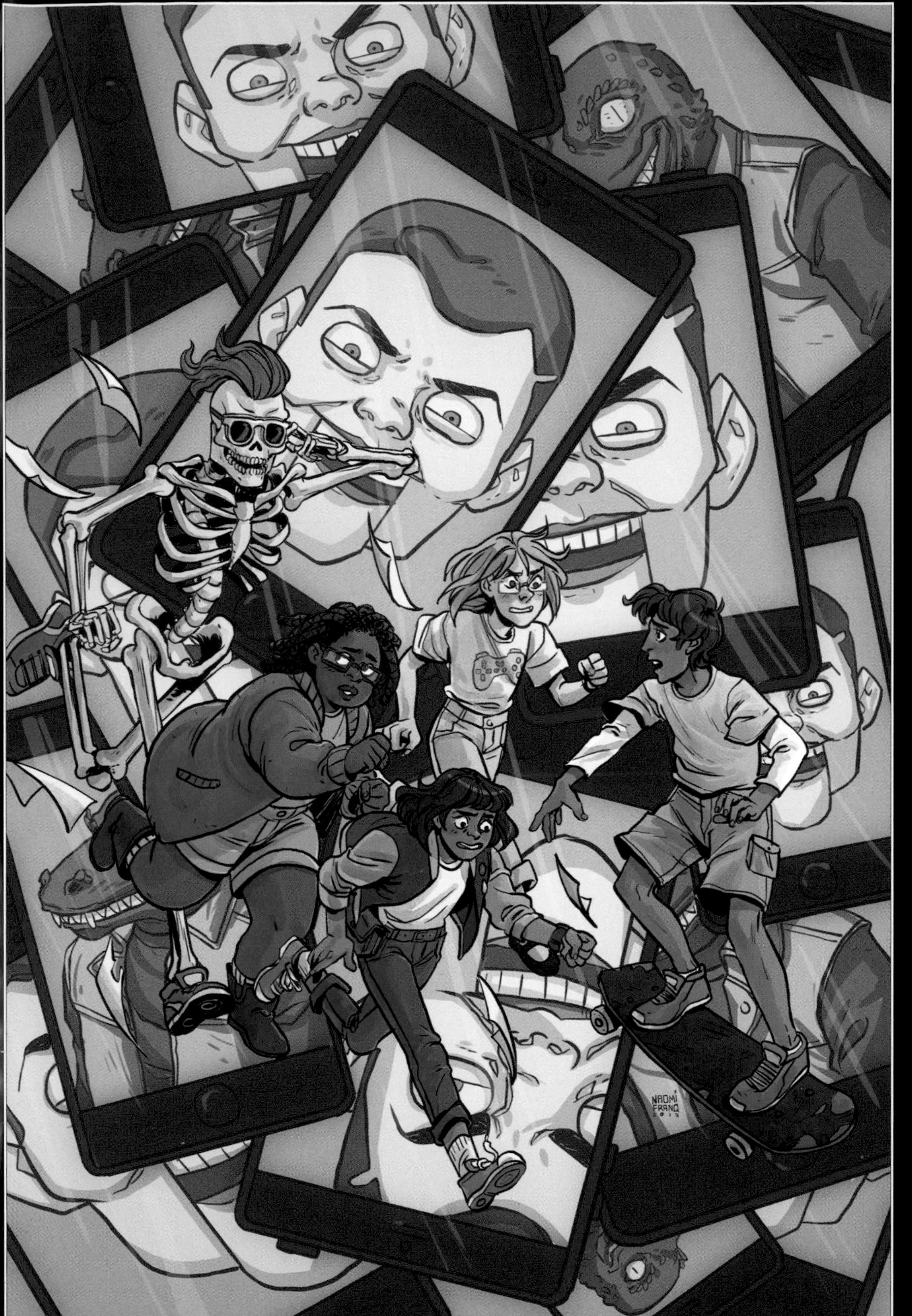
NAOMI FRANQ 2017

ART BY
NAOMI FRANQUIZ

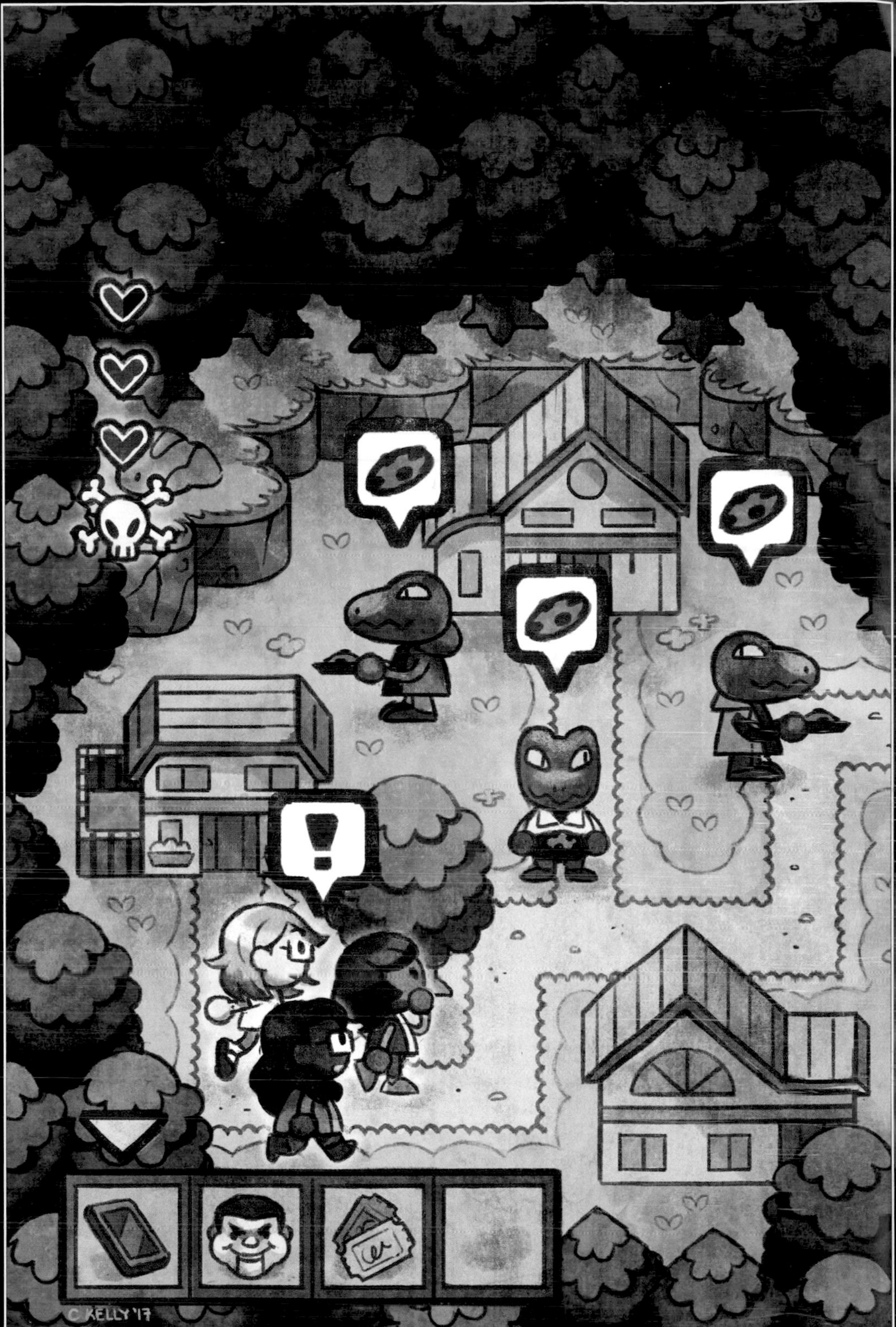
C KELLY '17

ART BY
CHRISTINA KELLY

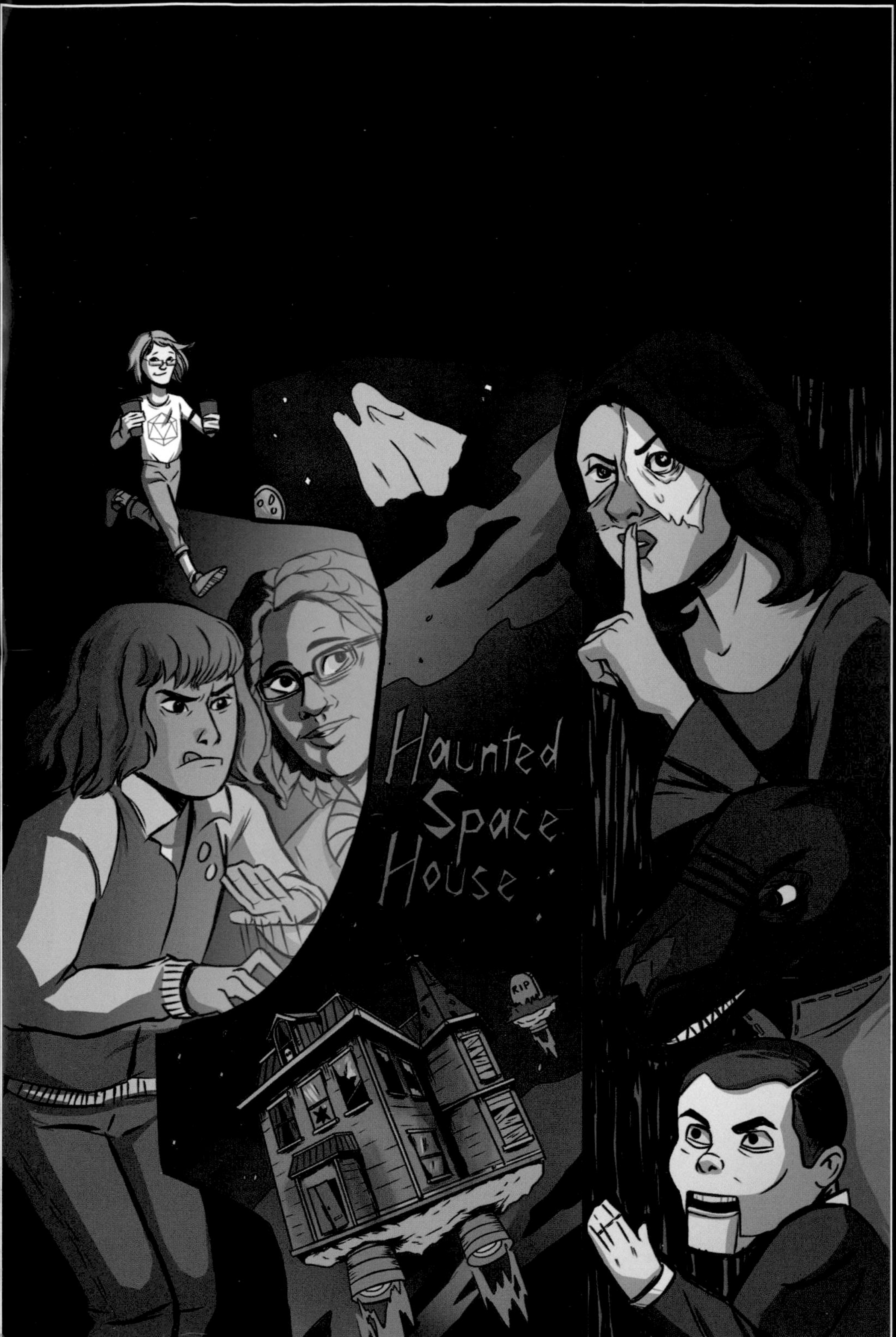
Haunted Space House

ART BY
JEN VAUGHN